W9-CFG-743

THE EVENTS IN THIS BOOK ARE REAL.

NAMES AND PLACES HAVE BEEN CHANGED
TO PROTECT THE LORIEN,
WHO REMAIN IN HIDING.

OTHER CIVILIZATIONS DO EXIST.

SOME OF THEM SEEK TO DESTROY YOU.

THE LORIEN LEGACIES

BY PITTACUS LORE

Novels

I AM NUMBER FOUR

THE POWER OF SIX

THE RISE OF NINE

THE FALL OF FIVE

THE REVENGE OF SEVEN

Novellas

I AM NUMBER FOUR: THE LOST FILES #1: SIX'S LEGACY

I AM NUMBER FOUR: THE LOST FILES #2: NINE'S LEGACY

I AM NUMBER FOUR: THE LOST FILES #3: THE FALLEN LEGACIES

I AM NUMBER FOUR: THE LOST FILES #4: THE SEARCH FOR SAM

I AM NUMBER FOUR: THE LOST FILES #5: THE LAST DAYS OF LORIEN

I AM NUMBER FOUR: THE LOST FILES #6: THE FORGOTTEN ONES

I AM NUMBER FOUR: THE LOST FILES #7: FIVE'S LEGACY

I AM NUMBER FOUR: THE LOST FILES #8: RETURN TO PARADISE

I AM NUMBER FOUR: THE LOST FILES #9: FIVE'S BETRAYAL

Novella Collections

I AM NUMBER FOUR: THE LOST FILES: THE LEGACIES

(Contains novellas #1–#3)

I AM NUMBER FOUR: THE LOST FILES: SECRET HISTORIES

(Contains novellas #4–#6)

I AM NUMBER FOUR: THE LOST FILES: HIDDEN ENEMY

(Contains novellas #7–#9)

THE REVENGE OF SEVEN

BOOK FIVE OF THE LORIEN LEGACIES

PITTACUS LORE

HARPER
An Imprint of HarperCollins*Publishers*

The Revenge of Seven

 For information address HarperCollins Children's Books, a division of HarperCollins Publishers, 195 Broadway, New York, NY 10007.

www.epicreads.com

Library of Congress Control Number: 2014942407

ISBN 978-0-06-219472-5 (trade bdg.)

ISBN 978-0-06-234705-3 (intl. ed.)

ISBN 978-0-06-236719-8 (special ed.)

Typography by Ray Shappell

14 15 16 17 18 CG/RRDC 10 9 8 7 6 5 4 3 2

❖

First Edition

CHAPTER ONE

THE NIGHTMARE IS OVER. WHEN I OPEN MY EYES, there's nothing but darkness.

I'm in a bed, that much I can tell, and it's not my own. The mattress is enormous, somehow contoured perfectly to my body, and for a moment I wonder if my friends moved me to one of the bigger beds in Nine's penthouse. I stretch my legs and arms out as far as they'll go and can't find the edges. The sheet draped over me is more slippery than soft, almost like a piece of plastic, and it is radiating heat. Not just heat, I realize, but also a steady vibration that soothes my sore muscles.

How long have I been asleep, and where the heck am I?

I try to remember what happened to me, but all I can think of is my last vision. It felt like I was in that night-mare for days. I can still smell the burned-rubber stench of Washington, D.C. Smog clouds lingered over the city, a reminder of the battle fought there. Or the battle that will be fought there, if my vision actually comes true.

The visions. Are they part of a new Legacy? None of the others have Legacies that leave them traumatized in the morning. Are they prophecies? Threats sent by Setrákus Ra, like the dreams John and Eight used to have? Are they warnings?

Whatever they are, I wish they'd stop happening.

I take a few deep breaths to clean the smell of Washington out of my nostrils, even though I know it's all in my head. What's worse than the smell is that I can remember every little detail, right down to the horrified look on John's face when he saw me on that stage with Setrákus Ra, condemning Six to death. He was trapped in the vision, too, just like I was. I was powerless up there, stuck between Setrákus Ra, self-appointed ruler of Earth, and . . .

Five. He's working for the Mogadorians! I have to warn the others. I sit bolt upright and my head swims—too fast, too soon—rust-colored blobs floating through my vision. I blink them away, my eyes feeling gummy, my mouth dry and throat sore.

This definitely isn't the penthouse.

My movement must trigger some nearby sensor, because the room's lights slowly grow brighter. They come on gradually, the room eventually bathed in a pale red glow. I look around for the source of the light and discover it pulsing from veins interwoven through the chrome-paneled walls. A chill goes through me at how precise the room looks, how severe, lacking any decoration at all. The heat from the blanket increases, almost as if it wants me to curl back up beneath it. I shove it away.

This is a Mogadorian place.

I crawl across the mammoth bed—it's bigger than an SUV, big enough for a ten-foot-tall Mogadorian dictator to comfortably relax in—until my bare feet dangle over the metal floor. I'm wearing a long gray nightgown embroidered with thorny black vines. I shudder, thinking about them putting me into this gown and leaving me here to rest. They could've just killed me, but instead they put me in pajamas? In my vision, I was sitting alongside Setrákus Ra. He called me his heir. What does that even mean? Is that why I'm still alive?

It doesn't matter. The simple fact is: I've been captured. I know this. Now what am I going to do about it?

I figure the Mogs must have moved me to one of their bases. Except this room isn't like the horrific and tiny cells that Nine and Six described from when they were captured. No, this must be the Mogadorians' twisted idea of hospitality. They're trying to take care of me.

Setrákus Ra wants me treated more like a guest than a prisoner. Because, one day, he wants me ruling next to him. Why, I still don't understand, but right now it's the only thing keeping me alive.

Oh no. If I'm here, what happened to the others in Chicago?

My hands start to shake and tears sting my eyes. I have to get out of here. And I have to do it alone.

I push down the fear. I push down the lingering visions of a decimated Washington. I push down the worries about my friends. I push it all down. I need to be a blank slate, like I was when we first fought Setrákus Ra in New Mexico, like I was during my training sessions with the others. It's easiest for me to be brave when I just don't think about it. If I act on instinct, I can do this.

Run, I imagine Crayton saying. *Run until they're too tired to chase you.*

I need something to fight them with. I look around the room for anything I can use as a weapon. Next to the bed is a metallic nightstand, the only other furniture in the room. The Mogs left a glass of water there for me, which I'm not dumb enough to drink even though I'm insanely thirsty. Next to the glass, there's a dictionary-sized book with an oily, snaky-skin cover. The ink on the cover looks singed, the words indented and rough around the edges, as if it were printed with acid for ink.

The title reads *The Great Book of Mogadorian Progress*, surprisingly in English. Under it are a series of angular boxes and hash marks that I assume is Mogadorian.

I pick up the book and open it. Each page is divided in half, English on one side and Mogadorian on the other. I wonder if I'm supposed to read this thing.

I slam the book closed. The important thing is that it's

heavy and I can swing it. I won't be turning any Mogadorian guards into ash clouds, but it's better than nothing.

I climb down from the bed and walk over to what I think is the door. It's a rectangular panel cut into the plated wall, but there aren't any knobs or buttons.

As I tiptoe closer, wondering how I'm going to open this thing, there's a mechanical whirring noise from inside the wall. It must be on a motion sensor like the lights, because the door hisses upward as soon as I'm close, disappearing into the ceiling.

I don't stop to wonder why I'm not locked down. Clutching the Mogadorian book, I step into a hallway that's just as cold and metallic as my room.

"Ah," says a woman's voice. "You're awake."

Rather than guards, a Mogadorian woman perches on a stool outside my room, obviously waiting for me. I'm not sure if I've ever seen a female Mog before, and definitely not one like her. Middle-aged, with wrinkles forming in the pale skin around her eyes, the Mog looks surprisingly unthreatening in a high-necked, floor-length dress, like something one of the Sisters would wear back at Santa Teresa. Her head is shaved except for two long, black braids at the back of her skull, the rest of her scalp covered by an elaborate tattoo. Instead of being nasty and vicious, like the Mogs I've fought before, this one is almost elegant.

I stop short in front of her, not sure what to do.

The Mog glances at the book in my hands and smiles.

"And ready to begin your studies, I see," she says, getting up. She's tall, slender and vaguely spiderlike. Standing before me, she dips into an elaborate bow. "Mistress Ella, I shall be your instructor while—"

As soon as her head comes low enough, I smack her across the face with the book as hard as I can.

She doesn't see it coming, which I guess is strange because all the Mogs I've encountered have been ready to fight. This one lets out a short grunt and then hits the floor with a fluttering of fabric from her fancy dress.

I don't stop to see if I've knocked her out or if she's pulling a blaster from some hidden compartment in that dress. I run, choosing a direction at random and hurtling down the hallway as fast as I can. The metal floor stings my bare feet and my muscles begin to ache, but I ignore all that. I have to get out of here.

Too bad these secret Mogadorian bases never have any exit signs.

I turn one corner and then another, sprinting through hallways that are pretty much identical. I keep expecting sirens to start blaring now that I've escaped, but they never do. There aren't any heavy Mogadorian footfalls chasing after me either.

Just when I'm starting to get winded and thinking about slowing down, a doorway opens on my right and two Mogadorians step forward. They're more like the ones I'm used to—burly, dressed in their black combat gear, beady eyes glaring at me. I dart around them, even though neither of them makes any attempt to grab me. In fact, I think I hear one of them laughing.

What is going on here?

I can feel the two Mog soldiers watching me run, so I duck down the first hallway that I can. I'm not sure if I've been going in circles or what. There isn't any sunlight or outside noises at all, nothing to indicate that I might be getting closer to an exit. It doesn't seem like the Mogs even care what I do, like they know I've got no chance to get out of here.

I slow down to catch my breath, cautiously inching down this latest sterile hallway. I'm still clutching the book—my only weapon—and my hand is starting to cramp. I switch hands and press on.

Up ahead, a wide archway opens with a hydraulic hiss; it's different from the other doors, wider, and there are strangely blinking lights on the other side.

Not blinking lights. Stars.

As I walk under the archway, the metal-plated ceiling gives way to a glass bubble, the room wide-open, almost like a planetarium. Except real. There are various consoles and computers protruding from the floor—maybe this is some kind of control room—but I ignore them, drawn instead to the dizzying view through the expansive window.

Darkness. Stars.

Earth.

Now I understand why the Mogadorians weren't chasing me. They know there's nowhere for me to go.

I'm in space.

I get right up to the glass, pressing my hands against it. I can feel the emptiness outside, the endless, ice-cold, airless space between me and that floating blue orb in the distance.

"Glorious, isn't it?"

His booming voice is like a bucket of cold water dumped on me. I spin around and press my back to the glass, feeling like the void behind me might be preferable to facing him.

Setrákus Ra stands behind one of the control panels, watching me, a hint of a smile on his face. The first thing I notice is that he's not nearly as huge as he was when we fought him at Dulce Base. Still, Setrákus Ra is tall and imposing, his broad physique clad in a stern black uniform, studded and decorated with an assortment of jagged Mogadorian medals. Three Loric pendants, the ones he took from the dead Garde, hang from around his neck, glowing a subdued cobalt.

"I see you've already taken up my book," he says, gesturing to my dictionary-sized club. I didn't realize I was clutching it to my chest. "Although not necessarily in the way I'd hoped. Fortunately, your Proctor wasn't badly injured . . ."

Suddenly, in my hands, the book begins to glow red,

just like the piece of debris I picked up back at Dulce Base. I don't know exactly how I'm doing it, or even what I'm doing.

"Ah," Setrákus Ra says, watching with a raised eyebrow. "Very good."

"Go to hell!" I scream, and fling the glowing book at him.

Before it's even halfway to him, Setrákus Ra raises one huge hand and the book stops in midair. I watch as the glow I'd infused it with slowly fades.

"Now, now," he chides me. "Enough of that."

"What do you want from me?" I shout, frustrated tears filling my eyes.

"You already know that," he replies. "I showed you what's to come. Just as I once showed Pittacus Lore."

Setrákus Ra hits a few buttons on the control panel in front of him and the ship begins to move. Gradually, the Earth, seeming both impossibly far and also like it's so close I could reach out and grab it, drifts across my view. We aren't moving towards it; we're turning in place.

"You are aboard the *Anubis*," Setrákus Ra intones, a note of pride in his gravelly voice. "The flagship of the Mogadorian fleet."

When the ship completes its turn, I gasp. I reach out and press my hand against the glass for support, knees suddenly weak.

Outside, in orbit around the Earth, is the Mogadorian

fleet. Hundreds of ships—most of them long and silver, about the size of small airplanes, just like the ones the Garde have described fighting before. But among them are at least twenty enormous warships that dwarf the rest—looming and menacing, mounted cannons jutting off their angular frames, aimed right at the unsuspecting planet below.

"No," I whisper. "This can't be happening."

Setrákus Ra walks towards me, and I'm too shocked by the hopeless sight before me to even move. Gently, he drapes his hand on my shoulder. I can feel the coldness of his pale fingers through my gown.

"The time has come," he says, gazing at the fleet with me. "The Great Expansion has come to Earth at last. We will celebrate Mogadorian Progress together, granddaughter."

CHAPTER TWO

FROM THE CRACKED SECOND-FLOOR WINDOW OF an abandoned textile factory, I watch an old man in a ragged trench coat and filthy jeans crouch down in the doorway of the boarded-up building across the street. Once he's settled, the man pulls a brown-bagged bottle from his coat and starts drinking. It's the middle of the afternoon—I'm on watch—and he's the only living soul I've seen in this abandoned part of Baltimore since we got here yesterday. It's a quiet, deserted place, and yet it's still preferable to the version of Washington, D.C., I saw in Ella's vision. For now at least, it doesn't look like the Mogadorians have pursued us from Chicago.

Although technically, they wouldn't have to. There's already a Mogadorian among us.

Behind me, Sarah stomps her foot. We're in what used to be the foreman's office, dust everywhere, the floorboards swollen and mildewed. I turn around just in time to see her frowning at the remains of a cockroach on the bottom of her sneaker.

"Careful. You might go crashing right through the floor," I tell her, only half joking.

"I guess it was too much to ask for all your secret bases to be in penthouse apartments, huh?" Sarah asks, fixing me with a teasing smile.

We slept in this old factory last night, our sleeping bags laid on the sunken floorboards. Both of us are filthy, it's been a couple of days since our last real shower, and Sarah's blond hair is caked with dirt. She's still beautiful to me. Without her at my side, I might've totally lost it after the attack in Chicago, where the Mogs kidnapped Ella and destroyed the penthouse.

I grimace at the thought, and Sarah's smile immediately fades. I leave the window and walk over to her.

"This not knowing is killing me," I say, shaking my head. "I don't know what to do."

Sarah touches my face, trying to console me. "At least we know they won't hurt Ella. Not if what you saw in that vision is true."

"Yeah," I snort. "They'll just turn her into a brainwashed traitor, like . . ."

I trail off, thinking of the rest of our missing friends and the turncoat they traveled with. We still haven't heard anything from Six and the others, not that there's an easy way for them to get in touch with us. All their Chests are here and, assuming they could even try reaching us by more traditional methods, they wouldn't have the first clue how to find us, seeing as we had to flee Chicago.

The only thing I know for sure is that I have a fresh scar on my leg, the fourth of its kind. It doesn't hurt anymore, but it feels like a weight. If the Garde had stayed apart, if we'd kept the Loric charm intact, that fourth scar would've symbolized my death. Instead, one of my friends is dead in Florida, and I don't know how, or who, or what's happened to the rest of them.

I feel in my gut that Five is still alive. I saw him in Ella's vision, standing alongside Setrákus Ra, a traitor. He must have led the others into a trap, and now one of them won't be coming back. Six, Marina, Eight, Nine—one of them is gone.

Sarah wraps her hand around mine, massaging it, trying to ease some of the tension.

"I can't stop thinking about what I saw in that vision . . . ," I begin, trailing off. "We'd lost, Sarah. And now it feels like it's happening for real. Like this is the beginning of the end."

"That doesn't mean anything and you know it," Sarah replied. "Look at Eight. Wasn't there some kind of death prophecy about him? And he survived."

I frown, not stating the obvious, that Eight could be

the one who was killed down in Florida.

"I know it seems bleak," Sarah continues, "and, I mean, it is pretty bad, John. Obviously."

"Good pep talk."

She squeezes my hand, hard, and widens her eyes at me like *shut up.*

"But those guys down in Florida are Garde," she says. "They're going to fight, they're going to keep going and they're going to win. You have to believe, John. When you were comatose back in Chicago, we never gave up on you. We kept fighting and it paid off. Just when it seemed like we'd lost, you *saved* us."

I think about the state my friends were in when I finally awoke back in Chicago. Malcolm was mortally wounded and Sarah badly hurt, Sam nearly out of ammo and Bernie Kosar unaccounted for. They'd put it all on the line for me.

"You guys saved me first," I reply.

"Yeah, obviously. So return the favor and save our planet."

The way she says it, like it's no big deal, makes me smile. I pull Sarah close and kiss her.

"I love you, Sarah Hart."

"Love you back, John Smith."

"Um, I love you guys, too . . ."

Sarah and I both turn to find Sam standing in the doorway, an awkward smile on his face. Curled up in his arms is a huge orange cat, one of the six Chimærae that our new Mogadorian friend brought with him, drawn to us by Bernie Kosar's rooftop howling. Apparently, the stick BK took from Eight's Chest was some kind of Chimæra totem used to lead them to us, like a Loric dog whistle. We stuck to back roads on our way to Baltimore, careful to make sure we weren't tailed. The crowded van ride gave us plenty of time to brainstorm names for our new allies. This particular Chimæra, preferring a chubby cat-shape as its regular form, Sam insisted we name Stanley, in honor of Nine's old alter ego. If he's still alive, I'm sure Nine will be thrilled to have a fat cat with an obvious affection for Sam named after him.

"Sorry," Sam says, "did I spoil the moment?"

"Not at all," Sarah replies, stretching out one arm towards Sam. "Group hug?"

"Maybe later," Sam says, looking at me. "The others are back and setting everything up downstairs."

I nod, reluctantly letting go of Sarah and walking over to the duffel bag with our supplies. "They have any problems?"

Sam shakes his head. "They had to settle for just a couple of little camping generators. Not enough cash for something big. Anyway, it should be enough juice."

"What about surveillance?" I ask, pulling the white locator tablet and its adapter free from the duffel bag.

"Adam said he didn't see any Mog scouts," Sam answers.

"Well, out of anyone, he'd know how to spot them," Sarah puts in.

"True," I reply halfheartedly, still not trusting this so-called good Mogadorian, even though he's done nothing but help us since showing up in Chicago. Even now, with him and Malcolm setting up our newly purchased electronics on the factory floor below, I feel a vague sense of unease at having one of them so close. I push it down. "Let's go."

We follow Sam down a rusty spiral staircase and onto the floor of the factory proper. The place must've been closed down in a hurry because there are still racks of musty, eighties-style men's suits pushed up against the walls and half-full boxes of raincoats abandoned on conveyor belts.

A Chimæra in golden retriever form that Sarah insisted we call Biscuit tumbles into our path, her teeth clenched around the ripped sleeve of a suit, locked in a tug-of-war with Dust, the gray husky. Another Chimæra, Gamera, which Malcolm named after some old movie monster, trundles after the others but has trouble keeping up in his snapping turtle form. The two other new Chimærae—a hawk we dubbed Regal and a scrawny raccoon we named Bandit—watch the game from one of the inoperative conveyor belts.

It's a relief to see them playing. The Chimærae weren't in the best shape when Adam liberated them from Mogadorian experimentation, and they still weren't doing so hot when he brought them to Chicago. It was slow going, but I was able to use my healing Legacy to fix them up. There was something inside of them, something Mogadorian, that actually felt like it was pushing back against my powers. It even made my Lumen flare up briefly, something that's never happened when using my healing. Ultimately, though, whatever the Mogs did was washed away by my Legacy.

I'd never actually used my healing Legacy on a Chimæra before that night. Luckily, it worked, because there was one Chimæra in even worse condition than all our new friends.

"Have you seen BK?" I ask Sam, scanning the room for him. I had found him on the roof of the John Hancock Center, shredded by Mogadorian blaster fire and barely clinging to life. I used my healing on him, praying that it would work. Even though he's better now, I've still been keeping an extra-close eye on him, probably because the fates of so many of my other friends are unknown.

"There," Sam replies, pointing.

At one end of the room, against a wall covered with competing graffiti tags, are a trio of industrial-size laundry bins overflowing with piles of khaki pants. It's at the summit of one of these piles that Bernie Kosar rests, the antics of Biscuit and Dust seeming to tire him out. Despite my healing, he's still weak from the fight in Chicago—and also missing a jagged chunk from one of his ears—but with my animal telepathy I can sense a sort of contentedness coming off him as he watches the other Chimærae. When BK sees us enter, his tail thumps fresh dust clouds from the pile of old clothes.

Sam sets down Stanley, and the cat trundles over to the clothes piles with BK, settling into what I guess is the designated Chimæra napping zone.

"Never thought I'd have my own Chimæra," Sam says, "much less a half dozen of them."

"And I never thought I'd be working with one of *them*," I reply, my gaze settling on Adam.

At the center of the factory floor, steelwork benches are bolted into the floor. Sam's dad, Malcolm, and Adam are setting up the computer equipment they just purchased by trading in some of my waning supply of Loric gemstones. Because there's no electricity running to this old factory, they had to buy some small battery-powered generators for the trio of laptops and mobile hotspot. I watch Adam hooking up one of the laptop batteries—his deathly pale skin, lank black hair and angular features making him slightly more human looking than the usual Mogadorians—and remind myself that he's on our side. Sam and Malcolm seem to trust him; plus he's got a Legacy, the power to create shock waves, which he inherited from One. If I hadn't seen him use the Legacy with my own eyes, I'm not sure I'd even think it was possible. Part of me wants to believe, maybe even needs to believe, that a Mog wouldn't be able to just steal a Legacy, that he has to be worthy. That it happened for a reason.

"Look at it this way," Sam says quietly as we walk over to the others. "Humans, Loric, Mogs . . . we've got like the first meeting of the Intergalactic United Nations over here. It's historic."

I snort and step up to the laptop Adam has just finished connecting. He takes one look at me and must detect something—maybe I'm not doing such a good job concealing my conflicted feelings—because he looks down and steps aside, making room for me and moving on to the next laptop. He keeps his eyes fixed on the screen, typing quickly.

"How'd it go?" I ask.

"We got most of the gear we need," Malcolm replies as he fiddles with a wireless router. Even with his beard starting to get majorly unkempt, Malcolm looks healthier than he did when I first met him. "Anything happen here?"

"Nothing," I say, shaking my head. "It'd take a miracle for the Garde in Florida to track us down. And Ella . . . I keep hoping her voice will pop into my head and tell me where they took her, but she hasn't made contact."

"At least we'll know where the others are once the tablet is hooked up," Sarah says.

"With the gear we bought, I think we can run a hack on the John Hancock building's phone network," Malcolm suggests. "That way, if they try calling in from the road, we can intercept the call."

"Good idea," I reply, plugging the white locator tablet into the laptop and waiting for it to boot up.

Malcolm pushes his glasses up his nose and clears his throat. "It was Adam's idea, actually."

"Oh," I reply, keeping my voice neutral.

"That *is* a good idea," Sarah chimes in. She scoots in next to Malcolm and starts working on the third laptop, giving me a look like I should try saying something nice to Adam. When I don't, an awkward silence settles over the group. There have been a lot of those since we left Chicago.

Before it can get too weird, the tablet boots up. Sam peers over my shoulder.

"They're still in Florida," Sam says.

There's a solitary dot for me on the tablet, pulsing on the East Coast, and then miles to the south are the four dots for the surviving Garde. Three of the dots are bunched together, basically overlapping into one glowing blob, while a fourth is a short distance away.

Immediately, scenarios for that isolated dot begin cycling through my head. Was one of our friends captured? Did they have to separate after they were attacked? Is that Five apart from the others? Does that prove he's a traitor, like in my vision?

I'm distracted from these thoughts by the fifth dot on the tablet, literally an ocean away from the others. This one hovers over the Pacific, its glow a little dimmer than the rest.

"That must be Ella," I say, my brow furrowing. "But how—"

Before I can finish my question, Ella's dot flickers and disappears. A second later, before I can even process my panic, Ella blinks back to life, now hovering over Australia.

"What the hell?" Sam asks, staring over my shoulder.

"It's moving so fast," I say. "Maybe they're transporting her somewhere."

The dot disappears again, then reappears at an impossible point over Antarctica, nearly off the edge of the tablet's screen. For the next few seconds, it flickers in and out, bouncing across the map. I smack the side of the tablet with my palm out of frustration.

"They're scrambling the signal somehow," I say. "We've got no chance of finding her while it's like this."

Sam points to the others clustered around Florida.

"If they were going to hurt Ella, wouldn't they have done it already?"

"Setrákus Ra wants her," Sarah puts in, looking at me. I had told them all about that nightmare scene in D.C. and Ella ruling alongside Setrákus Ra. It's still hard for any of us to believe, but at least it gives us one advantage. We know what Setrákus Ra wants.

"I hate to leave her out there," I say grimly. "But I don't think he'll harm her. Not yet, anyway."

"At least we know where the others are," Sam insists. "We need to get down there before someone else . . ."

"Sam's right," I decide, driven by the sinking feeling that one of those dots could blink out at any moment. "They might need our help."

"I think that would be a mistake," Adam says. His voice is tentative, but there's still enough Mog harshness to make my fists clench from reflex. I'm not used to having one of them around.

I turn to stare at him. "What did you say?"

"A mistake," he repeats. "It's predictable, John. It's a reactionary move. This is why my people always catch up to you."

I can feel my jaw working, trying to form a response, but mostly I just want to punch his face in. I'm about to take a step forward when Sam puts a hand on my shoulder.

"Easy," Sam says quietly.

"You want us to just sit around here and do nothing?" I ask Adam, trying to keep my cool. I know I should hear him out, but this whole situation has me feeling cornered. And now I'm supposed to take advice from a guy whose species has been hunting me for my entire life?

"Of course not," Adam replies, looking up at me with those coal-colored Mogadorian eyes.

"Then what?" I snap. "Give me one good reason we shouldn't go to Florida."

"I'll give you two," Adam replies. "First, if the rest of the Garde are in danger or captured as you suspect, then their continued survival hinges on luring you in. They are useful only as bait."

"You're saying it could be a trap," I reply through gritted teeth.

"If they are captured, then yes, of course it is a trap. On the other hand, if they are free, what good will your heroic intervention do? Aren't they highly trained and perfectly capable of getting themselves out of trouble?"

What can I say to that? No? Six and Nine, pretty much the two most badass people I know, aren't capable of escaping from Florida and tracking us down? But what if they're down there waiting for us to come get them? I shake my head, still feeling like I want to throttle Adam.

"So what're we supposed to do in the meantime?" I

ask him. "Just sit around and wait for them?"

"We can't do that," Sam jumps in. "We can't just leave them. They have no way of finding us."

Adam spins his laptop around so I can see the screen.

"Between kidnapping Ella and killing a Garde in Florida, my people will believe they have you on the run once again. They won't be expecting a counter-strike."

On the laptop, Adam has pulled up satellite photographs of an expanse of suburbia. It looks like a totally generic, wealthy community. When I look a little closer, I notice a paranoid number of security cameras mounted on the imposingly tall stone wall that encircles the entire property.

"This is Ashwood Estates, just outside of Washington, D.C.," Adam continues. "It's home to the top-ranking Mogadorians assigned to North America. With the Plum Island facility wrecked and the Chimærae recovered, I think we should focus our attack here."

"What about the mountain base in West Virginia?" I ask.

Adam shakes his head. "That is a military installation only, kept out of sight so my people's forces can mass there. We'd have a hard time taking it down now. And anyway, the real power, the trueborn Mogadorians, the leaders—they reside in Ashwood."

Malcolm clears his throat. "I tried to relay everything

"It's possible we could find a way to restore your memories," Adam says, sounding eager to help Malcolm. "If the equipment wasn't too badly damaged."

What Adam's saying makes sense, but I can't quite bring myself to admit it. I've spent my entire life running and hiding from Mogadorians, fighting them, killing them. They've taken everything from me. And now, here I am, making battle plans alongside one. It just doesn't feel right. Not to mention we're talking about a full frontal assault on a Mogadorian compound with none of the other Garde backing me up.

As if on cue, Dust wanders over and sits down next to Adam's feet. He reaches down to absently scratch behind its ears.

If the animals trust him, shouldn't I be able to?

"Whatever we find in those tunnels," Adam continues, probably knowing I'm not sold, "I am certain it will provide valuable insight into their plans. If your friends are captured or being tracked, we will know for sure once I've accessed the Mogadorian systems."

"What if one of them dies while we're on this mission of yours?" Sam asks, his voice cracking a little at the thought. "What if they die because we didn't rescue them when we had the chance?"

Adam pauses, thinking this over. "I know this must be hard for you," he says, looking between me and Sam.

"I admit, it's a calculated risk."

"Calculated risk," I repeat. "Those are our friends you're talking about."

"Yeah," Adam replies. "And I'm trying to help keep them alive."

Logically, I know Adam really is trying to help. But I'm stressed and I've been brought up not to trust his kind. Before I know what I'm doing, I take a step towards him and jab a finger into his chest.

"This better be worth it," I tell him. "And if something happens in Florida . . ."

"I'll take responsibility," he replies. "It'll be on me. If I'm wrong, John, you can dust me."

"If you're wrong, I probably won't need to," I say, staring into his eyes. Adam doesn't look away.

Sarah loudly whistles between her fingers, getting everyone's attention.

"If we can put the whole macho posturing thing on hold for a second, I think you guys should take a look at this."

I step around Adam, telling myself to cool down, and look over Sarah's shoulder at the website she's pulled up.

"I was looking up news stories about Chicago and this popped up," she explains.

It's a pretty slick-looking website, except for the all-caps headlines and sheer amount of flying saucer GIFs cluttering the sidebars. The stories listed under Most Popular, all of the links in a neon green that I guess is supposed to look alien, include: MOGADORIANS UNDERMINING GOVERNMENT and EARTH'S LORIC PROTECTORS DRIVEN INTO HIDING. The page Sarah currently has open features a picture of the burning John Hancock Center along with the headline MOG ATTACK IN CHICAGO: IS THIS THE ZERO HOUR?

The website is called They Walk Among Us.

"Oh jeez," Sam groans, joining the huddle around Sarah's computer. "Not these creeps."

"What is this?" I ask Sarah, squinting at the story on the screen.

"These dudes used to be strictly into the old-school black-and-white zine style," Sam says. "Now they're on the internet? I can't decide if that makes them better or worse."

"The Mogs killed them," I point out. "How does this even exist in *any* form?"

"I guess there's a new editor," Sarah says. "Check this out."

Sarah clicks into the website's archives, going back to the first story ever posted. The headline reads PARADISE HIGH SCHOOL ATTACK START OF ALIEN INVASION. Below that is a grainy cell-phone picture of the destruction around our high school's football field. I quickly skim the article. The level of detail is astounding. It's like whoever wrote this was there with us.

"Who's JollyRoger182?" I ask, looking at the screen name credited in the post.

Sarah looks up at me with an odd smile, bewilderment mixing with something like pride.

"You're going to think I'm crazy," she says.

"What's a Jolly Roger, anyway?" Sam asks, thinking out loud. "The pirate flag?"

"Yeah," Sarah replies, nodding. "Like the Paradise High Pirates. Whose old quarterback happens to be one of the only other people outside our group to know what went down at the high school."

I widen my eyes at Sarah. "No way."

"Yes way," she replies. "I think JollyRoger182 is Mark James."

CHAPTER THREE

"'THE MOGADORIANS, ALONG WITH THEIR CRONIES from the corrupted branches of national security, are believed to have fought a protracted battle in New Mexico against the heroic Garde,'" Sam reads aloud. "'My sources believe the Mogadorians were forced to retreat after their leader sustained an injury. The whereabouts of the Garde remain unknown.'"

"He's right on the money," Malcolm says, turning to me. "But where is he getting his information?"

"No idea," I reply. "We didn't exactly stay in touch after Paradise."

I lean over Sam's shoulder to check out the next story. I'm baffled by the amount of information Mark James—or whoever this is—has posted to They Walk Among Us. There are details of our battle at Dulce Base, early speculation about the attack in Chicago, frightening essays about what Mogs look like and what they're capable of, and posts rallying humanity in support of the Loric. There are also articles covering topics that I've never considered, even ones about which members of the U.S. government are in league with the Mogadorians.

Sam clicks through to a story where Mark accuses the secretary of defense, a man named Bud Sanderson, of using his political clout to pave the way for a Mogadorian invasion. Another click yields a second article about Sanderson, one with the tabloid-friendly headline CORRUPT S.O.D. USING MOGADORIAN GENETIC TREATMENTS. The story is tied to an image of Sanderson from five years ago juxtaposed with one of him from a few months ago. In the first, Sanderson looks like a haggard man in his late seventies—his face is age-spotted and he has a double chin and a steep paunch. In the second, he's lost weight and has a healthy glow and a full head of silver hair. It's almost as if he's time-traveled. In fact, I bet most people would think the picture was a hoax, like it's a photo of Sanderson from twenty years ago with a fake time stamp. But if you take Mark at his word, something's definitely changed with the secretary of defense—something way bigger than diet and exercise, or even plastic surgery.

Sam shakes his head, not buying it. "How would Mark possibly know all this? I mean, Sarah, you went out with him. Did he even know how to read?"

"Yes, Sam," Sarah replies, rolling her eyes. "Mark could read."

"But he was never, uh, journalistically inclined, was he? This is like WikiLeaks over here."

"People tend to change when they find out aliens are real," Sarah responds. "It looks to me like he's been trying to help."

"We don't know for sure that it's Mark," I say, frowning.

I look over at Adam. He's been quiet since we started exploring the They Walk Among Us website, listening to us with a hand on his chin, thoughtful.

"Could this be some kind of trap?" I ask him, figuring it's best to consult the expert.

"Of course," he says without hesitation. "Although if it is, it's an elaborate one. And, even for the sake of trapping you, I find it hard to believe Setrákus Ra would admit to being driven off from Dulce Base."

"Is it true?" Malcolm asks. "What he's written about the secretary of defense?"

"I don't know," Adam replies. "It very well could be."

"I'm going to email him," Sarah announces, opening up a new browser tab.

"Hold on," Adam says quickly, a bit more polite than when he slammed my idea to try rescuing the others. "If this Mark person really does have access to all this highly secret intel—"

Sam chuckles.

"—my people will almost certainly be monitoring his communications," Adam concludes, raising an eyebrow at Sam. He turns back to Sarah. "They'll also definitely be monitoring your email."

Sarah slowly lifts her hands away from the keyboard. "Can't you do anything about that?"

"I know how their cyber-tracking systems work. It was something I . . . excelled at during my training. I could write an encryption code, reroute our IP address through servers in different cities." Adam turns to me, like he wants permission. "They'd unravel it eventually. We'd have to leave this place within twenty-four hours to be safe."

"Do it," I tell him. "Better that we keep moving, anyway."

Adam immediately begins typing commands into his laptop. Sam rubs his hands together and leans over Adam's shoulder. "You should reroute them to as many crazy places as possible. Make them think Sarah's in Russia or something."

Adam smirks. "Consider it done."

It takes Adam about twenty minutes to write some code that will reroute our IP address through a dozen far-flung locations. I think back to the elaborate computer system Henri always had set up and the even more complicated grid that Sandor built in Chicago.

Then, I imagine a hundred Mogadorians, just like Adam, hunched over keyboards, stalking us. I never doubted our Cêpans were justified in their paranoia, but seeing Adam work I finally realize just how necessary it was.

"Whoa," Sarah says when she's finally able to open her email. The list of boldfaced unread mail consists entirely of messages from Mark James. "It really is him."

"Or the Mogs hacked his email," Sam suggests.

"Doubtful," Adam replies. "My people are thorough, sure, but this seems kind of . . . roundabout."

I glance over the email headings—lots of exclamation points and capital letters. A few months ago the idea of Mark James spamming my girlfriend would've gotten under my skin, but now it seems like our rivalry was something that happened to someone else, something from another life.

"When was the last time you checked this?" I ask.

"Weeks ago? I don't really remember," Sarah replies. "I've been a little busy."

She opens the most recent message from Mark and we all lean in to examine the contents.

Sarah—

I don't know why I keep sending these emails. Part of me hopes that you're reading them, using them to help the Loric, and can't reply for your own safety. Another part

of me worries that you aren't even out there, that you're gone. I refuse to believe that but . . .

I need to hear from you.

I thought I had a lead on you in New Mexico. All I found there was a deserted military base. It looked like a major battle went down. Way bigger and nastier than what happened in Paradise. I hope you guys got out safe.

I hope like hell I'm not the only one left to fight these assholes. That would suck.

A friend of mine set up a safe house for me. Way off the grid. A place where we can work on exposing those pale freaks to the world. If you can get in touch, I'll find a way to send you the coordinates. We're on to something big. Something international. I don't even know what to do with it.

If you're reading these, if you're still in contact with John, now would be a really good time to show up. I need your help.

—Mark

Sarah turns to me, her eyes wide with sudden passion, face set determinedly—I've seen that look before, know it well. It's the look she gives me right before telling me she wants to do something dangerous.

Without her even saying anything, I already know that Sarah wants to find Mark James.

The dashboard clock reads 7:45. We've got fifteen minutes until the bus leaves for Alabama.

I've got fifteen minutes left with Sarah Hart.

Fifteen minutes was about how long it took Adam to encrypt Sarah's email against any Mogadorian hackers. She got off a quick note to Mark, who replied almost immediately with an address for a restaurant in Huntsville. He told Sarah he'd watch the place for the next few days and, if she really was Sarah Hart, he'd pick her up there and spirit her off to his secret hideout. *At least Mark's being careful,* I told myself. That gives me confidence that Sarah will be safe. After that brief communication, Adam immediately wiped both email accounts from the internet.

Now, here we are.

We're parked in front of the bus station in downtown Baltimore, the place bustling with activity even at sunset. I'm behind the wheel, Sarah in the passenger seat next to me. We fit right in, just two teenagers sitting in a crappy car, in the middle of saying good-bye.

"I keep waiting for the part where you try talking me out of going," Sarah says, her smile a little sad. "You'll say it's too dangerous, we'll argue, you'll lose and I'll end up going anyway."

"It is dangerous," I reply, turning so I can face Sarah. "And I don't want you to go."

"That's more like it."

She takes my hand, lacing her fingers through mine. With my other hand, I run my fingers through her hair, eventually letting them rest gently on the back of her neck. I pull her in a little closer.

"But it's no more dangerous than staying here with me," I finish.

"That's the overprotective John I know and love," she replies.

"I'm not—" I start to protest, but cut myself off when I see her teasing smile.

"These good-byes never get any easier, do they?"

I shake my head. "No. They really don't."

We fall silent, holding tight to each other, watching the minutes on the dashboard clock slowly blink away.

Back at the textile factory, we didn't need to have a huge discussion about Sarah going to find Mark James. Everyone seemed to agree that it was the right thing to do. If Mark really had managed to acquire some crucial information on the Mogadorians, and if he was risking his life to help us, then we needed to return the favor. But the rest of the Garde was still missing. And Adam's plan to strike the Mogadorian stronghold in D.C. seemed more and more like the smartest play, a necessary strike to gather intelligence and show those bastards that we were still in this fight. There's too much happening for us to put all our resources into catching up with Mark.

Sarah made it easy by volunteering.

Of course, sending her off alone on a potentially dangerous mission involving an ex-boyfriend isn't exactly my favorite idea. But I can't shake the feeling that the grim future I saw in Ella's dream is racing towards us. We need all the help we can get. If there's even the tiniest possibility that sending Sarah to Alabama could help us win this war, it's a chance we have to take, my own selfish feelings be damned.

And anyway, she won't be totally alone on the trip.

In the backseat, Bernie Kosar stands with his paws braced against the closed window, tail wagging furiously as he watches all the people zipping in and out of the bus station. My old friend seemed pretty wiped out after the battle in Chicago, but some of his energy came back when we got on the road. Once, in Paradise, he'd been my protector. Now he will do the same for Sarah.

"I don't want you to think of me as your girlfriend right now," Sarah says out of the blue, totally composed.

I lean back a bit, squinting at her. "That's going to be hard for me."

"I want you to think of me as a soldier," she persists. "A soldier in this war who's doing what needs to be done. I don't know exactly what I'll find down south, but I have this weird feeling that I'll be able to help you better from there. At the very least, when it comes to battles, I won't be around to slow you down."

"You don't slow me down," I insist, but Sarah waves this objection away.

"It's okay, John. I want to be with you. I want to see that you're okay, I want to see you win. But not every soldier can be on the front lines, you know? Some do more good when they're away from the action."

"Sarah . . ."

"I've got my phone," she continues, motioning to the hastily packed backpack at her feet. Inside it she has a disposable cell phone that Malcolm bought, along with a few changes of clothes and a handgun. "I'll check in every eight hours. But if I don't, you have to keep going, keep fighting."

I get what she's trying to do. Sarah doesn't want me rushing off to Alabama if she misses one of her check-in phone calls. She wants my head in the game. Maybe she can sense it, too—that we're nearing the end of this fight, or at least crossing a point of no return.

Sarah looks into my eyes. "This is bigger than us, John."

"Bigger than us," I repeat, knowing it's the truth yet wanting to fight against it. I don't want to lose her, and I don't want to say good-bye. But I have to.

I look down at our interlinked hands and remember how simple things were, at least for a little while, back when I first moved to Paradise.

"You know, the first time my telekinesis started

working was during that Thanksgiving at your house."

"You never told me that," Sarah replies, an eyebrow raised, not sure why I'm suddenly getting sentimental. "Did my mom's cooking inspire you?"

I chuckle. "I don't know. Maybe. That was the same night Henri had his run-in with the original *They Walk Among Us* crew, along with the Mogadorians who were using them. Afterward, he wanted to leave Paradise, and I refused. Actually, I didn't just refuse, I used my telekinesis to pin him to the ceiling."

"Sounds like you," Sarah says, shaking her head and smiling. "Stubborn."

"I told him I couldn't go back to living on the run. Not after Paradise. And you."

"Oh, John . . ." Sarah puts her forehead against my chest.

"I used to think this war wasn't worth fighting if I couldn't be by your side," I tell her, gently lifting her chin. "But now, after everything that's happened, after everything I've seen—I realize that I'm fighting for the future. *Our* future."

The dashboard clock looms impossibly large in the corner of my eye. Only five minutes left. I focus on Sarah, wishing I had a Legacy where I could freeze time, or store this moment up. Tears slip down Sarah's cheeks and I wipe them away with my thumbs. She puts her hand over mine, squeezing hard, and I can tell she's trying to steel herself. She takes a deep, shuddering breath and fights back more tears.

"I have to go, John."

"I trust you," I whisper urgently. "I don't just mean to find Mark. If things get bad, I trust you to stay alive. I trust you to come back to me in one piece."

Sarah grabs the front of my shirt, pulls me in. I feel a few of her tears against my cheek. I try to let everything go—my missing friends, the war, her leaving me—and just live for a while in her kiss. I wish I could go back to Paradise with her, not as it is now, but the way it was months ago—sneakily making out in my temporary bedroom while Henri was grocery shopping, stealing looks during class, the easy, normal life. But that's over. We're not kids anymore. We're fighters—soldiers—and we have to act the part.

Sarah pulls away from me and, in one fluid motion, not wanting to drag this painful moment out any longer, she opens the door and hops out of the van. She shoulders her backpack and whistles. "Come on, Bernie Kosar!"

BK clambers into the front seat, head cocked at me, as if wondering why I'm not getting out of the van, too. I scratch him behind his good ear and he lets out a little whine.

Keep her safe, I tell him telepathically.

Bernie Kosar puts both his front paws on my leg and

sloppily licks the side of my face. Sarah laughs.

"So many good-bye kisses," she says as BK jumps down from the van. Sarah clips on his leash.

"This isn't good-bye," I say. "Not really."

"You're right," Sarah replies, her smile getting shaky, a note of uncertainty creeping into her voice. "I'll see you soon, John Smith. Stay safe."

"See you soon. I love you, Sarah Hart."

"I love you, too."

Sarah turns away, hurrying towards the sliding doors of the bus station, Bernie Kosar trotting along at her heels. She looks back at me only once, right before she disappears through the doors, and I wave. Then, she's gone—into the bus station and eventually off to some secret location in Alabama, searching for a way to help us win this war.

I have to stop myself from running after her, so I clutch the steering wheel until my knuckles are white. Too white—my Lumen kicks in unexpectedly, my hands glowing. I haven't lost control of that since . . . well, since back in Paradise. I take a deep breath and calm myself down, glancing around, making sure no one outside the bus station noticed. I turn the key in the ignition, feel the van rumble to life and pull away from the bus station.

I miss her. I already miss her.

I head back towards one of Baltimore's rougher

neighborhoods, where Sam, Malcolm and Adam are waiting for me, planning an assault. I know where I'm going and what I'm doing, but I still feel adrift. I remember my brief scuffle with Adam in the destroyed John Hancock penthouse, how I almost fell out the window. That feeling of emptiness behind me, of teetering right next to the edge, that's how I feel now.

But then I imagine Sarah's hands pulling me away from that empty space. I imagine what it will be like when we meet again, what it will be like with Setrákus Ra vanquished and the Mogadorians beaten back into the cold emptiness of space. I imagine the future and I smile grimly. There's only one way to make that happen.

It's time to fight.

CHAPTER FOUR

WE HIKE THROUGH THE DARKNESS, DOWN A MUDDY road carved out of the swampland, the rhythmic sucking noises from our waterlogged sneakers and the incessant chirping of bugs the only sounds. We pass by a solitary wooden pole, slanted and close to being totally uprooted, the streetlight out, power lines sagging under the overgrown trees, disappearing into them. It's a welcome sign of society after two days spent in the swamps, hardly sleeping, turning invisible at the slightest noise, plodding our way through muck.

It was Five who led us into the swampland. He knew the way, of course. It was his ambush. We didn't have an easy time finding our way out. It's not like we could've gone back to the car we drove down here, anyway. The Mogs would definitely be watching that.

A few steps ahead, Nine slaps the back of his neck, squashing a mosquito. At the noise, Marina flinches, and the field of cold she's been giving off since the fight with Five momentarily intensifies. I'm not sure if Marina's having trouble getting control of her new Legacy or if she's intentionally cooling the air around us. Considering how humid the Florida swamps have been, I guess it hasn't been so bad trekking around with a portable air conditioner.

"You all right?" I ask her quietly, not wanting Nine to overhear and yet knowing that's impossible with his heightened hearing. She hasn't spoken to Nine since Eight was killed, has barely said anything to me.

Marina looks over at me, but in the dark I can't get a read on her. "What do you think, Six?" she asks.

I squeeze her arm and find her skin cool to the touch.

"We'll get them," I tell her. I'm not much for these leader-style speeches—that's what John does—so I keep it blunt. "We'll kill them all. He won't have died in vain."

"He shouldn't have died at all," she replies. "We shouldn't have left him out there. Now they have him, doing Lord knows what to his body."

"We didn't have a choice," I counter, knowing it's true. After the beating we endured at the hands of Five, we were in no shape to fight off a battalion of Mogadorians backed up by one of their ships.

Marina shakes her head and falls silent.

"You know, I used to always want Sandor to take me camping," Nine butts in out of nowhere, looking at us over his shoulder. "I hated living in that cushy-ass penthouse.

But man, after this? I sort of miss it."

Marina and I don't respond. That's the way Nine's been talking since our battle with Five—these forced anecdotes about nothing, weirdly upbeat, like nothing serious happened out here. When he wasn't rambling, Nine made it a habit to hike ahead of us, using his speed to put some distance between us. When we caught up, he'd have already caught some animal, usually snake, and be cooking it over a small fire he built on a rare dry patch of land. It's like he wanted to pretend we were just on some fun camping trip. I'm not squeamish; I'd eat whatever Nine caught. Marina never did, though. I don't think the roasted swamp creatures bothered her so much as the fact it was Nine doing the hunting. She must be running on empty by now, even more so than me and Nine.

After another mile, I notice the road getting a little more packed down and well traveled. I can see light up ahead. Soon, the nonstop buzzing of the local insect life gives way to something equally annoying.

Country music.

I wouldn't exactly call this place a town. I'm sure it doesn't show up on even the most detailed map. It looks more like a campground that people forgot to leave. Or maybe this is just a place where the local hunters come to bro around and escape their wives, I think, noticing an overpopulation of pickup trucks in the nearby gravel parking lot.

There are a couple dozen crude huts scattered throughout this cleared stretch of swamp coast, all of them pretty much indistinguishable from an old-school outhouse. The huts basically consist of some pieces of plywood hastily nailed together, and they look like a strong breeze could knock them over. I guess when you're building at the edge of a Florida swamp, there's no point in putting too much effort in. Hung between the huts, lighting this grim little vista, are strings of blinking Christmas lights and a few gas-powered lanterns. Beyond the huts, where the solid ground sinks back into the swamp, there's a rickety dock with a few tied-up pontoon boats.

The source of the music—the center of this "town"—and the only solid structure built here is Trapper's, a skeevy-looking bar housed in a log cabin, the name proudly displayed along the roof in sizzling green neon. A row of stuffed alligators line the bar's wooden porch, their jaws open and searching. From inside, above the music, I can hear men shouting and pool balls cracking.

"All right," Nine says, clapping his hands. "My kind of place."

The place does sort of remind me of the off-the-grid spots I used to hit up when I was alone and on the run, places where the tight-knit and gritty locals made it easy to spot out-of-place Mogadorians. Even so, as I notice a scrawny middle-aged guy with a mullet and a tank top staring at us, chain-smoking in the shadows of the porch,

I wonder if we should find a safer place for us to poke our heads in.

But Nine is already halfway up the creaky wooden steps, Marina right behind him, and so I go along. Hopefully this place has a phone so we can at least get in touch with the others back in Chicago. Check to see how John and Ella are doing—hopefully better, somehow, especially now that we know the cure-all Five claimed to have in his Chest was a bunch of crap. We have to warn the others about him. Who knows what information he might've been feeding to the Mogadorians.

When we push through the swinging saloon doors of Trapper's, the music doesn't screech to a stop like in the movies, but everyone in the bar does turn their heads to stare at us, almost in unison. The place is cramped, not much to it besides the bar, a pool table and some beat-up lawn furniture. It stinks of sweat, kerosene and alcohol.

"Hoo boy," someone says, then whistles loudly.

I quickly realize that Marina and I are the only two women here. Hell, we might be the first women to ever set foot inside Trapper's. The drunks staring at us range from tremendously overweight to alarmingly skinny, all of them dressed in halfway-open plaid shirts or sweat-stained wifebeaters, some of them flashing gap-toothed leers, others smoothing down unkempt beards as they size us up.

One guy, in a ripped heavy-metal T-shirt and with a

lower lip stuffed with chewing tobacco, breaks away from the pool table to sidle up next to Marina.

"This must be my lucky night," the guy drawls, "because you gi—"

The rest of the pickup line is lost to the ages because the moment this guy tries to slide his arm around her shoulders, Marina roughly snatches his wrist. I can hear the moisture on his arm crackle as it flash freezes, and a second later the guy is crying out as Marina twists his arm behind his back.

"Do not come near me," she says in a measured tone, loud enough so the whole bar knows that the warning doesn't go just for the dude whose arm she's almost breaking.

Now, the room truly does go quiet. I notice one guy let his beer bottle slip down in his hand so he's holding it by the neck, all the better for swinging. A couple of burly guys at a back table exchange looks and stand up, eyeballing us. For a moment, I think the whole bar might try rushing us. That would end badly for them, and I try to communicate that with my stare. Nine, who with his tangled black hair and dirty face fits right in here, cracks his knuckles and lolls his head back and forth, watching the crowd.

Finally, one of the other hicks at the pool table hoots. "Mike, you dumbass, say excuse me and get over here! It's your shot!"

"Sorry," Mike whimpers to Marina, his arm turning blue where she's touching him. She shoves him away and he goes to rejoin his friends, rubbing his arm and trying to avoid looking at us.

Just like that, the tension breaks. Everyone goes back to what they were doing, which pretty much means guzzling beer. I figure scenes similar to that—little fights, stare downs, maybe a stabbing or two—must happen in Trapper's all the time. No big deal. Like I figured, this is one of those places where nobody asks any questions.

"Keep it under control," I tell Marina as we walk to the bar.

"I am," she replies.

"Didn't look like it."

Nine reaches the bar a step ahead of us, clearing a space between two hunchbacked drunks and slapping the chipped wooden surface.

The bartender, who looks just a tad more alert and cleaner than his customers, probably because he's wearing an apron, looks us over with weary disapproval.

"You should know I keep a shotgun under the bar. I don't want any more trouble," the bartender warns.

Nine grins at him. "It's cool, old man. You got anything to eat back there? We're starving."

"I could fry you up some burgers," the bartender replies after a moment's thought.

"It's not possum meat or something, is it?" Nine asks,

then holds up his hands. "Never mind, I don't want to know. Three of your finest, my man."

I lean across the bar before the bartender can retreat into the kitchen. "You got a phone?"

He jerks his thumb towards the bar's darkened back corner, where I notice a pay phone hanging cockeyed from the wall. "You could try that. It works part of the time."

"Looks like everything in here only works part of the time," Nine mutters, glancing at the TV mounted above the bar. The reception is bad at the moment, a news report swallowed up by static, the crooked rabbit ears emerging from the set not doing their job.

As the bartender disappears into the kitchen, Marina sits down with a couple of stools buffering her from Nine. She avoids eye contact, engrossed by the popping static on the TV. Meanwhile, Nine drums his hands on the bar, looking around, almost daring one of the drunks to say something to him. I've never felt so much like a babysitter.

"I'm going to try calling Chicago," I tell them.

Before I can go, the scrawny chain-smoker from outside squeezes into the space at the bar next to me. He flashes a smirk that's probably supposed to be charming, except he's missing a couple of teeth, and it doesn't quite reach his eyes, which look wild and desperate.

"Hey, honey," he says, obviously having missed Marina's demonstration about what happens when drunks try flirting with us. "Buy me a drink and I'll tell you my story. It's a doozy."

I stare at him. "Get away from me."

The bartender returns from the kitchen, the smell of cooking meat coming with him and making my stomach growl. He notices the scrawny guy next to me and immediately snaps his fingers in his face.

"Thought I told you not to come in here if you don't have any money, Dale," the bartender barks. "Go on, now."

Ignoring the bartender, Dale fixes me with one last pleading look. Seeing that I won't be budged, he slinks down the bar to beg one of the other patrons for a drink. I shake my head and take a deep breath; I need to get out of this place, I need a shower and I need to hit something. I'm trying to keep it cool, to be rational about things, especially considering my two companions aren't acting all that stable, but I'm angry. Furious, really. Five knocked me out, practically took my head clean off. In that time I was unconscious, the whole world changed. I know I couldn't have seen it coming—I never expected one of our own would turn traitor, even a freak like Five. Still, I can't help but feel it would've been different if I'd had my guard up. If I'd been fast enough to dodge that first punch, Eight might still be alive. I didn't even get a chance to fight, and it makes me feel cheated and useless. I bottle that rage up, saving it for the next time I see a Mogadorian.

"Six," Marina says, her voice suddenly fragile, not so

distant and cold. "Look at this."

The TV over the bar has started coming in, a rolling band of static disrupting the picture now and then, but a news broadcast is otherwise clearly visible. On it, a wind-blown reporter stands in front of a line of police tape, the John Hancock Center looming in the background.

"What the hell?" I say under my breath. The roof shakes from a sudden peal of thunder outside. That was me, letting some of that rage slip.

The newscast switches over from the reporter to taped footage of the top floors of the John Hancock Center in flames.

"This can't be happening," Marina says, her eyes wide, looking to me for confirmation that this is just some sick joke. I've been trying to be the stable one, but I can't find anything reassuring to say.

The bartender clicks his tongue, watching the TV, too. "Crazy, right? Freakin' terrorists."

I lunge across the bar and grab him by the front of his apron before he can even think of reaching for his hidden shotgun. "When did this happen?" I snap.

"Damn, girl," the bartender says, sensing something in my eyes that makes him decide not to struggle. "I dunno. Like, two days ago? It's been all over the news. Where the hell you been?"

"Getting our asses handed to us," I mutter, and shove him away. I try to pull myself together, to beat back the panic. Nine's been completely silent since the report came on. When I look over at him, his expression is completely blank. He stares at the television, watching footage of our penthouse headquarters and his former home burning, his mouth open just a little, his body completely still, almost rigid. He looks like he's shutting down, as if his brain isn't capable of processing this latest blow.

"Nine . . . ," I start, and my voice breaks his trance. Without a word to me or Marina, without so much as a look, he spins around and heads for the door. One of the pool players isn't quick enough to get out of Nine's way and gets shouldered to the floor.

Trusting that Marina won't freeze anyone to death in my absence, I chase after Nine. By the time I'm out on Trapper's porch, Nine has already made it into the parking lot, stalking intently towards the gravel road.

"Where are you going?" I shout after him, hopping the porch railing and jogging to catch up.

"Chicago," he answers bluntly.

"You're going to walk to Chicago?" I ask him. "That's your plan?"

"Good point," he replies, not slowing down. "I'll steal a car. You guys coming or what?"

"Stop being an idiot," I snap, and when that doesn't slow him down, I reach out with my telekinesis and grab him. I turn him around so he's facing me, his heels digging divots in the gravel as he tries to fight.

"Let me go, Six," Nine growls. "Let me go right now."

"Stop and think for a second," I insist, realizing as I start that I'm not just trying to convince Nine but also myself. My fingernails dig into my palms—not sure if that's from the concentration required to hold Nine with my telekinesis or from me straining to keep it together. Back on the roof of the John Hancock Center, I'd told Sam that we were at war and that there would be casualties. I'd thought I was prepared for that, but losing Eight—and now maybe losing the others in Chicago—no, I can't handle that. That can't have been my last conversation with Sam. It can't.

"They wouldn't be in Chicago anymore," I continue. "They'd run. That's what we'd do. And we know John is still alive or we'd have another scar. He's got the tablet; he's got his Chest. They've got a better chance of finding us than we have of finding them."

"Uh, last time I saw John he was comatose. He's not up for finding anyone."

"An exploding building tends to wake a person up," I counter. "He got out. We'd know if he didn't."

After a moment, Nine nods reluctantly. "All right, all right, let me go."

I let him loose from my telekinetic hold. He looks away immediately, peering down the darkened road, his broad shoulders slumped.

"I feel like we're screwed, Six," Nine says, his voice

hoarse. "Like we already lost and no one's got around to telling us."

I walk up next to him and put my hand on his shoulder. Our backs to the neon lights of Trapper's, I can't really see Nine's face, but I'm pretty sure his eyes are wet with tears.

"Bullshit," I reply. "We don't lose."

"Tell that to Eight."

"Nine, come on—"

Nine shoves both his hands through his tangled black hair, almost like he's going to pull some out. Then, he brings his hands down over his face, rubbing it. When he drops them back to his sides, I can tell he's trying to be stoic.

"It was my fault, too," he continues. "I got him killed."

"That's not true."

"It is. Five kicked my ass and I couldn't help myself. Had to keep talking, had to show him. It should've been me. You know it; I know it; Marina damn sure knows it."

I take my hand off Nine's shoulder and punch him in the jaw.

"Ow! Damn it!" he yelps, staggering away from me and nearly losing his footing in the gravel. "What the hell?"

"Is that what you want?" I ask, stepping towards him, fists clenched and ready. "Want me to kick your ass a little bit? Punish you for what happened to Eight?"

Nine holds up his hands. "Cut it out, Six."

"It wasn't your fault," I tell him evenly, unclenching

my fists and then jabbing him hard in the chest with my fingers. "Five killed Eight, not you. And the Mogadorians are to blame. Got it?"

"Yeah, I got it," Nine replies, although I can't be sure if I've actually gotten through to him or if he just wants me to stop assaulting him.

"Good. Enough with this mopey crap. We need to figure out what we're doing next."

"I've already figured that out," Marina chimes in.

I was so intent on beating some sense into Nine that I didn't hear her approaching. Neither did Nine, and I can tell by the embarrassed look on his face that he's wondering how much Marina overheard. At the moment, Marina doesn't seem concerned with Nine's meltdown. She's too busy dragging along the scrawny guy from the bar, Dale, the one who wanted to trade me his awesome story for a beer. Marina leads him across the parking lot towards us, holding his ear like a cruel teacher escorting a delinquent to the principal's office. I notice the slightest coating of frost forming on the side of Dale's face.

"Marina, let him go," I say.

She complies, yanking Dale ahead of her so that he stumbles into the gravel, ending up on his knees right in front of me. I give her a look—I understand where the violent streak comes from, but I don't like it. Marina ignores me.

"Tell them what you told me," Marina orders Dale. "Your *amazing* story."

Dale looks at the three of us, eager to please yet obviously terrified, probably thinking we're going to kill him if he doesn't listen.

"There's an old NASA base out in the swamp. Got decommissioned in the eighties when the swamp started rising," Dale begins haltingly, rubbing the side of his face to warm it up. "I go out there sometimes, looking for stuff I can sell. Normally, it's deserted. But last night, man, I swear I saw UFOs floating around out there. Creepy guys who didn't look right with guns like I ain't never seen guarding the place. You ain't with them, are you?"

"No," I answer. "We most definitely are not."

"Dale's volunteered to show us the way," Marina says, nudging Dale with the toe of her sneaker. He swallows hard and then nods enthusiastically.

"It's not far," he says. "Couple hours through the swamp."

"We just spent two days hiking out of that swamp," Nine says. "Now you want to go back in?"

"They *have* him," Marina hisses, pointing into the dark. "You heard Malcolm's story about what they did to Number One. They stole her Legacies."

I give Marina a sharp look. Even if most of it doesn't make any sense to him, Dale's still listening intently to our conversation. "Should we really be talking about this?"

Marina snorts. "You're worried about *Dale*, Six?

They're killing us and blowing up our friends. Keeping secrets from this drunk is the least of our worries."

Dale raises his hand. "I swear I won't say nothing about . . . about whatever you're talking about."

"What about Chicago?" Nine asks. "What about the others?"

Marina affords Nine only a quick glare. She keeps her eyes on me when she answers. "You know I'm worried about them. But we don't know where John and the others are, Six. We *know* where Eight is. And I am not, under any circumstances, letting those sick bastards keep him."

The way she says it, I know there's no way to convince Marina otherwise. If we don't go with her, she'll go by herself. Not that I even consider not going. I'm spoiling for a fight almost as bad as she is. And if there's a chance Eight's body is still out there—in the clutches of Mogadorians still lingering in Florida, maybe with Five—then we have to at least try recovering it. Leave no Garde behind.

"Dale," I say, "I hope you've got a boat we can borrow."

CHAPTER FIVE

THE SLAB OF MEAT IN FRONT OF ME LOOKS LIKE a soggy piece of uncooked fish, except it's lacking any texture whatsoever. I poke it with my fork and the pale slab jiggles like gelatin. Or maybe it's still alive and trying to escape, those unappetizing tremors its attempt to slowly wiggle off my plate. If I look away, I wonder if the thing will pick up the pace and try crawling into one of the air vents.

I want to vomit.

"Eat," Setrákus Ra commands.

He called himself my grandfather. That thought makes me more nauseous than the food. I don't want to believe him. This could be just like the visions, some sick game meant to get under my skin.

But why go through all the trouble? Why bring me here? Why not just kill me?

Setrákus Ra sits across from me, all the way down at

the opposite end of a ridiculously large banquet table that looks as if it was carved from lava. His chair is thronelike, made of the same dark stone as the table, but definitely not large enough to accommodate the mammoth warlord we fought at Dulce Base. No, at some point when I wasn't watching, Setrákus Ra shrunk down to a more reasonable eight feet tall so that he could comfortably hunch over his own plate of Mogadorian cuisine.

Could his size changing be a Legacy? It works really similarly to my ability to alter my age.

"You have questions," Setrákus Ra rumbles, observing me.

"What are you?" I blurt out.

He cocks his head. "What do you mean, child?"

"You're a Mogadorian," I say, trying not to sound too frantic. "I'm Loric. We can't be related."

"Ah, such a simplistic idea. Human, Loric, Mogadorian—these are just words, dear one. Labels. Centuries ago, my experiments proved that our genetics could be changed. They could be augmented. We needn't wait for Lorien to gift us with Legacies. We could take them as we needed them, utilizing them like any other resource."

"Why do you keep saying *we*?" I ask, my voice cracking. "You're not one of us."

Setrákus Ra smiles thinly. "I was Loric once. The tenth Elder. Until the time came when I was cast out. Then, I became what you see before you: the powers of a Garde combined with the strength of a Mogadorian. An evolutionary improvement."

My legs start shaking under the table. I hardly listen after he mentions the tenth Elder. I remember that from Crayton's letter. He said my father was obsessed with the fact that our family once had an Elder. Could that have been Setrákus Ra?

"You're crazy," I say. "And you're a liar."

"I am neither of those things," he replies, patiently. "I am a realist. A futurist. I altered my genetics to become more like them, so they would accept me. In return for their fealty, I helped their population grow. I brought them back from the brink of extinction. Joining the Mogadorians gave me a chance to continue the experiments that so frightened the Loric. Now, my work is almost finished. Soon, all life in the universe—Mogadorian, human, even what's left of the Loric—will be improved under my gently guiding hand."

"You didn't improve life on Lorien," I snap back. "You killed them all."

"They opposed progress," Setrákus Ra states, like the death of a whole planet is nothing.

"You're sick."

I'm not afraid to talk back to him. I know that he won't hurt me—not yet, at least. He's too vain for that, wants too badly to convert another Loric to the cause. He wants things to be just like in my nightmare. Since I woke up here, he's had a team of female Mogadorians attending to me. They dressed me in this long, black formal gown, very similar to the one I was wearing in my vision. It itches like crazy, and I have to keep tugging at the neckline.

I stare openly at his hideous face, hating myself for trying to find some resemblance. His head is bulbous and pale, covered in intricate Mogadorian tattoos; his eyes are empty and black, just like the Mogs; his teeth are filed down and sharp. If I look hard enough, I can almost see the Loric cast to his features, like crumbling architecture buried beneath the paleness and gross Mog artwork.

Setrákus Ra looks up from his food, meeting my gaze. Facing him head-on still gives me a chill and I have to force myself not to turn away.

"Eat," he says again. "You need your strength."

I hesitate for a moment, not sure how far I should push my insubordination, but also really not wanting to sample the Mog version of sushi. I make a point of dropping my fork so that it clatters loudly against the side of my plate. It echoes in the high-ceilinged room—Setrákus Ra's private dining area—which is only slightly more furnished than the other cold rooms aboard the *Anubis*. The walls are covered in paintings of Mogadorians bravely charging into combat. The ceiling is open, providing a breathtaking view of Earth, the planet imperceptibly rotating below us.

"Do not push me, girl," Setrákus Ra growls. "Do as you're told."

I push my plate away from me. "I'm not hungry."

He studies me, a condescending look in his eyes, like a parent trying to show a bratty child how patient they can be.

"I can put you back to sleep and feed you through a tube, if you'd prefer. Perhaps you'd be better mannered when I next woke you, once the war was won," he says. "But then we wouldn't be able to talk. You wouldn't be able to enjoy your grandfather's victory firsthand. And you wouldn't be able to entertain your futile notions of escape."

I swallow hard. I know we'll be going down to Earth eventually. Setrákus Ra isn't going to have his warships orbit Earth for a while and then float peacefully away. There's going to be an invasion. I've been telling myself that once we land I'd have a chance to run for it. Obviously, Setrákus Ra knows that I'd rather die than be his prisoner or his coruler or whatever he's got in mind. But, from the smug look on his face, he doesn't seem to care. Maybe he thinks he can brainwash me before we return to Earth.

"How am I supposed to eat with your nasty face right there?" I ask him, hoping to see his self-satisfied look falter. "It's not exactly appetizing."

Setrákus Ra stares at me like he's trying to decide whether to leap across the table and throttle me. After a moment, he reaches to the side of his chair where his cane is propped. Ornately carved from a shimmering golden metal with an ominous black eye on the handle, it's the same cane I saw Setrákus Ra use during the fight at Dulce Base. I brace myself for an attack.

"The Eye of Thaloc," Setrákus Ra says, noticing me eyeing the staff. "Like Earth, it will one day be part of your Inheritance."

Before I can ask a follow-up question, the obsidian eye in the cane's handle flashes. I flinch, but it quickly becomes clear that I'm not in any danger. Instead, it's Setrákus Ra who begins to convulse. Bands of red and purple light project from the Eye of Thaloc and scan over his body. Although I don't exactly know how, I can sense energy moving from the cane into Setrákus Ra. He writhes and contorts as his skin peels away from his body, expanding outward and shifting, like a bubble forming in candlewax.

When it's over, Setrákus Ra looks human. Actually, he looks like a movie star. He's assumed the form of a handsome older guy in his mid-forties, with immaculately arranged salt-and-pepper hair, soulful blue eyes and just a modest amount of stubble. He's tall, but no longer intimidatingly so, and he's wearing a stylish blue suit and pressed dress shirt, casually open at the collar. Of his previous appearance, only the three Loric pendants remain, their cobalt jewels matching his shirt.

"Better?" he asks, his usual scratchy voice replaced by this man's smooth baritone.

"What . . . ?" I look at him, dumbfounded. "Who are you supposed to be?"

"I chose this form for the humans," he explains. "Our research shows they're naturally drawn to middle-aged Caucasian men of these specifications. Apparently, they find them leaderly and trustworthy."

"Why . . ." I try to gather my thoughts. "What do you mean, it's *for the humans*?"

Setrákus Ra gestures towards my plate. "Eat and I will answer your questions. That's not unreasonable, is it? I believe the humans call it quid pro quo."

I look down at my plate and the pale blob waiting for me there. I think about Six and Nine and the rest of the Garde and wonder what they would do in my situation. It seems like Setrákus Ra wants to spill his guts, so I should probably let him. Maybe while he's trying to subtly win me over, he'll let slip the secret to beating the Mogadorians. If that even exists. Either way, taking a bite of the boiled slug on my plate seems like a small price to pay if it means gathering some important information. I shouldn't think of my situation as being held prisoner; it's more like I'm on a mission behind enemy lines.

I'm a freaking spy.

I pick up my knife and fork, cut a small square off the edge of the meat and plop it into my mouth. There's hardly any taste at all, it's almost like chewing a wadded-up ball of notebook paper. It's the texture that really bothers me—the way the meat starts to fizz and melt as soon as it touches my tongue, breaking down so quickly that I don't even really chew. I can't help but think of the way Mogadorians disintegrate when they're killed and have to stop myself from gagging.

"It isn't what you're used to, but it's the best the *Anubis* is equipped to produce," Setrákus Ra says, almost apologetically. "The food will improve once we've taken Earth."

I ignore him, not really caring about the finer points of Mogadorian cuisine. "I ate, now answer my question."

He inclines his head, looking charmed by my directness. "I chose this form because the humans will find it comforting. It's what I will wear to accept surrender of their planet."

I gape at him. "They're not going to surrender to you."

He smiles. "Of course they will. Unlike the Loric, who pointlessly fight against impossible odds, the humans have a rich history of subjugation. They appreciate demonstrations of superior force and will gladly accept the tenets of Mogadorian Progress. And those who don't will perish."

"Mogadorian 'Progress.'" I spit the words. "What are you even talking about? You're going to make everyone like you? A mon—"

I don't finish my question. I was going to call him a monster, but then I thought back to my vision. I callously ordered Six's execution right in front of John, Sam and a crowd of people. What if something like Setrákus Ra is already lurking inside me?

"I believe there was at least one question in all that

vitriol," Setrákus Ra says. He maintains his infuriating smile, made even worse now that he's wearing a handsome human face, and gestures towards my plate. I shovel down another bite of the horrible food. He clears his throat like he's about to give a speech.

"We share the same blood, granddaughter, which is why you will be spared the fate of those Garde who foolishly oppose me. Because, unlike them, you are capable of change," Setrákus Ra explains. "I may have been Loric once, but over the centuries I have made myself into something better. Once I control the Earth, I will have the power necessary to change the lives of billions. All they need do is accept Mogadorian Progress. Then my work will at last bear fruit."

I squint at him. "Power? From where?"

Setrákus Ra smiles at me, touching the pendants that hang around his neck. "You will see when the time is right, child. Then, you will understand."

"I already understand," I reply. "I understand that you're a disgusting, genocidal freak who gave himself a bad Mogadorian makeover."

Setrákus Ra's smile flickers and for a moment I wonder if I've pushed my luck too far. He sighs and drags his fingers across his throat, the skin of his assumed form parting to reveal the thick purple scar around his throat.

"Pittacus Lore gave me this when he tried to kill me," he says, his voice cold and level. "I was one of them, but he and the other Elders cast me out. Banished me from Lorien because of my ideas."

"What? Did they not want to elect you supreme ruler or something?"

Setrákus Ra passes his hand across his throat once again and the scar tissue disappears.

"They already had a ruler," Setrákus Ra replies, his voice dropping lower, as if the memory makes him angry. "They just refused to admit it."

"What's that supposed to mean?"

This time, he doesn't make me take a bite of food. He's on a roll now. "My dear, the Elders were ruled by the planet itself. Lorien made their choices for them. Who would be Garde and who would be Cêpan. They believed we should live as caretakers and let nature determine our fates. I disagreed. The Legacies granted by Lorien are simply a resource, like anything else. Would you let the fish in the ocean dictate who is fit to eat them, or allow the iron in the ground decide when to be forged? Of course not."

I try to digest all this information and compare it with what I learned from Crayton and his letter.

"You just wanted to be in control," I say after a moment.

"I wanted progress," he counters. "The Mogadorians understood. Unlike the Loric, they were a people ready to be elevated."

"You're insane," I say, pushing my plate away, done with this whole question-and-answer thing.

"You are an unenlightened child," he replies, that condescending patience back. "When your studies begin, when you see what I have accomplished for you and what the Loric have denied you, then you will understand. You will come to love and respect me."

I stand up, even though I have nowhere to go. Setrákus Ra has been gentle with me so far, but it's been made crystal clear that I can only move around the sterile hallways of the *Anubis* as he allows it. If he wants to keep me here and force me to finish my dinner, he will. It would probably be smoother for me if I let all his distortions and half-truths go unchallenged, but I just can't do it. I think of Nine, Six and the others—I know they'd never hold their tongue when faced with this monster.

"You destroyed our planet and all you've ever accomplished is hurting people," I say, trying to mimic my grandfather's mocking patience. "You're a monster. I will never not hate you."

Setrákus Ra sighs, his handsome features creasing briefly in consternation.

"Anger is the last refuge of the ignorant," he says, holding up his hand. "Let me show you something they denied you, granddaughter."

A coil of bright red energy begins to swirl around his raised hand. Nervous, I take a step backwards.

"The Elders chose who would escape from Lorien, and you were not meant to be among them," Setrákus Ra continues. "You were denied the advantages of the other Garde. I will rectify that."

The energy coalesces into a crackling orb in front of Setrákus Ra's hand, hovers there for a moment, and then zips towards me. I dive to the side and the orb alters course, making a beeline for me like it has a mind of its own. I hit the cold floor in a roll and try to avoid the energy, but it's too fast. It burns through the hem of my dress and attaches to my ankle.

I scream. The pain is excruciating; it's as if a live wire is being dragged across my skin. I pull my leg in towards me and try to slap at the spot where the orb hit, like I'm on fire and need to pat out the flames.

That's when I first see it. The twisting red energy is gone, leaving behind a band of jagged, pink scar tissue around my ankle. It's reminiscent of the angular tattoos I've seen etched on dozens of Mogadorian skulls, but there's also something unsettlingly familiar about it.

It's a scar very similar to the ones the Garde have signifying the Loric charm.

When I look up at Setrákus Ra, I have to bite my lip to choke off a scream. The bottom half of his pant leg has burned away, an identical charm freshly branded into his own ankle.

"Now," he says, smiling beatifically, "just like them, we are linked."

CHAPTER SIX

I GUESS IN A WAY WE'VE KIDNAPPED DALE. HE doesn't seem to mind. The scrawny redneck is having a grand old time lounging at the rear of his decades-old pontoon boat, pulling from his flask of moonshine, and brazenly ogling me and Marina. This boat of his is literally held together in places by duct tape and shoelaces, and we can't travel through the winding swampland streams too quickly for fear of overheating the engine. Also, every so often, Nine has to use a bucket to scoop dark brown swamp water out of the boat before the foot wells collect too much and we sink. Not exactly traveling in style, but Marina remains convinced that Dale stumbled on a Mogadorian encampment. So, for now, he's our guide.

Last night, Dale insisted it was too dark to try navigating the swamp but promised he would lead us to this decommissioned NASA base in the morning. It turned out that the bartender at Trapper's rented the shanties surrounding his place to any swamp people passing through. He gave one to us for next to nothing, floated us our meal, too, probably sensing that not helping us would just create more trouble.

No one trusted Dale not to run off at his first opportunity, so we decided to take turns keeping watch on him. Nine drew first shift and ended up sitting with Dale outside our little shack, listening to stories about all the interesting things Dale had scavenged from the swamp.

Marina and I lay down side by side on the flea-bitten mattress tossed on the floor of the shack, the only other furnishings a hot plate, a rusted-out sink that I don't think connected to any pipes, and an oil lantern. Considering we'd spent the last couple of days hiking through the swamps and barely resting, this was about the most comfortable I'd been in days. As we lay there, I noticed that Marina had stopped radiating the aura of cold she'd been giving off since Eight was killed. I thought maybe she'd fallen asleep, but then she started whispering to me in the darkness.

"I feel him out there, Six."

"What do you mean?" I whispered back, not understanding. "Eight is . . ." I hesitated, not able to bring myself to state the obvious.

"I *know* he's dead," she replied, rolling over to face me. "But I can still feel his—I don't know, his essence or something. He's calling to me. I don't know why, or how, I just know it's happening and that it's important."

I fell silent. I remembered Eight's story about meeting a mysterious old man while hiding out in India. I think his name was Devdan. The old guy taught him about Hinduism and martial arts and, eventually, disappeared back to wherever he came from. Eight really cherished what he learned about Hinduism—I think it helped him cope with his Cêpan's death. Hell, maybe there's something to all that reincarnation stuff. Eight was definitely the spiritual one of us, and if anyone would call out from beyond the grave, it'd probably be him.

"We'll find him," I said quietly, although I wasn't exactly confident that would be true. I thought about what Nine said during his freak-out earlier that night—that we'd already lost the war and no one had told us. "I just don't know what we're going to do afterward."

"It will reveal itself to us when the time comes," Marina replied peacefully, squeezing my hand, the nurturing Marina I'd gotten to know briefly resurfacing, replacing the angry revenge seeker I'd been surviving with the last couple of days. "I know it will."

So, this morning, we returned to the swamp. The trees are thick on both sides of the murky water and we frequently have to slow down to navigate around gnarled but ambitious roots that have spread into the water. The canopy of branches over our heads is dense, letting sunlight through in patches. Rotten logs drift by, their bark not always distinguishable from the craggy scales of the alligators roaming these waters. At least the bugs have stopped biting me. Or maybe I've just gotten used to them.

Marina stands at the front of the boat, her gaze straight ahead, moisture from the air dampening her face and hair. I stare at her back, wondering if she's lost it, or if this sixth sense about Eight's body is another new Legacy manifesting. It's at times like these we could really use a Cêpan; Marina's having a hell of a time controlling her freezing Legacy. Nine and I haven't brought it up with her—he's probably scared she'll bite his head off, and I'm just counting on her learning to control it at the same time she gets a grip on all that anger. So either this return to the swamp is happening because of a potentially haywire new Legacy, old-fashioned intuition, grief or legitimate contact with the spirit world. Maybe a combination of all four.

It doesn't matter, really. We're doing this.

It was only a few days ago that Five led us through waters similar to these. We'd been happier then—I remember Marina and Eight clinging to each other, something sparking there, and Nine whooping and acting stupid every time he spotted an alligator. I run a hand through my hair—it's damp from the humidity and knotted from the days spent out here—and remind myself that this is no time for reminiscing. We're heading into danger, but at least this time we know it.

"How much farther?" I ask Dale.

He shrugs. He's gotten a lot more comfortable around us since Marina half-froze his face last night. Probably on account of whatever's in that flask.

" 'Bout an hour," he says.

"You better not be screwing with us," I tell him. "If this is bullshit, we'll leave you out here."

That makes him sit up a little straighter. "I swear it's true, ma'am. I saw some weird-ass aliens out here. You bet."

I glare at him. Nine, finished dumping water over the side of the boat, snatches the flask from Dale's hand.

"What've you got in here, anyway?" Nine asks, sniffing at the flask. "Smells like paint thinner."

"I mean, it ain't *all* paint thinner," Dale counters. "Try some."

Nine rolls his eyes and hands him back the flask, then turns to me.

"Seriously?" he asks, lowering his voice, more concerned that Marina will overhear than Dale, who's sitting right next to us. "We're relying on this guy?"

"Not just him," I reply, shooting a look at Marina. "She senses something."

"Since when does she . . . ?" Nine trails off, for once taking a moment to consider his words. "It still seems a little nuts to me, Six. That's all."

Before I can respond, Marina waves her hand at us, getting our attention.

"Cut the engine!" she hisses.

Dales snaps to and turns off the engine, still not wanting to piss off Marina. Our boat drifts forward silently.

"What is it?" I ask.

"There's someone up ahead."

I hear it then, too. A motor—one that does a lot less hiccupping than Dale's—getting louder as it moves increasingly closer. With the zigzag pattern this tributary takes through the trees, we can't yet see this other boat.

"Are there other dirtbag swamp people out this far?" Nine asks, eyeballing Dale.

"Sometimes," Dale replies. He looks around at us, as if something has just occurred to him. "Now, hold on. Are we in danger? Because I didn't sign up for that."

"You didn't sign up for anything," Nine reminds him.

"Hush," Marina snaps. "Here they come."

I could turn us invisible. It occurs to me to grab hold of Marina and Nine, use my Legacy and make it look like Dale's alone out here. But I don't. Marina and Nine don't look like they're in any mood to hold hands either.

If there are Mogadorians out there, we want this fight.

I watch a dark outline pass through the clutter of trees and glide into the water in front of us. It's a pontoon boat just like ours except much sleeker and probably with a few dozen less leaks. As soon as we come into view, the second boat also cuts its engine. It drifts about thirty yards in front of us, its wake causing us to bob on a gentle wave.

The boat is manned by three Mogadorians. Because of the heat, they've removed their stupid black leather trench coats and stripped down to tank tops, their arms shining pasty white, their blasters and daggers clearly visible along their belts. I wonder what they're doing out here, brazenly out in the open, and then realize that they're probably looking for us. After all, the swamps are our last known location. These unlucky Mog scouts must've drawn swamp duty.

Everyone is very still. We stare at the Mogs, and I wonder if they'll even recognize us in the state we're in. The Mogs stare back, not making any move to restart their boat and get out of our way.

"Friends of yours?" Dale slurs.

His voice breaks the standoff. In unison, two of the Mogs reach for their blasters, the third spinning around to restart their engine. I shove forward with my telekinesis, hitting the front of their boat with as much force as I can muster, causing the ship's bow to rise up from the water. The Mog going for the engine falls overboard, and the other two go staggering backwards.

A split second after my telekinetic attack, Marina leans over the side and plunges her hand into the swamp water. A sheet of ice spreads out from her towards the Mogs' boat, the water cracking and popping as it flash freezes. Their boat is stuck on a tilt, half out of the water, as the ice floe coalesces around it.

Nine bounds out of our boat, gracefully runs across Marina's ice floe and hurdles over the side of the Mogs' boat. He grabs the nearest Mog around the neck, his momentum and the boat's sloped deck causing them to stumble towards the boat's rear. The second Mog gets his blaster up and aims at Nine, but before he can fire, Nine plants his feet and tosses the first Mog at his buddy.

The scout who fell overboard tries to climb out of the water and onto Marina's patch of ice. That's a mistake. A jagged icicle rises from the floe's edge, impaling the Mogadorian. Before that Mog has even turned to ash, I use my telekinesis to tear the icicle through him and send it plunging into one of the Mogs on the boat. The final Mog, dagger drawn, charges at Nine, but he grabs the Mog by the wrist, twists backwards and stabs him through the eye with his own blade.

Just like that, it's over. The whole fight lasted less than a minute. Even as dysfunctional as we seem right now, we can still kill the hell out of some Mogs.

"Now that was refreshing!" Nine yells, grinning at me from the other boat.

I hear splashing from over my shoulder and turn around just in time to see Dale swimming frantically through the swamp water. He must have jumped overboard, and now he's dog-paddling away from us as fast as his scrawny arms and drunkenness will allow.

"Where are you going, idiot?" I shout after him.

Dale reaches a muddy outcropping of roots and pulls himself onto it, gasping for breath. He stares at me and the others with wide, wild eyes.

"You people are freaks!" he screams.

"That's not very nice," Nine says, laughing, as he carefully makes his way back onto Dale's boat, the ice floe Marina created already beginning to melt in the Florida heat.

"What about your boat?" I shout to Dale. "You gonna swim back to Trapper's?"

He squints at me. "I'll figure something out that don't involve mutant powers, thank you very much."

I sigh and raise my hand, intending to telekinetically drag Dale's stupid ass back onto his boat, but Marina touches my shoulder and stops me.

"Let him go," she says.

"But we need him to find the base," I reply.

"We're close enough," Marina says, shaking her head. "And besides—"

"Uh, holy shit," Nine interrupts, shielding his eyes and staring up at the sky.

"I think we can just follow that thing," Marina finishes.

The day suddenly gets very dark. I look up as a shadow passes overhead, cutting off the limited light that was squeezing through the swamp's canopy. Through the leaves, all I can see is the armor-plated hide of a Mogadorian ship as it begins to descend. It's nothing like the dinky saucer-style crafts that I was able to knock out of the sky with a few well-placed lightning bolts. This ship is enormous, the size of an aircraft carrier, ferocious gun turrets protruding from its belly. The local birds squawk and take flight, darting away from this terrifying giant.

Instinctively, I reach out and grab Nine and Marina, turning the three of us invisible. A boat of Mogadorians is one thing. I don't think we're ready for something this big. The warship above us doesn't care, though. It doesn't notice us. To a ship that size, we're as insignificant as the mosquitoes. As it passes, gliding above the swampland and gradually allowing light to reenter, I feel like I've shrunk, like I'm small again.

Like I'm a child.

And then I remember that last day on Lorien. The nine of us and our Cêpans running for the ship that would take us to Earth. The screams all around us, the heat of fire from the city, blaster fire hissing through the air. I remember looking up into the night sky and seeing ships just like the one passing over us, blotting out the stars, their turrets blazing, their cargo doors falling open to let loose hordes of blood-hungry Piken. Above us, I realize, is a Mogadorian warship. It's what they will use to take Earth once and for all.

"They're here," I say, the breath nearly sucked out of me. "It's starting."

CHAPTER SEVEN

GRADUALLY, THE SUBURBS OUTSIDE WASHINGTON, D.C., start to change. The houses become bigger and farther apart, until eventually they aren't visible from the road at all. Outside the van windows are immaculately maintained meadows or miniature parks where the trees are spaced at obsessively equal intervals, designed to keep the houses behind them hidden from prying eyes. The side streets branching off from the main road all have prestigious-sounding names like Oaken Crest Way or Goldtree Boulevard, all of them protected by severe PRIVATE PROPERTY signs.

In the backseat, Sam whistles. "I can't believe they live out here. Like rich people."

"No kidding," I reply, my hands sweating on the steering wheel. I was thinking the same thing as Sam but don't really feel like talking about it, worried that I won't be able to keep the jealousy out of my voice. I've spent my entire life on the run, dreaming about living in places like this—stable, quiet places. And here are the Mogs, carving out a normal life for their trueborn upper class, living the high life on a planet they're only looking to exploit and destroy.

"The grass is always greener," Malcolm says.

"They do not appreciate it, if that's any consolation," Adam says quietly, the first words he's spoken since we started on these last few miles to Ashwood Estates, his former home. "They are taught not to enjoy something unless they can possess it."

"What's that mean, exactly?" Sam asks. "Like, if a Mogadorian went to the park . . . ?"

"'One takes no satisfaction from that which one cannot hold,'" Adam recites, suppressing a sneer when he finishes the quotation. "That is from Setrákus Ra's Great Book. A Mogadorian wouldn't care about your park, Sam, not unless the trees were his to chop down."

"Sounds like a *great* book," I say dryly.

I glance over at Adam, next to me in the passenger seat. He's staring out the window, a distant look on his face. I wonder if this is strange for him—it's basically a homecoming, even though he's not actually from Earth. Adam turns his head, notices me looking at him and seems almost embarrassed. His expression quickly changes to one I'm familiar with—cold Mogadorian composure.

"Pull over here," he instructs. "It's only a mile farther on."

I pull the van over to the side of the road and kill the engine. Without the noise from the van, the constant chirping from behind me seems even louder.

"Jeez, guys, calm down," Sam says to the box of excited Chimærae sitting on the bench between him and Malcolm.

I turn around to look down at the Chimærae, all of them in bird form. Regal, whose resting form is a stately hawk, perches next to a trio of more common birds—a pigeon, a dove and a robin. Then there's a sleek gray falcon that must be Dust and an overweight owl that has to be Stanley. All of them have lightweight leather collars strapped gently around their necks.

This is step one of our plan.

"Is everything working?" I ask Sam, who looks up from the laptop resting on his legs and grins at me.

"Check it out," Sam says proudly, turning the laptop to face me. Using the Chimærae in this way was his idea.

Tiled on the laptop screen are half a dozen grainy video feeds, each of them showing my face from a slightly different angle. The cameras are working.

On our way from Baltimore to Washington we stopped at a dark little storefront called SpyGuys that specializes in cameras and home-security gear. The clerk didn't ask Malcolm why he needed to purchase more than a dozen of their smallest wireless cameras; he seemed grateful for the business and even showed us how to install the necessary software on one of our laptops. After that, we picked up the collars at a pet store. The others carefully attached the cameras to them while I drove south towards Washington.

The Mogadorians have spent so much effort running surveillance on us, stalking us. Now we're going to turn the tables.

"Spread out around Ashwood Estates," I tell the Chimærae, punctuating my command with a mental picture of the satellite photos of Ashwood that I've been studying since yesterday and sending that on to the flock telepathically. "Try to cover every angle. Focus especially on where the Mogadorians are."

The Chimærae respond with enthusiastic cawing and a fluttering of wings.

I nod to Sam and he throws open the van's side door. What follows is a wild flurry of activity, our half dozen shape-shifting spy birds taking off all at once, a funnel of squawking and flapping wings as they fly out of the van. As serious as our situation is, there's something awesome about the sight; Sam is grinning and even Adam allows himself a small smile.

"This is going to work," Malcolm says, patting Sam

on the back. Sam's smile increases just a little bit more.

The view on the laptop screen is disorienting, the Chimærae all swooping and gliding in different directions. The first to settle into some trees position themselves right above the wrought-iron gates of Ashwood Estates. A gate is built into a brick wall there; the wall stretches for a few yards and then, presumably once it's no longer visible from the road, turns into a more sinister-looking barbed-wire fence.

"Guards," I say, pointing out the trio of Mogadorians, two of them sitting in the gatehouse, one of them pacing in front of the gate itself.

"That's it?" Sam asks. "Only three of them? That's nothing."

"They do not expect a frontal attack. Or any attack, really," Adam explains. "Their purpose is mainly to scare off any drivers who might make a wrong turn."

As the remaining Chimærae settle onto rooftops and tree branches, the video feeds snapping into focus, I start to get a clearer idea of Ashwood Estates' layout. Beyond the front gate is a short but winding entrance road with very little cover. That road leads to what is essentially a very large cul-de-sac, about twenty well-appointed houses arranged around a central recreation area. Apparently, the Mogadorians have picnic tables, basketball hoops and a pool. All in all, it's an idyllic swath of suburbia, except there's no one around.

"Seems quiet," I say, scanning the feeds. "Is it always like this?"

"No," Adam admits. "Something isn't right."

One of the Chimærae takes flight and repositions itself, getting an angle on one of the houses that we couldn't see before. A trash truck is parked at the curb, its engine off.

"There's someone," Sam says, enlarging the feed.

A solitary Mogadorian holding a tablet computer stands next to the truck. He looks bored as he thumbs something into the tablet.

Adam squints at the tattoos on the Mogadorian's scalp. "An engineer," he says.

"You can tell that?" I ask.

"It's in the tattoos. For trueborn, those are symbols of honor and what they've accomplished. The vatborn get job titles," Adam explains. "Makes it easy to order them around."

"There's more," Sam points out.

We watch as four Mogadorian warriors carry a refrigerator-sized piece of computer equipment out of the house. They take it towards the curb and set it down in front of the engineer, then wait around while he circles the machine and inspects it.

"Looks like a server," Malcolm observes. He turns

to Adam. "Could they be replacing the equipment you destroyed?"

"Possibly," Adam replies, but he doesn't sound certain. He points out a two-level house with a porch a few doors down from where the Mogadorians are working. "That's my old home. I know for certain there's an access point to the tunnels through there, but the other houses likely have access, too."

While Adam's talking, the engineer finishes his inspection of the server. He shakes his head, and the other Mogs pick the equipment back up. They toss it into the trash truck, then return to the house.

"I guess they aren't big on recycling, huh?" Sam says.

Before the first group of Mogs can head back into the house, a second group emerges. They're carrying what looks like a barber's chair from a bad sci-fi movie, the thing equal parts futuristic and frightening, wires and nodes dangling from it. The engineer hustles forward to meet this second group, helping them to ease the equipment gently onto the grass of the front yard.

"I recognize that," Malcolm says, an edge to his voice.

"Dr. Anu's machine," Adam says, turning to me. "That's what they used on Malcolm. And on me."

"What're they going to do with it now?" I ask,

watching the engineer begin his inspection.

"This looks like a salvage team," Adam explains. "I did some damage to the tunnels the last time I was here. Now, they're saving what equipment they can and getting rid of the rest."

"What about all the trueborns who were supposed to be here?"

Adam grimaces. "They might have been evacuated until this place can be brought up to spec."

I widen my eyes at Adam. "So we drove out here for nothing? The trueborn are already gone and the machine is busted."

"No," he says, and I can see the gears turning behind his eyes. "If we can take out this salvage team before they get off a distress call, we'd have complete access to what's left of Ashwood. From there, we can get onto their network—"

"And that gets us what?"

"It's like if one of my people could open one of your Chests, John. We'll know their secrets. What they're planning."

"We'll be one step ahead," I say.

"Yes." Adam nods, watching the engineer as he evaluates Dr. Anu's machine. "But we should get in there. What the salvage team decides to destroy could still be useful to us."

"All right," I say, watching the Mog salvage team

head back into the house. "So, is there a secret entrance or something?"

"At this point, I think a direct assault is our best bet." He looks at me. "That all right with you?"

"Hell yes," I reply. Originally, we'd planned to use our network of Chimærae surveillance to observe the Mogs for a while, figure out the most strategic approach to attacking. But, now that we're here, I find myself itching to go into battle. I need some payback for everything they've done—for taking Ella, destroying Nine's home, killing one of my friends. If Adam says we need to rush in, I'm ready to go.

Malcolm grabs a box from under the seat. From within, he produces two earbuds, one for me and one for Adam. The devices are connected to the pair of walkie-talkies Sam and Malcolm will be using. I slip mine into my ear and Adam does the same.

"Are we at all concerned with the local authorities?" Malcolm asks. "A firefight in broad daylight might attract some attention."

Adam shakes his head. "They're bought off," he says, then looks at me. "We will want to be quick, though. Kill them before they can call for reinforcements. If I can get past them into my old house, I should be able to cut off their communications."

"I can do quick," I reply.

I strap my Loric dagger to my calf, hidden under my

pant leg. Next, I clip my red bracelet around my wrist. The amber jewel in its center that expands to form a shield shimmers in the midday sun. Immediately, the bracelet jolts me with icy pinpricks, warning me there are Mogs in the area. Of course it would—there's one sitting right next to me. Adam's presence is going to really wreak havoc on my danger sense.

"Ready?" I ask him.

Next to me, Adam pulls on an over-the-shoulder holster, a silenced handgun now hanging under each of his armpits. He nods.

"Whoa, hold on," Sam says. "Check out this guy."

Adam and I turn back to the laptop, watching as another Mogadorian emerges from the house the salvage team is currently unloading. He's tall and broad shouldered, bigger than the others, and with a more regal bearing. Unlike the others, he has a huge sword strapped across his back. While we watch, he barks some orders at the engineer, then disappears back into the house. When I glance over at Adam, his face is somehow more pale than usual.

"What is it?"

"Nothing," he says, too quickly. "Just watch out for that one. He's a trueborn general, one of Setrákus Ra's most trusted men. He . . ." Adam hesitates, watching the spot on the monitor this general just occupied. "He has killed Garde before."

I feel heat rushing to my hands. If I wasn't ready for a fight already, I definitely am now.

"He's dead," I say, and Adam merely nods, opens his door and gets out of the van. I look to Sam and Malcolm. "We'll approach on foot, take out the guards and then you pull up to cover our back."

"I know, I know," Sam says. "I'll watch the monitor and shout in your ear when I see trouble."

Malcolm has already started unpacking his sniper rifle from its case. I saw him use that thing in Arkansas—he saved my ass. There's no one I'd rather have watching my back than the Goodes.

"Be careful," Malcolm says, raising his voice so Adam can hear. "Both of you."

Sam and I slap hands. "Give them hell," he says.

And then I'm out of the van, moving at a brisk jog towards the Mogadorian stronghold. Adam keeps up alongside me.

"John," he says, our feet crunching in the gravel on the side of the road. "There is something else you should know."

Of course. Just when I was beginning to let my guard down around this guy, right when we're going into battle together, he's going to spring something on me.

"What is it?"

"The General is my father."

CHAPTER EIGHT

I ALMOST SKID TO A STOP, BUT ADAM DOESN'T seem to be slowing down any, so I keep pace with him.

"You're kidding me."

"No." Adam frowns, focusing on the road ahead. "We don't exactly get along."

"Are you going to . . ." I don't even know how to phrase this. "Will you be able to . . . ?"

"Fight? Kill?" Adam replies. "Yes. Show him no mercy, because he won't show any to us."

"Your own father, man? I mean, even for a Mogadorian, that's pretty cold."

"At this point, defeating him in battle is likely the only way he'll ever feel pride for me," Adam replies, adding weakly, "not that I care."

I shake my head. "You guys are so screwed up."

We fall silent as the entrance to Ashwood Estates comes into view. The Mogadorian in front of the gates spots us and shields his eyes from the sun, trying to get a better look. We keep up a steady pace and don't make any attempt to conceal ourselves. We're separated from the gates by about fifty yards and closing fast, but to the Mog we might look like just a couple of joggers. He won't notice the guns strapped to Adam just yet.

"Wait until we're a little closer," I say through gritted teeth, and Adam nods.

At thirty yards, the Mog turns his head, saying something to his two buddies in the gatehouse. Warning them that something might be up. I see them stand up, silhouetted in the window, peering out at us. The Mog in front edges back a bit, his fingers inching towards the blaster surely hidden under his coat. But he hesitates, probably still thinks he's being paranoid.

They really never thought we'd come for them. They aren't prepared.

With twenty yards to go, I fire up my Lumen, flames roaring across my hands. Next to me, in stride, Adam draws both his guns and takes aim.

The closest Mog tries to pull his blaster, but he's way too slow. Adam fires two shots, one from each gun, both of them muffled by silencers. Struck twice in the chest, the Mog teeters for a moment and then explodes into a cloud of ash.

I launch a fireball at the gatehouse. The Mogadorians inside are scrambling around but, like their friend, are also too slow. The fireball explodes through the window, sending glass everywhere, and causing one of the Mogs to go up in flames. The other one manages to throw himself out the door, flames dancing up his back. He's standing right in front of Ashwood's locked entrance, so I reach out with my telekinesis and tear the wrought-iron gate off its hinges, crushing the Mog.

"Think the others heard us?" I ask Adam, as we step around the bent metal gate and into Ashwood Estates.

"Our entrance did lack subtlety," Adam observes.

Sam's voice crackles in my ear.

"Four of them running up the access road," Sam warns. "Blasters ready."

The access road is uphill with a slight bend at the top after which we'll be at the housing development. There isn't a whole lot of cover on the way.

"Stay behind me," I tell Adam.

Just then, the Mogs come around the bend. They don't ask any questions before unleashing a volley of blaster fire. Adam leaps behind me just as my shield deploys—it's like a parachute exploding out of my arm, the rippling crimson material spreading to absorb the blasts. Adam grabs hold of the back of my shirt.

"Go forward," he says.

I do, the shield absorbing more blaster fire as I press towards the Mogs. The bracelet is now a steady, numbingly painful buzz against my wrist. Carefully following my steps to keep from getting shot, Adam pops around the edge of the shield, gunning down two of the Mogs in one go. Realizing they're not making any progress, the other two try to retreat. I lower my shield and launch a fireball that explodes between them, knocking them both to the ground. Adam finishes them off with some well-aimed gunfire. Out of danger for now, my shield retracts back into my bracelet.

"Not bad," I tell him.

"We're just getting started," he replies.

We run down the access road around the bend, and the opulent homes of Ashwood Estates finally come into view. There's no one out and all the windows are dark; the whole place feels like a ghost town. To our right, I see Adam's old house, and a few houses down from that is the trash truck and the high-tech chair the engineer was inspecting. The salvage teams, the engineer and the General are nowhere to be seen.

"They're coming from the backyard!" Sam yells.

Both Adam and I spin around in time to see a squadron of Mog warriors sneaking towards us between two of the houses. It would've been a pretty good ambush if we didn't have scouts perched in their trees. As they raise their blasters, Adam is ready. He stomps the ground and a concussive wave of force rolls in their direction, pavement and chunks of grass rippling upward. The closest Mogs are completely thrown off their feet, others stagger and one of them accidentally discharges his blaster into another's back.

"I'll finish them off!" I tell Adam. "You go make sure they aren't calling reinforcements."

Adam nods, then sprints across the lawn towards his old house. Meanwhile, next to the stunned Mogadorians, I notice a metal tank that came unmoored from where it was attached to a house. With my hearing focused, I can hear a faint hiss emanating from the tank. I almost laugh at my luck.

It's a gas line.

I launch a fireball at the Mogs before they can collect themselves. It whizzes right by the lead Mog, who I think actually smirks at me, thinking that I've missed in those two seconds before the propane tank explodes, incinerating the lot of them. The windows of the two adjacent houses are all blown inward from the force, large black singe marks forming on the outside, grass burning. I have to stop myself from appreciating the destruction—it feels almost cathartic to destroy this place, to tear down what the Mogs have built, after how many times they've torn down my attempts at a normal life.

"Damn, dude," Sam says in my ear. "We felt that over here."

I yank my walkie-talkie off the back of my jeans. "What's it look like, Sam?"

"You're clear," he says. "It's weird. I thought there'd be more of them."

"They could be down in the tunnels," I reply, starting towards the house Adam rushed into. I scan the empty windows as I go, wary of any Mogs who might be lying in wait. It's just too damn quiet.

"And that huge-ass general guy," Sam says. "He wasn't with the ones you blew up."

I'm crossing the lawn towards Adam's house when the front window shatters and Adam's body comes flying out. His legs smack hard against the porch railing and he's turned head over heels, flipped like a rag doll into the front yard. I run to him as he shakily tries to pick himself up.

"What happened?" I shout.

"Father . . . isn't happy," he groans, looking up at me as I crouch down over him. There's a huge piece of glass sticking out of his cheek, a trickle of dark blood running down his neck. He yanks it out and tosses it aside.

"Can you get up?" I ask, grabbing his shoulder.

Before Adam can answer, a booming voice interrupts. "Number Four!"

The General strides confidently through the front door, looking down at me from the porch. He's huge and muscular. The tattoos splashed across his pale skull are way more intricate than any Mog I've seen outside of Setrákus Ra. I sense motion behind him—other Mogadorians, I can't be sure how many. They don't come out of the house. It's almost like the General wants to do this alone.

I stand up and face him, my hands glowing and hot, a fireball floating in my palm.

"You know who I am, huh?" I ask him.

"Indeed. I have long hoped we would meet."

"Uh-huh. If you know me, then you know you don't stand a chance against me." I crane my neck to look past him. "None of you do."

The General actually smiles. "Very good. Bravado. A welcome change of pace. The last Loric I encountered ran. I had to stab him in the back."

I decide I've had enough talk and whip the fireball at him. The General sees it coming, hunkers low and in one surprisingly fluid motion draws his sword from its sheath. He slices the air in front of him just as the fireball gets close, and the glowing Mogadorian blade absorbs my attack.

Not good.

The General leaps off the porch, sword raised above his head, and brings it down in a vicious arc towards me. He's fast—way faster than the other Mogs I've been fighting—and my shield barely has time to deploy before his sword would cleave me in two. The shield rebuffs the blade with a loud clang, but the force is still enough to knock me backwards and off my feet.

"John!" Adam shouts, and the General, having landed right next to him, takes a moment to kick his son hard across the face. Adam screams, rolling away.

"You are a perpetual disappointment," the General seethes at Adam, so low I can barely hear his words. "Stay down and I may yet show you mercy."

I pop onto my knees quickly, channeling another fireball. The General points his sword at me and I feel something like a rush of air, almost like the blade is sucking in the energy around it. My fireball gutters and shrinks, forcing me to focus harder to build it bigger. Meanwhile, the grass around the General goes from green to brown, the blade draining the life from it. I haven't seen one of the Mogs armed with a weapon like this since that fight in the woods outside Paradise High.

"Don't let it hit you!" Adam warns, spitting blood.

But his warning is too late. A dagger-shaped bolt of energy tears loose from the General's blade and screams towards me; the energy is black, or more like devoid of any color at all, and changes the very texture of the air that it passes through, sucking up life and oxygen, like a mini black hole.

I don't have a chance to dodge it. My shield deploys, expanding in the usual umbrella-like way, but immediately turns black and brittle when the General's blast hits. Frozen like that, my shield slowly begins to crumble, blown away like so much Mogadorian ash. Dark, rustlike veins begin to spread through the bracelet itself, and I hurriedly snap it off before they make contact with my skin. When it hits the ground, my bracelet breaks in half.

The General smiles at me again and asks, "Now will you run?"

CHAPTER NINE

THE MOGADORIANS WHO WERE TAKING COVER inside the house start to laugh. One by one, they filter onto the porch, eager to get a closer look as their great general dispatches one of the Garde. There's a couple dozen of them, the salvage team plus some warriors and scouts, all of them vatborn. Not exactly the high-priority targets we were hoping for, but that doesn't matter now. There are only two trueborn Mogs in Ashwood Estates—one of them is Adam, and he's laid out in the grass just a few yards from me, dark blood dripping from his face.

The other is charging right at me.

As the General bears down on me, sword leveled at my throat, there's a moment where I think we might have bitten off more than we can chew, Adam and me trying to take on an entire Mogadorian town.

But then I remember it isn't just the two of us.

With a shriek, Dust, still in falcon form, dive-bombs the General. His talons sink deep into the General's face, the huge Mogadorian grunting in pain before he manages to backhand Dust away.

It's exactly the distraction I need. Quickly, I form another fireball and pitch it at the General. This time, he doesn't have a chance to get his sword up, and the fire hits him right in the chest. I expect him to at least be knocked off his feet, but the General merely stumbles back a few steps. The front of his uniform burns away, revealing a carapace of obsidian Mogadorian armor beneath.

Dust, stunned by the blow, flops into the grass at the General's feet. He brings his sword down hard at the Chimæra, but Dust transforms into a snake at the last second and manages to slither through the grass away from the blade. The General, fresh claw marks across his face, swings his gaze back to me.

"Hiding behind your pets!" the General bellows. "Disgraceful. Fight me with honor, boy. No more tricks."

I hold up my hand and smile at the General, noticing the birds fluttering in from all sides. "Hold on. Just one more trick."

And that's when the rhinoceros drops from the sky.

One moment the Chimæra—I'm not even sure which one—is a robin flying innocently above the heads of the Mogadorians; the next it's a half-ton African rhino belly-flopping on top of them. A couple of the Mogs on the porch are crushed outright, the wood breaking and splintering, the front of the house even sinking a little at the beast's weight. Another Mog is gored by the rhino as it starts to rampage around. The other Mogs spill into the yard, blasters firing. They aren't laughing anymore. This whole noble execution the General had them watching has been ruined by our small army of Chimærae.

It's chaos. All around us, birds are morphing into more lethal forms—a bear, a couple of jungle cats and a lumbering lizard thing that I think is a Komodo dragon—and running down the Mogadorians. I see some of the Chimærae sustain blaster burns as the Mogs fire madly at them, trying desperately to regroup. They won't be able to hold out long. For once, we've got the element of surprise.

"Looks like *you* should be the one running," I yell at the General as I square up with him. Truth be told, I'm not sure what to do with him. He is Adam's father, after all. Adam told me to show no mercy, but it still feels wrong to kill a father in front of his son, even if they are Mogadorians. I glance over to Adam, hoping he'll at least give me a thumbs-up or thumbs-down, but he's still crumpled in the grass, struggling to pick himself up. Dust is next to him in wolf form, also looking a little beaten up, gently licking Adam's face.

"My name is already written in the histories as a killer of Garde!" the General roars back at me, not even caring about the decimation of his men going on behind him. "If today is the day I die, I will take you with me."

He charges me, sword stabbing right for my sternum. I hold up my arm, expecting my shield to deploy and deflect the blow. It takes me a split second to remember my wrist is bare, my shield destroyed. The General almost skewers me for my overreliance on my bracelet. I have to spin to the side at the last second and can feel how close I came, his blade tearing through the back of my shirt.

The General's sword might miss, but his elbow doesn't. Using his momentum to swing around, he catches me right in the temple. He must be wearing that Mogadorian armor all over his body, because the elbow feels more like a hammer. I stumble to the side, seeing stars. The General slashes at me again, and I just barely manage to lash out with my telekinesis, shoving him backwards. His heels dig up tufts in the grass as he refuses to leave his feet.

Instead of charging back at me, the General levels his sword, another minivortex developing at the blade's tip. I'm caught out—no shield, no cover—and I know I can't let that life-draining energy hit me. I brace myself, ready to dive aside.

Before the sword can discharge, the General's right

hand explodes. He roars and drops his blade, holding up his hand to look at the nickel-sized hole through the palm that wasn't there a second ago.

"Dad says, 'You're welcome,'" Sam's voice chirps in my ear.

I glance over my shoulder to see our van parked on the access road. Malcolm Goode stands next to the driver-side door, using it for cover as he peers through the scope of his rifle.

"Interlopers," the General growls. Before Malcolm can fire another shot, the General takes off at a sprint, using the trash truck for cover. He's surprisingly fast considering his bulk and that full suit of armor.

Well, I'd wanted him to run.

I chase after him, thoughts of how he hunted and killed Garde fueling me. Out of the corner of my eye, I see a Mog warrior draw a bead on me with his blaster. As he fires, a Chimæra in the shape of a black panther leaps onto his back. The blast sails wide and ends up shearing in half the chair Dr. Anu used in his experiments. I know our goal was to keep this Mog technology in tact, but that doesn't matter to me now. I'm seeing red. The General—so proud of killing Garde. Killing children.

I'm going to write the last chapter in his precious history. Right now.

As I come around the trash truck, I see the General

has made it to the basketball courts and stopped. He beckons me onward, waiting for me at center court. I charge in, ignoring the part of me that knows he's setting me up for some kind of trap. Whatever it is, it won't stop me.

The General growls something in Mogadorian. It sounds like a command. Under my feet, beneath the asphalt, a generator of some kind vibrates to life.

I feel a static charge as a dome-shaped force field rises up over the basketball court, trapping me with the General. Everything is suddenly very quiet, the noise of the Chimærae mauling the Mogadorians blocked out by the force field.

I take a step away from the nearest wall, sensing the same type of electric jolt that we encountered at the base in West Virginia. I remember how sick I was after that—it took me days to recover—and know that I can't get too close.

Even as I'm thinking this, an overeager Chimæra in the shape of a tiger flings herself at the General. The blue energy repulses the pouncing Chimæra, shocks her and leaves her in a convulsing heap on the ground, still very much outside the force field.

"We used to fight Piken against each other in this place," the General muses, waving his hand at the enclosed space. "It was a reward for the vatborn. Pity more of them aren't here to witness today's contest."

"You want some alone time with me, is that it?" I taunt the General, making sure to put some distance between me and the force field.

"I want to kill you in peace," he replies. "With your many friends watching helplessly."

"Good luck with that."

Without hesitation, I charge towards the General, pitching fireballs at him as I go. He absorbs each of them. Huge chunks of his uniform burn away, but I don't seem to be doing any damage to the armor underneath. Not letting any pain register on his face, the General rushes right for me, like he's going to barrel into me.

He probably weighs a solid two hundred pounds more than me with that armor. But screw it.

We crash together and the wind goes out of me, but I manage to stay upright. I press my hand, still engulfed by the flames of my Lumen, against the side of the General's face. He lets out a grunt of pain, but that's his only reaction to me burning his face, his pale skin searing black and popping. Both of his hands wrap around my throat, big enough that his fingers overlap at the back of my neck.

He squeezes my neck and immediately dark spots form in my vision. I can't breathe. With the hand not burning the side of the General's face, I pry at his fingers. It feels like my throat will completely collapse if I let his grip get any tighter.

It's hard to concentrate with him choking me, but I manage to keep up the intensity of my Lumen while simultaneously using my telekinesis. I maneuver my dagger out from beneath my pant leg. Without a free hand, I gather as much telekinetic force as I can muster and send the blade lancing towards the General's heart.

My dagger deflects off his armor. Before I can stab at him again, he tightens his grip on my throat and I lose control of my telekinesis. Feeling faint, it's all I can do to keep my Lumen burning against the side of his face.

"Who do you think will die first, boy?" the General sneers, smoke from his own burned face spilling out of his mouth when he speaks. I try to backpedal, to break away from him, but he puts all his weight down, forcing me to my knees.

Suddenly, a Mogadorian sword is thrust towards my face. Unable to move my head, I can only flinch backwards. The tip of the glowing blade stops just short of my eye. The General's grip slackens and then drops away entirely. I fall onto my side, gasping for breath, trying to figure out what just happened.

"Through the back. Isn't that how you do it, Father?"

Adam holds the General's broadsword in two hands—it's almost too heavy for him—and yanks it out of his father's back. He drove it straight through the General's chest, the glowing blade piercing that Mogadorian armor as if it were made of tinfoil. I was too busy fighting for my life to notice the force field come down. Luckily, the General was, too. He stares at Adam, stunned. The General must realize his mistake—all the Mogs know the voice command to bring down the force field, but one of them wasn't fighting on his side.

The General gropes at the wound on his chest and for a moment I think he's going to keep coming. But then he staggers, reaching out to grasp at Adam, almost as if he wants to hug him. Or maybe strangle him. It's hard to tell.

Adam steps aside, a detached look on his face, and allows the General to fall face-first onto the pavement. Beyond the court, the fighting is over, the Mogadorians all dead. Back in Adam's front yard, Sam kneels over a wounded Chimæra. Malcolm stands a few feet off from us, on the sideline, watching the scene with the General, a look of concern on his face. I pick myself up and stand next to Adam.

"Adam, are you . . . ?" My voice is hoarse, throat raw and sore. Adam holds up a hand, cutting me off.

"Look," he says flatly.

At our feet, the General begins to disintegrate. It doesn't happen quickly like I've seen with the many vatborn scouts and warriors I've killed. The General decomposes slowly, parts of him flattening out faster than others. In some spots, his flesh melts away but not the bone beneath, leaving a skeletal elbow jutting up from the ground next to a rib cage, all attached to a half-disintegrated skull.

"You can see where Setrákus Ra augmented him," Adam says, his voice almost clinical as he explains. "Healed wounds, cured diseases, improved his strength and speed. He promised immortality. But the unnatural parts disintegrate, like the vatborn. The rest, what's left, that is trueborn, real flesh."

"We don't have to get into this now," I manage to say, still trying to catch my breath. It's not that I don't appreciate the information. It's just that Adam's dad is lying dead at our feet and he's giving a lesson in Mogadorian genetics like nothing happened.

"They're too far gone to realize it, but this is the fate Setrákus Ra offers my people. Ashes and spare parts," Adam says, staring at his father's remains. "I wonder how much more would be left if the *Great Leader* had never poisoned his body and mind."

Adam lets go of the sword and it thunks heavily to the ground. I put my hand on his shoulder, the revulsion I felt for him over the last couple of days forgotten. He just saved my life and killed his own father to do it.

"Adam, it's okay," I start, not really sure what to say in this crazy situation.

"I hated him," he replies, not looking at me. He stares at the burned uniform, piles of ash and random bones that used to be the General. "But he was my father. I wish things could have ended differently. For all of us."

I crouch down over the General's remains and carefully remove the simple black leather sheath that he wore across his back. It's a little singed but still holding together. I pick up the sword from where Adam dropped it, sheath it and hold it out to him.

"I don't want that," Adam says, staring at the sword with a look of disgust.

"Things *can* end differently," I tell him. "Use this in a way that your father never did. Help us win this war and change the fate of both our people."

Adam hesitates for a moment before accepting the sword from me. He holds the blade in both hands and stares down at it. After a long moment of contemplation, Adam slings the sheath over his shoulder. He grunts at the weight but manages to stand up straight.

"Thank you, John," he says quietly. "I swear to you, this blade will never again be used against a Loric."

Sam walks over to us. "You guys all right?"

Adam nods. I touch the skin of my throat, which already feels swollen and puffy from where the General strangled me.

"Yeah, I'm good," I reply, then look to Adam. "Are we done, though? Or are there more coming?"

He shakes his head. "I shut down communications right before my—right before the General caught up with me. There won't be any reinforcements."

"Nice," Sam replies, looking out at the empty windows of Ashwood Estates. "So we just took over a Mogadorian base."

Before I can bask in any sense of accomplishment, I notice a dark look on Adam's face. He's no longer staring down at his father. Instead, his eyes are turned towards the horizon, like he's expecting to see something bad headed our way at any moment.

"What is it?" I ask him.

"There was something else," he says slowly, choosing his words carefully. "I was only on the communications network for a few moments, but I picked up some chatter. Troop movements. Mass relocations of trueborn to the West Virginia fortress. Deployments of warrior groups to population centers."

"Whoa, whoa," I say, holding up my hands. "What does all that mean?"

"Invasion," Adam replies. "Invasion is imminent."

CHAPTER TEN

SETRÁKUS RA HAS SOME OF HIS MINIONS STICK me in a cold room without any windows. No more polite conversations over nasty dinners, I guess. It's so small in here that I can stand at the center, stretch out my arms and almost brush the opposing walls with my fingertips. There's a little dome-shaped protrusion in the middle of the ceiling. I bet it's a camera. Against one wall is a small metal desk with a chair that looks like it's designed for maximum discomfort. On the desk is a copy of *The Great Book of Mogadorian Progress.*

I'm supposed to sit here and study my grandfather's masterwork. Read three sections and spend at least twenty minutes in deep contemplation of each.

No thanks.

I'm not sure if it's the same copy I used to hit that Mogadorian lady on my first day here. There are a lot of these books lying around the *Anubis*. It's like the only thing the

Mogs read. Anyway, they've chained this one to the desk to make sure I don't turn it into a weapon.

Instead of studying, I lean against the wall farthest from the desk and wait for the Mogs to run out of patience. I try to ignore the itching sensation coming from the Mogadorian charm freshly burned into my ankle. If they're watching me—and I'm almost certain that they're *always* watching me—I don't want them to see me looking uncomfortable.

I definitely don't want them to know how disgusted I am at the idea of being connected to Setrákus Ra. The Mogs hate the Loric, but they fall over themselves to please their "Beloved Leader," even though he used to be one of us. Based on what he told me at dinner, Setrákus Ra turned himself into some freakish hybrid species made from the powerful Legacies of an Elder and the technological advancements of the Mogs. Or so he says. It's hard to figure out what's fact and fiction with him. Whatever he is now—Loric, Mog or something in between—Setrákus Ra has spent centuries making the Mogs view him as a savior. As a god. Where he came from doesn't matter to them anymore. And even though I get a few sideways looks from some of the soldiers aboard the *Anubis*, to most of the crew, I'm on Setrákus Ra's level.

I'm the granddaughter of a self-proclaimed god. So far, that's keeping me safe.

As if being blood relatives wasn't enough, now we're bonded by his version of a Loric charm. I remember feeling left out when I discovered all the other Garde were connected in the same way, all of them once protected by the same force. I wanted to be part of that. Now I've got two thick and jagged bands of scar tissue around my ankle.

Be careful what you wish for, Ella.

I'm zoning out, trying to think up a way to test what the charm does without hurting myself, when a noise starts playing in the room. It sounds almost exactly like a smoke alarm. At first it's like a ringing in my ears, but seconds later it's amplified enough that it drowns out my thoughts. I cover my ears, but the sound only gets louder. It's coming through the walls from every direction at once.

"Turn it off!" I yell to the Mogs I'm sure are watching me. In response, the volume increases. My head feels like it might split open.

I stumble away from the wall and the volume immediately lowers from a deafening shriek to a piercing whistle. When I take another step towards the Great Book, the volume drops another fraction. I get the hint. When I finally open up the book, the noise drops to an annoying buzz.

So that's how Setrákus Ra intends to "educate" me—by making it so the only peace I can find is literally in the pages of his Mogadorian encyclopedia.

Maybe I should try to make the most of this. There might be some information I can use against him in Setrákus Ra's painfully boring book. It can't hurt to skim a little. There's no way I'll ever believe any of the lies on these pages.

The ringing cuts off entirely when I start to read the first page. Even though I resent it, I can't help but let out a little sigh of relief.

> **There is no greater achievement for a species than the shouldering of one's own genetic destiny. It is for that reason that the Mogadorian race must be considered the most elevated of all life throughout the universe.**

Ugh. I can't believe this thing goes on for like five hundred pages, or that it's become required reading for an entire species. I'm not going to find anything useful in here.

As soon as my eyes drift away from the page, the heinous buzzing resumes, more intense than before. I grit my teeth and look back at the book, skimming over a couple more sentences until something occurs to me.

I grab the top of the first thirty pages or so and tear them out of the bindings. The piercing noise in my ears reaches siren level, my eyes watering, but I force myself to go on. I hold up the pages so that whichever Mogadorian is watching can see, and then I tear them down the middle. Then I tear them into fourths, smaller and smaller, until I've got two handfuls of Great Book confetti to toss into the air.

"How am I supposed to read it now?" I shout.

The wailing goes on for another couple of minutes. It

gets to the point where my neck and back start to ache from the way my shoulders are bunched up, like they're trying to cover my ears. I continue tearing more pages out of the book. I can't even hear the paper ripping.

And then, all of a sudden, the noise stops. The bones in my face, my teeth—everything hurts. But I've beaten them, and the silence in that tiny, uncomfortable room is the best I've ever experienced.

My reward is a couple of hours of alone time. Not that I can even really tell how much time is passing. I sit on the edge of the uncomfortable chair, rest my head on the desk and try to nap. My thoughts sound louder in my head than they should, and the ringing in my ears won't let me sleep. That, and the feeling that I'm being watched. When I open my eyes, it feels like the room has actually gotten smaller. I know it's just my imagination, but I'm starting to freak out a little.

My ankle is itching like crazy. I pull up the hem of my dark Mogadorian gown—a fresh one, not the one Setrákus Ra burned—and stare at the raw flesh on my leg. I'm failing at my goal of giving nothing away, but I can't help myself. I reach down and massage my ankle, letting out a deep sigh as I do. I press my palm against the brand and wish that the scar will be gone when I lift my hand. Of course it's still there, but at least the clammy sweat on my palm actually feels sort of good against the seared flesh.

Something occurs to me then. What if I use my Aeternus

to return to a younger age? Would the skin on my ankle heal?

I decide to try it. I close my eyes and picture myself as I was two years ago. The feeling of getting smaller is like letting out a held breath. At least this time when I open my eyes the room seems to have gotten bigger.

I look down at myself. I've shrunk down a few inches, made myself skinnier, the muscles I'd started developing over the last few months smoothed away. And yet, the jagged Mogadorian symbol on my leg remains, pink and achy as ever.

"Aeternus. We have that in common."

It's Setrákus Ra. He stands in the now open doorway of my little study room. Still in that infuriatingly plastic human form. He observes me with a casual smile, leaning against the door, his arms folded across his chest. "It's useless," I reply bitterly, covering up my ankle. I close my eyes and ease back into my true age. "What I get for being related to you. The dumbest Legacy of all."

"You won't feel that way when you're my age," Setrákus says, ignoring my insult. "You will be young and beautiful forever, if you wish. It will be an inspiration to your subjects to see their leader radiant and ageless."

"I don't have any subjects."

"Not yet. But soon."

I know exactly who Setrákus Ra means for me to lord over, but I refuse to acknowledge it. I regret using my

Aeternus. Now he knows something else about me, another way for him to try finding common ground with me, like we're the same.

"Is the charm bothering you?" he asks gently.

"It's fine," I reply quickly. "It's like it's not even there."

"Hmm. The irritation should pass in a day or so." He pauses, his hand on his chin in reflection. "I know it hurts now, Ella. But in time you will come to appreciate the lessons you are learning. You will thank me for my benevolence."

I frown at him, sure that he's going to ramble no matter what I say. So I don't say anything at all.

I glare up at him. "So what? You're, like, protecting me with this thing? Is that the point?"

"I would see no harm come to you, child," Setrákus Ra replies.

"Does this charm work like the one the Garde had?" I take a step towards him and the doorway. "If I run out of here and one of your minions tries to stop me, will anything he does to hurt me be reflected back at him?"

"No. Our charm does not work like that," Setrákus Ra answers patiently. "And *I* would stop you, granddaughter. Not one of my *minions*."

I take another step towards him, wondering if he'll back away. He doesn't. "If I get too close, will the charm break?"

Setrákus Ra doesn't move. "Just as each charm works differently, so does each one have a unique weakness. If only I'd discovered that bringing the Garde together would have broken the Elders' craven charm sooner, I would have already obliterated the Garde." He touches the three glowing Loric pendants dangling from around his neck. "Although, I must admit, I have enjoyed the hunt."

I try my best to sound casual and sincere. "Shouldn't I know what that weakness is? I don't want to accidentally go breaking our connection, Grandfather."

Setrákus Ra actually grins at me. I'm beginning to realize that he appreciates it when I'm duplicitous. Then, his eyes drift towards the shredded pages of his book and his grin falters.

"Perhaps soon, when you are ready, when you trust the purity of my motives," he replies, then abruptly changes the subject. "Tell me, granddaughter, besides the Aeternus, what other Legacies have you developed?"

"Only whatever I used to hurt you at Dulce Base," I lie, figuring it's a good idea to keep my telepathy a secret. I've tried using it to reach out to the Garde, but the distance from the *Anubis* to Earth must be too great. Once we land, I'll try again. Until then, the less Setrákus Ra knows about me, the better. "And I can't control that one. I don't even know what it is."

"I was hardly hurt," Setrákus Ra scoffs. "Your other Legacies will develop soon, dear. In the meantime, would you like me to show you the extent of your power?"

"Yes," I reply, almost surprised at my own eagerness. I

tell myself that it's smart to learn how to use my Legacies, even if my teacher is the biggest monster in the universe.

In response, Setrákus Ra smiles. Almost like he thinks he's gotten through to me. He hasn't, but let him go on thinking that I'm becoming an eager pupil. He waves his hand at the mess I've made of his book.

"First, clean this up," he commands. "I will see you have a chance to practice your Legacies once your betrothed arrives."

My *what*?

CHAPTER ELEVEN

SUNSET IN THE EVERGLADES WOULD BE PRETTY if not for the massive Mogadorian warship blotting out the horizon. Whatever alien metal the warship is made from, it reflects nothing, the pink and orange light of the dying day simply absorbed into the hull. The behemoth doesn't land—there's not enough cleared space in the swampland for it to set down, unless it wants to crush the smaller Mogadorian ships parked on the narrow runway below. Instead, the warship hovers, metal gangways unfurling from the ship's underside and connecting to the ground. Mogadorians scurry up and down the ramps, loading equipment into the ship.

"We should wipe them out," Marina says matter-of-factly.

Nine blinks at her. "Are you serious? I count at least a hundred Mogs and the biggest goddamn ship I've ever seen."

"So what?" Marina counters. "Don't you love to fight?"

"Fights I can *win*, yeah," Nine replies.

"And if you can't win, you just run your mouth, right?"

"Enough," I hiss before Nine can say anything more. I don't know how long Marina's going to hold this grudge against Nine or what it'll take to ease the tension, but now is definitely not the time to deal with it. "Bickering isn't getting us anywhere."

We're on our stomachs in the mud, shielded from the busy Mogadorians by overgrown tallgrass, right at the edge of where the swamp begins to encroach on the man-made clearing. There are two buildings in front of us; one is a glass-and-steel one-story that looks almost like a greenhouse, and the other is an aircraft hangar with a narrow landing strip, perfect for small propeller planes or the saucer-shaped Mogadorian crafts, nowhere near large enough for the warship floating above us. Just like Dale told us before he fled, the whole place looks like it was abandoned until recently. The swamp is beginning to creep back in and crack the asphalt, the metal struts of the greenhouse are rusted over, and the NASA logo has almost completely faded from the side of the hangar. Of course, these conditions don't appear to have deterred the Mogs from setting up a small base here.

But now, it looks like they're packing up.

"Marina, do you sense anything?" I ask. At this point, we've got nothing else to go on except this intuition of hers. It's gotten us this far—right into a swarming nest of Mogadorians. Might as well let it take us a little further.

"He's here," she says. "I don't know how I know, but he's here."

"Then we're going in," I say. "But we're doing it the smart way."

I reach out and grab both of their hands, turning the three of us invisible. If a Mogadorian was to look over here now, we'd be nothing more than three strange indentations in the mud. As a group, we stand up, confident that the horde of Mogs won't be able to see us.

"Marina, you lead the way," I whisper.

As we step out of the swamp, Nine trips over a root and nearly topples over, our chain almost breaking. That would've been the shortest covert mission in history. I squeeze his hand hard.

"Sorry," he says quietly. "It's just weird not being able to see my legs."

"That can't happen again," I warn him.

"I'm reconsidering that whole rushing-in-and-killing-them-all thing," Nine replies. "Being sneaky isn't exactly my strong suit."

Marina makes an annoyed noise, so I squeeze her hand hard, too.

"We need to move as a unit," I say through gritted teeth, hoping we can regain some of that instinctual team-work we managed during the earlier fight with Mog scouts.

"Take it slow, be quiet and don't bump into anything."

With that, we start slowly forward. I'm not too worried about the noise our footfalls make on the uneven pavement; the Mogadorians are busy loading heavy gear from the greenhouse to the warship, the wheels on their dollies squeaking and grinding. I'm used to moving around while invisible, trusting my instincts, but I know that it can be hard for the others. We approach slowly, grasping on to each other, keeping as quiet as possible.

Marina takes us towards the greenhouse first. The Mogs are concentrated around that area, wheeling out carts loaded up with bizarre, mad scientist–looking devices. I watch as one Mog pushes a wheeled shelving unit cluttered with potted plants—flowers, patches of grass, saplings—all of them things found on Earth, and yet all of them veined with a strange gray fluid. They look droopy, on the verge of dying, and I wonder what kind of experiments the Mogs were running on them.

There's a tall Mogadorian at the base of the ramp leading to the warship. His uniform is different from the usual warrior garb—those Mogs are at least sort of trying to fit in on Earth, even if they're dressed like gothic weirdos. This guy is definitely some kind of military officer, his attire formal and severe, all black, covered in shining medals and studded epaulets. The tattoos across his scalp are much more elaborate than any I've seen. He holds a computer tablet in his hands, checking items off with a swipe of his finger as the Mogs load them onto the ship. He barks the occasional order at the others in harsh Mogadorian.

Marina tries to move us closer to the greenhouse, but I tighten my grip and plant my feet. Nine bumps into my back, letting out an annoyed grunt that we're stopped. The path in front of us is like a Mogadorian obstacle course—they're everywhere. Any closer and we run the risk of a stray Mog walking right into us. If Eight is in that greenhouse with their experiments and cargo, our only chance to get him would be a full-on assault. I'm not ready to go down that road yet. Sensing my reluctance, Marina's hand grows a little colder in mine.

"Not yet," I hiss at her, my words barely louder than a soft breath. "We check the hangar first."

We make it about ten more steps before an animal groan stops us in our tracks. From the greenhouse, a team of Mogs wheel out a large cage. Inside is a creature that might have been a cow at one point but has since been transformed into something seriously nasty. The animal's eyes are wet and jaundiced, painful-looking horns jut out of its skull, and its udder is immensely swollen and covered in the same grayish veins I noticed on the plants. The creature looks lethargic and depressed, barely alive. Whatever experiments the Mogs were running down here are truly disgusting and, like Nine, I'm starting to reconsider Marina's idea of just wiping out all these bastards, massive warship or no massive warship.

"Hold up," Nine whispers in my ear. "I've got an idea."

Exposed as we are, I'm not sure it's a great time for one of Nine's crazy ideas. But, a moment after he stops us, the cow-beast in the cage groans again and lumbers awkwardly to its feet. It staggers to the side and pushes all its weight against one side of the cage, causing the Mogs pushing it to yell for assistance as the whole thing threatens to topple. Then, the monster mule-kicks one of its huge cloven hooves at the bars, nearly smashing the face of a Mog.

"I asked it to give us a distraction," Nine whispers, more Mogs closing in on the cage to try sedating their experiment. "Poor thing was happy to help."

Nine's animal telepathy works like a charm. As if it's at last discovered a purpose in life, the cow thrashes about, bulling towards the sides of its cage, even catching one Mog in the shoulder with its horn. The chaos creates an opening for us to slip through the mass in front of the greenhouse and make our way towards the hangar.

We all stop at the sound of a Mog blaster being fired. Turning around, I see the officer holstering his blaster, a smoking hole in the side of the cow's head. It slumps in the cage, unmoving. He yells some orders, and the Mogadorians begin loading the corpse onto the warship.

As I tense up, Nine whispers to me, "Better this way. It was in a ton of pain."

With some distance between us and the highest concentration of Mogs, I feel comfortable enough to whisper back. "What were they doing to it?"

Nine pauses before answering. "I couldn't, like, have a heart-to-heart with the thing. But I think they were trying to figure out how they could make it more efficient. They're, uh, experimenting with the ecology."

"Demented," Marina mutters.

We pick up some speed as we move towards the hangar. On our right, at the edge of the runway, are a trio of the smaller, saucer-shaped Mogadorian ships. A maintenance crew of five Mogadorians huddles around one of them, pulling circuit boards out of the ship's underbelly and generally looking befuddled. I guess Mogadorians can have technical difficulties, too. Other than those guys, the coast is clear.

The huge, sheet-metal doors of the hangar, wide enough for a small plane to pass in and out, are only open a few feet, just enough to let a person pass through. There are lights on inside the hangar, but all I can see through the gap is empty space.

Marina slows down as we reach the doors and then stops fully to peek inside. While she's doing that, I look over my shoulder. Nothing's changed—the Mogs are still loading materials onto the warship, completely unaware that we just snuck through their ranks.

"Anything?" Nine whispers, and I can sense him

craning his neck, trying to see through the crack in the hangar doors. Before I can answer, I hear Marina's breath catch in her throat. My hand stings, shot through with cold, like I'm suddenly clutching a block of ice.

"Shit, Marina!" I hiss, but she's not listening. Instead, she's lunging through the doors. Considering my hand is numb, it takes all my willpower to keep hold of her. I tug Nine along behind me and his shoulder strikes the steel door, his grunt covered by the echoing metallic rattling.

The hangar is almost completely empty, the Mogadorians having already cleared all their gear out. Large floodlights shine down from the rafters, illuminating the metal table and chair in the center of the room. They're the only things left in the hangar, and the lights from above cast long shadows across the concrete floor.

Eight's body is on the table.

He is wrapped in a black body bag, unzipped to the waist. He's shirtless, the quarter-sized wound where Five stabbed him through the heart plainly visible on his chest. His brown skin is ashen, but Eight still looks very much like himself, like at any moment he'll teleport off the table and play some annoying joke on me. There are black electrodes with short, fragile-looking antennae attached to Eight's temples and a few more running down his sternum. The electrodes generate some kind of field that's barely visible to the eye, like a low and steady current of electricity is passing over Eight's body. I think it's something the Mogs attached to Eight to keep his body intact for their experiments. In addition to the electrodes, someone has cleaned the blood off him and, surprisingly, they've left his Loric pendant around his neck, the jewel shimmering dully against his chest. It kills me to see him like this, but Eight looks almost peaceful.

Of course, Eight isn't the reason Marina shoved through the hangar doors, or the reason that she's currently giving my hand a wicked case of frostbite.

Seated next to Eight, head in his hands, is Five.

Five sits crouched forward, almost like he wishes he could fold in on himself. There's a thick pad of gauze over the eye Marina stabbed back in the swamp, a very faint pink stain beginning to soak through. His good eye is red-rimmed; it looks as if he's been crying or hasn't been sleeping—or both. Five's head is freshly shaven since we last saw him, and I wonder how far off he is from getting a set of his own Mogadorian tattoos. He's dressed in Mogadorian formal attire similar to the officer directing traffic at the warship. However, his uniform is severely wrinkled, the buttons around the neck undone, everything looking a little too tight.

There's no way the one-eyed traitor didn't hear us enter. Thanks to Marina, we made a ton of noise coming through the door, and the emptiness of the hangar amplifies everything to the point where I'm suddenly extremely conscious of my breathing. Even worse, I can hear a low growl coming from Marina, like she's fighting back an intense scream, ready to throw herself at Five. Behind me, I can sense Nine basically holding his breath.

Five's good eye flicks briefly in our direction. He definitely heard us, but he can't see us. Maybe there's hope he'll just write it off as noise from the Mogs outside. I want another go at the renegade Garde, too—one where he doesn't sucker punch me into unconsciousness before the fight even starts—but we have to pick our battles. Facing off against Five in an enclosed space with a Mogadorian warship at our back is definitely not the battle we want. We'll need to figure out another way to recover Eight's body.

I pull at Marina's arm, the icy pinpricks in my hand now replaced by full-on numbness, trying to communicate to her just how terrible an idea charging in would be. She tugs against me for a moment, but then I start to feel her calm down, which I can tell because my hand starts to warm up.

But as Marina slowly and quietly releases a deep breath, I see it mist in front of her, the air around her too cold. A cloud of breath from an invisible girl, floating in the bright lights of the hangar.

Five sees it, his eye narrowing. He stands up from his chair and looks right at the spot where we're standing.

"I didn't mean to do it," he says.

CHAPTER TWELVE

I CLENCH MARINA'S AND NINE'S HANDS, HOPING that will be enough to keep them from saying anything back to Five and totally giving away our position. I'm not ready to lose our one advantage—invisibility—just yet. Thankfully, they both manage to control themselves, Five's words hanging out there unanswered.

"I know you won't believe me," Five continues. "But no one was supposed to get killed."

Five's beseeching gaze is still aimed right at us, so slowly, quietly, I begin leading the others to the side. We move just inches at a time, careful of each other, not making any noise. Gradually, we slip out from under Five's gaze, flanking him. Now, he's staring at truly empty space, stupidly waiting for a response.

With a grunt, Five turns away. It's like he was never talking to us at all. Instead, he starts speaking directly to Eight's body.

"You shouldn't have done what you did, diving in front of Nine," Five lectures, his voice almost wistful. "It was heroic, I guess. I kinda admire you for it. But it wasn't worth it. The Mogadorians are going to win anyway, you know? A levelheaded guy like you would've learned his place. You could've helped with the rebuilding and unification. Nine, though . . . he's too brain-dead to know when he's beat. He's no good to anyone."

I feel muscles tense in Nine's arm, but for now he resists the urge to throw himself at Five. That's good—he's learning. Or maybe, like me, he's stunned this is happening at all, Five just rambling away like this, pretending we're not here.

Five puts his hand gently on Eight's shoulder. The sleeve of his uniform rides up and I notice the leather sheath strapped to his arm, the one that holds the needle-shaped spring-loaded dagger that he used to kill our friend.

"He told me—" Five's voice breaks a little as he continues addressing Eight. "He told me I'd have a chance to talk you guys into joining. No one would have to get hurt if you just accepted Mogadorian Progress. He kept his word before, I mean, I'm living proof, right? When the charm broke, he could've killed me, but he didn't."

Five must be talking about Setrákus Ra, about a deal he struck with the Mogadorian leader. He walks around the table, turning his back on us. Marina takes a step towards him, but I don't let her go any farther. I don't know why Five is talking so much, but he has to know we're here. I'm not sure if this is a trap, if he's baiting us, or what is going on. But I want to listen.

"I didn't expect you to be so brainwashed," Five says, standing over Eight, his hunched back presenting a perfect target. "Thinking about everything in black and white, heroes and villains."

Five reaches down and lifts Eight's pendant, squeezing the jewel in his fist. His Legacy—Externa, he called it, where his skin takes on the quality of whatever he touches—kicks in, Five's skin briefly flashing the shimmering cobalt of Loralite. After a moment, he lets the pendant go with a sigh, and his flesh returns to normal.

"But then, maybe I'm the brainwashed one, right? Isn't that what you guys said to me?" Five lets loose a low laugh, then reaches up to carefully adjust the gauze over his destroyed eye. "They fill your head with all this shit—the Elders, the Great Book. All these rules about who we're supposed to be. But I don't care about any of it. I'm just trying to survive."

I feel Nine's hand sweating in mine; he must be struggling to hold himself back from attacking. Marina, meanwhile, isn't radiating the furious cold she was moments ago, probably because the scene unfolding before us is so misguided and pathetic. If Five's speech—clearly for our benefit—has revealed anything, it's that he's pretty much lost his mind.

Five brushes a speck of something gently from Eight's forehead, then shakes his head.

"Anyway, the point is, I'm sorry, Eight," Five says, that know-it-all tone still in his voice but mixed with an undercurrent of sincerity. "I know it doesn't mean anything. I'll be a coward, a traitor, a murderer for the rest of my life. That won't change. But I want you to know that I wish things could've turned out differently."

Behind us, someone clears his throat. All of us were so wrapped up in Five's unhinged monologue—Five included—that we didn't notice the Mogadorian officer enter. He eyes Five warily, his posture stiff and formal. Looking at him, standing there like a soldier ready to deliver a report, it occurs to me that this Mogadorian might actually take orders from Five. If that's the case, he seems way disgusted by it.

"We are finished loading the ship," the officer says.

The Mog waits for Five to acknowledge him, but Five stays silent for a long, awkward moment. He stays hunched over Eight's body, breathing slowly. I tense up and wonder if his strange game is over and if now he's thinking about sounding the alarm.

The Mogadorian officer does a bad job of hiding how much Five's silence perturbs him. "One of the hunting parties hasn't reported back," he continues. "And the mechanics are having difficulties getting one of the scout vessels to work."

Five sighs. "That's fine," he says. "We'll leave them behind."

"Yes, those were my orders," the officer replies, not so subtly asserting his power. "Are you ready to leave?"

Five turns to the officer, a malicious twinkle in his remaining eye. "Yeah. Let's get out of here."

Five walks towards the hangar doors, his movements mockingly sluggish. We stand to the side, watching all this transpire, staying quiet. The officer arches an eyebrow, not stepping out of Five's way.

"Aren't you forgetting something?" the officer asks Five when the two are nearly face-to-face.

Five scratches his head. "Huh?"

"The body," the officer says, annoyed. "Your instructions are to bring the Loric's body. And the pendant."

"Oh, that," Five replies, and glances back at the metal table where Eight rests. "The body's gone, Captain. The Garde must have slipped in here and taken it. Only explanation."

The Mogadorian captain doesn't know what to say. He makes a show of craning his neck, looking past Five to where Eight is still very much on the table. Then, he studies Five's face, his eyes narrowed impatiently.

"Is this some kind of game, Loric?" the captain hisses. "Or are you blind in both eyes now? The Garde is *right there.*"

Five ignores the insult and shakes his head at the

Captain, clicking his tongue.

"Happened on your watch, too," Five says. "You let them steal a war asset from right under your nose. That's basically treason, my man. You know what the punishment for that is."

The Mogadorian opens his mouth for another disbelieving protest. He's cut off by a scrape of metal, Five's blade popping out from beneath his sleeve. Without hesitation, he drives the point into the underside of the officer's jaw and straight up into his brain. Before he starts to disintegrate, there's a look of total surprise on the Mog's face.

Five doesn't move as the Mog turns to ash. He disintegrates slower than the many other dying Mogs I've seen, and when it's finished there are jagged bones poking out of his crumpled uniform. Five pushes his blade back into the mechanism on his forearm and kicks the officer's remains away from the doors. Then, he carefully brushes himself off and straightens his coat.

From where we're standing, Five is in profile, and the eye that's visible is the one covered by the gauze bandage. Because of that, it's not easy to get a read on his expression.

"Good luck," Five says, then steps through the hangar doors, easing them closed behind him.

No one says anything or even moves for about a minute, all of us a little worried that a squadron of Mogs will be storming in here at any second. Finally, Nine shakes off my grip, popping back into the visible world.

"Okay. What the *holy hell* was that about?" he exclaims. "Is that kid trying to buddy up now or is he just totally loony tunes?"

"It doesn't matter," I reply. "We've got Eight, that's what's important. We can deal with Five another time."

"He's alone and lost," Marina says softly, letting go of my hand as well. She notices me rubbing some warmth back into it, the chilled feeling still lingering, and frowns. "Sorry, Six. He brought it out of me."

I wave it off, not wanting to get into Marina's Legacy control at the moment. I tiptoe to the hangar doors and edge them open just a crack. I'm just in time to see Five disappearing up the ramp and onto the warship, the last one aboard. Once he's inside, the ramp curls back into the warship's underbelly and the huge ship begins to rise up, its engines purring with a softness that seems almost impossible for a vessel that size. Once it reaches a certain height, the warship starts to flicker and I begin having trouble distinguishing its outline from the purple clouds. Hulking, virtually silent, and equipped with some kind of cloaking device—how are we supposed to fight something like that?

"You sound like you feel sorry for him," Nine says to Marina.

"I don't," she snaps at Nine, but I can hear some doubt creeping into Marina's voice, that tough exterior she's been putting on showing some faults. "I . . . did you see his eye?"

"I saw a hole in his head covered by a Band-Aid," Nine replies. "Dude has that and more coming to him."

"Do you think Eight would want that?" I ask, honestly wondering. "He died trying to keep us from killing each other."

The warship risen out of sight, I turn around to face the others. Nine chews his lip and stares at the floor, considering what I just said. Marina has taken a seat in Five's former chair at Eight's side. She tentatively touches the electrodes and waves her fingers through the energy field. When nothing happens, Marina gently brushes her fingers through his curly hair. Her eyes shine with fresh tears, but she holds them back.

"I knew I'd find you," she whispers. "I'm sorry I ever left you."

I walk over to join Marina at the table, gazing down at Eight. Maybe it's my imagination, but it seems like he has the faintest smile on his lips.

"I wish I'd known you better," I say to Eight, reaching out to place my hand lightly on his shoulder. "I wish our lives had been different."

Nine hesitates but eventually joins us at the table, standing next to Marina. At first, he avoids looking directly at Eight's body, his lips pursed, the muscles in his neck twitching like he's trying to lift something heavy.

He's ashamed, I realize. It seems to take a great effort on his part, but after a moment Nine manages to look at Eight. Immediately, he reaches out to zip up the body bag a little more, enough so that Eight's wound is hidden from view.

"Oh man," he says quietly. "I'm sorry for . . ." Nine shakes his head, running a hand through his hair. "I mean, thank you for saving my life. Five was right, uh, you probably shouldn't have. If I'd just shut my mouth you'd probably still be . . . shit, I'm sorry, Eight. I'm so sorry."

Nine takes a shuddering breath, obviously holding back tears. Marina puts her hand softly on his back and leans against him.

"He would forgive you," she says softly, adding, "I forgive you."

Nine puts his arm around Marina and pulls her into a hug that's tight enough to make her squeak. He buries his face in her hair, hiding his tears. My mind is and has always been racing—wondering about John, Sam and the others, worrying about how we're going to find our way back to them, if they're even still alive and uncaptured—but seeing Marina and Nine like this, coming together, starting to heal, it gives me hope. We're a strong people. We can get through anything.

"We need to get moving," I say gently, reluctant to end this moment but knowing that I have to.

Nine finally releases Marina, and I carefully zip up Eight's body bag. Nine reaches down and, with an equal amount of care, lifts Eight's body into his arms.

Just as we turn towards the hangar doors, they rumble open.

The group of Mogadorians who were working on the scout ship. I forgot all about them. They stand in the doorway, caught in the middle of pushing their broken ship into the hangar. They look about as surprised to see us as we are to see them.

Before we can do anything, a mechanical grinding emanates from the ship. The front—or at least the side of the saucer aimed directly at us—opens up, a blaster turret clanking into view and whirring to life with an electric sizzle. There must be a Mog inside.

"Get down!" Nine shouts.

There's no cover in this empty hangar except the metal table, and it's way too late to go invisible. Marina flips over the table, Nine crouches with Eight's body still in his arms, and I dive to the side, hoping that we're fast enough as the turret opens fire.

CHAPTER THIRTEEN

"DOES THE NAME GRAHISH SHARMA MEAN ANY-thing to you?" Sarah asks.

I think for a moment, trying to pluck the name out of my memory. "Sounds kind of familiar. Why?"

I'm standing in the yard outside Adam's old house, Sarah's voice arriving long-distance over the disposable cell phone. Beyond the empty basketball courts, the sun is just beginning to dip below the horizon. A large bird cuts across the orange sky and I wonder if it's one of ours—we've set the Chimærae up as sentries all around the grounds of Ashwood Estates with orders to find us if any intruders should appear. So far, it's been quiet. If I didn't know better, it'd seem like I was hanging out in a peculiarly quiet suburb, one where everyone's still at work.

"He's from India," Sarah explains. "He's the

commander of something called the Vishnu Nationalist Eight."

The name clicks at the mention of Eight and I snap my fingers. "Oh, right. That's the army guy who was protecting Eight in the Himalayas."

"Hmm," Sarah says. "So his story checks out."

I pace across the lawn, picturing Sarah with her blond hair pulled up in a studious bun, pens and pencils stuck through it, poring over some documents in the new offices of They Walk Among Us. Never mind that those offices are located in an abandoned ranch fifty miles outside of Huntsville, Alabama. Never mind that Sarah was escorted there by her ex-boyfriend Mark, who's actually turned out to be surprisingly capable at this cloak-and-dagger stuff. It's the image of Sarah that I focus on.

"What story is that?"

"Well, it's a lot of rumor and internet weirdness that we're trying to cut through. But this Sharma guy is claiming to have shot down an alien spacecraft and captured its crew."

"Some of the Mogs who were after Eight, probably," I reply.

"Right. Took them alive and everything. Even though it happened in India, it should still be national news, but it's not. Someone's keeping a lid on it. Mark's trying to make contact with Sharma. He wants to run the story on They Walk Among Us, hopefully expose the Mogs to the general public."

"Huh," I say, rubbing the back of my neck and thinking out loud. "Might help rally some support if things get bad."

"How bad are things going to get, John?"

I swallow hard. Even though I used my healing Legacy shortly after battle, I can still feel the General's fingers clenched around my throat.

"I don't know," I say, not sure why I'm hiding Adam's theory on imminent invasion from Sarah. I guess maybe I'm still trying to protect her. I quickly change the subject. "How's Mark doing, anyway?"

"He's doing fine," Sarah replies. "He's changed a lot."

"How so?"

Sarah hesitates. "I . . . it's hard to explain."

I don't dwell for very long on the present state of Mark James. It isn't what I want to talk about. Really, after nearly dying this afternoon, all I want is to hear Sarah's voice.

"I miss you," I say.

"I miss you, too," Sarah replies. "After a long day of fighting alien invaders and unraveling international conspiracies, I wish we could just snuggle up on that old couch in my basement and watch a movie."

That makes me laugh, the feeling bittersweet as I

picture the kind of normal life Sarah and I might be leading if we weren't trying to save the world.

"Soon," I tell her, trying to sound confident.

"I hope so," she replies.

I sense movement behind me and turn around to find Sam standing on the ruined porch of Adam's house. He motions for me to come inside.

"Sarah, I've gotta go," I say, feeling reluctant to hang up the phone. We've been checking in with each other every eight hours like we planned, and I feel a sense of relief every time I hear her voice. Every time I disconnect, I start thinking about the next time . . . the time when she won't call. "Be careful, okay? Things might be getting pretty heavy soon."

"Things aren't already heavy?" she asks. "You be careful, too. I love you."

I say good-bye to Sarah and tilt my head at Sam. He looks almost excited, like he's gotten some good news in the last five minutes.

"What's up?"

"Come down," he says. "We figured something out."

I climb onto what's left of the porch after this afternoon's skirmish and follow Sam through the half-sunken doorway into the living room. The interior of the house matches the exterior—the perfect idea of human suburbia—except the furniture looks like it was arranged exactly as seen on the pages of a catalog.

There's absolutely no sense of it being lived in. I try to imagine what it was like for Adam growing up here, try to picture him bashing little Piken action figures together on the floor, and just can't do it.

At the back of the living room is a massive metal door secured by a series of locks operated by a keypad covered in Mogadorian symbols. The door is the one thing that breaks the suburban illusion and it's actually kind of surprising to me that the Mogs didn't try hiding it behind a bookcase or something. I guess they never thought their enemies would make it this far. The door is already open, unlocked by Adam earlier, and it's through there that Sam and I descend into the tunnels beneath Ashwood Estates.

We walk down a long metal staircase, the phony hominess above immediately replaced by sterile stainless steel and buzzing halogen lights. The labyrinthine network of tunnels beneath Ashwood is much more in keeping with my idea of the Mogadorians—functional and cold. It's not quite as sprawling down here as the hollowed-out mountain in West Virginia, but it definitely puts Dulce Base to shame. I wonder how long it took them to carve all this out, the Mogs tunneling into the Earth during those years I was on the run with Henri, expanding their reach without us even realizing it.

There's a jagged and long crack in the wall that starts about halfway down the steps and runs ahead deeper into the tunnels. Sam reaches out to drag his hand along it, coating his fingers with concrete dust.

"We're sure this place isn't going to collapse, right?"

"Adam doesn't think so," Sam replies, clapping his hands clean, the noise echoing. "It creeps me out down here, though. Seriously claustrophobic."

"Don't worry. We won't be staying long."

We pass other cracks as we navigate the twisting hallways, places where the foundation shifted, broken sections of concrete grinding against each other. The damage was caused the last time Adam was here, when he unleashed his earthquake Legacy to rescue Malcolm. There are some hallways where the ceilings have outright collapsed.

Down the hall, we pass by a large, well-lit room that looks like it might have been a laboratory at one point, lots of nozzles and levers and worktables, but no equipment. Everything must have gotten destroyed in Adam's attack, and the Mog salvage team never got the chance to replace it. Next to the lab, we pass a row of oppressive eight-by-eight rooms with thick doors made from bulletproof glass. Cells. All of them currently unoccupied.

"The archives are up here," Sam tells me. "Dad's been in there nonstop. The Mogs recorded *everything*."

We stop by a small room—almost like an office—with a huge bank of monitors. Malcolm sits behind the room's single computer terminal, bleary-eyed from watching who knows how many hours of footage. On-screen, a Mogadorian scout speaks directly into the camera.

"It has been three days since we leaked rumors of a Loric presence in Buenos Aires," the scout reports. "There has yet to be any sign of Garde, but surveillance continues—"

Malcolm pauses the video when he notices us, rubbing his eyes.

"Find anything useful?" I ask.

Malcolm shakes his head and pulls up a list of files on the computer. He brushes a finger down the touch screen, and the files begin an endless scroll. There are thousands of them, and all their titles are in Mogadorian.

"From what I can gather, this is almost five years' worth of Mogadorian intelligence," Malcolm explains. "I'd need an entire team to go through it all. Even with Adam translating these titles, which are basically just dates and times, it's hard to figure out where to begin."

"Maybe we can hire some interns," Sam suggests, then tugs my arm. "Come on, we gotta see Adam."

"Do what you can," I tell Malcolm before Sam drags me away. "Even the smallest bit of information might help."

A few more steps down the hall and we reach the

room Adam described as the control center. The room is pretty much undamaged, so it's where we set up shop. The walls are covered in monitors, security-camera footage from Ashwood streaming over some, but also video feeds from other places, including one hacked security camera outside the barricaded John Hancock Center. Beneath the monitors are a row of computers, not exactly user-friendly since all the keys are in Mogadorian.

I put my hands on my hips and survey this place, watching the camera feeds that not too long ago would've been trained on me. It feels strange to be on the other side. Like Sam, this place makes me uneasy.

"Are we safe here?" I ask. "All these cameras . . . there aren't any pointed back at us?"

"I've disabled them," Adam replies. He's in a swivel chair at one of the computers, typing out a string of commands. He turns around to face me. "Using the General's authorization, I've sent a code back to the Mogadorian command in West Virginia reporting that the salvage team uncovered a toxic chemical leak. It'll take some time to clean up. They'll assume the failed cameras have something to do with the salvage team's work."

"How much time does that buy us?"

"A couple of days? A week?" Adam replies. "They'll become suspicious when the General doesn't check in, but we should slip through the cracks for a while."

"What do we look for in the meantime?"

"Your friends," Adam replies. "In fact, I believe I've already found them."

"Yeah, Florida," I say. "We already knew that."

"No, he *found* them. Like, exactly," Sam replies, grinning at me. "That's why I came to get you. Check this out."

Sam points at one of the screens, this one displaying a map of the United States. The map is covered in triangles of various sizes. There's a small triangle over our location along with a few similar-sized indicators scattered throughout the country. There are bigger triangles glowing on top of population centers. New York, Chicago, Los Angeles, Houston—all these cities are marked on the map. The biggest triangle of all is to the west of us, right around where the Mogs' mountain base is hidden in West Virginia.

"This is a, uh . . ." Sam looks over at Adam. "What'd you call this thing?"

"Tactical asset overview," Adam replies. "It shows where my people have ongoing operations."

"They're massing in the major cities," I say, studying the map.

"Yeah," Adam replies, grimly. "In preparation for the invasion."

"Let's not focus on the i-word right now, okay?" Sam says. "Look at this."

Sam has plugged the tablet displaying the location of the other Garde into one of the computers. He hands it to me and my eyes immediately shoot to Florida. My heart skips a beat; there's only one blinking dot on the map. It takes me a moment to realize that the four dots symbolizing each of the remaining Garde have actually gotten so close together that they perfectly overlap.

"They're almost on top of each other," I say. "All four of them."

"Yep," Sam replies, taking back the tablet. "And look at this."

He holds the tablet up next to the map of Mogadorian activity. The four dots perfectly line up with one of the smaller orange triangles in Florida.

"The Mogs have them," I say, gritting my teeth. "Adam, is that a base of some kind?"

"A research station," he replies. "The records show there was some genetic experimentation being done there. It isn't the kind of place we'd normally keep prisoners, especially not Garde."

"Why even take prisoners at this point?" Sam asks. "I mean, I get Setrákus Ra has some weird thing for Ella. But the others . . ."

"They aren't prisoners," I say, hitting Sam on the arm in excitement as this dawns on me. "The others are up to something. They're on the attack."

"I'm working on getting us a visual of the base,"

Adam says, his fingers racing across the keyboard.

"How're you going to do that?" I ask.

I sit down in the swivel chair next to Adam and watch his hands flick across the Mogadorian keyboard. Whatever he's doing seems almost like second nature.

"I've locked down a scout ship so they won't be able to operate it. That was the easy part. Accessing and isolating its onboard surveillance while still keeping the craft inoperable is proving trickier."

"You're hacking into a ship?" Sam asks, leaning over the back of Adam's chair.

I watch the monitor directly in front of Adam crackle with static. "How does that help us?"

"This control room is a nerve center, John," Adam explains, taking a moment away from typing to gesture around. "Information from all the other bases feeds to here. It is just a matter of accessing it."

"Accessing it how?"

"Hunting the Loric for so many years has made my people paranoid to ever miss a potential lead. Every operation is recorded. There's surveillance everywhere." Adam strikes a key with a triumphant flair. "Even aboard our own ships."

The monitors above flicker briefly and then display grainy footage of a runway in the middle of a swamp.

"If the Garde are nearby, we might be able to see them," Adam explains.

"If they're not invisible," I say, squinting at the monitor.

Beneath the camera, a handful of Mogadorians look frustrated as they yank engine parts from the scout ship's hull. They clean these parts, reattach them and, when nothing happens, start taking apart something else.

"What're they doing?" Sam asks.

"Trying to fix what I've done," Adam replies excitedly, seeming pleased that he's outsmarted his people. "They assume engine failure, not automated systems override. It will take them awhile to catch on."

Another Mogadorian, this one wearing an impressive-looking uniform similar to the General's, approaches them. He yells at the mechanics, then walks offscreen in a huff.

"Does the camera move?" I ask.

"Of course."

Adam hits a button and the camera begins to scan to the side, following the dressed-up Mogadorian. At first, there isn't much to see except pavement and, in the distance, some swampland. However, after a short walk, the dressed-up Mogadorian disappears into an airplane hangar.

"Do you think they're in there?" I ask.

"This camera should be equipped with heat vision, if I can figure out how to access it," Adam replies, tentatively tapping a few of the keys in front of him.

Before Adam can figure it out, Five walks through the hangar doors. Even though I'd guessed he was a traitor from Ella's vision, I'd been holding on to a foolish hope that it wasn't true. Or, dark as it might seem, that Five was the one killed in battle. But there he is, in a rumpled Mogadorian uniform, and with a bandage covering his right eye.

I can hear Sam suck in a breath; he's stunned. The only part of my visions that I hadn't told anyone about was seeing Five, not wanting to smear his name if I was wrong.

"He's . . ." Sam shakes his head. "That son of a bitch traitor. It must've been him who told the Mogs about Chicago."

"One of your own," Adam says quietly. "That is unexpected."

I have to look away from Five's image before my blood boils. "You didn't know about this?" I ask Adam through clenched teeth.

"No," he says, shaking his head. "I would've told you. Setrákus Ra himself must have been keeping him a secret."

I force myself to look back at the screen. I keep calm, studying my new enemy. His slumped shoulders, his freshly shaved head, the dark look in his remaining eye. What could have brought one of our own to such a terrible place?

"I knew there was something off about that jerk," Sam says, pacing now. "John, man, what are we going to do about him?"

I don't reply, mainly because the only solution I can think of at that moment, seeing Five in the enemy's uniform, is to kill him. "Where's he going? Follow him," I tell Adam.

Adam does. The camera follows Five across the runway until he reaches a ramp that leads onto the biggest spaceship I've ever seen, so massive that its entire bulk isn't even picked up on camera.

"Damn," I breathe, my eyes widening. "What the hell is that thing?"

"Warship," Adam answers, a note of awe sneaking into his voice as he squints at the screen. "I can't tell which one."

"Which *one*?" Sam exclaims. "How many of those things do they have?"

"Dozens? Maybe more, maybe less. They run on the old fuel of Mogadore and whatever my people managed to mine from Lorien. Not the most efficient things. And slow. When I got in trouble as a boy, my mother would threaten to ground me until the fleet's arrival . . ." He realizes he's rambling and trails off, looking up at us.

"You don't care about this, do you?"

"Maybe not the best time for reminiscing," I reply, watching as Five boards the ship. "But what else can you tell us about the fleet?"

"They've been traveling since the fall of Lorien," Adam continues. "Mog strategists believe they've got enough firepower left for one last siege."

"Earth," I say.

"Yeah," Adam replies. "Then, my people will settle here. Maybe rebuild the fleet if Setrákus Ra finds a reason."

"You mean if there's any life in the universe left for him to conquer," I say.

Sam shakes his head, still marveling at the hulking warship. "So they have a secret weakness, right? Like how you can shoot that one spot on the Death Star and the whole thing blows up?"

Adam's brow furrows. "What's a Death Star?"

Sam throws up his hands. "We're screwed."

"If they've been taken prisoner and are aboard that thing . . ." I don't finish the thought, mainly because a course of action just isn't coming to me. Taking over a mostly abandoned Mogadorian base is one thing; finding a way aboard a massive warship is another entirely.

Especially when that massive warship is slowly rising into the sky. Maybe Sam's right and we are screwed.

The three of us watch in silence as the warship

climbs. Before it's entirely offscreen, the ship's carapace flickers and the whole thing disappears from view. Well, not entirely—the ship's outline is still vaguely visible, as if the light around it is bending in strange ways. The distortion is almost like trying to focus on an object that's underwater.

"Cloaking," Adam says. "All of the warships have it."

"Hey, look at the tablet," Sam says. "Maybe everything isn't totally depressing."

As the now invisible warship floats upward, one of the dots on the tablet slowly pulls away from the others. Five's dot. After a few seconds, it begins to flicker erratically across the screen. We've now got two Garde indicators bouncing spastically over the map.

"Just like Ella," Sam says, furrowing his brow.

"The warship must be returning to orbit," Adam says. "Which means . . ."

"Ella is already aboard one of those things," I finish the thought. "They brought her up to the fleet."

"How are we going to get up there?" Sam asks.

"We won't have to," Adam responds. "The fleet will come to us."

"Oh, right," Sam says. "Worldwide invasion. So we're planning to just wait for that?"

I tap my finger on the tablet, pointing out the three dots still in Florida. "The plan is to get the others.

They're still there. We just have to—" I stop myself when I look back at the screen. The runway is starting to move. "I thought you disabled the ship. Why are they moving?"

With a hurried series of keystrokes, Adam cranes the camera down. From this angle, we can see the crew of Mogadorians grimacing as they push the scout vessel manually towards the hangar.

"I guess they gave up on getting it started," Sam observes.

One of the Mogs runs ahead to slide open the metal doors and there, caught out in the middle of the empty hangar, are Nine, Marina and Six. Sam lets loose an excited shout that he cuts off quickly, the harsh math sinking in, that there are three Garde where there should be four, and that Nine is carrying in his arms what is obviously a body bag.

"Eight," Sam says, swallowing. "Shit."

I turn to Adam, not ready to grieve yet.

"Does this ship you've hacked have any guns?"

CHAPTER FOURTEEN

AFTER A BARRAGE OF NEAR-DEAFENING BLASTER fire in the wide-open space of the hangar, the scout ship goes eerily silent. Marina and I crouch next to each other, both of us huddled behind the flipped-over metal table. We exchange a look—the table didn't sustain even a single shot of blaster fire. In fact, it doesn't seem like the ship's turret came even close to hitting us.

"Nice aim, dipshit!" Nine shouts, laughing. He's off to the side of the table, flat on the ground, half shielding Eight's body with his own.

I poke my head out from behind the table. Between us and the scout vessel are a dozen piles of ash, formerly the Mogadorian mechanics. The ship's gun turret is still smoking but hangs dormant now, not the least bit interested in us. Cautiously, I stand up. Marina joins me.

"What the hell is going on?" I ask.

"Who cares?" Nine says, hefting Eight's body. "Let's get out of here."

"Perhaps some kind of malfunction?" Marina proposes, inching closer to the ship, which still blocks our way out. The three of us spread out, making sure not to stand directly in the path of the blaster.

"It only shot the Mogs," I say. "That's one convenient malfunction."

All three of us jump when the ship's cockpit opens up with a hydraulic hiss. There's a burst of static from a speaker in the cockpit, and then a familiar voice rings out.

"Guys? Can you hear me?"

"John?" I exclaim, not believing my ears. The last I saw him, he was in a coma along with Ella. I sprint to the ship and jump onto its front end, standing over the open cockpit to better hear his voice.

"It's me, Six," John says. "It's good to see you."

"See me?" I ask, then notice the small camera mounted over the cockpit entrance. It wiggles back and forth, almost nodding in greeting.

"Dude, what happened?" Nine asks, eyeing the cockpit skeptically. "Is your brain, like, trapped in a Mogadorian ship now?"

"What? No, don't be an idiot," John replies, and I can picture the look of annoyed amusement on his face. "We've taken over a Mogadorian base and used their tech to hack into this ship."

"Nice," Nine replies, like that's all he needed to hear. He jumps effortlessly onto the ship's hood, still holding Eight, and lands right beside me. Our side of the saucer-shaped vessel dips a little at his weight before righting itself, the landing gear whining. Nine kicks the metal hull with his heel, testing it out. "So this is our ride?"

In answer, the ship's engine begins to vibrate beneath our feet. I look down into the cockpit—there are six hard plastic seats in there, along with a blinking dashboard covered in random Mogadorian symbols and a set of controls that look similar to what you'd find on an airplane. Not that I've ever flown one of those before, much less one made by Mogadorians.

"We saw what happened in Chicago," Marina says, also climbing onto the ship.

"Is everyone all right?"

"Yeah," John replies quickly, then seems to reconsider. "They took Ella, but I don't think she's in danger yet."

Marina's eyebrows shoot up in alarm, and I can feel the cold start to roll off her. "What do you mean they *took* her?"

"I'll explain everything when you get in the air," John says. "First, let's get you out of there."

"Sounds good," Nine replies, and hops down into the cockpit, gently placing Eight's body across a couple of the seats.

"Uh, John, one problem," I say, following Nine into the antiseptic-smelling Mog ship. "How are we supposed to fly this thing?"

There's a pause on John's end and then a different voice responds, this one with a harsh accent that makes my shoulders tense.

"I could fly you remotely, but I'm worried hacking into the ship's computer might have damaged some of the auto-navigation protocols. It'll be safer if you do it manually with me walking you through it," the Mogadorian explains quickly. Then, as if realizing we might be freaked out, the guy adds, "Hey. I'm Adam."

"The guy Malcolm told us about," I say, remembering that dinner conversation.

"Don't worry, Six," Sam's voice interjects, and I can't help but grin at the sound of it. "He's totally not evil."

"Oh, well, in that case, let's fly," Nine says sarcastically, but settles into one of the hard-backed plastic seats all the same. I hop into the pilot's chair. Marina hesitates for a moment, giving the console where the Mog's voice came from a look of distrust.

"How do we know that's really John?" she asks. "Setrákus Ra can change forms. This might be some kind of trap." In my excitement to hear John and Sam, I hadn't even considered the possibility that this could be a ploy. Behind me, Nine shouts towards the communicator.

"Hey, Johnny, remember back in Chicago? When you

were claiming to be Pittacus Lore and we had a debate about whether to go to New Mexico?"

"Yeah," John's voice sounds like it's coming through clenched teeth.

"How'd we settle that?"

John sighs. "You dangled me off the edge of the roof."

Nine grins like that's the best thing ever. "It's definitely him."

"Marina," John says, probably thinking Nine's little test wasn't good enough. "The first time we met, you healed two bullet wounds in my ankle. And then we almost got hit by a missile."

A small smile forms on Marina's face, the first I've seen in days. "I thought you were about the coolest guy I'd ever met, John Smith."

Nine barks out a laugh at that, shaking his head. Marina climbs aboard, taking a seat next to Eight's body. She drapes a hand protectively on the body bag and settles in.

"Watch your heads," Adam warns as the cockpit hisses closed above us. There's a moment where I feel a sense of panic at being sealed inside a Mogadorian ship, but I shove that feeling down and tightly clutch the steering apparatus. It's dim in the cockpit, the glass having a tinted sunglasses-like look. Streams of data in compressed Mogadorian symbols are projected directly onto the glass, the readouts something only a Mog pilot could make sense of.

"All right," I say. "What now?"

"Hold up," Nine interjects, leaning forward. "How come you get to drive?"

Adam's voice comes through clear, patient but authoritative. "Turn the wheel in front of you. That will rotate the ship."

I do as he instructs, the wheel turning easily, the saucer portion of the ship doing a 180 without the wheels moving at all. I stop turning when we're pointed towards the hangar's exit.

"Good," Adam says. "Now, the lever on your left moves the wheels."

I grip the lever and push it just a tad. The ship jerks forward almost immediately. The controls are sensitive, and it doesn't take much pressure to get us slowly rolling out onto the runway.

"Give it some gas, Six, damn," Nine complains. "Drive it like we stole it."

"Don't listen to him," Marina says, hugging herself.

"If you're out from under the hangar, you can stop," Adam instructs.

I look up through the glass of the cockpit, see only sky and so let go of the lever. The ship creaks to a stop.

"Okay," Adam says. "Now, grasp the wheel in front of you at three and nine. Do you feel the triggers?"

I take the wheel again and feel around for the two buttons indented in its underside. "Got 'em," I reply, testing out the trigger on the left by squeezing it. As soon as I do, the vibration from the ship's engine reaches a bone-rattling crescendo and we rise into the air.

"Ho, shit!" Nine yells. Next to me, Marina squeezes herself a little tighter, closing her eyes.

"Be careful, Six," she whispers.

I let go of the button and the ship effortlessly maintains its elevation. We're hovering about twenty yards off the ground.

"You weren't supposed to do that yet," Adam admonishes.

"Uh, yeah, sorry. First time flying a spaceship," I reply.

"No big deal," Adam replies. "The trigger on your left increases your elevation. The one on your right decreases it."

"Left up, right down. Got it."

"Also," Adam says. "you're in what my people call a Skimmer. It isn't built for interplanetary travel, so it isn't quite a *space*ship."

Nine makes a loud snoring noise. "Is this dude about to give us a lesson in Mogadorian aviation or something? The hell?"

"You know I can hear you, right?" Adam replies over the mic. "And no, I am not."

"Sorry about Nine," I say, giving him a dirty look over my shoulder. "Does this thing come with ejector seats?"

"Yes, actually," Adam replies.

"Whoa, now," Nine says, edging forward so his butt isn't entirely on the seat. "Don't get any ideas, Six."

I shush Nine when I hear a series of clanking noises emanating from the ship's underbelly.

"What is that?" I ask.

"Don't worry," Adam replies. "I just remotely put up your landing gear."

When the clanking finishes, two small panels on the steering wheel slide aside, revealing thumb-sized buttons positioned so they can be pressed at the same time as the elevation triggers.

"You should see a couple of buttons," Adam continues. "Depress them to accelerate. Simply let them go to brake."

I grip the steering wheel more tentatively than before and gently squeeze the buttons, careful not to hit the triggers on the wheel's underside. The Skimmer zips forward, then lurches to a stop when I let the button go.

"It's like a video game," Nine says, leaning over the back of my chair. "Any idiot could work this thing. No offense, Mog guy."

"None taken."

I press down the accelerator a little more forcefully and the ship shoots forward. A diagnostic on the screen starts flashing—a warning in any language—right before I scrape the bottom of the Skimmer against the top of a tree. I hear branches breaking and, craning my neck, see them hit the ground below.

"Oops," I say, and glance sidelong at Marina.

"Six, I swear," she says, flashing me a half-panicked look.

"You'll want to get some more elevation," Adam says. "And, um, consider steering."

Nine laughs and leans back. I pull the trigger for vertical and we rise up higher. As we clear the dense trees of the swampland, the horizon becomes visible. A laser-fine dotted line appears on the cockpit glass, superimposed over the view, like a trail.

"I've plotted your course," Adam says. "Just follow the line."

I nod and give the ship some juice, following the laser-path north.

"All right, boys," I say. "Here we come."

The flight from Florida to Washington takes about two hours. On Adam's instructions, I keep our altitude low enough that we won't be picked up on satellites or accidentally cross paths with any airplanes, but high enough that there won't be a rash of UFO sightings along the Eastern Seaboard. Although, considering how serious the threat of all-out Mogadorian invasion seems, maybe we should let our stolen ship be seen, shoot off some fireworks, warn the locals.

After the initial rush of elation at hearing John and Sam, at knowing our friends are alive, the conversation turns grim. Over the radio, they describe what went down at the John Hancock Center. After that, John tells us about what he saw in the nightmare vision he shared with Ella and why he thinks Setrákus Ra doesn't want to hurt her. John's pieced together a theory that Ella could be related to Setrákus Ra and that the Mogadorian ruler could actually be some kind of twisted Loric, the banished Elder mentioned in Crayton's letter. I'm not ready to grapple with that yet.

Once John's caught us up, it's our turn to fill in the others on what happened in Florida. Even over the radio, I can tell John's trying not to press us too much. I think about the days that John's been living with a fresh scar on his ankle, wondering which one of us wouldn't be making it back—as much as it hurts to talk about, he deserves to know what happened to Eight. However, neither Marina nor Nine are very forthcoming, so it falls to me to describe how Five betrayed us, how he murdered Eight technically by accident, but only because he was actually trying to murder Nine. I was unconscious for most of the fight, so I keep the description bare bones, just the facts, not sugarcoating anything. Then, I give them the details of rescuing Eight's body from the Mogadorian encampment and tell them about what Five did to his Mogadorian pal. When I'm finished, a grim mood settles inside the cockpit and we ride in silence until we reach suburban D.C.

I land the ship in the middle of a basketball court. We're

in a fancy-ass suburban development, one made extraordinarily eerie by all its darkened windows and general emptiness. The cockpit opens for us and Marina flashes me a relieved look as she stands up. Carefully, Nine picks up Eight's body and climbs out of the ship. Marina stays close to him, her hand on Nine's elbow, making sure that Eight doesn't get jostled too much. It's still hard to believe that's our friend in that body bag, and it feels wrong to be carrying him around so much.

"Your travels are almost over," I overhear Marina whisper to Eight's body. She must feel the same as I do.

Marina and I hop down to the ground and turn around to help Nine lower Eight's body. Instead of passing Eight down, Nine squints into the darkness around us.

"Whoa," he says. "There are, like, some random creatures watching us right now."

"Creatures?" I reply, looking up at him. Nine's expression has gone blank—well, blanker than usual—the way he gets when he's using his animal telepathy.

"Oh, I forgot to mention we found some new friends!"

It's John, jogging towards us from the crooked doorway of a house that looks half smashed, like the ground tried to swallow it up but couldn't quite finish. Sam is a few steps behind him, beaming at me, although when he notices me noticing him, he quickly tones down the wattage of his smile, going for something a little less eager. Behind John and Sam, pushing a gurney, are Malcolm and a pale, lanky guy that I assume must be Adam, the dark hair hanging in his face making him look half-Mog and half-emo rock star.

"So many Chimærae," Nine says, nodding excitedly as he gazes out into the darkness. "That's awesome."

"We named the chubby, lazy one after you," Sam replies.

"Less awesome."

Upon reaching us, John wraps Marina in a tight hug. It's dark out, but I can see days of worry etched in the dark bags under his eyes. I remember that wide-eyed kid I found fighting Mogadorians at his high school and wonder if John felt like that again, like he was back to being alone against the world. It should be a relief that we're reunited, but we're one less, and I know John well enough to know that he's been beating himself up over our loss for days.

"You made it," John says as he lets Marina go and hugs me next. His voice is quiet, for me only. "I didn't know what I was going to do if—"

"You don't have to say anything," I reply, squeezing him back. "We're here now. We're going to fight. We're going to win."

John takes a step back from me, a relieved look briefly passing across his face, like he needed someone to tell him that. He nods to me and then walks over to the ship, taking Eight's body in his arms so that Nine can jump down. Everyone falls silent as Malcolm wheels the gurney forward so that John can set down the body.

"The Mogs put something on him," Marina says. She takes a lurching step towards the gurney. "Some electrical field."

Adam takes a tentative step forward and clears his throats. "Electrodes? Over the heart? On the temples?"

"Yes," Marina replies without looking at Adam, her eyes fixed on Eight's body bag.

"The Mogs use that to, uh . . ." Adam pauses, then finishes awkwardly. "To keep specimens fresh. It won't harm the remains, just preserve them."

"Specimens," Nine repeats dryly.

"I'm sorry about your friend," Adam says quietly, pushing a hand through his hair. "I just thought you should know . . ."

"It's all right. Thanks, Adam," John says. He puts a hand on Marina's shoulder. "Come on. Let's get him inside."

"What—" Marina chokes up and has to take a deep breath. "What're you going to do with him?"

"We've set aside a quiet room inside," Malcolm replies gently. "I'm not sure what customs the Loric have for burials . . ."

I look first at John, whose face is scrunched up in thought, then at Nine, who looks absolutely baffled.

"We don't know them either," I say. "I mean, when was the last time we had a chance to properly honor one of our fallen?"

"We can't bury him here, though," Marina says. "This is a Mog place."

Malcolm nods, understanding, and touches Marina softly on the shoulder. "Do you want to help me bring him inside?"

Marina nods. Together, she and Malcolm wheel Eight's body back towards the sunken house. Adam follows them at a respectful distance, his hands clasped awkwardly behind his back. After a moment, Nine claps John hard on the back, breaking the tension.

"So did I mishear over the communicator, or did you send your girlfriend off on a super-sexy secret mission with her ex-boyfriend?"

"We're fighting a war here, Nine, it's not a joke," John replies sternly. After a moment's awkward pause, a begrudging smile breaks on his face. "Also, shut up. It's not super sexy. What does that even mean?"

"Wow, you really need my guidance," Nine says. He throws his arm around John's shoulders and leads him towards the house. "Come on. I'll explain what sexy is."

"I know what it—ugh, why am I even discussing this with you?" John shoves Nine in frustration, but Nine just holds on tighter. "Get off me, idiot."

"Come on, Johnny, you need my affection now more than ever."

I roll my eyes as the guys walk towards the house, having their little bro moment. That leaves me alone with Sam, standing a few feet away, looking at me intently. I can see him trying to figure out what to say, or more likely working up the nerve to say it. The guy's probably been chewing on this moment for hours, working on his amazing speech to the girl he wasn't sure he'd ever see again.

"Hey," is what he settles on at last.

"Hey back," I reply, and before he can get another word out, I wrap my arms around him and kiss him hard enough that I probably knock the wind out of him. Sam seems stunned at first but kisses back after a moment, trying to match my intensity. I grab him by the front of the shirt and pull him so that we're pressed up against the side of the Skimmer—not exactly the most romantic place in the world, but I'll take it. I grab Sam's hands and put them on my hips, then clutch the sides of his face and run my fingers up through his hair, all this desperate energy pouring out of me and into this kiss.

After a couple of minutes, Sam breaks away from me, breathless. "Six, whoa, what is going on?"

The look on Sam's face isn't what I was expecting. Yes, there's flushed bewilderment, but mixed in with that surprise is an undercurrent of concern. It makes me look away.

"I just really wanted to do that," I reply, telling him the truth. "I didn't know if I'd get another chance."

I press my face against the side of Sam's neck and feel his heartbeat against my cheek. I've spent the last few days putting on a strong front, trying to keep it together with Marina and Nine both on the verge of falling apart. Finally, at least while we're out here in the dark, I can let myself go a little bit. Sam has me around the waist, so I sink against him, let him hold me up and take a shuddering breath against his neck.

"It can just end so quickly . . . ," I whisper, leaning back to get a look at him. "I didn't want to *not* have done that, you know? I don't care if it complicates things."

"Me neither," Sam says. "Obviously."

We start to kiss again, this time a lot gentler, Sam's hands slowly moving up my sides. When the wolf howls—loud, echoing, nearby—my first instinct is that it's Nine spying on us from the house and making stupid noises. But then a second and third wolf make a howling chorus and I lean back to peer at Sam.

"What the hell is that?" I ask. "Wolves in the suburbs?"

"I don't know—" he starts to reply, but then his eyes widen. "The Chimærae. They're warning us."

A moment after he says it, I hear the *whup-whup-whup* of at least three helicopters bearing down on us. If I squint, I can see their outlines approaching in the night sky. And then there are the blue flashing lights coming from the housing development's only access road; the lights are attached to a caravan of black SUVs, all of them speeding in our direction.

CHAPTER FIFTEEN

AT THE SOUND OF SCREECHING TIRES AND HELICOPTER rotors, Nine and I burst back outside, leaping over the house's broken porch and onto the lawn. We're just in time to see a lightning strike slice down from the sky, courtesy of Six. It's a warning shot; the bolt erupts a piece of asphalt right in front of a black SUV that's careening up the access road, causing it to swerve.

"The hell is this?" Nine growls. "I thought we were done with the feds."

"Adam said they're supposed to leave this place alone," I reply. "Some deal with the Mogs."

"I guess that ended when you killed them all, huh?"

There are three choppers overhead, circling like vultures. Some signal must pass between them, because they all turn on spotlights at the same time. One of them trains on me and Nine, another on the entrance of the house behind us and a third on Six and Sam. In the bright light, I notice Sam, unarmed, quickly climbing into the Skimmer for cover. Six, her hands splayed in the air, in the process of summoning some nasty weather for our uninvited guests, goes invisible before the spotlight can really get a fix on her.

Meanwhile, undeterred by the lightning strike, a parade of black SUVs files up the access road, blue lights flashing beneath their windshields. They skid to a stop next to each other in a tight formation, eventually creating a blockade of bulletproof glass and shiny, dent-resistant paneling. Their doors fling open and a bunch of agents in identical navy-blue Windbreakers leap out. The ones who aren't yelling into walkie-talkies have guns trained on us, all of them hunkered behind their car doors for cover. It takes them less than a minute to have us pinned down in the cul-de-sac.

"Do they really think this will stop us?" Nine asks as he takes a step away from the house, almost daring the agents to try shooting him.

"I don't know what they're thinking," I reply. "But they don't know about the Chimærae."

I can sense them lurking in the shadows just off the access road. These government guys might think they've got us surrounded, but the glowing eyes in the darkness would argue otherwise. The Chimærae hold their position, waiting for a signal.

I hear a creak behind me and half turn to find

Marina on the porch, jagged icicles extending from her hands like twin daggers. That's new. Next to her, using the doorway for cover, is Adam, holding a Mogadorian blaster.

"What do we do?" Marina asks.

I notice storm clouds gathering overhead. Six is ready to throw down if we need to. But so far, the government guys haven't done anything except make a lot of noise. They didn't come in shooting, which is the only reason I haven't fired up my Lumen.

"I don't want to hurt them if we don't have to," I say. "But we don't have time for any bullshit. I'm damn sure not being taken in for questioning."

Apparently, Nine interprets my words as encouragement to do something crazy. He strides forward and picks up the base of Dr. Anu's chair, which got sheared in half by blaster fire during this afternoon's battle. The thing must weight close to two hundred pounds, but Nine hefts it easily with one hand, swinging it back and forth as a demonstration.

"You guys are on private property!" Nine shouts. "And I don't see any warrants!"

Before I can stop him, Nine flings the entire chunk into the air, putting it just inches from the nose of the nearest helicopter. It's pretty obvious from my vantage point that the chopper isn't in any real danger, but I guess the human pilot isn't used to having superstrong

Garde chucking scrap metal at him. The pilot pulls back on his controls and the chopper shakily gains altitude, its spotlight making erratic trails across the lawn. The chair piece comes down with a loud crash in the middle of the street.

"That was unnecessary," Adam observes from the doorway.

"Eh, agree to disagree," Nine says.

As he bends down to pick up another piece of the chair, I hear the telltale cocking of guns from the line of SUVs. Six must hear them too from wherever she's lurking, because a wave of fog suddenly rolls across the lawns of Ashwood Estates, making us much harder to target.

I light my Lumen and step forward, putting myself between Nine and the SUVs. I hold up my hands so the agents can clearly see that they're enveloped in fire.

"I don't know why you're here," I yell towards the line of cars, "but you're making a mistake. This is a fight you seriously cannot win. Smartest thing you can do is go back to your bosses and tell them there was nothing here."

To punctuate the speech, I send a telepathic command to our Chimærae. Howls rings out from the darkness on the SUVs' flanks. Suddenly panicked, some of the agents start aiming their guns into the shadows, and one of the choppers uses its spotlight to begin combing the fields alongside the access road. We've got them scared.

"Last warning!" I shout, letting a basketball-sized fireball float up from my palm.

"Jesus Christ!" a woman's voice shouts from the line of cars. "Everybody stand down!"

One by one, the agents at the cars lower their weapons. As they do, one of them squeezes between a pair of SUVs and walks towards us, her hands raised in surrender. Through the fog, I recognize her rigid posture and severe ponytail.

"Agent Walker? Is that you?"

Next to me, Nine laughs. "Oh, come on. You going to try arresting us *again*?"

Walker grimaces as she gets closer, her sharp features more lined than I remember. She's pale, an alarming streak of gray running through her red hair. I try to remember how badly she was hurt back at Dulce Base. Could she still be feeling the effects of that?

Before she can get too close, Six manifests behind Walker and grabs her by the ponytail. "Not another step," she snarls.

Walker, eyes wide, obediently stops. Six reaches down and takes the gun off her hip, dropping it into the grass.

"I'm sorry for the commotion," Walker says, her voice slightly strangled thanks to the angle Six has her head at. "My agents saw that Mogadorian ship land and we thought you might be under attack."

I let the Lumen in my hands go out, tilting my head at her. "Wait. You came rushing in here because you thought *we* were under attack?"

"I know you have no reason to believe me," Walker says, her voice hoarse. "But we're here to help."

Next to me, Nine scoffs. I stare hard at Walker, waiting for the punch line, or the secret signal for her men to open fire.

"Please," she says. "Just hear me out."

I sigh and motion towards the house. "Bring her in," I tell Six, then turn to Nine. "If the rest of them try anything even a little suspicious—"

Nine cracks his knuckles. "Oh, I know what to do."

Six shoves Walker up the broken steps of Adam's house and through the front door. I follow a few steps behind, leaving the rest of our friends to keep an eye on the small army of government agents.

"Is that a Mogadorian I saw out there?" Walker asks as Six pushes her into the living room. "You have one of them prisoner?"

"He's an ally," I say. "Right now, *you're* the prisoner."

"Understood," Walker says, sounding more tired than anything. Without Six having to push her, Walker sits down heavily on one of the sofas. In the light of the living room, I can see that there's definitely something off about her. Maybe it's owing to the odd streak of gray in her hair, but Walker looks drained. She notices the entrance to the Mogadorian tunnels but doesn't look particularly interested or surprised.

"Ah, a guest," Malcolm says as he appears in the doorway between the living room and the kitchen, his rifle slung over his shoulder. "And she brought lots of friends. Is everything all right?"

"I'm not sure yet," I reply, an edge to my voice, keeping my guard up. Six circles around the couch so she can stand where Walker can't see her.

"Hm," Malcolm says. "I was about to put a pot of coffee on. Would anyone else like some? I think I saw some tea in the kitchen, too."

A shaky smile forms on Walker's face. "Is this some kind of good-cop, bad-cop routine?" She looks from Malcolm to me. "Is he one of your . . . what do you call them? Cêpans?"

Six raises her hand to Malcolm. "I'll take a cup, actually." When I flash her an annoyed look, she shrugs. "What? Trust me, I can drink some coffee and take down this lady at the same time, if I need to."

Agent Walker glances over her shoulder at Six. "I believe her."

I stride forward so I'm standing right in front of Walker and snap my fingers in her face. "All right, stop wasting time. Say what you came here to say."

"Agent Purdy is dead," Walker states, looking up at me. "Had a heart attack at Dulce Base."

"Aw, I remember him," Six says. "What a shame."

I remember Agent Walker's partner, too—an older guy, white hair, crooked nose. I shrug, not seeing what this has to do with us. "Condolences, I guess. So what?"

"Guy was a prick," Walker replies. "It isn't so much that he croaked, it's what happened after."

Walker shows me her hands, then very slowly reaches into the front pocket of her FBI-issue Windbreaker. She removes a stuffed manila folder, rolled-up and rubber-banded. She opens it up, reaches inside and pulls out a Polaroid photograph. Walker hands it to me and I find myself examining a close-up of a dead Agent Purdy—or what's left of him. Half his face is melted away, disintegrated into ash on the concrete underneath him.

"I thought you said it was a heart attack," I say.

"It was," Walker replies. "Thing is, afterward, Purdy started to dissolve away. Just like one of the Mogadorians."

I shake my head. "What does that mean? Why?"

"He'd been getting treatments," Walker says. "Augmentations, the Mogs call them. Most of the senior MogPro people have been getting them for years."

The term "MogPro" rings a bell from They Walk

Among Us, but I don't know how this all adds up with the augmentations Adam told us about.

"Back up," I tell her. "Start at the beginning."

Walker self-consciously touches her streak of gray hair and for a moment I wonder if she's having second thoughts about this confession. But then she hands me the folder she's been clutching, meeting my eyes.

"First contact was ten years ago," she says. "The Mogadorians claimed they were hunting fugitives. They wanted to use our law-enforcement network, have free rein to move around the country, and in exchange they'd provide us with weapons and technology. I was just out of the academy when all this happened so I obviously wasn't invited to any meetings with the aliens. I guess no one wanted to piss them off or turn down weapons more powerful than any we'd ever seen, because our government caved real quick. The director of the bureau himself was in on the negotiations. This was before he got promoted. Might've been *why* he got promoted, in fact."

"Let me guess," I say, remembering the name from Mark's website. "The old director was Bud Sanderson. Now secretary of defense."

Walker looks momentarily impressed. "Right. You connect the dots, you'll find a lot of people who negotiated with the Mogs ten years ago have done real well for themselves since."

"What about the president?" Six asks.

"That guy?" Walker snorts. "Small fish. The ones who get elected, who give speeches on TV—they're just glorified celebrities. The real power's with the people who get appointed, who work behind the scenes. The ones you've never heard of. They're who the Mogs wanted and that's who they've kept around."

"He's still the president," Six counters. "Why doesn't he do something?"

"Because he's kept in the dark," Walker says. "And anyway, the VP is a MogPro guy. When the time comes, the president will either go along with the Mogs, or he'll get removed."

"I'm sorry," I say, holding up my hands. "What the hell is MogPro?"

"Mogadorian Progress," Walker explains. "It's what they're calling the, quote, intersection of our two species, unquote."

"You know, if you ever want a second career, I know a website you could write for," I tell Walker as I start paging through the documents in her file. There are specifications for Mogadorian blasters, transcripts of conversations between politicians, pictures of important-looking government guys shaking hands with Mogs in officer uniforms. It's the kind of document dump a site like They Walk Among Us would kill for.

Actually, a lot of this stuff was *already* on Mark's website. Could Walker have been the one feeding him information?

"So your boss sold out humanity for some upgraded weapons?" Six asks, leaning over the back of the couch to glare at Walker.

"That sums it up. We weren't the only country to sign up either," Walker continues, her tone bitter. "And they knew how to keep us on the hook, too. After the weapons, they started promising medical advances. Genetic augmentation, they called it. Claimed they could cure everything from the flu to cancer. They were basically promising immortality."

I look up from the file, stopping at a picture of a soldier with a rolled-up sleeve, the veins on his forearm blackened as if his blood had turned to soot.

"How's that working out?" I ask, tapping the photo.

Walker cranes her neck to look at the picture, then locks eyes with me. "What you're looking at is one week's withdrawal from Mogadorian genetic injections. That's how it's working out."

I show the photo to Six and she shakes her head in disgust.

"So basically they're killing you slowly," Six says. "Or turning you into Mogs."

"We didn't know what we were getting into," Walker says. "Seeing Purdy disintegrate like that, though . . .

it opened some eyes. The Mogs aren't saviors. They're turning us into something inhuman."

"And yet you guys are still dealing with them, aren't you?" I reply. "I heard there's people trying to go public on some captured Mogadorians, but someone's squashing the story."

Walker nods. "The Mogs claim their genetic augmentations will only get better with time. A lot of the good old boys in Washington want to stick it out and stay the course. They've never seen a human being disintegrate, I guess. Guys like Sanderson and some of the other high-ranking MogPro cronies, they've already started receiving more advanced treatments. All the Mogs want in exchange is our continued cooperation."

"Cooperate how?"

Walker raises an eyebrow at me. "If you haven't figured that out yet, then I've definitely picked the wrong side and we are well and truly screwed."

"Maybe if you'd picked the right side years ago instead of helping to hunt down children—" I catch a look from Six and check my anger. "Whatever. We know they're coming. No more hiding in the shadows or the suburbs. They're coming in force, right?"

"Right," Walker confirms. "And they expect us to hand over the keys to the planet."

Malcolm returns from the kitchen with two cups of coffee. He hands one to Six and one to Walker, the agent looking surprised but grateful.

"Excuse me, but how will that work?" Malcolm says. "In a first-contact situation, there's certain to be widespread panic."

"Plus, they look like pasty-faced freaks," Six adds. "People are gonna lose their shit."

"Don't be so sure about that," Walker replies, and gestures with her mug to the folder I'm still holding. After flipping through a couple more pages, I come to a set of photographs. Two guys in suits are eating lunch in a fancy restaurant. The first is a guy in his late sixties with thinning gray hair and a face like an owl I recognize from Mark's website; he's Bud Sanderson, the secretary of defense. The other, a handsome middle-aged guy who looks vaguely like a movie star, I've never seen before. There's something hanging around his neck, mostly hidden by his suit and the bad camera angle. It stirs some recognition in me, so I hold the picture out to Walker.

"I know Sanderson," I say. "Who's this other guy?"

Walker raises an eyebrow at me. "What? You don't recognize him? I'm not surprised. Guy has a couple of different looks, apparently. Me, I didn't recognize him when he was destroying you kids at Dulce Base, big as a goddamn house, with some flaming whip. Actually, I guess that was about the time I decided MogPro wasn't for me."

My eyes widen and I take another look at the picture. The actual pendants are hidden beneath his suit coat, but the man clearly wears three chains around his neck. "You're kidding me."

"Setrákus Ra," Walker says, shaking her head. "Sealing the deal for Mogadorian-human peace."

Six comes around the couch to take the picture from me. "Damn shape shifter," she says. "He's been doing all this while we've been on the run. Setting all this up while we scrambled around."

"He might be ahead, but it isn't over," Malcolm says.

"Well, that's some heartening optimism," Walker says, and sips her coffee. "But it will be over in two days."

"What happens then?" I ask.

"The UN convenes," Walker explains. "Conveniently, the president won't be able to make it, so Sanderson will appear in his stead. He'll be there to introduce Setrákus Ra to the world. A nice bit of political theater about how the sweet little aliens mean us no harm. There will be a motion to allow the Mogadorian fleet safe passage onto Earth, let them dock here, be good neighbors in the intergalactic community. The world leaders he's bought off already will support it. Believe me, they've got a majority. And once they're here, once we let them in . . ."

"We saw one of those warships in Florida," Six says,

giving me a grim look. "They'd be hard enough to take down even with an army that's ready for battle."

"But there won't be a battle." I say, finishing her thought. "Earth won't even put up a fight. And by the time they do realize they've let in a monster, it'll be too late."

"Exactly," Walker says. "Not everyone in the government is on board with Sanderson. Of the FBI, CIA, NSA, the military—about fifteen percent are for MogPro. Lots of powerful friends, they made sure of that, but most people are still entirely in the dark. I figure the Mogs established the same ratio in other countries. They know how many humans they need to control to get this done."

"And you're what? The one percent that's fighting back?" I ask.

"Less than one," Walker replies. "It's a lot to go up against if you don't have superpowers and—what was that out there? An army of wolves? Anyway, my crew have been staking out Ashwood, waiting for a chance to strike or, I don't know, do *something*. When we saw you take the place over—"

"All right, Walker, I get it," I say, cutting her off and setting aside the file. "I believe you, even if I don't really trust you. But what are we supposed to do? How do we stop this?"

"Get to the president?" Six suggests. "He has to be able to do something."

"That's one idea," Walker says. "But he's one man, and seriously well guarded. And even if you could get to him, explain to him about aliens and bring him around to your side? There's still plenty of MogPro pricks waiting to stage a coup."

I stare at Walker, knowing she already has a plan and is just stringing us along. "Spit it out. What do you want us to do?"

"We need to win over the people who're still in the dark. To do that, we need something big," Walker says, totally cavalier, like she's talking about taking out the trash. "I'd like you to come with me to New York, assassinate the secretary of defense and expose Setrákus Ra."

CHAPTER SIXTEEN

I WATCH FROM THE OBSERVATION DECK AS THE warship approaches, at first just a dark speck against the blue Earth but steadily growing larger until it blots out the planet below. The warship slows once it's relatively close to the *Anubis—relatively* because we could be miles apart up here, the vastness of space making depth and distance hard to figure. I'm far away from Earth. Far from my friends. That's the only distance that matters.

A port on the other warship opens and a small transport ship pops into view. It's white, perfectly spherical, like a pearl floating through space's dark ocean. The little ship bobs along in my direction and I can hear a grinding of gears and a whoosh of decompressed air, the *Anubis*'s own docking bay, right beneath my feet, preparing to accept the visitor.

"At last," Setrákus Ra says, and squeezes my shoulder. He sounds excited for this new arrival, a wide smile on his stolen, human face. We stand side by side on the observation deck right above the docking bay, rows of scout ships and a smaller collection of the orb-shaped transports anchored below us.

We're awaiting my "betrothed." Even thinking the word makes me want to vomit. Setrákus Ra's hand resting all fatherly on my shoulder makes it all the worse.

I keep my face completely neutral. I'm getting better at hiding my emotions. I'm determined not to give anything more away to this monster. I pretend like I'm excited, too, maybe just a little nervous. Let him think that he's worn me down or that I've checked out. Let him think my lessons in Mogadorian Progress are taking effect, that I'm becoming the ghostly version of myself that I was in my vision of the future.

Sooner or later, I know, I'll be able to escape. Or I'll die trying.

I turn away from the window and gaze down from the observatory's balcony, watching as the ship arrives at our docking bay doors. Lights flash below, warning any Mogs that they'll be sucked into space if they don't clear the area. Setrákus Ra already took care of them, sending the Mog technicians away so that we could greet this new arrival in private. The heavy doors open and I can feel the pull of space even through the observatory's closed airlock; the pressure changes, like water coming unclogged from my ear. Then, the transport ship glides aboard, the doors seal behind it and everything is quiet again.

"Come," Setrákus Ra commands, striding out from the observatory, through the now-open airlock and down the spiral staircase that leads to the docking bay. I follow along obediently at his heels, footsteps echoing on the metal deck as we pass between the rows of scout ships. Cautiously, not wanting to look too interested, I peer around Setrákus Ra to catch a glimpse of the ship as it opens up. I'm expecting one of the younger Mogadorian trueborn, some high-ranking up-and-comer hand selected by Setrákus Ra, like the ones I've seen nervously delivering status reports to their "Beloved Leader."

Try as I might to keep cool, I still can't help emitting a little gasp when Five steps out of the ship.

Setrákus Ra looks back at me. "You two are already acquainted, yes?"

One of Five's eyes is hidden beneath a gross-looking gauze bandage, a smudge of dark brown blood in the center, the edges sweat stained. He looks ragged and exhausted, and when his good eye flicks towards me, his thick shoulders become even more slumped. He stops right in front of Setrákus Ra, his gaze downcast.

"What is she doing here?" Five asks quietly.

"We are all together now," Setrákus Ra answers, and grasps Five by the shoulders. "The liberated and the enlightened, poised on the brink of absolute Mogadorian Progress. In no small part thanks to you, my boy."

"Okay," Five grunts.

I remember Five being in my vision—he was there to escort Six and Sam towards their execution, Six spit right in his face—but I guess I'd glossed over that part, more concerned with my disturbing connection to Setrákus Ra. Now here he is, receiving a pat on the back from the Mogadorian leader, the future already taking shape. And apparently I've been promised to him for whatever creepy ritual passes for a Mogadorian marriage. Right now, though, that's not my most pressing concern. Because if Five is here, looking like he just got out of a fight . . .

"What—what did you do?" I ask, my voice squeakier than I'd like. "What happened to the others?"

Five looks at me again and his lips screw up. He doesn't reply.

"You gave them a chance, did you not?" Setrákus Ra asks Five, but I can tell he's speaking for my benefit. "You tried to show them the light."

"They wouldn't listen," Five replies quietly. "They gave me no choice."

"And look how they repaid you for your attempt at mercy," Setrákus Ra says, brushing his fingers against the bandage on Five's face. "We will have that repaired immediately."

I take a surprised step backwards when Five slaps away Setrákus Ra's hand. It's a stinging blow, the impact echoing off the ships around us. I can't see his face, but I can see the muscles in Setrákus Ra's back tighten, his already rigid posture stiffening that much more. I get the sense of an immense bulk hiding inside that human form, just waiting to explode outward.

"Leave it," Five says, voice shaky and quiet. "I want to keep it this way."

Whatever rebuke Setrákus Ra might have been ready with doesn't come. He seems almost taken aback by Five's fervor to remain half blind.

"You're tired," Setrákus Ra says, finally. "We will discuss it further once you've rested."

Five nods and takes a cautious step around Setrákus Ra, as if he's uncertain whether the Mogadorian overlord will actually let him pass. When Setrákus Ra doesn't try to stop him, Five grunts and slouches his way towards the exit.

He makes it about halfway there before Setrákus Ra calls after him.

"Where is the body?" he asks, stopping Five in his tracks. "Where is the pendant?"

Five clears his throat, and I notice his hands start to shake, at least before he makes a conscious effort to steady himself. He turns back around to face Setrákus Ra, who is looking towards the open ship, obviously expecting something to be waiting for him.

"What body?" I ask, feeling a tightness in my chest. When they ignore me, I raise my voice higher. "What body? Whose pendant?"

"Gone," Five says simply, answering Setrákus Ra.

"I asked you a question, Five!" I shout. "What bo—"

Without looking at me, Setrákus Ra waves a hand in my direction. My teeth click together as he telekinetically shuts my mouth. It's like being slapped, and my cheeks grow hot with anger. Someone is dead, I know it. One of my friends is dead, and these two bastards are ignoring me.

"Elaborate," Setrákus Ra growls at Five, and even in his handsome human form, I can tell his patience is beginning to wane.

Five sighs like this whole exchange is a waste of his time. "Commander Deltoch decided he would watch over the body personally, and I didn't want to question his orders. I found Deltoch's remains right before we left. The Garde must have snuck in and escaped with their friend."

"You were supposed to bring him to me," Setrákus Ra hisses, his eyes burning holes into Five. "Not Deltoch. *You.*"

"I know," Five replies. "He wouldn't listen when I told him those were your orders. At least he died for his insubordination."

I watch a dark cloud pass over Setrákus Ra's face, wheels turning behind his stolen blue eyes, as if he knows Five is playing him somehow, the rage building up. I feel his telekinetic grip on my jaw loosen. He's distracted, now focused entirely on Five. Before he can say or do anything more, I step between the two of them, raising my voice a little higher. This time, they have to pay attention to me.

"*What* body? Who are you talking about?"

Finally, Five's good eye lands on me. "Eight. He's dead."

"No," I say, the word practically a whisper as I try, too late, to stop myself from reacting. My knees feel weak, and Five's impassive face becomes blurry as my eyes fill with tears.

"Yes," Setrákus Ra chimes in, and all the rage has been drained from his voice, replaced by something more coiled and sinister—his tone showy and overly congenial. "Five here saw to that, didn't you, my boy? All in the service of Mogadorian Progress."

I take a step towards Five, my fists clenched. "You? You *killed* him?"

"It was—" For a moment, it looks like Five might deny it. But then he glances quickly at Setrákus Ra and simply nods. "Yes."

Just like that, all my effort to show no emotion around Setrákus Ra slips away. I feel a scream building up inside me. I want to attack Five. I want to throw myself at him and tear him apart. I know that I wouldn't stand a chance—I saw the way he handled himself in the Lecture Hall, the way he can turn his skin to metal or anything else he touches—but I'll do as much damage as I can. I'll break my hands on his metal skin if it means getting just one punch in.

Setrákus Ra puts his hand on my shoulder, stopping me.

"I believe now would be an excellent time for that lesson we discussed," he says to me in that same phony tone.

"A lesson in what?" I spit, glaring at Five.

Five looks almost relieved that Setrákus Ra's attention now seems focused on me. "May I be excused?" he asks.

"You may not," Setrákus Ra replies.

From next to one of the ships, Setrákus Ra grabs a cart covered in tools—wrenches, pliers, screwdrivers all made for servicing the Mogadorian ships, but not so different from the ones on Earth—and wheels it over next to us. He looks down at me and smiles.

"Your Legacy, Ella, is called Dreynen. It gives you the ability to temporarily cancel the Legacy of another Garde," Setrákus Ra lectures, his hands clasped behind his back. "It was one of the rarest on Lorien."

I wipe my forearm across my eyes and try to stand up a little straighter. I'm still glaring at Five, but my words are for Setrákus Ra. "Why are you telling me this now? I don't *care*."

"It's important to know one's history," he replies, undeterred. "If you believe the Elders, Legacies arose from Lorien to suit the needs of Loric society. I wonder, then, what benefit is derived from a power only useful against other Garde?"

Five remains perfectly still, refusing to meet my eyes. Distracted by my anger, I forget to moderate my words, to keep it cool.

"I don't know," I snap sarcastically. "Maybe Lorien saw freaks like you two coming and knew someone would have to stop you."

"Ah," Setrákus Ra replies, his voice overloaded with professorial smugness, like I've stepped right into his trap. "But if that is the case, why did the Elders not select you to be among the young Garde saved? And, if Lorien does somehow shape Legacies to suit the needs of the Loric, why would it bestow Legacies to those ill suited to use them? The mere existence of Dreynen suggests a fallibility in Lorien that the Elders would seek to deny. It is chaos that needs to be tamed, not worshipped."

I try to take a step towards Five, but Setrákus Ra uses his telekinesis to keep me in place. I choke back my anger and remind myself I'm a prisoner here. I have to play along with Setrákus Ra's stupid game until the time is right. Revenge will have to wait.

"Ella," Setrákus Ra says. "Do you understand what I'm telling you?"

I sigh and turn away from Five to stare dully at Setrákus Ra. Obviously, he already has this whole philosophical lecture mapped out. It's probably one of the longer sections in his book. There's no point in trying to argue with him.

"So everything's random and we should exploit it and blah blah blah," I say. "Maybe you're right, maybe you're wrong. We'll never know since you went and destroyed the planet."

"What did I destroy, exactly? A planet, perhaps. But not Lorien itself." Setrákus Ra toys with one of the pendants dangling from his neck. "It is more complicated than you know, my dear. Soon, your mind will open and you will understand. Until then—" He reaches over to the cart, plucks up a Mogadorian wrench and tosses it to me. "We practice."

I snag the wrench out of the air and hold it in front of me. Setrákus Ra turns his attention to Five, still standing there silently, waiting to be dismissed.

"Fly," Setrákus Ra orders.

Five looks up, confused. "What?"

"Fly," Setrákus Ra repeats, waving to the high ceiling of the docking bay. "As high as you can."

Five grunts and slowly levitates until he's about forty feet in the air, his head nearly brushing the rafters of the docking bay. "Now what?" he asks.

Instead of replying, Setrákus Ra turns to me. I've already got an idea what he wants me to do. My palm is sweating against the cold metal of the wrench. He kneels down beside me and lowers his voice.

"I want you to do what you did at the Dulce Base," Setrákus Ra says.

"I told you, I don't know *how* I did that," I protest.

"I know you are afraid. Afraid of me, of your destiny, of this place you find yourself," Setrákus Ra says patiently, and for a terrifying moment his voice sounds almost like

Crayton. "But for you, that fear is a weapon. Close your eyes and let it flow through you. Your Dreynen will follow. It is a hungry thing, this Legacy that lives within you, and it will feed on what you fear."

I squeeze my eyes shut. Part of me wants to resist this lesson, my skin crawling at the sound of Setrákus Ra's voice. But another part of me wants to learn to use my Legacy, no matter the cost. It doesn't seem so unnatural—there's an energy inside me that wants to get out. My Dreynen *wants* to be used.

When I open my eyes, the wrench glows with red energy. I've done it. Just like at Dulce Base.

"Very good, Ella. You can use the Dreynen by touch or, as you have just accomplished, charge objects with it for long-range attacks," Setrákus Ra explains. He takes a quick step back when I thrust the wrench towards him. "Easy now, my dear."

I stare at Setrákus Ra, unblinking, holding the wrench like I might hold a torch if I was trying to scare off a wild animal. I wonder if I could hit him with it, drain his Legacies and then bash his head in. Would Five try to stop me? Would I even be able to pull it off? I'm not yet sure of the full extent of Setrákus Ra's Legacies, or what other tricks he might have up his sleeve, or what might happen with the charm that now binds us together. But maybe it would be worth it.

A slow smile spreads across Setrákus Ra's face, as if he

can tell I'm making these mental calculations and he appreciates them.

"Go on," he says, and his eyes flick towards the ceiling. "You know what to do next. He failed me. And he killed your friend, didn't he?"

I know that I should resist, that I shouldn't do anything Setrákus Ra wants me to do. But the wrench, charged with my Dreynen, feels almost eager in my hand, like it's hungry and needs release. And then I think of Eight, dead somewhere down on Earth, killed by the chubby boy currently in a midair sulk right above me, who my grandfather apparently has designs about marrying me off to.

I turn around and hurl the wrench at Five.

I'm not sure my throw has the accuracy or the distance, so I give it a boost with my telekinesis. Five must see it coming, but he doesn't try to move out of the way. That's what makes me start to regret my decision—his resignation and willingness to receive this punishment.

The wrench hits Five right in the sternum but without much force. Even so, it sticks to his chest like it's magnetized. He sucks in a sharp breath, his bored look failing him as he claws at the wrench. That only lasts for a second, though, until the glow briefly intensifies and Five plummets out of the air.

Five's landing is ugly; his legs crumple beneath him, his hands fail to brace the impact and his shoulder cracks against the floor. He ends up lying on his face, breathing hard. He tries to pick himself up, but his arm isn't quite working right, and he only manages to push himself an inch off the floor before sagging back down. The wrench falls from his chest, the damage done, his Legacies canceled. Setrákus Ra pats me approvingly on the back. That's when I really start to feel some guilt, seeing Five like that, even knowing what he did to Eight. It occurs to me that maybe he's just as much a prisoner as I am.

"Get yourself to the infirmary," Setrákus Ra orders Five. "I do not care what you do about your eye, but I need you able-bodied when we descend to Earth."

"Yes, Beloved Leader," Five croaks, straining his neck to look up at us.

"That was well done," Setrákus Ra says to me as he shepherds me towards the exit. "Come. We will return to your studies of the Great Book."

Even though I'm still furious about what he did to Eight, as we pass Five's prone body, I reach out to him telepathically. I refuse to lose my sense of right and wrong while I'm stuck here.

I'm sorry, I tell him.

I don't think he'll answer, considering how he could barely even look at me before. Just as I'm about to cut off our telepathic link, his response comes.

I'm fine, he replies. *I deserved it.*

You deserve worse than that, I reply, although I can't quite manage the malice I want. It's hard while I'm mentally picturing Eight, laughing, joking around with me and Marina.

I know, Five responds. *I didn't—I'm sorry, Ella.*

I pick up something else from his mind. That's never happened before—maybe my Legacy is getting stronger. I don't think too much about it, because through my mind's eye I'm seeing Eight's body, left behind on purpose in an empty hangar. I try to make sense of the image, but Five's thoughts are a confused jumble. There are so many conflicting impulses in his brain, and I'm not a skilled enough telepath to make sense of them all.

I've already walked past him, but after our telepathic conversation, I hazard a glance over my shoulder. Five has managed to prop himself up. He works a metal ball bearing across his knuckles, over and under, waiting for his Legacies to return. He looks right at me.

We have to get out of here, he thinks.

CHAPTER SEVENTEEN

ASHWOOD ESTATES IS QUIET JUST BEFORE SUNrise, a light fog greeting the gray day. I could hardly sleep, which isn't exactly a new development. I sit next to the living-room window in Adam's old house and take cell-phone photographs of the documents Agent Walker turned over, sending them on to Sarah. We're going to leak them online via They Walk Among Us, because at least that way we can ensure the information gets out there. Walker has a list of journalists and other media people who she believes to be trustworthy, but she's got a list the same length of reporters in the pocket of MogPro. There's no surefire way to get this intel out there except on our own. It's going to be an uphill battle. In the years we've spent on the run, the Mogadorians have gotten too far ahead, become too entrenched in the military, government and even the media. The smartest thing they ever did was chase us into hiding.

According to Walker, it's going to take something big to turn the tide. She wants us to cut the head off of MogPro, meaning take out the secretary of defense. I'm not sure how that's supposed to get us any support from humanity. Walker says we can carry out the assassination covertly. I haven't decided if we're going along with that part of the plan, but it's okay to let Walker think we're down with doing her dirty work. For now.

More important than Sanderson, we're supposed to expose Setrákus Ra, using whatever human-Mog photo op he's got planned for the United Nations against him. The plan is to make a big enough scene that humanity will see the Mogs for what they really are and rally against the invasion. A population that's been duped for a decade will finally be out of the dark. Once the humans see aliens firsthand, we're hoping people will take a niche site like They Walk Among Us seriously. I just hope we figure out a way to pull all this off. Without dying.

Dark thoughts still gnaw at me. Even if we manage to form a resistance bigger and stronger than the ragtag bunch we've assembled at Ashwood Estates, there's no guarantee we can turn back the Mogadorians. For as long as I've been on Earth, our war with the Mogadorians has been fought in the shadows. Now, we're about to involve millions of innocent people. It seems like all we're struggling for is to give humanity and us remaining Loric the *opportunity* to fight a long and bloody war. I wonder if this is what the Elders had planned for us. Were we supposed to have already defeated the Mogs with humanity none the wiser? Or was their plan when they sent us to Earth just as desperate as ours is now?

No wonder I can't sleep.

Through the window, I watch a couple of FBI agents share a cigarette on the porch across the street. I guess I'm not the only one suffering from impending invasion insomnia. We let Walker's people camp out in the empty houses around Ashwood. They secured the perimeter, guards posted at the gate Adam and I wrecked earlier in the day, pretty much making this place the home base of the brand-new Human-Loric Resistance.

I still don't entirely trust Agent Walker or her people, but the looming war has forced me to take on a lot of strange allies. So far, they've panned out. If my luck with trusting old enemies doesn't hold, well, we're pretty much all doomed anyway. Desperate times call for desperate measures and all that.

The floorboards creak behind me and I turn around to find Malcolm standing in the doorway leading up from the Mogadorian tunnels. His eyes are droopy with exhaustion and he's in the process of stifling a yawn.

"Morning," I say, closing up the folder of Walker's documents.

"Already?" Malcolm replies, shaking his head in disbelief. "I lost track of time down there. Sam and Adam were helping me earlier. I thought I just forced them to take a break a little while ago."

"That was hours ago," I reply. "Did you spend your entire night going through those Mogadorian recordings?"

Malcolm nods his head mutely, and I realize that he's more than just overtired. He's got the punch-drunk look of a man who's just witnessed something shocking.

"What did you find?" I ask.

"Me," he answers after a moment's pause. "I found myself."

"What do you mean?"

"I think you better gather the others" is his only reply before he disappears back into the tunnels.

Marina is asleep in one of the upstairs bedrooms, so I wake her up first. As she heads downstairs, she pauses in front of the master bedroom; once upon a time it was occupied by the General and Adam's mother, but now it's the temporary resting place for Eight. Marina lays her hand gently on the doorframe as she passes. I noticed when I woke her that she's taken to wearing Eight's pendant. I wish there was more time for me to grieve with her.

Adam is asleep in the remaining upstairs bedroom, his sword propped against the side of the bed within arm's reach. I hesitate for only a moment before waking him, too. He's one of us now. He proved that yesterday when he saved my life from the General. Whatever Malcolm's discovered on those Mogadorian recordings, Adam's insight could be invaluable.

Sam and the rest of the Garde slept elsewhere in Ashwood Estates, so I dispatch some Chimærae to track them down. Nine shows up after a few minutes, his long hair all unkempt and wild, looking about as fatigued as I feel.

"I slept on the roof," he explains when I shoot him a weird look.

"Uh, why?"

"Somebody had to keep an eye on those government dorks you've got camping out."

I shake my head and follow him down the steps into the tunnels. Malcolm and the others I'd gotten hold of are already assembled in the Mogadorian archives, silent and uneasy, Marina sitting about as far from Adam as possible.

"Sam and Six?" Malcolm asks me when I enter.

I shrug my shoulders. "The Chimærae are looking for them."

"I saw them go into one of the abandoned houses,"

Nine says, a sly smile on his face. I give him a questioning look and he wiggles his eyebrows at me. "End of the world, you know, Johnny."

I'm not sure exactly what Nine means until Six and Sam come hustling through the door. Six is all business, her hair pulled back, looking like she's cleaned up and gotten some good rest since her ordeal in the swamp. Sam, on the other hand, is flushed, his hair sticking up at odd angles, and his shirt is buttoned all wrong. Sam catches me studying him and turns a darker shade of red, giving me a sheepish smile. I shake my head in disbelief, fighting back a grin in spite of the dour mood. Nine whistles between his teeth and a smile even flits briefly across Marina's face. All this only causes Sam to blush more, and for Six to increase the defiant look she's skewering us with.

Malcolm, of course, is oblivious to all this. He's focused instead on the computer, queuing up one of the Mogadorian videos.

"Good. We're all here," Malcolm says, glancing up from the keyboard. He looks around the room, almost nervously. "I feel like a failure, having to show you this."

Sam's post-hookup blush turns into a look of concern. "What do you mean, Dad?"

"I—" Malcolm shakes his head. "They tore this information out of me and even now, having seen what

I'm about to show you, I don't actually remember it. I let you all down."

"Malcolm, come on," I say.

"We've all made mistakes," Marina says, and I notice her gaze drift towards Nine. "Done things we regret."

Malcolm nods. "Regardless. Late in the game as it is, I still hope this video will show another way forward."

Six tilts her head. "Another way instead of what?"

"Instead of total war," Malcolm answers. "Watch."

Malcolm presses a button on the keyboard and the video screen on the wall comes to life. The face of a gaunt, older Mogadorian appears. His narrow head fills most of the screen, but in the background a room similar to this one is visible. The Mogadorian begins speaking in his harsh language, his tone sounding formal and academic, even though I can't understand him.

"Am I supposed to be able to understand this creep?" Nine asks.

"He's Dr. Lockram Anu," Adam says, translating. "He created the memory machine that . . . well, you know. You chucked a piece of it at a helicopter last night, actually."

"Oh, that," Nine says, grinning. "That was fun."

Adam continues. "This is old, taped during the machine's first trials. He's introducing a test subject, one he says was mentally tougher than the others he's worked on. He'll be demonstrating how his machine can be utilized for interrogation . . ."

Adam trails off as Dr. Anu steps aside, revealing a younger Malcolm Goode strapped into an insanely complicated metal chair. Malcolm is thin and pale, the muscles in his neck standing out, largely thanks to the awkward angle his head is forced to recline at. His wrists are buckled to the titanium arms of the chair; an IV cord runs into the back of his hand, nutrients arriving via a nearby bag. An assortment of electrodes are stuck to his face and chest, their cords attached to the circuit boards of Dr. Anu's machine. His eyes stare directly into the camera, but they're unfocused and unblinking.

"Dad, oh my God," Sam says quietly.

It's difficult to look at the Malcolm on-screen, and it gets even worse when Anu starts asking him questions.

"Good morning, Malcolm," Anu says, now in English, his tone the kind usually reserved for children. "Are you ready to resume our conversation?"

"Yes, Doctor," the Malcolm on-screen answers, his mouth sagging through the words, a glimmer of drool appearing at the corner of his mouth.

"Very good," Anu replies, and glances down at a clipboard on his lap. "I want you to think about your encounter with Pittacus Lore. I want to know what he was doing on Earth."

"He was preparing for what is to come," Malcolm

replies, his voice distant and robotic.

"Be specific, Malcolm," Anu insists.

"He was preparing for the Mogadorian invasion and the rebirth of Lorien." On the screen, Malcolm looks suddenly alarmed. He jerks his arms against his bonds. "They're already here. Hunting us."

"Indeed, but you're safe now," Anu says, and waits for Malcolm to calm down. "How long have the Loric been visiting Earth?"

"Centuries. Pittacus hoped that humanity would be ready when the time came."

"When the time came for what?"

"To fight. To restart Lorien."

Anu drums the clipboard with his pen, growing annoyed by Malcolm's hypnotized vagueness. "How will they restart Lorien from here, Malcolm? The planet is light-years away. Are you lying to me?"

"Not lying," Malcolm mumbles. "Lorien is not simply a planet. It is more than that. It can exist in any place where the people are worthy. Pittacus and the Elders have already made the preparations. Loralite runs beneath our feet even now, circulating through the Earth. Like blood coursing through veins, it only needs a heartbeat to give it purpose. All it needs is to be awoken."

Anu leans forward, suddenly very interested. I find

myself doing the same thing, bending towards the screen, my head tilted.

"How will they accomplish this?" Anu asks, clearly trying to keep the excitement out of his voice.

"Each of the Garde possesses what Pittacus called Phoenix Stones," Malcolm replies. "When the Garde come of age, the Stones can be used to re-create the features of Lorien—the plant life, Loralite, the Chimærae."

"But what of the Legacies? What of Lorien's true gifts?"

"Those, too, will come once Lorien is awoken," Malcolm answers. "The Phoenix Stones, the pendants, everything has a purpose. When they are committed to the Earth in the Elders' Sanctuary, Lorien will live once again."

Anu glances back at the camera, his eyes wide. He composes himself and presses on.

"Where is this Sanctuary, Malcolm?"

"Calakmul. Only the Garde may enter."

Here, Malcolm pauses the recording. He looks around the room; his lips are squeezed into a somber line, but there's a hopeful glimmer in his eyes. Everyone's stunned faces peer back at him, none of us quite done digesting what we've just seen.

Nine raises his hand, frowning. "I don't get it. What the hell is Calakmul?"

"It's an ancient Mayan city located in southeast Mexico," Malcolm replies, a ripple of excitement stirring his voice.

"Why didn't we know any of this?" Six asks, still staring at the paused screen. "Why didn't the Elders tell us? Or our Cêpans? If this is all so important, why keep us in the dark?"

Malcolm pinches the bridge of his nose. "I don't have a good answer for that, Six. The Mogadorian invasion caught the Elders off guard. You were rushed to Earth, your Cêpans completely unprepared as well. Your survival was top priority. I can only assume all this—the Phoenix Stones, your pendants, the Sanctuary—was meant to be revealed when you came of age, once you had Legacies and were ready to fight. To tell you before that would've made your secrets too vulnerable. Although"—Malcolm looks forlornly at his image on the screen—"we can see how poorly secrecy served us."

"Maybe that's why Henri came to Paradise looking for you, Dad," Sam suggests, glancing between his father and me. "Maybe it was time."

My mind is racing. Without even realizing it, I've started to pace back and forth. It takes a look from Six to get me to stop.

"I always thought we'd win this war and return to Lorien," I say slowly, trying to catch hold of my thoughts. "I thought that's what Henri meant about restarting it."

"Maybe he meant here," Six suggests. "Maybe we're supposed to restart Lorien here."

"What would that even mean?" Sam asks. "What would happen to Earth?"

"Can't be worse than what'll happen when the Mogs get here," Nine replies. "I mean, I remember Lorien being pretty sweet. We'd be doing Earth a favor."

"On the tape you made it sound like an entity of some kind," Marina says, looking at Malcolm.

"I—" Malcolm shakes his head. "I wish I could remember more, Marina. I don't have the answers."

"It could be like a god," Marina says, a hushed reverence in her voice.

"It could be like a weapon that comes busting out of the Earth to kill all the Mogs," Nine suggests.

Adam clears his throat uncomfortably.

"Whatever it is, Malcolm said we need the Phoenix Stones to wake it," I say, trying not to let the group get sidetracked.

"And the pendants," Six says, then tilts her head as something occurs to her. "Maybe that's why Setrákus Ra keeps them. They could be more than trophies to him."

"We went through our Chests back in Chicago," Nine groans, probably remembering how bored he was cataloging our Inheritance. "I've got more rocks and shit than I know what to do with."

"We should bring it all," Marina says, certainty in her voice. "Our Inheritances. Our pendants. Bring it to the Sanctuary and commit it to the Earth, like Malcolm said."

Malcolm nods. "I know it's vague, but it's something."

"It could be the advantage we're looking for," I say, thinking it over. "Hell, it could be what we were sent here to do in the first place."

Nine crosses his arms, looking skeptical. "Yesterday I was staring at the biggest goddamn Mogadorian ship I've ever seen. Burying our stuff in some dusty-ass temple might've been a cool idea like months ago, but we're *this close* to full-on war and I'm pretty sure we've got some bad guys to kill."

Before I can reply, Malcolm steps forward. "The Sanctuary might be our best hope," he says. "But it's best not to put all our eggs in one basket."

"Nine's sort of right. As much as I hate the idea of splitting up again," Six says, "some of us should stick with Walker's plan to take the fight to the Mogs and their people."

Nine pumps a fist. "This guy."

"And some of us should head to Mexico," I say, finishing Six's thought.

"I want to go," Marina says immediately. "I want to see this Sanctuary. If it's a place for Loric, a place where we lived, maybe that's where we should bury Eight's body."

I nod and look over at Six, waiting for her decision. "Well? New York or Mexico?"

"Mexico," she says, after a moment. "You're better at dealing with these government types than I am. And if we need a Loric representative at the UN, you're the obvious choice."

"Thanks. I think."

"She's saying that because you're such a boy scout," Nine adds in a loud whisper.

I glance over at Sam, who seems like he's about to speak, his mouth half open. He's cut off by Six, who subtly shakes her head at him.

"I'll stay here, too, I guess," Sam says after an awkward moment, sounding more than a little deflated. He forces a smile for me. "Someone has to keep you and Nine in line."

That leaves only Adam. Our Mogadorian ally has maintained a respectful silence this whole time, probably trying not to step on any toes as the secrets of our race are revealed. When I turn to him, he's still gazing at the screen. He looks lost in memory, maybe remembering Dr. Anu and his machine. He frowns when he notices the rest of us watching him.

"They'll be waiting for you in Mexico," Adam says. "If there's a source of Loric power there, you know my people will have spent the last few years trying to access it."

"Only the Garde can get in, though, right?" Sam asks, looking from Adam to his dad.

"It's what I said," Malcolm replies, lips pursed in uncertainty.

"Just like only we can have Legacies?" Nine replies, eyeballing Adam. "You're saying this could be another trap, Mog?"

"It's not a trap when you know it's there," Adam says, sparing a quick glance for Nine before turning his eyes towards Six. "I don't know exactly what you'll find down there, but I can guarantee a Mogadorian presence. I can pilot the Skimmer better than you, maybe outmaneuver them if they've got ships in the air."

"Well, I sure as hell wasn't going to walk to Mexico," Six replies, dryly. She looks at me. "You trust this guy, right?"

"I do."

She shrugs. "Then welcome to Team Calakmul, Adam."

I hear Marina suck her teeth, but she doesn't make any other protest.

"Great. We're sending a Mogadorian to investigate a Loric holy place," Nine complains, shaking his head.

"Doesn't anyone else think that's sorta disrespectful?"

"Didn't you just refer to it as *dusty-ass*?" Sam asks.

"Statement of fact," Nine says. "Just like this whole good-Mog thing is still hella weird. No offense."

I silence the banter when I reach under my shirt and pull my Loric pendant over my head. I feel an odd coldness against my heart when it's gone. I can't remember the last time that I was without it. With the room suddenly gone quiet again, I hold out the pendant to Six.

"Take it," I say. "Make sure it gets to the Sanctuary."

"No pressure," Six says, smirking, as she accepts the pendant.

"Now," I say, looking around. "Let's win this war and change the world."

CHAPTER EIGHTEEN

WE SAY GOOD-BYE LATER THAT MORNING, ALL OF us gathered around the Skimmer on the Ashwood Estates basketball court.

It feels strange to be wearing a Loric pendant around my neck again. And I don't mean literal physical weight—the pendants themselves aren't heavy at all. They just contain all the Legacies of Lorien, apparently. All the power of our nearly extinct people, imbued into a few glistening Loralite stones.

Yeah. No big deal.

"Is that everything?" Marina asks. She's on her knees in front of her open Chest, gently rearranging its contents. We've got Eight's Chest as well. Its contents are forever locked up, possibly destroyed, but we figured it couldn't hurt to bring it to the Sanctuary with the rest.

I don't have a Chest of my own, so Marina has to put all

of our collected Inheritance into hers. After our meeting earlier, John and Nine went through their Chests and gathered together anything that wasn't a weapon, a healing stone, or otherwise combat related. Besides the handful of Loric gemstones yet to be traded for penthouses or computer equipment, John handed over a bundle of dried leaves tied with a yellowed piece of twine that make the sound of the wind when my fingers brush against them, and Nine gives up a pouch of soft, coffee-dark soil. Marina carefully put these items into her Chest, alongside a vial of crystal clear water, a stray piece of Loralite and a tree branch with the bark pared away.

"So, because we don't know what exactly these Phoenix Stones are, we'll just dump anything that's close, right?" I say, then hastily correct myself. "I mean, not dump. *Commit to the Earth.* What brainwashed Malcolm said."

John laughs a little. "If we come up with a better plan, I'll let you know."

"Dad's still down there watching more tapes," Sam offers. "Maybe he'll find something else."

"Right now, winging it seems like the only option. On pretty much every front," John says. "There's something else I want you to take to the Sanctuary, Six."

John crouches down to reach into his Chest. I was wondering why he'd brought it with him to the basketball court after we already went through it inside. I understand when he holds out a small can that I immediately recognize.

Henri's ashes.

"John . . . ," I say, not accepting the can right away.

"Take him," John replies, gently. "He belongs at the Sanctuary."

"But don't you want to be there? To say good-bye?"

"Of course I do. But with everything that's happening, I don't know if I'll have a chance." When I start to protest again, John cuts me off. "It's okay, Six. I'll feel better knowing he's with you, headed to the Sanctuary."

"If it's what you want," I say, accepting the ashes. "I'll take care of him. I promise."

I carefully place the can of Henri's ashes in Marina's Chest with the rest of our stuff. We all fall silent, the mood turning somber. It's hard to have this kind of moment when you're being watched, though. The government agents keep their distance, although I can see some of them, including Walker herself, watching us from a nearby porch.

"You going to be all right with them?" I ask John.

He looks around, noting all the prying eyes. "They're on our side now, remember?"

"I have to keep reminding myself," I reply, my gaze involuntarily turning towards the Skimmer. "Seems like I'm doing that a lot."

Adam is already on board the Skimmer, along with Dust, the Chimæra that's bonded with him. I'm taking

John at his word that we can trust the wiry Mogadorian currently running diagnostics in the cockpit. I'm not sure Marina feels the same; she hasn't said anything outright, but I can feel cold radiating from her whenever Adam's near. After everything that's happened, I can't blame her for being suspicious. I've resigned myself to a very chilly flight to Mexico.

"Check in often," John reminds me, tapping the phone that he's clipped to the hip of his jeans like a total dork. Both Marina and I are now in possession of satellite phones, too bulky to wear as fashion accessories, so they're stored with the rest of our supplies. The gear arrived courtesy of the U.S. Government, or at least the rebel-faction that Walker has ties with. Both Adam and Malcolm looked over the phones and assured us they aren't bugged.

"Yeah, yeah," I reply. "You, too, John. Stay in touch. Stay alive."

"And take care of all our stuff," Nine grumbles. He's standing a few paces off, watching Marina mess with her Chest, his eyebrows furrowed. "I want some of those gems back, if possible. You know, for after. Need to buy a new place to live thanks to my shitty house-sitter over here."

I shoot Nine a look. "Are you serious right now?"

He shrugs. "What? Gotta plan for the future!"

Marina looks up from her Chest and, with a sigh, tosses Nine a pair of dark gloves. "Here. I never figured out what to do with these."

"Sweet," Nine says, and pulls them on immediately. He flexes his fingers inside the leatherlike material, then violently thrusts his palms out towards John. "Did you feel anything, dude?"

John ignores Nine, looking at Marina. "Can we be sure those aren't important? What if they're a Phoenix Stone?"

"They're gloves, Johnny," Nine says, not taking them off. "You ever heard of an ancient ritual that involves burying a pair of stylish-ass gloves? Come on."

John shakes his head, giving up. His eyes linger on Henri's ashes until Marina closes her Chest, and then his gaze drifts towards the Skimmer. "I wish I could come with you. I'd like to be there for . . . for both of them."

Eight's body is already on board the Skimmer, strapped securely to one of the seats.

"After," Marina says, and she reaches out to squeeze John's hand. She's still walking around with a lot of sadness—we all are—but I'm slowly seeing signs that the old, gentle Marina is melting all that ice. "Eight would understand. Once we've won, there will be time for us to pay our respects properly. All of us, together."

Nine stops screwing with his new gloves and gets serious for a moment, looking at Marina. "I'd like that," he says.

"Ready?" I ask Marina.

She nods and uses her telekinesis to float her Chest into the Skimmer's entrance. "Be safe, all of you."

One by one, Marina hugs the boys, and I do the same. Sam is last for me, and when he wraps me up in a big hug, I get the same feeling that I did before when we were all assembled in the Mogadorian tunnels, that everyone is watching us and tittering about how precious we are. I bristle a little bit, but before I know it the hug has lasted way longer than the others', and our friends have drifted a few steps away as if to let us have a discreet moment.

"Six—," Sam says quietly against my ear, and I pull back enough to look at him, cutting him off.

"Don't make this weird, Sam," I whisper, and tuck a loose strand of hair behind my ear, glancing surreptitiously towards the others.

So, we spent last night together. Maybe that wasn't the wisest move on my part. I love Sam, in my way, and I don't want to string him along or hurt his feelings. I'm just still not sold on having any kind of relationship until this is all over, especially with how stupid and complicated things got with John after just some flirting. But, after everything that happened in Florida, I needed something good for a change—something warm and safe and approaching normal—and that was Sam. I thought he understood that I didn't want to get into some dopey John/Sarah-style, star-crossed-lovers thing with him. But here we are, having a moment, and blunt as I'm trying to be, I'm not exactly pulling away either.

"I'm not making it anything," Sam says, screwing up his face at me. "I just—I don't get why you didn't want me coming with you."

"You'll do more good here, with your dad," I tell him. "And you'll need to keep John and Nine in line."

"The last time I went on a mission with John, he left me inside a mountain," Sam says, not buying it. "Come on, Six. What is it really?"

I sigh, simultaneously wanting to strangle him and kiss him. For a second, I'm not sure which instinct will win out. I want something more with Sam, I think. Eventually. I just don't want to think about it right now. Last night was one thing, but now I'm back to fighting a war.

"I don't want the distraction, Sam. All right?"

"Oh," he says, looking like I've just murdered his pride. "You mean, like you'd have to keep saving me from Mogs or stop me from stepping on some ancient Mayan spike trap or whatever. Because I thought we were past that. I can handle myself, Six. And I only accidentally shot you that one time in practice and—"

I kiss him. Mostly just to shut him up and illustrate my point, but also because I just can't help myself. I hear Nine make an *oohing* noise off to the side and make a mental note to destroy him the next chance I get.

"*That's* the distraction I'm talking about," I say quietly, my face still close to his.

Sam is blushing again, and his mouth is still working

like he wants to say something more. He's probably trying to come up with some smooth way to say good-bye, but I'm sick of these drawn-out moments, so I take one last look at his sweet, dumbstruck face and turn away. A few seconds later, I'm strapped into the Skimmer's seat next to Adam, ignoring the raised eyebrow and smirk Marina's fixing me with.

"Shall we?" Adam asks.

We nod and Adam throws some switches, handling the Skimmer's controls with much more confidence than I did. As we slowly rise up, I look out the window to see Sam and the others below, waving good-bye to us. I wonder if my life will ever be without these moments—the painful good-byes before we all go off to risk our lives. John always talks about how much he can't wait for some boring normal life, but would I be happy like that? We gain altitude, trees zipping by beneath us, and I think about Sam. If it wasn't for this war, the constant chaos, we'd have never even gotten together. What would it be like for us without the looming threat of Mogadorian destruction?

I'd like to find out.

CHAPTER NINETEEN

NINE LEANS ACROSS ME SO THAT HE CAN GET A good look at Sam, saying to him in a stage whisper, "All right, dude. What's the deal with you and Six?"

Sam pointedly looks out the window of the van. "What? Nothing."

"Psshh," Nine snorts. "Come on, man. It's like a four-hour drive to New York. You gotta give up some details."

In front of us, in the passenger seat, Agent Walker clears her throat.

"Fascinating as I find the sex lives of teenage boys, maybe we could use this time to go over our operational parameters," she says dryly.

"Agreed," I say, shoving Nine back in his seat so he can't leer at Sam anymore. "We need to focus on the mission."

Nine frowns at me. "All right, John. I'm gonna focus

my ass off for the rest of this car ride."

"Good."

Sam flashes me a grateful smile and I nod. Part of me really does think we should be thinking about the impossible odds we're facing, but another part of me just doesn't want to hear any details about Sam and Six. I'm happy for them, I guess. Glad they could find some comfort together. But I can't get over the feeling that Sam is going to end up with his heart broken. I remember my vision of the future, the way Sam screamed right before the Mogadorians executed Six. Maybe that's why I get the sinking feeling this is going to end badly.

Or maybe I'm just jealous. Not because Sam hooked up with Six, but more because the love of my life is miles away. Of course, there's no way I'm expressing any of that in front of Nine, or Walker and the silent FBI-guy driving the car. Yeah, let's focus on the mission.

We're driving up I-95, from Washington to New York. Malcolm stayed behind at Ashwood Estates to finish going through the Mogadorian archives, hoping to turn up something else that might be useful. The vast majority of Walker's renegade agents stayed back, too. They're holding down the fort, using it as a base of operations to coordinate their efforts to undermine MogPro. I still don't entirely trust Walker's people, and

I probably won't ever reach that level after everything the government put us through, so I left behind our five remaining Chimærae with orders to protect Malcolm at all costs.

Besides Walker and our driver, there's another SUV filled with agents following along behind us. That makes a grand total of six agents, plus me, Nine and Sam. Not much of an army. But then, the war hasn't started yet. Maybe, if everything goes according to my plan, it won't start at all.

"Secretary of Defense Sanderson is staying at a hotel in midtown Manhattan, close to the UN," Walker says. She glances down at her phone, which she's been typing away on all morning. "I had a mole on his security team, but . . ."

"But what?"

"They were pulled this morning," Walker replies. "All his bodyguards, replaced by a new team. Pale guys in dark trench coats. Sound familiar?"

"Mogadorians," Nine says, grinding his fist into his palm. "Keeping their pet politician safe before his big sellout speech."

"I think it actually works to our advantage," Walker says, looking at me. "My people weren't looking forward to fighting through their own on the way to Sanderson. I mean, some of these guys are just doing their jobs."

"Yeah, we aren't in the habit of fighting humans either," I say, giving Walker a pointed look. "Unless they make us."

"So, that's the whole plan?" Sam asks, skeptical. "We go to his hotel, fight our way through a bunch of Mogs and then kill this Sanderson guy?"

"Yes," Walker answers.

"No," I say.

Everyone looks at me. Even our stoic driver is staring at me in the rearview mirror.

"What do you mean, *no*?" Walker asks, her eyebrows raised. "I thought we were clear on this."

"We're not killing Sanderson," I say. "We don't fight humans. We sure as hell don't kill them."

"Kid, I'll pull the trigger if you get me in front of him," Walker replies.

"You can arrest him, if you want," I say. "Charge him with treason."

"The penalty for treason is *death*," Walker exclaims, sounding exasperated. "Anyway, his MogPro cronies won't let an arrest go through. And you think anything in the courts is going to matter once Setrákus Ra is here?"

"You said it," I reply. "Setrákus Ra is who's important."

"Right. Instead of Sanderson, it'll be you guys there

to greet him at the UN. We'll show the world the difference between good aliens and bad aliens. Meanwhile, behind the scenes, my people will dismantle MogPro." Walker rubs her temples. "I've got other agents already in position. Around the time we take out Sanderson, a dozen other MogPro traitors will—"

I cut her off. "If you're about to tell me about more assassinations, I don't want to know."

Nine raises his hand. "I want to know."

"That's not what we do, Walker," I continue. "It's not what we're about."

"Kid, you want to get the word out about the Mogs, sooner or later you're gonna have to get your hands dirty."

"And what if Sanderson gets the word out for us?"

Walker squints at me. "What're you talking about?"

"He's giving a speech at the UN, right? Going to talk up Setrákus Ra, tell humanity how it's safe to welcome the Mogadorian fleet." I shrug, trying to seem nonchalant about this, confident in my plan. "Maybe he gives a different speech. Maybe he delivers a warning."

"You're talking about *turning* him?" Walker exclaims. "This late in the game? You're out of your mind."

"I don't think so," I reply, glancing left and right at Nine and Sam. "My friends and I are pretty persuasive."

"Yeah," Nine jumps in, grinning fiercely at Walker. "I'm convincing as all hell."

Walker stares at me for a long moment, then turns around and goes back to typing coded messages into her phone. "I didn't realize I was teaming up with some hippy-dippy peacenik aliens," she sighs. "Fine. If you can talk Sanderson into flipping sides in front of the UN, go for it. But if I'm not convinced, I'm shooting him."

"Sure," I reply to Walker. "You're in charge."

We stop at a gas station in New Jersey to fill up the SUVs. Since I've got a few minutes alone, I decide it's a good time to check in with Sarah. I take out my phone and wander across the parking lot. As I do, I can feel Walker's eyes boring into my back.

"Where are you going?" she calls after me.

"To call my girlfriend," I say, raising the phone. "Remember? You illegally detained her that one time."

"Oh, great," Walker replies. I can hear her mutter to the driver. "We're depending on a bunch of horny teenagers to save the world."

Better us than people like Walker, I think, but pretend not to have heard her snide remark.

The phone rings five times, each one causing my heart to beat a little faster, before Sarah answers, narrowly evading the dump to voice mail.

"Before you say anything," she begins, not even saying hello, her voice shaky, "I just want you to know that I'm okay."

"What happened?" I ask, trying to keep that first rush of panic out of my voice. I can hear the sound of traffic in the background. Sarah's in a moving car.

"We went into town for supplies and had a run-in with some Mogs," Sarah says, still catching her breath. "I guess they tracked us down somehow, not too happy about the They Walk Among Us thing. Don't worry, we're all fine. Bernie Kosar handled them."

"Are you somewhere safe?"

"We will be soon," she replies. "Mark's hacker buddy GUARD gave us directions to his home base in Atlanta."

Mark had some details about GUARD in one of his emails to Sarah. He's another conspiracy junkie, like one of those guys from the old version of They Walk Among Us. But he's also an excellent hacker and, according to Mark, has access to a surprising amount of information. It makes me a little nervous that Sarah and Mark are headed to meet him without us knowing his identity.

"What does Mark know about this guy?" I ask.

Sarah repeats my question to Mark. I can't quite make out his reply over all the noise from the road.

"Mark says he's probably some nerd hiding out in

his mom's basement," Sarah repeats dryly. "But that he's a 'solid dude' and that we can trust him."

I roll my eyes at Mark's scouting report. "That's heartening. Just in case, I'm going to text you the location of somewhere safe. It's a base in Washington that we took over, loaded with government guys who are on our side. If you need somewhere to run to, you could head there."

I hear two engines rumble to life behind me. I turn around to see all of Walker's agents piled into the cars. Nine and Sam still stand outside our SUV, waiting for me. Nine makes an impatient wrap-it-up motion.

"What's going on there?" Sarah asks me. "On your way to do something stupid but possibly world saving?"

"Pretty much," I reply, allowing myself a faint smile. "Did you get those documents I sent you?"

"Yeah," Sarah replies. "We'll have a chance to upload them once we're in Atlanta."

"Perfect. I've got a feeling They Walk Among Us is about to get a lot more hits." I pause, reluctant to get off the phone. "The others are waiting for me. I've gotta go."

"Mark says to go kick some ass. And I love you." Sarah catches herself, laughing. "Mark didn't say that last part. That was from me."

We say our good-byes and I'm left with that same feeling of longing mixed with dread that I get after every one of these phone conversations. I trudge back to the SUV. Everyone else is already inside except for Sam.

"So you're putting all of Walker's documents on They Walk Among Us?" Sam asks. "It's a good idea. Like anti-Mogadorian propaganda."

"It's a desperate idea, is what it is," I say glumly. "No one's going to be digging through search results while their cities are getting bombarded."

"There's a comforting thought," Sam replies, frowning. "But seriously, that's a lot of heavy reading. If you're trying to get people on our side, it shouldn't just be about the Mogadorians. You shouldn't just be trying to scare people. They'll be scared enough as it is. You've gotta give them some hope."

"What do you suggest?"

Sam thinks about it for a second, then shrugs. "I don't know yet. I'll come up with something."

I nod and pat Sam on the shoulder, the two of us climbing back into the car. I know he's just trying to help, and that's why I don't tell him that whatever he comes up with . . . it might be too late.

We make it to New York about an hour later. I've never been here before and neither have Nine or Sam. I wish our visit could be under different circumstances. As we inch along in heavy traffic through a canyon of skyscrapers, I find myself craning my neck to look out the window. Chicago is a huge city, but the frenetic jostle of pedestrians on the sidewalks here is something else entirely. There are flashing signs advertising Broadway shows, yellow cabs darting in and out of traffic, a hum of activity all around us.

And these people have no idea what's heading their way.

As we drive farther uptown towards Sanderson's hotel, we pass a dude wearing a cowboy hat and underwear, strumming an acoustic guitar for a crowd of tourists. Nine snorts.

"Look at this," he says, shaking his head. "That shit wouldn't fly in Chicago."

I lean forward to get Walker's attention. "Are we close?"

"A few more blocks," she replies.

I reach down to make sure my Loric dagger is still fastened securely to my leg. I also touch my wrist, reflex telling me to check for my shield bracelet, except that it's gone, destroyed by the General.

"Did your guy on the scene tell you how many Mogs we should be expecting?" I ask Walker.

"A dozen. Maybe more."

"That's nothing," Nine says, pulling on the gloves

that Marina gave him. He clenches his fists and I inch away from him, wary that he's going to accidentally trigger some kind of weapon. Thankfully, nothing happens.

"You're wearing those into a fight?" Sam asks, eyeing Nine incredulously. "You don't even know what they do."

"What better way to find out?" Nine replies. "These Loric things, man, they have a way of not helping you until you've given up on them."

"Or maybe they're just for keeping your hands warm," Sam suggests.

"Just don't do anything stupid," I tell Nine, and he stares at me, his expression getting deathly serious.

"John, I won't," he says. "For real. You can trust me out there."

I can tell Nine is still carrying around what happened down in Florida and is eager to prove himself. I just nod at him, knowing he wouldn't want me to make a big deal out of it. I'm glad he's got my back.

Walker turns around to look at Sam. "These guys shoot fireballs and have magic gloves, apparently. But what do you do?"

Sam looks momentarily taken aback, and I notice him reach down to touch the scars burned into his wrists. After a moment's consideration, he looks Walker in the eye.

"I've probably killed more Mogs than you have, lady," Sam replies.

Nine elbows me, and I can't help but grin. To her credit, that actually looks like the answer Walker was hoping for. She opens the glove compartment, pulls out a holstered handgun and holds it out to Sam.

"Well, I'm officially arming a minor," she says. "Do your country proud, Samuel."

A minute later, our driver pulls over to the side of one of Manhattan's quieter blocks, double-parking. The other SUV rolls up behind us. Across the street and down the block a bit is the entrance to a posh hotel. There's a wide awning out front and a red carpet, a place for guests to turn over their car keys to a valet and drop their bags onto one of the waiting luggage carts.

Except there's no activity outside the hotel. No tourists strolling the sidewalk, no valets waiting for tips. Nothing. Everything's been cleared away or scared off by the trio of Mogadorians standing guard at the door, their coats brazenly open to reveal the blasters hanging from their belts.

It's like they're not even bothering to hide anymore.

"We want to do this quick and clean," Walker says to us, hunching low in her seat so she can look at the Mogs in her side-view mirror. "Take down the Mogs and get to Sanderson before they can send up an alarm, radio for backup, or whatever they do."

"Yeah, got it," I reply quickly. I pull up the hood on my sweatshirt so that it hides my face. "We've done this before."

"Let my people lead," Walker says. "We'll flash some badges, maybe confuse them. Then you hit them hard."

"Sure, you distract 'em," Nine says. "But then get the hell out of our way."

Walker picks up a walkie-talkie and radios to the agents in the second car. "You guys ready?"

"Affirmative," a male voice answers. "Let's do this."

"Here we go," says an excited Nine, and claps his gloved hands together.

The concussion of sound that detonates from Nine's hands when he claps isn't quite sonic-boom loud, but it's definitely close. It's like a thunderclap in the backseat; all of the SUV's windows explode outward, and the car even bounces a few inches into the air. The SUV behind us doesn't fare much better—its windows also shatter, but inward, spraying the agents huddled inside. The windows of nearby storefronts break, too, and a pedestrian walking by is knocked clear off her feet. Next to me, Sam is squeezing the sides of his head, looking dazed. For the first few seconds, I can't hear much except a low chirping that I soon realize is car alarms going off up and down the block.

I turn to Nine, wide-eyed, and catch him staring at his gloved hands, also wide-eyed. I can't hear what he says, and I'm not much of a lip reader.

But I'm pretty sure it's "Oops."

At the entrance of the hotel, one Mogadorian is down on his knees, clutching his head. The other two are pointing right at our SUV and raising their blasters.

So much for the element of surprise.

CHAPTER TWENTY

WITH THE WAY MY EARS ARE RINGING, I DON'T really hear the first volley of Mogadorian blaster fire. But I feel it. The SUV is rocked to the side as the jagged energy bolts shear across the car's bulletproof paneling. Walker huddles for cover behind her door, keeping her head down. Our driver isn't so lucky; a blast comes sizzling through the window and hits him in the side of the neck. His flesh is burned badly and he immediately starts convulsing.

"Go!" I shout, unable to hear myself and not sure if anyone else can either. "Go!"

Nine rips open the back door of the SUV, literally. As he gets out of the car, he holds the door in front of him, using it as a shield to absorb the Mogs' fire.

I lunge into the front seat and press my hands onto the FBI agent's blaster wound, letting my warm healing energy flow into him. Slowly, the injury begins to knit itself closed, and his convulsions stop. The agent looks up at me with wide, grateful eyes.

I sense movement to my left and turn my head. Outside the driver-side window is the pedestrian who got knocked down when Nine's thunderclap went off. She's a pretty, college-aged girl with big brown eyes. She looks shell-shocked and seems to be rooted in place—except she's not so stunned that she failed to get her phone out of her purse. She's just finished recording me healing our driver and is filming my face as I shout at her to run.

Another volley of Mog blaster fire bounces over the hood of our SUV, nearly hitting the girl. Sam springs out of the backseat and grabs her. He drags her farther down the sidewalk and puts her in cover behind some parked cars.

Months ago, my face on video after using my Legacies would've been a disaster. But now, I don't even care. However, we can't let any more innocent people wander into our war zone.

"Turn the car!" I shout in our driver's ear. I'm not sure he can hear me, so I make a steering wheel motion with my hands. "Block the street off!"

He gets it and peals out—I can smell the burned rubber but don't quite hear it. He gets the car parked perpendicular across the middle of the road, blocking any traffic.

I hop out of the SUV and turn towards the hotel just in time to see a Mogadorian warrior sheared in half and turned to dust by our car door, which Nine flung through the air discus style. Meanwhile, the agents in the second car have managed to collect themselves. Seeing our maneuver, their driver throws his SUV into reverse and they quickly block access to the road from the other direction. Then, they jump out, using their SUV as cover, and return fire on the remaining Mogadorians. Their gunfire is barely audible popping in my damaged ears.

One of the Mogs keels over from a well-placed bullet to the forehead. Outnumbered, the remaining Mog ducks into the hotel doorway for cover. I reach out with my telekinesis, grab a luggage cart parked behind the Mog and jerk it forward so that it takes out the back of his legs. As he stumbles out of the doorway, Walker's agents light him up.

Nine glances back to me and I nod. Together, we rush towards the entrance. I look over my shoulder to check on Sam and see him still talking to that bystander, gesturing emphatically at her cell phone. No time to worry about that now.

Inside, the posh hotel lobby is completely deserted except for a frightened clerk cowering behind the front desk. Beyond the marble columns and leather couches of the waiting area is the elevator bank. Oddly, two of the three elevators are out of service, and the third is stuck up at the penthouse level. The Mogs might not have expected an assault, but they definitely took precautions.

With a moment to catch my breath, I press my hands to the sides of my head and let some of that healing energy flow into my ears. They pop and crackle, but sound slowly returns, like a volume dial in my head being gradually turned up. From outside, I can hear sirens, screeching tires, and Walker's people yelling at local cops to stay back. Our plan to do this covertly is already shot; now we just have to be quick.

I grab Nine before he can make it to the elevators and clap my hands to the side of his head, healing him as well. When I'm done, he shakes his head back and forth, like he's trying to dislodge water from his inner ear.

"You're an idiot," I tell him.

Nine shakes the sonic gloves at me before stuffing them in his back pocket. "At least now we know what they do."

Seeing that we aren't gun-toting Mogadorians, the guy at the front desk slowly comes out of hiding. He's skinny and middle-aged, and from the bags under his eyes, he looks as if he's having one terrible day.

"What—what is going on?" the clerk asks us.

Before we can answer, Walker strides through the

door. She flashes the clerk her badge and then shouts, "What floor is Sanderson on?"

The wide-eyed clerk glances from Walker to us and then back. "Pent-penthouse," he stammers. "Those-those *things* you killed are with him. They cleared out the entire hotel this morning except for me and some of the staff. And I'm not even a *manager*."

Nine stares at the clerk, trying to make sense of him. "Why would they keep *you* around?"

"They've been ordering room service," he responds incredulously, his voice squeaky. "Acting like they own the place and we're their servants."

"That's some ballsy shit," Nine says, shaking his head. "Like they've already taken over or something."

Walker squints at the clerk like she could strangle him, then turns to me, her voice still incredibly loud. "Goddamn it. I can't *hear* this guy."

I wave her over and press my hands to her ears. While I'm healing Walker, I look over at the clerk. "You should get out of here. Go outside very slowly, with your hands up. We'll send out anyone else we come across."

The clerk nods mutely, then begins taking baby steps towards the exit, his hands raised above his head.

Walker shakes off my hands as soon as her hearing is back. "What did he say?"

"He said we're going up," I reply, pointing to the elevator.

"Actually," Nine says, "they're coming down."

The hotel's one working elevator has begun to descend, the little lights above ticking off the floors. I light my Lumen, the whoosh of flames feeling good. Walker adjusts her grip on her pistol.

"Easy, guys," Nine says. "I've got this."

Nine picks up one of the leather sofas and holds it like a battering ram. Walker and I both step aside, giving him room. When the elevator dings and the doors slide apart, the four Mogadorians sent downstairs to reinforce the ones we've already dispatched are greeted by Nine screaming and shoving a sofa into them. One of them manages to get a burst of blaster fire off, but it sizzles harmlessly against the floor. The entire unit is pinned inside the elevator, the centermost Mog crushed outright behind Nine's weight. Walker easily darts around Nine and picks the Mogs off with her handgun.

"That still doesn't make up for the whole glove thing," I tell Nine as he effortlessly tosses the sofa back into the lobby.

"Come on," Nine complains, grinning. "It was an accident."

"Are there any other alien gadgets I need to be aware of?" Walker asks as we pile into the elevator and hit the button for the top floor.

"Well, there's this," Nine replies, and pulls a string of three emerald-green stones out of his pocket. I remember that thing from before—when Nine throws it, the string creates a miniature vacuum, sucks up whatever's close and then spits it violently back out. He must have taken it out of his Chest before turning over the rest of his Inheritance to Marina and Six.

"What does that do?" Walker asks.

"You'll see," I reply, looking at Nine. "You know there will be more waiting for us outside the elevator, right?"

"My thoughts exactly," he replies, grinning.

I pull Walker close so that we're pressed against the side of the elevator, right up against the buttons. Nine takes cover against the opposite wall, lazily swinging his string of stones like a bolo.

"You might need to hold on to me," I tell Walker. "You've seen how Nine does with gadgets."

"Hey," Nine says, wounded. "This one I actually know how to work."

Seconds later, the elevator doors open and a barrage of blaster fire hammers the elevator's back wall, the Mogs up here adopting a strategy of shoot first and ask questions later. Without poking his head out of cover, Nine tosses the strand of stones outside the elevator.

I imagine Nine's weapon working like it did back at the cabin—the beads hovering in a perfect circle, spinning slowly forward, sucking up anything in their path.

I can hear the whoosh of air, followed by Mogadorian screams, and a lot of futile shooting. Glass breaks as framed pictures are torn from the hallway walls, the pieces sucked into the miniature vacuum.

Nine snaps his fingers and everything the vacuum collected explodes outward. Violently expelled from the suction, one Mogadorian comes flying into the elevator. His head smashes hard against the back wall, his neck broken. Outside, everything is quiet.

When it's over, I stick my head outside the doors. The air is filled with swirling dust particles that might be Mogadorian remains. A blaster that somehow became wedged against the ceiling clatters to the floor. Aside from that, the only thing in the hallway is a room-service cart that looks like it's gone through a grinder, its legs bent and twisted. There's only one door at the end of the short hallway, the one for the penthouse, and it's now half broken off its hinges.

"What the hell was that thing?" Walker asks, incredulous.

"The Mogs aren't the only ones with kick-ass weaponry," Nine says, picking up the harmless-looking stone strand from where it landed on the floor.

"Don't get any ideas," I say to Walker when I catch her craning her neck to get a look at the stones. "Our technology isn't for sale."

Walker frowns at me. "Yeah, well, judging by that bullshit with the gloves, you don't know how to work it anyway."

From the broken doorway up ahead, I hear the droning of a television. It's turned to cable news, I think, some talking head rambling on about stock prices. Other than that, the hallway is totally quiet. There isn't any sign of more Mogadorians. Even so, we advance cautiously towards the penthouse door.

Wary of an ambush, I nudge the door with my telekinesis before we get too close. It comes off the hinges easily and falls into the penthouse with a thud. The living room inside is dark, all the curtains drawn, and lit only by the blue glow of the television.

"Come on in," a gravelly voice calls from inside. "There's no one in here who can hurt you."

"That's Sanderson," Walker whispers.

I exchange a quick look with Nine. He shrugs and waves towards the door. I go first, Nine right behind me and Walker bringing up the rear.

The first thing I notice is a damp, moldy smell in the hotel room. It smells like rot with an undercurrent of minty, old-man joint cream. A map of New York City is spread across the table in the suite's dining area, notes in Mogadorian scribbled at various locations. Next to the table is a knocked-over chair, as if someone got up in a hurry. There are also Mogadorian cannons propped up against one wall along with some dark canvas backpacks of gear—I notice a laptop, a few cell phones and a thick leather-bound book.

None of that interests me as much as the old man seated at the edge of the suite's slept-in king-size bed. He watches the TV through the open bedroom doorway, maybe too weak to walk himself into the penthouse's living room.

"Goddamn, dude," Nine exclaims, upon seeing Sanderson. "What is wrong with you?"

I've seen a lot of pictures of Bud Sanderson over the last few days. The first was on They Walk Among Us, Sanderson as an old man with thinning white hair, jowls and a paunch. On the website, in a tabloid-style story I didn't think too much about, Mark James accused Sanderson of using some kind of Mogadorian antiaging treatment. The next time I saw Sanderson was in Agent Walker's file, having lunch with a disguised Setrákus Ra, hale and hearty, silver hair full and slicked back, looking like he might jog a few miles after his Cobb salad.

The Sanderson in front of me doesn't look like either of those pictures. Nine and I walk into the bedroom to get a closer look, Walker lingering behind. The secretary of defense is a frail old man, his hunched body wrapped up in a puffy hotel robe. The right side of his face looks saggy and collapsed—his eye socket droops, and his jawline disappears beneath folds of loose skin. His white hair is badly thinned, a comb-over barely managing to hide a smattering of age spots. He smiles at us—or maybe it's a grimace—his teeth yellow, gums receding. In the open neck of his robe and along his forearms, I notice some prominent veins that are discolored black.

"Number Four and Number Nine," Sanderson says, pointing a shaky finger at me and then Nine. He doesn't seem offended at all by Nine's grossed-out reaction, doesn't even seem to have noticed. "Your pictures have been crossing my desk for years. Furtive shots from security cameras and the like. I practically watched you boys grow up."

Sanderson sounds like a reminiscent, doddering grandfather. I'm completely taken aback. I'd been expecting a sellout politician to try hitting me with talking points on Mogadorian Progress. This guy barely looks capable of getting up from his bed, much less giving a speech in front of the UN.

"And you . . ." Sanderson tilts his head to get a look at Walker. "You're one of mine, aren't you?"

"Special Agent Karen Walker," she replies, stepping into the doorway. "Not one of yours. I serve humanity now, sir."

"Well, that's nice," Sanderson says dismissively. He doesn't seem at all interested in her. The way his beady, black eyes settle on Nine and me, like we're his long-lost relatives gathered around his deathbed, makes me seriously uncomfortable. Even Nine has slipped into an awkward silence.

I notice a small kit on the bed next to Sanderson. It contains a few sleek syringes filled with a dark liquid that reminds me vaguely of Piken blood.

I take a step towards him, my voice low. "What did they do to you?"

"Nothing I didn't ask for," Sanderson replies, sadly. "I wish you boys would have found me sooner. Now it's too late."

"Like hell," Nine says.

"Even if you kill me, it won't make any difference," Sanderson rasps, resignedly.

"We're not here to kill you," I reply. "I don't know what they've told you, what they've filled your mind and body with, but we're not done fighting."

"Oh, but I am," Sanderson replies, and pulls a small handgun out of his robe's front pocket. Before I can stop him, he holds the pistol next to his temple and pulls the trigger.

CHAPTER TWENTY-ONE

IF I'D HAD TIME TO THINK ABOUT IT, I PROBably wouldn't have been able to do it.

There's about a millimeter of space between Bud Sanderson's temple and the barrel of his gun. It's in that space that I manage to stop the bullet, holding it there with my telekinesis. The precision required makes me grunt from exertion. Every muscle in my body is tensed, my fists clenched and toes curled. It's like I flung my entire body into stopping that bullet.

I can't believe I just did that. I've never done anything so precise before.

A ring-shaped burn from the pistol's barrel forms on Sanderson's temple, but otherwise his head is totally intact.

It takes until the pistol's report stops echoing for the secretary of defense to realize his suicide attempt didn't work. He blinks his watery eyes at me, not quite understanding why he's still alive.

"How—?"

Before Sanderson can pull the trigger again, Nine lunges forward and slaps the gun out of his hand. I exhale very slowly and allow my body to uncoil.

"That's not right," Sanderson says to me accusingly, his lower lip shaking as he rubs his wrist where Nine struck him. "Just let me die."

"Seriously," Walker interjects, her hands tightening around her own gun. "Why'd you stop him? Could've solved all our problems right there."

"It wouldn't have solved anything," I say, shooting her a look as I let the bullet drop harmlessly onto Sanderson's unmade bed.

"He's right," Sanderson says to Walker, his shoulders slumping. "Killing me won't change anything. But keeping me alive is simply cruel."

"You don't get to decide when you check out, old man," I tell Sanderson. "When we win this war, we'll let the people of Earth decide how they deal with traitors."

Sanderson chuckles dryly. "The optimism of youth."

I crouch down to look him in the face. "There's still time to redeem yourself," I say. "To do something of value."

Sanderson raises an eyebrow, and his eyes seem to focus up a bit. But then the right side of his mouth droops and he has to wipe away a blob of drool with the cuff of his robe. Looking utterly defeated, Sanderson averts his eyes.

"No," he says quietly. "I think not."

Nine sighs from boredom and picks up the kit of syringes laid out next to Sanderson. He studies the tar-colored sludge inside the injector for a moment, then waves it in Sanderson's face.

"What is this shit they're giving you, huh?" Nine asks. "This what you traded the planet for?"

Sanderson peers longingly at the vials but then weakly shoves them away.

"They healed me," Sanderson explains. "More than that. They made me young again."

"And look at you now," Nine grunts. "Fresh as a daisy, right?"

"You know their leader has lived for centuries," Sanderson counters, his eyes swinging wildly between me and Nine. "Of course you do. He promised us that. He promised immortality and power."

"He lied," I say.

Sanderson looks down at the floor. "Yes."

"Pathetic," Walker says, but the venom's gone out of her. Like me, I don't think Sanderson has turned out to be the villain Walker expected. Maybe he was once the puppet master of an international conspiracy in support of Mogs, but at this point he's been entirely chewed up and spit out by Mogadorian Progress. This isn't the game changer Walker was hoping for. I'm worried that we've wasted what precious little time we have left.

Sanderson ignores Nine and Walker. For some reason, maybe because I forced him to keep on living, he appeals directly to me. "The wonders they had to offer . . . can't you understand? I thought I was ushering in a golden age for humanity. How could I say no to them? To *him*?"

"And now you have to keep taking this stuff, is that it?" I ask, glancing to the syringes that I bet contain something like the unnatural genetic brew the Mogs use to grow their disposable soldiers. "If you stop, you'll break down like one of them."

"Old enough to turn to dust, anyway," Nine grumbles.

"It's been two days, and look at me . . ." Sanderson waves a hand at himself, at his body that looks like a slug with salt poured on it. "They used me. Kept giving me treatments in exchange for favors. But you freed me. Now I can finally die."

Nine throws up his hands and looks at me. "Dude, screw this. This guy's a lost cause. We need to figure something else out."

A sense of desperation begins to sink in now that Walker's lead on the secretary of defense has turned up only a broken old man and gotten us no closer to thwarting the imminent Mogadorian invasion. But I'm not willing to give up just yet. This lump sitting in front of me used to be a powerful man—hell, the Mogs had a protection detail on him, so he still is. There has to be a way to fix him, to make him willing to fight.

I need him to see the light.

Some combination of desperation and intuition causes me to turn on my Lumen. I don't crank it up to fire level; instead, I produce just enough juice so that a beam of pure light shoots from my hand. Sanderson's eyes widen and he inches back on the bed away from me.

"I already told you, I'm not going to hurt you," I say, as I lean in towards him.

I shine my Lumen on the palsied, saggy part of his face, wanting to get a good look at what I'm dealing with. The skin is grayed and almost dead looking, fine, ash-colored veins running through it. The dark particles under Sanderson's skin actually seem to float away from my Lumen, almost like they're trying to burrow deeper.

"I can heal this," I say, resolutely. I'm not sure if it's actually true, but I have to try.

"You—you can fix what they did?" Sanderson asks, a note of hope in his gravelly voice.

"I can make you like you were," I reply. "Not *better*,

in the way they promised. Not younger. Just . . . as you should be."

"Old people get old," Nine puts in. "You gotta deal with it."

Sanderson looks at me skeptically. I must sound just like the Mogadorians did years ago, when they first convinced him to join their side.

"What do you want in exchange?" he asks, like a high price is a foregone conclusion.

"Nothing," I reply. "You can try killing yourself again for all I care. Or maybe you can find what's left of your conscience and do what's right. It'll be up to you."

And with that, I press my palm against the side of Sanderson's face.

Sanderson shudders as the warm healing energy of my Legacy passes into him. Normally, when using my healing powers, I get a sensation that the injury is knitting itself back together, of cells rearranging themselves beneath my fingertips. With Sanderson, it feels as if a force is pushing back against my Legacy, as if there are dark, cellular pits into which my healing light plunges down and gutters out. I still feel Sanderson healing, but it's slow going, and I have to concentrate much harder than usual. At one point, something actually sizzles and pops beneath his skin, one of his discolored veins burning up. Sanderson flinches away from me.

"Are you hurt?" I ask, short of breath, my hand still

poised next to his face.

He hesitates. "No—no, it actually feels better. Somehow . . . cleaner. Keep going."

I keep going. I can feel the Mogadorian sludge burrowing deeper into Sanderson, retreating from my Legacy. I intensify my healing, chasing it through his veins. I find that I'm squinting from the exertion and a cold sweat dampens my back. I'm so focused on beating back the darkness I detect inside Sanderson that I must lose track of time or enter some kind of trance state.

When I'm finished at last, I stumble backwards, my legs wobbly, and run right into Sam. I wasn't even aware he'd come upstairs. He's holding out a phone—did he steal it from that bystander we knocked over?—and recording my healing of Sanderson. He stops when I bump into him and, for a moment, Sam is the only thing holding me up.

"That was awesome," Sam says. "You were, like, *glowing*. Are you okay?"

I draw myself up with some effort, not wanting to show any sign of weakness in front of Walker or Sanderson, even though I feel drained. "Yeah. I'm good."

I catch Walker staring at me with that same look of awe her driver had after I healed his neck. Sanderson, still sitting in front of me, looks close to tears. The black spiderwebs that crisscrossed beneath his skin have disappeared; his face no longer droops, his muscles aren't atrophied. He's still an old man, deep-set wrinkles lining his face, but he looks like a *real* old man, not one who's slowly had the life drained out of him.

He looks human.

"Thank you," Sanderson says to me, his words barely above a whisper.

Nine looks at me, checking to see how I'm holding up, then turns to Sanderson and snorts derisively. "It's all for nothing, Grandpa, if you let those pasty-faced asshats land on Earth."

"I'm ashamed of what I've done, what I became . . . ," Sanderson says, his gaze pleading and confused. "But I don't understand what you expect me to do. *Let* them? How can I stop them?"

"We don't expect you to stop them," I say, "just slow them down. You need to rally people against them. When you give your speech tomorrow at the UN, you need to make it clear that the Mogadorian fleet can't be allowed to land on Earth."

Sanderson stares at me, confused, then slowly swivels his gaze towards Walker. "Is that what your mole told you? Is that what you think will be happening tomorrow?"

"I *know* what's happening," Walker replies, no less caustic now that Sanderson seems to be coming around to our side. "You and the other leaders who the Mogs have bought off will get up onstage and convince the world we should coexist peacefully."

"Which is really just code for surrender," Nine adds.

"Yes, that's planned for tomorrow," Sanderson says, with a dark, hopeless laugh. "But you've got the order confused. You think I give some speech *and then* their Beloved Leader lands his ships? You think he cares about the slow-turning wheels of human politics? He's not waiting for *permission*. The UN will convene to save lives, to calm a frightened population, because a military resistance is doomed *against that*—"

Sanderson gestures wildly through the door, at the television still buzzing in the other room. Slowly, we each turn, leaving Sanderson's bedroom for the penthouse living room, drawn in by the ashen face of a cable news anchor. She stumbles over her words as she tries to explain the unidentified flying objects manifesting in the air over dozens of major cities. The reception goes in and out, the bursts of static getting more and more frequent, as something interferes with the signal.

". . . reports coming in that the ships have been sighted overseas as well, in places like London, Paris and Shanghai," the newscaster says, eyes wide as she reads from her teleprompter. "If you're just joining us, something literally out of this world is happening, as ships of alien origin have appeared over Los Angeles, Washington . . ."

"It's happening," Sam says, stunned, looking at me for some kind of guidance. "The warships are coming down. They're making their move."

I don't know what to tell him. Grainy footage of a massive Mogadorian warship sliding out of the clouds in the sky over Los Angeles appears on-screen. It's everything I dreaded, coming to pass. The Mogadorian fleet is gliding slowly towards a woefully unprepared Earth. It's Lorien, all over again.

"I tried to tell you," Sanderson calls to us. "It's already too late. They've already won. All that's left is surrender."

CHAPTER TWENTY-TWO

"I'M DONE DOING WHAT THEY TELL ME. WHAT *ANY* of them tell me."

My eyes snap open. I'd been in a deep sleep, one that I didn't think would be possible in my giant Mogadorian bed with its strange, slippery sheets. I'm becoming uncomfortably adjusted to life aboard the *Anubis*. I thought I heard a voice in my sleep, but maybe it was just my imagination, or the remnant of some dream. Not taking any chances, I stay very still and keep my breathing even, like I'm still asleep. If there is an intruder, I don't want them to know I'm awake.

After a few seconds of silence filled only by the ever-present hum of the warship's engines, a voice resumes speaking.

"One side drops us on this strange planet and basically forces us to fight for our lives. The other side, they talk about peace through progress, but that's all just fancy talk for killing anyone who stands in their way."

It's Five. He's in my room somewhere. I can't locate him in the near darkness. I can only hear his mumbled under-the-breath rambling. I'm not even sure if he's talking to me.

"They all just wanted to use us," Five hisses. "But I'm not going to let them. I'm not going to fight in their stupid war."

He shifts then, and I can finally make out Five's outline. He's sitting on the edge of my bed, his skin the dark, slick texture of my sheets. He blends right in to my covers, and it must be because he's touching them, using his Externa. That means his Legacies are back. It also means that he's seriously creeping me out, like a monster came crawling out from under my bed.

"I know you're awake," Five says to me without turning his head. "The ship is descending, we aren't in orbit anymore. If you want to go, now is the time."

I scoot up in bed, keeping the covers close. For a second, I consider making Five powerless again by charging the sheets with my Dreynen. But what good would that do? I decide not to attack him. For now.

"I thought you were on their side," I say. "Why would you help me?"

"I'm not on anybody's side. I'm done with this whole thing."

"What do you mean, *done*?"

"For a while, after my Cêpan died, I was alone. It wasn't

so bad. I'd like to go back to that," Five says. "You know how many little islands there are in the oceans? I'm going to pick one out and stay there until this is over. I don't give a shit who wins, so long as they stay far away from me."

"That's cowardly," I reply, shaking my head. "I'm not going to some deserted island with you."

Five snorts. "I didn't invite you, Ella. I'm getting off this ship and I thought you might want to come along. That's as far as we go."

I consider the possibility that this could be some kind of test orchestrated by Setrákus Ra. But remembering the way Five acted earlier, I decide to take my chances that he's for real. I hop out of bed and pull on my thin-soled Mogadorian slippers.

"Okay, what's your plan?"

Five stands up and his skin reverts to normal. As the automatic lights come on in my room, I can finally see his face. He's changed the bandage over his eye so that it isn't crusty with blood anymore, but he still hasn't gotten it healed. His remaining eye twinkles like he's excited to get into some trouble. Seeing him makes me second-guess my decision to join forces.

"I'm going to open up one of the airlocks and jump out," Five says, illustrating his brilliant plan.

"That's nice for you. You can *fly*. What am I supposed to do?"

Five reaches into his back pocket and casually tosses me

a round object. I catch the stone in my hands and cradle it. I recognize it as one of the objects from John's Chest.

"Xitharis stone," Five explains. "I, uh, borrowed it from our friends."

"You stole it."

He shrugs. "I charged it with my flight Legacy. Use it to fly off and save the planet."

I hide the stone inside my dress, then look up at Five. "So that's it? You think we're just going to walk off this ship?"

Five raises an eyebrow at me. I notice that he's not wearing any shoes or socks, probably so his bare feet are in constant contact with the metal paneling of the *Anubis*. Also, attached to his forearm is some kind of contraption that looks like it might be a weapon.

"They won't be able to stop me," Five says, a dark confidence in his voice. It isn't exactly inspiring, but it's the best hope I've got.

"Okay, lead the way."

The door to my room slides open for Five. He pokes his head out, checking to see that the coast is clear. When he's satisfied, Five hustles into the hallway, motioning for me to follow. We navigate the labyrinthine halls of the *Anubis* at a brisk walk.

"Just act normal," Five tells me, keeping his voice low. "He's got scouts watching us, always. But they're also afraid of us. You, in particular, are supposed to be treated like royalty. They won't interfere if we don't look suspicious. And, even if they do think something's wrong, by the time one of them actually works up the guts to tell Beloved Leader, we'll be gone . . ."

He's talking a lot. That tells me that he's nervous. Without thinking about it—because if I actually thought about it, I might get too repulsed—I reach out and take Five's hand.

"We're just a newly betrothed couple, getting to know each other," I say. "Enjoying a nice walk through the cozy halls of a massive warship."

Five's hand is sweaty and cold. He tries to jerk away from me, his initial instinct not to be touched, but after a moment he calms down and lets his dead-fish hand be held.

"Betrothed?" he grunts. "He wants us to get married?"

"That's what Setrákus Ra said."

"He says a lot of things." Five's face is red, the blush traveling all the way up into his scalp. I'm not sure if he's embarrassed or angry or some combination of the two. "I didn't agree to that. You're a *child*."

"Um, obviously I didn't agree either. You're a gross, murdering, weirdo—"

"Shut up," Five hisses, and for a second I think that I've actually offended him. But then I realize we're passing by the open entranceway of the observation deck.

I can't help but slow my steps as we sneak by. The empty

darkness of space I'd gotten used to has been replaced by the familiar, bright-blue atmosphere of Earth. The *Anubis* is still making its descent, but already the outline of civilization is visible, roads boxing up green fields, tiny houses arranged into perfect suburbs. Dozens of Mogadorians have gathered to watch Earth approach, an excited energy in the air as they whisper to one another, probably talking about which swath of land they'll pillage first.

Five leads me around the next corner and crashes right into two Mog warriors who were jogging towards the observation deck. The nearest one lifts a corner of his mouth in a disdainful sneer, eyeing us.

"What are you two doing?" the Mog asks.

In response, I draw myself up, trying to look as regal as possible. I fix the overcurious Mog with a cold stare. The Mog's sneer quickly fades as he remembers himself—or, more likely, remembers that I'm not just some Lorien but the blood of his Beloved Leader—and he looks down at the floor. He begins to mutter something apologetic when a metallic *shink* cuts him off.

A needlelike blade extends from the leather contraption on Five's forearm. In a blur, Five drives the blade right through the first Mog's forehead, instantly turning him to ash. The other Mog's eyes widen in panic and he tries to run. A delighted grin spreads across Five's face. Before the Mog can get even a few steps down the hall, Five's non-blade arm takes on a rubbery consistency and stretches after him. Five's arm snakes around the Mog's neck and then yanks him backwards so Five can finish him off with his blade.

The whole thing is over in about ten seconds.

"We were supposed to be acting normal," I say to Five in a loud whisper, mindful that we're not all that far from the crowded observation room.

Five blinks at me, almost like he's not sure what just came over him. Carefully, he presses the blade back into its holster.

"I lost my cool, okay?" Five anxiously rubs his hand across the stubble on top of his head. "It doesn't matter now. We're almost there."

I stare at this unhinged monster standing in front of me. He gulps down a few deep breaths, his shoulders shaking, fists balled from the excitement. Minutes ago, he sounded almost fragile, rambling in the darkness of my room. He's broken, a total mess—I have to remind myself that he murdered Eight in order to squelch the swelling of sympathy I feel for him. Sympathy, yes, but also fear. He flew off the handle with zero provocation, and almost seemed happy killing those Mogs.

This screwed-up, violent, cowardly traitor is my only real hope of getting off the *Anubis*.

I shake my head. "Let's go," I sigh.

Five nods and we jog on, tossing out the whole hand-holding thing, and just careening towards our destination.

As we run, I notice Five clenching and unclenching his hands. They're both empty.

"How'd you do that with your arm?" I ask him, thinking about those rubber and steel balls he used to change his skin in the Lecture Hall. "I thought you needed to be touching something . . ."

Five turns his head so his good eye is on me. He touches the fresh bandage over his face.

"Losing an eye gave me some new, uh . . . storage possibilities," he says.

"Ugh," I reply, grossed out as I picture the rubber ball shoved into Five's eye socket. "How'd you lose it, anyway?"

"Marina," he answers, simply, no malice in his voice. "I had it coming."

"I'm sure."

We round the next corner, and the hallway opens up, the ceiling rising as we enter the huge docking bay. I can see crisp, blue sky through the portholes, sunlight pouring across the dozens of docked Mogadorian scout vessels. Other than the ships, the docking bay is empty. The mechanics and crew must be on the observatory deck, gazing out upon the world they plan to conquer.

We're so close.

"Hold on," I say. "If we open the airlock, are we going to be sucked out right away?"

"We're in the atmosphere now, not space," Five says impatiently. He leans over a nearby console, studying the interface. "It'll be windy. You're not going to chicken out, are you?"

"No," I say, looking around the docking bay. "Do you think we could blow some of this stuff up? Maybe bring down the *Anubis* before it has a chance to do anything?"

Five turns to me, looking slightly impressed. "You have any explosive Legacies?"

"No."

"Me neither. Know how to make a bomb?"

"Uh, no."

"Then we're going to have to settle for escaping," Five says. Five hits a button on the console and a thick metal door thuds into place behind us. It's the airlock—sturdy enough to keep the ship safe from the vacuum of space. It effectively seals us off from the rest of the ship.

"That'll slow them down," Five says, referring to pursuers we don't yet have.

"Good thinking," I admit as I peer through the small window on the airlock, expecting to see Mogs chasing us down at any moment.

Five taps out a few more keystrokes and, with a hydraulic whine and a gust of chilled air, the docking-bay doors at the far end of the room open up. The wind pulls at me and I let out a deep, relieved sigh. I reach into my dress and remove the Xitharis stone, clutching it. Slowly, I walk towards the open dock, wondering what it'll be like to pitch myself into that open blue sky. Way better than life on the *Anubis*, that's for sure.

"So, I just hold this stone and fly?" I ask, looking over my shoulder at Five.

"Supposed to be how it works," he answers. "Just imagine your body light as a feather, floating on air. That's how I learned to use my Legacy, anyway."

I glance towards the open air, the cloudless sky waiting for me.

"What if it doesn't work?"

Five starts towards me, sighing. "Come on. We'll go together."

"You won't be going anywhere."

Setrákus Ra steps out from between two of the ships. I'm not sure if he's been there the whole time, waiting for us, or if he just teleported into the room somehow. Either way—it doesn't matter. We're caught. Still in his human form, Setrákus Ra stands between us and the open docking bay, the wind gently blowing through his perfect brown hair, plucking at the lapels of his suit. He holds his golden staff—the Eye of Thaloc—in one hand.

Five puts a hand on my shoulder and tries to push me behind him. I shake him off. We face Setrákus Ra side by side.

"Get out of our way, old man," Five growls. He's trying to sound tough, but he can barely manage to meet Setrákus Ra's eyes.

"I will not," Setrákus Ra replies, his voice full of scorn

and disappointment. "I expected this kind of behavior from you, Ella. You have only recently joined us and it will take time to undo the brainwashing you endured at the hands of the Garde. But, Five, my boy, after everything I have done for you—"

"Shut up," Five says quietly, almost pleading. "You talk and talk and talk, but none of it's true!"

"Mine is the only truth," Setrákus Ra counters sternly. "You will be punished for your insolence."

Five still can't bring himself to look directly at Setrákus Ra, but his shoulders rise up and down rapidly, just like in the hallway with the Mog warriors. Inside his chest, a low rumble starts to build. It reminds me of a teakettle coming to a boil. I take a subtle step to the side, worried that Five might literally explode.

"Enough of this inanity, children," Setrákus Ra says, but his latest rebuke is partly drowned out by the rabid scream that tears loose from Five's lungs.

And then he charges.

At first, Five's bare feet make slapping sounds across the metal deck. But as he nears Setrákus Ra, his footfalls become metal clanging against metal, his Externa changing his skin to match the floor. Setrákus Ra merely raises an eyebrow at Five, not impressed or intimidated in the least.

I don't just stand around and watch. While Five charges in, I make a break for one of the nearby tool carts. If I can grab a wrench or any other object to charge with my

Dreynen, maybe I can re-create yesterday's lesson. Only this time, my target will be Setrákus Ra.

That plan, along with whatever Five intended to do, gets scrapped when Setrákus Ra sweeps his arm from side to side. A wave of telekinetic force blasts across us, knocking me completely off my feet and scattering the nearby tools to the far wall. His telekinesis is so powerful that some of the ships even rock to the side, their shocks grinding and creaking.

I land hard on my stomach and immediately roll over to reorient myself. Five was knocked into the air, too, but caught himself with his flight Legacy. He floats just a few yards from Setrákus Ra. Five's skin is no longer the dull gray of the docking-bay floor. It has changed to a glistening chrome, like the ball bearing I know he carries around. So that must be jammed into his eye socket as well.

"Stop at once," Setrákus Ra warns, but Five is way past the point of listening.

Five soars in towards Setrákus Ra, throwing big, looping punches with the intention of smashing his pretty human face. Setrákus Ra deflects the blows easily with his cane, although Five's sheer animalistic fury is enough to drive Setrákus Ra back towards the open docking-bay doors.

Their scuffle opens up a path for me. Let these two crazies duke it out. All I have to do is make a break for it, dive into the open blue sky, and hope the Xitharis stone does what Five said.

Just when I start to make my move, I notice Setrákus Ra's eyes flash. I feel an invisible field of energy pass over me, almost like the pressure in the room has changed. As he's in the middle of throwing a punch, Five's skin turns back to normal. His fist crunches against Setrákus Ra's upraised cane. At the same moment, Five falls out of the air with a shout.

It's just like at Dulce Base. Setrákus Ra has created some kind of field that cancels Legacies. He's an Aeturnus like me, and now I know that Setrákus Ra and I also share Dreynen. His technique is different from anything I've been able to learn. It's like he's charged the molecules in the air around him, creating a radius where Legacies are useless.

Except it doesn't work on me. I can still feel my Dreynen lurking within me, and I know that I could use my Aeturnus if I wanted. Somehow, I'm immune to Setrákus Ra's version of Dreynen. Is it because we're related? Or is one of my Legacies an immunity to Setrákus Ra? He said all that crap about our Legacies coming randomly and Lorien being nothing but chaos. But what if he's wrong and my Legacies have been specifically chosen to destroy him? More important—does Setrákus Ra know that his power doesn't affect me?

In that moment, Setrákus Ra isn't paying me any attention at all. He's completely focused on Five. I know I should make a break for it, but I find myself rooted in place. Even after everything he's done, can I really leave Five behind?

Five is on his knees in front of Setrákus Ra, clutching his injured hand to his belly. Setrákus Ra's unimposing human form has grown by a few feet—he's taller and broader now, inflated in a way that is vaguely grotesque. He reaches down and palms Five's head in one unnaturally large hand.

"All you needed to do was follow orders," Setrákus Ra seethes at Five. He jerks Five's head back so he can look him in the face. "We could have walked into the Sanctuary together, if you'd only brought me that damned pendant. And now, this—you *dare* raise a hand against your Beloved Leader. You disgust me, boy."

I don't know what Setrákus Ra means by *Sanctuary*, but I make a mental note of it. I also take a step towards him and Five, still torn between fleeing and helping, and uncertain of what I could even do in a fight against the Mogadorian ruler.

Five's head is cocked at an awkward angle, so he can only gurgle in response to Setrákus Ra's ranting.

"I should have known that no member of the Garde could truly be salvaged," Setrákus Ra continues. "You are my greatest failure, Five. But you will be my last."

Five cries out as Ra's hand tightens on his skull. My stomach turns over as I realize he's literally going to crush Five's head. I can't let that happen.

With all the telekinetic force I can muster, I shove Setrákus Ra towards the open docking-bay doors.

His eyes widen in surprise as he stumbles backwards,

the open air tugging at his fancy suit, which is now bulging at the seams from his inhuman growth spurt. Setrákus Ra loses his grip on Five's head, his nails scratching divots into his scalp. He manages to stop himself before I push him off the *Anubis*, and I can feel his telekinesis battle back against mine.

"Ella, how—," he starts to ask, surprise mixing with frustration.

But then Five is charging at him, his forearm blade extended.

"Die!" Five bellows. Setrákus Ra tries to step aside but can't entirely avoid Five. The blade plunges into his shoulder.

I scream as a piercing jolt of pain courses through me.

A hole in my shoulder opens up, warm blood pouring down my front. I stagger against one of the nearby ships, clutching the wound, trying to stop the bleeding with my fingers.

Five recoils from Setrákus Ra, his eyes wide. The Mogadorian looks unharmed. Setrákus Ra smiles as Five turns to gape at me. I'm run through right where he should've stabbed Setrákus Ra.

"Now look what you did," Setrákus Ra chides.

The Mogadorian charm, I realize, even as I start to feel faint. Any damage done to Setrákus Ra is instead done to me.

Five looks horrified by what he's done. Before he can

react, Setrákus Ra picks him up by the throat and slams the back of his head violently against the hull of the nearest ship. He does this again and again, until Five's body is limp.

Then, callously, Setrákus Ra tosses his unconscious body out the open doors of the *Anubis*. I try to reach Five with my telekinesis, but I'm too weak. His body plummets out of sight, towards the Earth below.

I collapse to the floor, blood seeping through my fingers. All the strength has gone out of me. I won't be escaping from the *Anubis* today. My grandfather has won.

Setrákus Ra stands over me, his human form returned to normal, although his suit is ruined. He shakes his head, his smile like a disappointed teacher.

"Come now, Ella," he says. "We must put this episode behind us."

I hold up my blood-covered hand for him to see. "Why? Why did you do this to me?"

"It was the only way for you to learn that Mogadorian Progress is more important than even your own life," he replies. Setrákus Ra gathers me up in his arms. As I start to lose consciousness, he whispers gently. "You won't disobey Beloved Leader again, will you?"

CHAPTER TWENTY-THREE

ADAM'S FLIGHT PLAN IS TO TAKE US DOWN THE Atlantic coast until we hit Florida, then dip back west over the gulf and finally arrive at the southeastern tip of Mexico. With the Skimmer flying at maximum speed and staying low enough to avoid any other aircraft, the trip should take about four hours.

It's a quiet ride. I lean back in my seat and watch the coast ebb and flow beneath us. Adam doesn't say much of anything; he keeps his eyes straight ahead, occasionally adjusting our course when his systems pick up another aircraft. Dust naps on the floor at his feet. As for Marina, she remains typically rigid, her whole fear-of-flying thing not getting any better with a Mogadorian at the controls.

"You know, you can rest for a few hours," Adam suggests eventually, his tone cautious. I'd already been close to dozing off, so he must be talking to Marina. She's sitting straight backed, a slight chill coming off her. She must be looming right in the corner of Adam's eye.

Marina seems to consider this for a moment, then leans forward so that her head is nearly on Adam's shoulder. He raises an eyebrow, but otherwise keeps his hands on the controls.

"The last trip Six and I made south was less than a week ago," Marina says, her voice measured. "We found out too late that we had a traitor traveling with us. I ended up stabbing him in the eye. That was me being *merciful*."

"I know what happened in Florida," Adam says. "Why are you telling me this?"

"Because I want you to know what will happen if you betray us," Marina replies, leaning back. "And don't tell me to *rest*."

Adam looks over at me for help, but I shrug my shoulders and turn away. Marina's still figuring out just how angry she wants to be, and I'm not going to get in her way. Besides, I don't think putting a little fear in our Mogadorian companion is such a bad thing.

I assume he's just going to let the conversation die, but after a few minutes Adam speaks up. "Yesterday, for the first time I picked up a sword that's been in my family for generations. I'd never been allowed to touch it before, only admire it from afar. It belonged to my father, General Andrakkus Sutekh. He was fighting Number Four—John. I drove that sword through my father's back and killed him."

Adam delivers this speech matter-of-factly, like he's reading the news. I blink at him, then glance over my shoulder at Marina. She's looking down at the floor, deep in thought. As the chill rising off her begins to die down, Dust picks himself up and goes over to her. The wolf rests his head in Marina's lap.

"Cool story," I say to Adam when it becomes painfully clear that someone needs to break the silence. "I've never known anyone who carried around a sword before."

"*Cool*," Adam repeats, frowning. "My point is, you don't need to doubt my loyalty."

"I'm sorry you had to do that to your father," Marina says after a moment. "I didn't know."

"I'm not," Adam replies brusquely. "But thanks for the sympathy."

To break the tension, I start messing with some of the dials on the Skimmer's console. "Does this thing have a freaking radio, or what? Are we just going to tell death stories the whole way?"

Adam is quick to readjust the dials right after me. I think I catch him smiling a little, probably relieved that the death-threat portion of the trip is over.

"There's no radio," he says. "I can hum some Mogadorian standards, if you'd like."

"Oh, barf," I reply, and Marina snickers in the backseat.

I realize Adam is giving me a funny look, his angular face more open than I've seen, that defensive stoicism he wears stripped away. For a moment, he almost looks comfortable being up here with two of his mortal enemies.

"What?" I ask, and he hurriedly looks away. I realize his mind was elsewhere.

"Nothing," he says, almost wistful. "For a second there, you just reminded me of someone I used to know."

The rest of the flight south is uneventful. I manage to doze off once or twice, although never for long. With Dust snuggled up against her, it seems like Marina is finally able to relax. Adam refrains from humming any Mogadorian anthems.

We're flying over the tropical forest of Campeche, Mexico, just another hour away from the Loric Sanctuary supposedly hidden amid the ruins of an ancient Mayan city, when a red warning light begins to flash on the Skimmer's translucent windshield. I only notice it when Adam tenses up.

"Damn it," he says, and immediately starts flicking switches on the Skimmer's control panel.

"What is it?"

"Someone's locked on to us."

The cameras mounted on the Skimmer send images to our screen, views from the underside of the ship and behind us becoming visible. I don't see anything but cloudless blue sky and the dense canopy of the forest beneath us.

"Where are they coming from?" Marina asks, squinting as she peers through the window.

"There," Adam says, jabbing his finger at the screen. On it, a Mogadorian scout ship just like ours drifts slowly towards us from below. Its roof is painted in overlapping shades of greens, camouflaged to match the forest it detached from.

"Can we outrun it?" Marina asks.

"I can try," Adam replies, pulling down the lever to give our Skimmer some more juice.

"Or we can just shoot it down," I suggest.

As we pick up a little speed, the blinking red light on the console multiplies into four blinking red lights. There are more of them. Two identical Skimmers rise up from the jungle right in front of us, another along our side. The first still sits right on our tail. Hemmed in, Adam has no choice but to stop. The other Skimmers surround us.

"They all have guns, too, right?" Marina asks.

"Yes," Adam replies. "We're at a distinct disadvantage."

"Not quite," I say, and focus on the sky outside. What was cloudless a moment ago slowly begins to darken, clouds rolling in at my beckoning.

"Hold on," Adam warns. "We don't want to give away you're all on board."

"You're sure they won't shoot us down?"

"Ninety percent," Adam says.

I let go of the storm I was whipping up, allowing the clouds to drift through the sky along their natural course.

A second later, a shrill beep emanates from our dashboard.

"They're hailing us," Adam says. "They want to talk."

Another plan has occurred to me, one that doesn't involve fighting a midair battle against bad odds.

"You said you're some general's kid, right?" I say to Adam. "So can't you, like, throw your weight around or something?"

As Adam considers this, the dashboard communicator bleats again.

"I should tell you, I'm not exactly well liked among my people," he says. "They might not listen to me."

"Yeah, well, that's a risk," I admit. "Worst-case scenario, they take you prisoner, right?"

Adam grimaces. "Yeah."

"So, we let them take us where we're going. Don't worry. We'll rescue you."

"Uh, you need to do *something*," Marina says, waving towards the windshield. The ship directly in front of us, getting impatient or suspicious, has brought its blaster turret around to aim at us.

"All right, go invisible," Adam says. I reach around my seat and grasp Marina's hand, disappearing the both of us. Sensing the situation, Dust shrinks down into a tiny gray mouse and skitters under Adam's seat.

Adam hits a button on the console, and a video feed crackles to life on our screen. A nasty-looking Mogadorian scout, his empty eyes too close together, his teeth short and sharp, stares at Adam with a look of fierce annoyance. He barks something in harsh Mogadorian.

"Immersion protocol dictates we speak English while on Earth, you vatborn cretin," Adam replies coldly. He draws himself up in his chair, suddenly so regal that I kinda want to slap him. "You are addressing Adamus Sutekh, trueborn son of General Andrakkus Sutekh. I am on urgent business from my father. Lead me to the Loric site immediately."

I have to give it to Adam, he's an excellent bullshitter. The scout's expression goes from annoyance to confusion and finally to outright fear.

"Yes, sir, right away," the scout replies, and in response Adam immediately cuts off the conversation. One by one, the Skimmers break up the ring they had us trapped inside and let us get back on course.

"That worked," Marina says, sounding a little stunned as she lets go of my hand.

"For now," Adam replies, frowning uncertainly. "He was low ranking. Whoever's in command will be a different story."

"Can't you just tell them your dad sent you down here to check their progress?" I ask.

"Assuming they don't know I betrayed our people and that my father essentially sentenced me to die? Yeah, that might work."

"You only need to distract them for a little bit," I say.

"Long enough for Marina and me to figure a way into the Sanctuary."

"There it is," Marina says, watching through the window as the Skimmers begin to descend towards Calakmul.

There are a bunch of ancient little buildings below, all of them constructed from limestone that's been eroding for centuries, the jungle creeping in to reclaim them. My eyes are drawn to the huge pyramid-shaped temple that towers over them all; built on a low hill, the temple is blocky, covered in steep and crumbling staircases that are chiseled right into the stone. I can't quite make it out from this distance, but there appears to be some kind of door at the top of the pyramid.

"How much you want to bet we need to climb up to that thing?" I say.

"It's the Sanctuary," Marina replies. "I'm certain of it."

"So are my people, obviously," Adam says.

The Mogadorians have cleared the jungle around the Sanctuary in a perfect ring, the trees all chopped down, an entire fleet of Mogadorian scout ships parked on the naked soil. Besides the dozens of Skimmers, I can make out an array of tents where the Mogs must be camping. There's also what looks to be a couple of heavy-duty missile launchers and blaster turrets, all of these weapons aimed at the temple, and yet the structure looks completely untouched. Oddly, at the base of the temple and creeping up the sides, there are still overgrown trees and vines, untended for years. It's a stark contrast to the severe neatness of the Mogadorian perimeter, where everything natural has been cleared away.

"It's like something kept them from getting too close," Marina says, noticing the same thing as me.

"Malcolm did say that only the Garde could enter," I reply.

Our escort of Mog ships float down to the makeshift airfield and Adam lands a few yards away from them. The Sanctuary looms in the distance. The only thing standing between us and the Loric temple is a strip of wide-open land and a small army of Mogadorians, many of whom have begun gathering in the airfield, all of them armed with blasters.

"Some welcoming committee," I say, glancing at Adam. He watches his people mass on the monitor, swallows hard and unbuckles himself from the pilot's seat.

"All right, I'll go first. Lead them away somehow. You guys get into the Sanctuary."

"I don't like this," Marina says. "There's a lot of them."

"It'll be fine," Adam says. "Just get inside and do what you have to do."

With that, Adam opens the cockpit and hops onto the Skimmer's hull. There are about thirty Mogadorians down below, waiting on him, with more walking over from the tents. Marina and I hunker down inside the Skimmer, my hand close to hers in case we need to go invisible.

"Who's in charge here?" Adam yells, standing tall and rigid, again putting on his trueborn airs.

A tall female warrior dressed in a sleeveless black overcoat steps forward. She has two thick braids that start on the sides of her head and wrap around it, encircling the traditional Mogadorian tattoos on her scalp. Her hands are wrapped in dusty white bandages, like they've recently been injured or burned.

"I am Phiri Dun-Ra, trueborn daughter of the honorable Magoth Dun-Ra," the warrior shouts to Adam. Her posture is nearly as imposing and rigid as his. "Why have you come here, Sutekh?"

Adam hops down from our ship, tossing his head to flip his hair out of his eyes.

"Orders from Beloved Leader himself. I am to inspect this site to prepare for his arrival."

A tremor passes through the crowd when Adam mentions Setrákus Ra. Many of the Mogs exchange nervous glances. Phiri Dun-Ra, however, appears nonplussed. She strides forward, letting her blaster dangle idly next to her hip. Something tightens up in my stomach at the sight of her. The predatory way she moves, the glint in her eye like trouble could spark at any moment. She's way sharper than the other Mog warriors I've encountered.

"Ah, Beloved Leader. Of course," Phiri says. She waves to the temple in the distance. "What would you like to see first, sir?"

Adam takes a step towards the Mog camp and opens his mouth to speak. Smoothly, without warning, Phiri lifts her blaster and cracks Adam across the mouth with the handle. As he falls to the ground, the rest of the Mogadorians level their blasters at him in unison.

"How about the inside of a cell, traitor?" Phiri snarls, standing over Adam, her blaster pointed at his face.

CHAPTER TWENTY-FOUR

I EXTEND MY HAND TO MARINA AND SHE GRASPS it immediately. Invisible, we carefully climb out of the ship, synchronizing our movements. Behind us, I hear a sudden flapping of wings. Dust takes flight in the shape of a tropical bird, his wings flecked with gray. None of the Mogs notice him soar out of the cockpit, and they don't hear Marina and me leap down to the ground.

They're too distracted by the show Phiri Dun-Ra is putting on with Adam.

"I know your father, Sutekh," Phiri is saying, projecting her voice so that the Mogs gathered in a semicircle around her and Adam can all hear. "He's a bastard, but at least he's noble. He believes in Mogadorian Progress."

If Adam manages a reply, I can't hear it over the murmur of agreement that comes from the other Mogs. I catch a glimpse of him through the crowd—he's crumpled at Phiri's feet, scrabbling in the dirt, trying to regain his feet but probably still seeing stars.

"In fact, your father gave me this assignment," Phiri continues. "I was responsible for a team that allowed a Garde to escape from the West Virginia stronghold. The punishment was either death or a journey here. Not much of a choice, really. You see, if we fail, we'll all be executed anyway. The only way to live is for us to deliver the *Sanctuary.*"

At the word "Sanctuary," Phiri makes a sarcastically dramatic gesture with her two bandaged hands that encompasses the whole of the temple. I hesitate for a moment to listen to what else she has to say.

"There's not a day goes by that I don't wonder if I made the wrong decision. Maybe a quick death would have been better. You see, Sutekh, all of us were sent here as punishment," Phiri explains. It occurs to me that she's not just talking to Adam—she's also trying to fire up her troops. Maybe morale gets low in the jungle. "We were sent to this forsaken place to bring down the impenetrable shield that surrounds whatever spoils the Loric have hidden within. For all of us, it is our last chance to impress Beloved Leader. It's the perfect place for a traitor like you."

Phiri crouches down in front of Adam.

"So do you know the secret to the Sanctuary? Have you come here to redeem yourself at last?"

"Yeah," comes Adam's groggy reply. "If it's a force field, try throwing yourself at it."

Phiri actually laughs at Adam's quip. It's that laugh that gets me moving again—it has an air of menace to it, like her little sideshow is about to wrap up. That means we have to hurry.

I tug Marina and we slip behind the gathered Mogadorians. Adam's created one hell of a diversion—if we were sticking to the plan, we could make it inside the perimeter of the Sanctuary easily. But I'm not willing to leave Adam to his fate, and I don't think Marina is either. Instead of heading for the temple, we move swiftly towards one of the mounted blaster turrets that the Mogs have been using to fruitlessly fire at whatever force protects the Sanctuary.

"Throw myself at it," Phiri is repeating, her laughter dying down. "That isn't such a bad idea, Sutekh. Why don't you go first?"

Out of the corner of my eye, I notice Phiri signal to a couple of the warriors in her command. They hustle forward and wrestle Adam to his feet. With Phiri leading the way, the Mogs drag Adam towards the invisible line that divides the cleared Mogadorian section of jungle with the untouched portion surrounding the temple.

"We've tried everything short of atomic bombardment to cross into the Sanctuary," Phiri says, conversationally. "It's said Beloved Leader knows a way in. It involves the Garde and their little pendants. As you know, they've proven to be . . . elusive. But if you believe the Great Book—and I do—then you know nothing can stand in the way of Mogadorian Progress. Which means this damned force field will come down. I intend to trample whatever Loric magic is keeping us out, in the name of Beloved Leader."

"Then why haven't you done it already?" Adam replies. "If nothing can stand in the way of Mogadorian Progress, why aren't you making any?"

"Maybe because I never had a pretty trueborn boy's face to use as a battering ram."

Marina and I reach the nearest turret. Together, we climb up the steps on the back of the blaster. The thing looks like a mounted jackhammer. There is a windshield with a crosshairs placed over the barrel. There are two handles for turning the gun, with triggers that look like the brakes of a bicycle set next to them.

"Will you be able to fire this thing?" I whisper to Marina.

"Aim, squeeze, shoot," Marina whispers back. "It's pretty intuitive, Six."

"All right," I reply. "Hold on."

The gun turret requires two hands to operate. Even though all the Mogs are facing away from us, I don't want to go visible and chance one of them glancing back and ruining our ambush. I carefully place my hand on the back of Marina's neck before letting go of her hand. This way, she's able to operate the turret while the two of us still remain invisible. Slowly, Marina starts moving the turret so that it's pointed at the Mogs. The gun needs oiling—it makes a metallic whine when she moves it. I wave my free hand in the air and quickly summon a strong gust of wind to cover the sound.

"Let me give you a preview of what you're in for," Phiri is saying. She's got Adam right in front of the invisible barrier now, her goons forcing him onto his knees. She unwraps the bandages around one of her hands, revealing horribly charred flesh. "This is what the Loric shield does when we mistakenly run up against it."

"You should be more careful," Adam replies.

At a nod from Phiri, the two warriors grapple Adam into a half-bent position, securing his arm so that they can press it against the force field.

Phiri leers down at Adam. "There are rumors about you, Sutekh. They say you're part Garde now. Maybe you're just what we need to get into the Sanctuary. Maybe a freak like you will short-circuit the force field and today will be the day we enter the Sanctuary in the name of Beloved Leader."

"One way or another, today's your last day at the Sanctuary," Adam replies through gritted teeth. "I promise you that."

Adam's words make Phiri hesitate. She glances back towards our ship, suddenly realizing that maybe Adam didn't come alone. She's too late.

Marina has the turret lined up on the crowd of Mogs.

"Ready?" she whispers to me.

"Light 'em up."

Marina's invisible hands squeeze down the turret's triggers. The gun roars to life with such force that I'm nearly knocked off the back. I manage to cling to Marina so that she doesn't turn visible. The closest group of Mogs don't even have a chance to turn around as glowing columns of sizzling blaster fire pummel their backs, turning them immediately to ash.

As soon as Marina opens fire, Dust comes screeching down from the sky. Now in the shape of a gray-winged falcon, the Chimæra rakes its talons across the face of one of the warriors holding Adam.

The Mogs shout and scatter. They're totally confused—it must look like their turret has been possessed by a ghost. Phiri Dun-Ra has the presence of mind to squeeze off some blaster fire that deflects off the turret's windshield, but then she ducks for cover. Marina continues to strafe them, although she's careful to avoid the area around Adam.

With Dust taking down one of the warriors, Adam elbows his second captor in the stomach. When he doubles over, Adam shoves him backwards, right into the invisible border around the Sanctuary. With a flare of cold, blue energy, the shield surrounding the temple reveals itself—it's like a giant electrical web stretched into the shape of a dome. The Mog flares up like the tip of a matchstick when he hits the force field. His body leaves a coating of ash that seems to float in the air once the shield disappears again, until a gentle gust of wind blows it away.

Freed from his captors, Adam throws himself onto his stomach. Right away, Marina swings the turret around to take out the Mogs cluttered around him. A few of them, including Phiri Dun-Ra, have made it to the cover of one of the parked ships. Even though they can't see us, they return fire on the turret. Our gun soon begins to belch smoke and rattle dangerously.

"It's overheating!" I yell. "Jump!"

Marina and I dive in opposite directions as the turret explodes in a cloud of acrid black smoke. We're visible and without any cover to speak of.

Before the surviving Mogs can take aim, Adam pounds his fist against the ground. A tremor ripples in their direction and knocks the Mogs off their feet. I use the distraction to roll beneath one of the other ships, already channeling my Legacy to call down a storm.

The sky darkens and it begins to rain. Out here in the jungle, it's a cinch to call up this kind of weather, but I'm still a few seconds away from channeling lightning and I'm not sure I'll be quick enough. Phiri and her troops are already drawing a bead on me, their blaster fire scoring the wet dirt in front of my position.

That's when a fist-sized hailstone strikes Phiri right in her bald head. She falls back, shielding herself.

I notice Marina hiding behind a stack of crates. She's focusing intently on the raindrops, turning them to ice around the Mogs and knocking them senseless with hail. I feel the storm above reach a boiling point and let loose with a jagged stripe of lightning. Phiri manages to dive aside at the last second, but her last two warriors are electrocuted into dust.

And then, to my surprise, Phiri Dun-Ra runs. Without even a look over her shoulder, the Mog trueborn bolts into the nearby jungle.

Adam leaps to his feet. Both his lips are split open where Phiri clubbed him, blood trickling down his chin. Otherwise, he looks unharmed and alert. He starts to run after Phiri, his feet sliding through the reddish-brown mud my storm has created. Phiri is out of sight before Adam can get very far. He pulls up short a few yards away from me.

"Let her go," I tell him, willing the storm I whipped up to taper off.

"Shouldn't we go after her?" Adam asks, spitting blood into the dirt. His eyes scan the nearby ruins and tree line, and I can tell he'd like a fair fight against the other trueborn. Dust, back in wolf form, lopes over and sits down next to Adam, lapping gently at his hand. He glances back to me. "Thanks for the save, by the way."

"Yeah, I figured since the whole distraction thing was my call, I kinda owed it to you to not let you get slaughtered."

"Glad you saw it that way," Adam replies, then looks back towards the ruins around the Sanctuary. "We should catch her. She's dangerous."

"Forget about Phiri what's-her-face," I say, turning away from the jungle and gazing up at the waiting temple.

"We've got more important things to do than chase down one Mog," Marina puts in as she walks over to join us. "No matter how nasty she might be."

I nod in agreement. "She's alone out there. Maybe something will eat her. We'll leave Dust back here to keep watch over the ships, in case she tries to double back."

Adam continues to stare into the jungle. After a moment, he finally nods his head. "Fine. I'll keep an eye on things while you guys go inside."

I exchange an inquiring look with Marina to make sure she doesn't have any misgivings with what I'm about to say. She shrugs her shoulders in response, then starts towards our ship to begin the unloading. I cock my head at Adam.

"You don't even want to *try* coming in with us?" I ask.

Adam stares at me. "Are you joking? Did you see what contact with that field did to Phiri Dun-Ra?"

"I'll heal you if that happens," Marina offers over her shoulder.

"I don't understand," Adam says. He turns to look up at the temple, his hands on his hips. He looks nervous. "Why would you even want me to go in there? It's a Loric place."

"Like that Phiri bitch said, you're part Garde now," I explain. "You're not Loric, but you've got Legacies."

"I've got one Legacy," Adam clarifies. "And it wasn't even mine to start with. I—I'm not even sure if I'm supposed to have it."

"Doesn't matter. If I understood what Malcolm told us—and I guess that's maybe a big if—there's a living piece of Lorien in that temple. That's where our Legacies come from. Which means you're connected to it, just like us."

"Everything has happened for a reason," Marina says as she climbs up onto our ship's hull. She looks back at us, a thoughtful frown straining her soft features. "Just look at Eight's prophecies."

Adam looks unconvinced. He swallows hard.

"We don't know what's waiting for us in there or what to expect. We might need you in there. So man up."

I'm not sure how Adam will respond to being called out. A smile flickers across his face, like that one in the cockpit when he was spacing out.

"I'm in," he says. "Assuming that invisible wall doesn't burn my face off."

We walk over to the ship to help Marina. She pulls the Chest with our gathered Inheritance out of the cockpit and floats it down to me with telekinesis. Then, she carefully floats Eight's body out of the ship. She has him hover right in front of her, almost like she was carrying him in her arms. To my surprise, she unzips the top half of the body bag. There's Eight, looking just as he did when he was alive, those Mogadorian electrodes preserving him.

"Marina? What are you doing?"

"I want him to see the Sanctuary," she says, then gently smooths some of Eight's curly hair back from his forehead. "You're going home," she whispers to him.

Marina climbs down from the ship, focusing her telekinesis so that Eight's body stays with her the entire way. There's a look of deep purpose on her face, and she doesn't even look at me or Adam before walking towards the temple. I realize that she's been waiting days for this moment, the time when she can properly lay Eight to rest. Wordlessly, Adam and I join her somber procession.

As we approach the edge of the land the Mogs cleared, the wild and overgrown temple looming before us, I feel a strange tickle against my chest. I look down to find John's pendant glowing brightly and rising up against the front of my tank top. I adjust my shirt and the pendant floats out in front of me, straining against its chain. It's like it's magnetically drawn to the Sanctuary. The two pendants Marina wears are doing the same thing.

Adam gives me a look and arches an eyebrow at my gravity-defying jewelry. I shrug in response. This is all new to me, too.

Marina is the first to pass over the threshold. The force field appears again, cobalt and electric, and there's a static popping as she passes through it. Loose tangles of her hair charged by the energy float up around her head, but otherwise nothing happens.

I'm only a few steps behind her. The force field gives my skin a fizzy feeling. It only lasts a second and then I'm standing on the other side, the cracked and vine-riddled steps of the Sanctuary rising up before me.

I turn back to check on Adam. He's stopped right in front of the force field. Cautiously, he extends his index finger and makes contact with the energy. It pops loudly and he jumps back, but he isn't scorched like the other Mogadorian was.

"You're sure this is a good idea?"

"Don't be a wimp," I reply.

Adam sighs, steels himself, and reaches forward again, this time with his whole hand. The energy crackles and sparks against his pale skin way more than it did with Marina and me, but it lets him through without incinerating him. I grin at him and he gives me a relieved look, wiping some sweat off his forehead.

"Now what?" he asks.

Marina has paused a few yards in front of us, still floating Eight's body. She reaches behind her head and takes off one of her pendants. Loosed from her neck, the pendant bobs slowly towards the stone steps of the temple, and then begins to rise up them.

"We climb," Marina says.

Her pendant glints blue in the sunlight and it occurs to

me that the Loralite is glowing a little brighter. Like it's charged up or something. I feel it, too. The Sanctuary is giving off some kind of energy beyond just the force field. There's a sense that every cell in my body has been suddenly invigorated. I glance up to the sky and know that I could call up a larger storm than ever before. I feel more in touch with my Legacies. And somehow, it all seems so natural—like I've known this feeling before.

Marina was right, I realize. We're home.

CHAPTER TWENTY-FIVE

IT TAKES US ABOUT THIRTY MINUTES TO CLIMB to the top of the Mayan pyramid. I try passing the time by counting the steps, but I lose track somewhere around two hundred. There are sections where the stone steps have crumbled into ankle-twisting crevices, and other spots where rain has eroded the ancient stonework down to smooth slopes. We use the overgrown vines that spill forth from the jungle to assist us over the difficult parts, ascending hand over hand. We don't talk much, except to tell each other when a particularly tricky section of steps is coming. Somehow, it seems rude to disturb the silence of the Sanctuary.

We take a break once we reach the top of the temple. Marina is sweating from the heat, the climb and the exertion of using her telekinesis to carry Eight's body for so long. I set down the Chest I've been carrying and flex my fingers. Adam stands with his hands on his hips and gazes out over the temple's edge.

"Some view," he says.

"It's beautiful," I agree.

At the temple's pinnacle, we are above the treetops. It's possible to see beyond the overgrown trees that crowd the pyramid, beyond the stripped ring of land the Mogs cleared and out to the rest of the Mayan ruins and the thriving jungle beyond. I imagine some old Mayan ruler standing up here and gazing out at his domain. And then, I imagine that same ruler turning his eyes to the heavens as a Loric ship descends from the clouds. The image seems so real and vivid; I get the strange feeling that my imagination didn't just conjure it up. Centuries ago, something like that really happened here—the Loric visited, and the Sanctuary remembers.

"You guys, look at this," Marina calls to us.

Adam and I turn away from the view and walk across the flat roof of the temple. At the centermost point is a stone door. At first, I think the door is carved from the same pale stone as the rest of the pyramid, but as I draw closer it becomes obvious that the door is smooth and unblemished, the ivory-colored material not showing the same effects of age as the rest of the temple. The door may have been here for some time, yet it's apparent that it was plunked down on top of the already built pyramid.

The door doesn't lead anywhere, a fact Marina demonstrates by walking in a circle around it. Her floating pendant hovers in front of the door, waiting for us to catch up.

I stop in front of the door and examine its surface. It is completely smooth—no handles, knobs, or anything like that—with the exception of nine round divots arranged in a circle at the door's center.

"The pendants," I say, brushing my fingers over cool stone.

Marina plucks her pendant out of the air and guides the stone into one of the notches. It fits perfectly and emits a crisp clicking sound. The door doesn't move, though.

"We only have three," I say, grimacing. "It isn't enough."

"We have to try," Marina says, already pulling off her remaining pendant.

She's right. We've come too far to turn back now. I pull off John's pendant and fit it into the notches on the stone door.

"Here goes nothing," I say, as I push the final pendant home.

Immediately, the Loralite stones begin to glow with the same energy as the force field. The glow spreads between the stones, connecting them, the energy filling the gaps where we're missing pendants. The circular symbol that takes shape on the door reminds me of the scars we get on our legs when one of the Garde dies.

And then, with an ancient grinding noise, the stone door slides down into the temple, leaving behind only a thin frame. Instead of jungle through the doorframe, I see a dusty room lit by the dim blue glow of Loralite.

"I thought we'd need more," I say. "We don't even have a majority."

"Or maybe the Sanctuary knows how badly we need to enter," Marina suggests.

"It's some kind of portal," Adam says, squinting into the room beyond the doorframe. "Is that inside the temple?"

"Let's find out," I say. I pick up Marina's Chest and step over the threshold.

Immediately, I get that disorienting, end-over-end, roller-coaster feeling that I used to have whenever Eight would use his teleportation Legacy. It only lasts a second, and then I'm blinking my eyes to adjust to the dimmer lighting of this inner sanctum. My ears pop from the pressure change, and I get the sense that I just stepped through a portal into the middle of the Mayan temple. Or maybe, considering the way the jungle sounds have been completely sealed out, we're even deeper than that. Maybe this Sanctuary is completely beneath the pyramid.

Marina—with Eight's body in tow—and Adam follow me through, the both of them squinting to adjust to the lower light. When they're on the other side, the doorway blinks out of existence. There's no exit in its place, only a solid limestone wall, although a circle of notches just like the one from the door are carved into it. Our pendants clatter to the floor and I hurriedly pick them up.

"The Sanctuary," Marina breathes.

"How long ago did your people put this here?" Adam asks.

"Hell if I know. We heard they'd been coming to Earth for centuries," I reply absently, peering around. "I guess this is what they were doing."

"They were preparing for this day," Marina adds, that eerie certainty back in her voice.

"What'd they leave us, though?" I ask, a little disappointed as I look around. "An empty room?"

The Sanctuary is one long, rectangular room with high ceilings and absolutely no doors or windows. It's as if our ancestors teleported into a solid chunk of rock, somehow managed to carve out a room, and then forgot to furnish it. There's nothing here. Veins of glowing Loralite are threaded through the stone walls and ceiling in chaotic patterns that cast the entire room in a cobalt hue. My eyes glide over the swoops and swirls of Loralite—there's something vaguely familiar there, something that I'm just not seeing.

"It's the universe," Adam says. "It's . . . more than we even know about. The Mogadorian star maps don't cover this much."

It takes me a moment to realize what he's saying. But

then I notice the way the Loralite veins pool into circles at some spots and I recognize the other veins as the swirling stars of the cosmos and beyond. It's just like the Macrocosms, only way bigger and covering way more universe. I find Lorien on one wall, the glowing puddle of Loralite at its heart shining much dimmer than some other spots.

"Our home," I say, and touch Lorien gently with my finger. A chill goes through me as the Loralite seems to pulse in answer, almost as if it recognizes me.

"My home," Adam says dryly. He points to an area that's notable only for its complete absence of Loralite, like a void existing in the glowing universe. He frowns. "At least your ancestors got the whole forbidding-darkness thing right."

"Those aren't our homes, not anymore," Marina says, tracing her fingers across the wall, following the exact trajectory our ship took from Lorien to Earth. "This is our home now."

The Loralite outline of Earth glows much stronger than any other section of the wall. Marina presses her fingers against it and the Loralite crackles and vibrates.

Something below us is moving.

Dust and dirt shake loose from the ceiling, the motes sparkling in the suddenly hypercharged light of the Loralite. I know I shouldn't be scared—this is a Loric place, it won't hurt us—but I can't help backing up to the nearest wall, the Sanctuary suddenly feeling very claustrophobic now that it's shaking around me. Adam stumbles in next to me, his eyes wide.

With an ancient groan and a grinding of stone, a circular section of the floor at the room's center rises up. It's like an altar or a pedestal extending up from the floor. The room stops shaking when the thing has risen to about waist high. This new extension is made from pure Loralite. The slab of plain limestone floor sits atop the Loralite cylinder, almost like a seal holding in whatever might be down below. Cautiously, the three of us approach.

"It looks like this piece comes off," I say, touching the limestone seal, but not yet removing it.

"It almost looks like a well," Adam says, musing. "What do you think is down there?"

"No clue," I reply.

"Look," Marina says. "The drawings."

I see them. They're similar to the cave paintings that Eight showed us back in India, except these are carved directly into the well's Loralite sides. I have to walk a circle around the well to take all the images in.

Nine silhouettes looming over a planet that looks like Earth, with nine smaller silhouettes standing on the planet below them.

A person—I can't tell if it's a male or female—standing in front of a hole in the ground and dumping the contents of a box into the opening.

Nine silhouettes again, this time arranged in front of a

castle, fending off something that looks like a tidal wave or maybe a three-headed dragon.

"More prophecies?" I ask.

"Maybe," Marina replies. She is paused in front of the carving of the person with the box. "Or maybe they're instructions."

I stand next to her. "Do you think this is the place? Where we, uh, commit our Inheritances to the Earth?"

Marina nods. She sets Eight's body gently down to the ground, then uses her telekinesis to push the slab of limestone that seals the well aside. It crumbles onto the ground with a huge thud, the old stone instantly breaking apart.

A column of pure blue light flows up from the well, so bright that I have to shield my eyes. It's like a spotlight. I can feel the warmth from the light deep in my bones.

"This is . . ." Adam trails off, unable to complete his thought. There's profound amazement in his dark Mogadorian eyes.

Marina kneels down in front of her Chest and opens it up. She cups her hands and removes a handful of Loric gemstones, then drops them into the Sanctuary's well. They glitter and flash as they slip through her fingers, falling into the light. In response, the whole room seems to get a little brighter. The Loralite veins in the walls pulse stronger.

"Help me, Six," Marina says excitedly.

I grab the pouch of soil from the Chest, open it up and

dump the contents down the well. A fragrant, greenhouse-like aroma fills the dusty chamber, and the light grows stronger still. Marina follows the soil with the bundle of dried branches and leaves. In that moment before they leave her hand, while they're bathed in the light, I could swear the branches look green and alive again. As they drop out of sight, a swirling breeze fills the chamber, cooling us down.

"It's working," I say, even though I'm not sure *what* exactly we're doing. I'm only sure that it feels right.

When we've emptied out the Chest of everything else, I pick up the can of Henri's ashes. Carefully, I remove the lid and empty it into the light. Each of the ashes briefly sparks as they swirl downward into the well. I wish John could've been here to see this.

I turn back to Marina, inclining my head gently towards where Eight's body rests on the ground. "Should we . . . ?"

Marina shakes her head, looking down at Eight. "I'm not ready yet, Six."

I take a moment to sweep my gaze over the room, checking to see if anything's changed. The light from the well is nearly as bright as the sun, but it doesn't really hurt my eyes anymore. The Loralite veins in the walls pulse with energy. Our Chest is empty and Henri's ashes have been spread.

"There's nothing else to do," I say to Marina. "It's time."

"The pendants, Six," Marina says. "We have to give it the pendants."

"Hold on," Adam says, stepping forward for the first time. He's been watching all this take place with awe, but Marina's words snap him back. "If you drop those pendants down there, we'll have no way out of here."

I'm still holding all of our pendants. I clutch them tightly as I think it over.

"We have to have faith, right?" I say, shrugging my shoulders. "We have to trust that whatever's down there, whatever the Elders left for us, that it'll show us a way out."

Marina nods. "Yes."

Adam looks at me for a moment, then to the light. Everything he's seen today must go against his Mogadorian instincts. But he has Garde in him, too.

"All right," Adam says. "I trust you."

I hold on to the pendants for a moment longer. I've worn an amulet around my neck for most of my life. There were many times that it reminded me who I was, where I was from, and what I was fighting for. It was heartbreaking to lose two pendants and I've never felt right without one. It's as much a part of who I am—who we all are—as the scars on our ankles. But it's time to let that go.

I drop the three pendants into the well.

The response is immediate and blinding. The light from within the well goes supernova. I shout and shield my eyes, and I'm pretty sure Marina and Adam do the same. There is a whooshing sound from down below, like thousands of wings taking flight, or a miniature tornado touching down beneath the Earth. There is a loud, baritone thump that sends vibrations through my teeth. A few seconds later, the sound repeats.

Thump, thump. Thump, thump.

The rhythm gets faster and stronger. Steadier.

It's a heartbeat.

I'm not sure how long I'm bathed in that pure blue light, how long I listen to the sonorous heartbeat of Lorien. It could be two minutes or it could be two hours. The experience is hypnotic and comforting. When the light begins to die down and the volume of the heartbeat lowers to a steady thrum in the background, I almost miss it. It's like waking up from a warm dream that you don't want to leave.

I open my eyes and immediately gasp.

Eight's body hovers upright over the Sanctuary's well, the column of blue light surrounding him. I snatch at Marina's hand.

"Are you doing this?" I ask, unintentionally shouting.

Marina shakes her head and squeezes my hand. There are tears in her eyes.

A few steps behind us, Adam is on his knees. He must've collapsed during the light show. He looks up at Eight, completely mystified.

"What's happening? What is this?"

"Look at him," Marina says. "Look."

I'm about to tell Adam I have no idea what's going on when I see Eight's fingers move. Was it just a trick of the light? No—Marina must have seen it too because she makes a little squeaking sound and covers her mouth with her free hand, her other squeezing down hard on mine.

Eight wiggles his fingers. Floating, he shakes out his arms and legs. He rolls his head as if working out a crick in his neck.

Then, he opens his eyes. They are pure Loralite. Eight's eyes glow the same cobalt shade as the deepest veins in the wall. When he opens his mouth, blue light comes flooding out.

"Hello," Eight says, in an echoing voice that doesn't belong to our friend. It's a melodic, beautiful voice, like nothing I've ever heard before.

It is the voice of Lorien.

CHAPTER TWENTY-SIX

MOST PEOPLE HAVE THE SENSE TO RUN. THESE New Yorkers have seen enough movies to know what happens when an alien spaceship parks itself over your city. They stream down the sidewalk in droves. Some even abandon their cars in the middle of the avenues, which makes it slow going for our convoy of black SUVs. Luckily, outside Sanderson's hotel, Agent Walker was able to convince the local cops who showed up in response to the shooting to help us. When it comes to alien invasions, I guess there's something about a federal agent in a black suit and sunglasses.

Even with the added sirens and flashers of the NYPD, it's hard cutting through the city. Through the chaos.

And yet, some people aren't running away from the East River, where the Mogadorian warship hovers ominously over the United Nations. They're running towards it. People with their phones out, recording, eager to catch a glimpse of alien life. I can't make up my mind if they're brave, crazy or just stupid. Probably a combination of the three. I want to shout out the window for them to turn and run, but there's no time.

I won't be able to save all of them.

"Michael Worthington, a senator representing Florida." Agent Walker barks the name into her cell phone, reading it off a yellow legal pad. She's in the passenger seat, looking harried and wild. She knows there's not enough time for her orders to make a difference, but she's giving them anyway.

"Melissa Croft, she's on the joint chiefs of staff. Luc Phillipe, the French ambassador." Walker pauses, reaching the end of her list. She glances into the backseat, where Bud Sanderson is sandwiched in between me and Sam. "Is that everyone?"

Sanderson nods. "Everyone that I know of."

Walker nods and speaks into the phone. "Arrest them. Yes, all of them. If they resist, kill them."

She hangs up the phone. The list of politicians associated with MogPro—dozens of names relayed one by one by Walker to her contacts—came courtesy of Sanderson. Even if the rogue agents Walker has in her command can pull it off, the arrests might not do much good now, at the zero hour. At the very least, we have to hope Walker and her people will knock the

Mog-friendly traitors out of power, leaving behind a government that's ready to resist. Although how much resistance they'll be able to mount remains to be seen.

How long did Henri tell me it took the Mogs to conquer Lorien? Less than a day?

Through the windshield, the Mogadorian warship is visible. It makes the city's skyscrapers look like toys and casts blocks-long shadows in every direction. The thing looks like a giant roach poised over New York. There are hundreds of blaster turrets along its sides and on its belly, and I think I can make out openings where smaller Mog ships are probably docked. Even with the full Garde, Legacies blazing, I'm not sure we could take down that hulk.

Agent Walker is staring at the ship, too. I guess it's probably impossible to ignore the massive, alien object that crowds the horizon. She turns to look at me.

"You can destroy that thing, right?"

"Sure," I reply, trying to mimic Nine's casual bluster. He's in the SUV behind ours, probably explaining to his escort of agents how he'll rip apart that warship with his bare hands. "We got this. No problem."

Next to me, Sanderson chuckles darkly, but shuts up when Walker fixes him with a menacing look. On the other side of the disgraced secretary of defense, Sam finally looks up from the cell phone he "borrowed" from that innocent bystander outside the hotel.

"The upload is done," he says to me. "Sarah's got the footage."

"Thanks, Sam," I reply, and pull my own phone out from my pocket, immediately dialing Sarah's number.

I wonder what Henri would think of me and Sam uploading footage of me using my Legacies to the website of They Walk Among Us. In my wildest dreams, I don't think I could've concocted a scenario where I'd willingly take my powers public. But here we are.

Sarah answers on the first ring. I can hear activity in the background—people talking, a television blaring.

"John, thank God! The Mogs are all over the news! Are you okay?"

"I'm fine," I tell her. "Just making my way towards the biggest Mogadorian ship I've ever seen."

"John, I hope you know what you're doing," Sarah replies, worry in her voice.

"It's nothing we can't handle—" I start to reassure her, until a blast of static cuts me off. "Sarah? Are you still there?"

"I'm here," she replies, sounding a little more distant than before. "I think something's interfering with the connection, though."

It must be the warships. I'm sure those huge things coming down from orbit aren't doing any favors for the cellular networks. Not to mention all the panicked phone calls like this one that must be going on around the country. I have to talk quicker in case I lose service.

"Sam just sent some video files to Mark's website. Did you guys get them? I think they could be useful." I remember what Sam said to me outside the gas station. "We don't want to just scare people. We also want to give them hope."

Next to me, Bud Sanderson snorts. I guess the old man doesn't have too much faith in anything we're doing on They Walk Among Us. I don't know if it's going to work either—like Walker's arrests, like anything we do today, it might be too late for it to matter. But we've got to cover every possible angle of fighting back against the Mogs.

"I'm looking at it now," Sarah says, and her breath catches. "John, it's—you're amazing. But I'm a sucker for handsome aliens performing miracles."

I've been trying to look stone-faced in front of my uneasy allies, so I have to turn away from Sanderson to hide my smile.

"Uh, thanks."

"We can definitely use this," Sarah says, and I can hear her already tapping out keystrokes. "What are you going to do now, though? That ship looks *huge*."

I glance at the chaos outside the window. "We're going to try to end this war before it gets started."

Sarah's voice sounds concerned. She knows I'm

about to tell her something crazy. "What do you mean, John? What's the plan?"

"We're going to the Mogadorian warship," I tell her, trying to sound confident about a plan that seems more desperate the closer we get to that looming warship. "We're going to lure Setrákus Ra out. And we're going to kill him."

Our convoy has to stop ten blocks short of the United Nations when the traffic becomes impassable. The streets are clogged with people trying to get a closer look at the warship. Some of them are even standing on top of cars or, in one case, a stalled city bus. There are cops everywhere trying their best to restore some order, but I doubt they're trained for first-contact scenarios; most of them are busy staring up at the ship, too. The crowd is buzzing and there's a lot of excited shouting.

Just a bunch of easy targets for the Mogadorians. I dread the moment those cannons along the sides of the warship open fire on this crowd. I want to tell everyone to run, but that might just start a panic. If anyone would even listen to me.

"Move! Get out of the way!" Walker screams as she gets out of the SUV. She's got her badge in the air, although no one's really paying attention to her.

The agents from the two SUVs along with the cops Walker recruited back at the hotel form a tight perimeter around me, Sanderson and Sam. Nine shoves his way in next to us, glaring at a group of teenagers cheering encouragement at the spaceship.

"Idiots," he grumbles, then looks at me. "This is nuts, Johnny."

"We need to protect as many as we can," I reply.

"They need to protect themselves," Nine says, then shouts over the shoulder of one of our agents. "Go home, you morons! Or get some guns and come back!"

Walker glares at him. "Please don't encourage the civilians to get armed."

Nine gives her a wild look and keeps shouting. "It's war, lady! These people need to get prepared!"

Some of the people around us have overheard, or maybe they're just unnerved by the growing police presence. I notice a few exchange nervous looks and people begin trickling back the way we came. Walker grimaces at Nine, then slaps one of the agents on the shoulder.

"Forward!" she shouts. "We need to move forward!"

There's still a mob separating us from the UN, and it shows no signs of really thinning out. Walker's agents and the cops start muscling through and we're carried along with them.

"Watch it, dude! No cutting in the line to get beamed

up!" shouts one bystander.

"Holy shit! It's the Men in Black!" screams another.

"Are they going to hurt us?" a woman we pass yells at Sanderson, maybe recognizing him as someone important looking. "Are we in danger?"

Sanderson averts his eyes and soon the woman is lost in the crowd. It's slow going, even with a dozen cops and agents bull-rushing ahead of us. These people need to get out of our way.

A wild-eyed guy with a scraggly beard who looks like the type to be waving handmade signs about the end of the world barrels right into Agent Walker. She's thrown off balance, and I reach out to steady her. Walker doesn't thank me—there's fury and frustration in her eyes. Fed up with the crowd, she reaches for the gun holstered on her hip, maybe thinking she'll fire a few shots in the air to clear the area. I stop her arm and shake my head when she glares at me.

"Don't. You'll start a panic."

"This is already a panic," she replies.

"Personally, I'd be panicking more if someone was shooting," Sam chimes in.

Walker makes an annoyed noise and goes back to pushing her way through the crowd. I elbow Nine in the ribs. "Let's help them," I tell him, adding, "But don't hurt anyone."

Nine nods and we begin using telekinesis to move

people out of our way. Nine's gentler than I would have expected. We create a sort of telekinetic bubble around us, the nearby bystanders sliding off it. No one gets trampled, and slowly the path starts to clear for Walker and the rest of our escort.

As we move closer to the UN, we come directly under the shadow of the Mogadorian warship. A chill goes through me, but I try not let it show. There are flags of every nation planted in the ground on both sides of the road we're pressing down, all these symbols flapping in a gentle spring breeze, caught beneath the looming Mogadorian vessel.

Up ahead, I see that a stage has been hastily erected at the front entrance of the UN. There is a more organized police force there—both local cops and the UN's private security. They keep people away from the stage and from storming the entrance to the main building. There's a concentration of press up ahead, too, all of them with cameras eagerly swinging between the stage and the hovering spacecraft.

I grab Sanderson around the shoulders and yank him close, pointing to the stage.

"What's the deal with that? What's supposed to happen here?"

Sanderson grimaces at me but doesn't try to wriggle away. "The Beloved Leader has a taste for theatrics. Did you know he wrote a book?"

"Reading is stupid," grunts Nine, more focused on the crowd.

"I don't care about his propaganda. Explain the stage, Sanderson."

"Propaganda, like you said," Sanderson replies. "Myself and some of the others from MogPro—the ones our dear friend Walker probably had arrested—we were supposed to greet Setrákus Ra. He was going to demonstrate the gifts the Mogadorians could offer humanity."

I remember the state we found Sanderson in, all black veined and nearly keeled over, all strung out on the Mogadorian's so-called medical advancements.

"He was going to heal you," I say, putting it together.

"Hallelujah!" Sanderson says, bitterly. "Our savior! Then, we'd invite him inside the UN for discussions and, come tomorrow, a peaceful resolution would be adopted to allow the Mogs into the airspace of every member nation."

"And that's it," Sam says. "Earth would be surrendered."

"At least it would be peaceful," Sanderson says.

"Don't you think people would freak out?" I ask Sanderson. "I mean, look around. Imagine what will happen when the Mogs actually show themselves?

Start walking around? Taking things over? There'd be panic, riots—even with your bullshit diplomacy. How was your plan ever going to work?"

"Of course he thought of that," Sanderson says. "That's how Setrákus Ra plans to identify the dissidents. The problem elements."

"So he'll know who to kill," Nine grunts.

"That's sick," Sam says.

"A small price to pay for humanity's survival," Sanderson argues.

"I've seen the future under Mogadorian rule," I tell Sanderson. "Believe me. It's a bigger price than you're willing to pay."

Sam gives me a worried look and I realize how cold I must sound, like war with the Mogadorians on Earth is inevitable, like there's nothing we can do at this point to keep people from getting hurt. In truth, I'm not sure that there is a way to resolve this without bloodshed. The war is here and it's going to be fought. But I need the others to keep up hope.

"It doesn't have to be that way," I add. "We're going to stop Setrákus Ra before this goes any further. But you have to help us."

Sanderson nods, his eyes fixed on the stage. "You want me to go through with it."

"Draw him out, just like he wants," I say, pulling up the hood on my sweatshirt. "And we'll take him down."

"You're powerful enough for that?"

As I look over at Sanderson to respond, I can see the same question in Sam's eyes. He wasn't at our last fight with Setrákus Ra, but he knows it didn't go well. That was with the whole Garde—now it's just me and Nine. Well, and all the guns Agent Walker can bring to bear.

"I have to be," I tell Sanderson.

As we get closer to the front of the UN and the stage, we pass by a guy dressed like a bike messenger surrounded by a few news cameras. It's noticeable because he's the only thing commanding any press attention around here besides the giant Mogadorian warship. I focus my senses to hear what he's saying.

"I swear, the guy fell out of the sky!" the bike messenger exclaims to a skeptical press corps. "Or maybe he floated down, I don't know. He hit the ground hard, but his skin was, like, covered in armor or something. He looked all sorts of messed up."

Nine's hand clamps down on my shoulder. He heard it, too, and he's so distracted that he stops telekinetically pushing people aside. The agents escorting us shuffle and groan as the crowd surges in, but they manage to keep them back.

"You heard that, right?" Nine asks, his eyes practically glowing with bloodlust.

"He could just be some nutjob," I say, referring to the bike messenger, although I don't really believe it. "This kind of thing definitely brings them out."

"No way," Nine says, excitement in his voice. His eyes dart around the crowd with a renewed interest. "Five is here, man. Five is here, and I'm going to smash his fat face in."

CHAPTER TWENTY-SEVEN

I FEEL NUMB.

In the docking bay, I catch a glimpse of myself in the pearl-colored armor paneling of the small ship we'll be taking to Manhattan. I look ghostly. There are huge bags under my eyes. They dressed me up in a new formal gown, black with red sashes throughout, and pulled my hair back in a ponytail so severe that my scalp feels like it's peeling away from my skull. Princess of the Mogadorians.

I don't really care. I've got a cloudy feeling, like I'm just floating along. A part of me knows that I should be focusing up, getting my head straight.

I just can't.

The entrance to the transport ship opens and a small staircase unfolds for me to climb up. Setrákus Ra gently places his hand on my shoulder and urges me forward.

"Here we go, dear," he says. His voice sounds far away. "Big day."

I don't move at first. But then a pain starts up in my shoulder where I was stabbed. It feels like little worms wiggling around under my skin. The ache only subsides when I put one foot in front of the other, climb up the steps and flop into one of the vessel's bucket seats.

"Good," Setrákus Ra says, and follows me aboard. He sits down in the pilot's seat and the ship seals up behind us. His human form has been restored after his scuffle with Five, and he's dressed himself in a sleek black suit with crimson flourishes. The color scheme doesn't complement the fatherly human face he's wearing—it makes him look stern and authoritative. I don't tell him that, both because I don't want to help him and because it seems like too much effort to talk.

I wish I could just sleep through this.

They did something to me after the gash opened up on my shoulder. I was in and out of consciousness from blood loss, so my memory is foggy. I can remember Setrákus Ra carrying me down to the medical bay, a place on the ship I hadn't had the bad luck to explore until then. I remember them injecting my wound with something black and oozing. I'm pretty sure that I screamed from the pain. But then my wound started to close. It wasn't like the times I'd been healed by Marina or John. In those cases, it felt like my injuries were knitting back together, like my flesh was regrowing. Under the Mogs' "care," it felt like my flesh was being replaced by something else, something cold and foreign. Something alive and hungry.

I can still feel it, crawling around beneath the perfect, pale skin of my now uninjured shoulder.

Setrákus Ra flips a few switches on the console, and our little spherical ship powers up. The walls become translucent. It's the Mogadorian version of tinted glass, though—we can see out, but no one can see in.

I turn my head to study the docking bay that's crowded with combat-ready Mogadorians. They all stand perfectly still, hundreds of them arranged in orderly lines, all of them with their fists clenched over their hearts. They're saluting their Beloved Leader as he sets out to conquer Earth. I look at their pasty, expressionless faces and their dark, empty eyes. Are these my people? Am I becoming one of them?

It seems easiest to give in.

Setrákus Ra is about to get us moving when a red light flashes on one of his video screens and a shrill buzzing sounds. The noise wakes me up a little. Some unlucky underling is trying to call Setrákus Ra right in the middle of his big day. Setrákus Ra's jaw sets in annoyance at the incoming message and, for a moment, I think he might ignore it. Finally, he jabs a button and a frazzled Mogadorian communications officer appears on-screen.

"What is it?" snarls Setrákus Ra.

"Deepest apologies for the interruption, Beloved Leader," the officer says, keeping his eyes downcast. "You have an urgent message from Phiri Dun-Ra."

"It had better be," Setrákus Ra grumbles. He waves a hand impatiently at the screen. "Very well. Put her through."

The screen flashes, crackles, and then a Mogadorian woman appears. She has two long braids pinned up around her bald head and a sizable cut above her eyebrow. She's surrounded on all sides by jungle. Apparently, a message from this trueborn is important enough to delay our flight down to New York. I try to sit up a little bit in my seat, fighting through the fog to pay attention.

"What is it, Phiri?" Setrákus Ra says, coldly. "Why have you contacted me directly?"

The Mog woman, Phiri, hesitates before she speaks. Maybe she's taken aback by the human face addressing her with such authority. Or maybe she's just scared of her Beloved Leader.

"They're here," Phiri says at last, a note of triumph in her voice. "The Garde have activated the Sanctuary."

Setrákus Ra leans back in his seat, his eyebrows arched in surprise. He laces his hands in front of him in consideration.

"Very good," he replies. "Excellent. Your orders are to keep them there, Phiri Dun-Ra. On your life. I will join you shortly."

"As you wish, Belo—"

Setrákus Ra severs the connection before Phiri Dun-Ra can finish. The mentions of the Garde and the Sanctuary have me a little more aware. I try to think of Six and Marina, of John and Nine—I know they would want me to fight through this. It's just so difficult to keep my mind from going blank, to keep my body from slouching.

"For years I've pursued them," Setrákus Ra says quietly, almost to himself. "To wipe out the last bit of resistance to Mogadorian Progress. To take control of what those Elder fools buried on this planet. Now, the day has come when everything I've fought for will be mine, all at once. Tell me, granddaughter, how can there be any doubt of Mogadorian superiority?"

He doesn't really want a response. Setrákus Ra just likes to hear himself talk. I let a slow, medicated smile form on my face. That seems to please him. My grandfather reaches out and pats me on the knee.

"You're feeling better, aren't you?" he says. He flips a few levers on the console and our ship's engines vibrate to life. "Come. Let us go take what is ours."

With that, Setrákus Ra navigates the ship forward. We zip through the docking bay, past the rows of Mogadorian warriors. They thump their fists against their chests as we go, shouting out gravelly Mogadorian encouragement. We exit through the same passage as Five's body. That part—seeing him brutalized and then tossed aside like so much garbage—I'm glad to lose to the fog.

We descend on Manhattan. I can see all the humans gathered below. There are thousands of them crowded in front of a fancy-looking set of buildings and its surrounding campus. I can make out a stage down there, too. It's all built on the bank of a gray, choppy river. I remember the Washington from my vision, the smoky smells that choked the air. That will be New York soon. I wonder if these people will throw themselves into the river when their city begins to burn.

The people below point up at our ship. I can hear them shouting and screaming out greetings. These humans—the ones who came closest to the *Anubis*—they don't think they're in any danger.

It occurs to me that we're traveling into this throng of people without any Mogadorian guards. I loll my head towards my grandfather, wet my lips and manage to find words.

"We're facing them alone?" I ask him.

He smiles. "Of course. I mean to elevate these people, not harm them. We have nothing to fear from the humans. My servants on Earth have arranged for a greeting that I find more than suitable."

He's up to something, obviously. Probably already has this whole event planned out. I know it's unlikely even a crowd of humans this size would stand a chance against Setrákus Ra and all his powers, but part of me hopes maybe one of them will see through whatever sideshow he's got planned and take some shots at the scary alien.

Of course, that would mean my death before they could

stop Setrákus Ra. At this point, it seems almost worth it. I feel whatever the Mogadorians injected into me crawling around beneath my skin. I can't endure any more of that.

The descent is over. We hover about fifteen feet above the stage. A nervous-looking older man in a suit, some kind of politician, waits for us there. There are flashbulbs going off like crazy. I blink my eyes and try to keep from sleep-walking through this.

"Come, Ella. Let us greet our subjects," Setrákus Ra says. He picks up his golden cane, the obsidian Eye of Thaloc catching the light. I'm not sure why he brought that with him. I guess he doesn't want to face our so-called subjects completely unarmed. Or maybe he thinks it makes him look noble—like a king with a scepter.

I stand up, slightly unsteady. Setrákus Ra offers me his arm. I hook my hand through it.

The door of our transport ship opens and a glowing staircase extends outward, creating a path for us to the stage. The crowd gasps as we emerge. Through my bleary eyes, I can see dozens of TV cameras trained on us. The crowd is hushed in amazement. What do we look like to them? Aliens . . . aliens that look exactly like humans. A handsome older man and his pale granddaughter.

Setrákus Ra raises his hand and waves to the people. It's a royal thing, courtly and showy. When he speaks, his voice booms like he's hooked up to a microphone.

"Greetings, people of Earth!" he bellows in perfect

English, his voice firm and reassuring. "My name is Setrákus Ra and this is my granddaughter, Ella. We have traveled a great distance to come humbly before you with wishes of peace!"

The crowd actually cheers. They don't know any better. Setrákus Ra gazes beatifically across all their upturned faces. But when his eyes settle on the old man standing on the stage, I feel a tension go through his arm.

"Hmm," Setrákus Ra says under his breath. Something isn't right. The greeter isn't what he expected. Or maybe there were supposed to be more humans waiting onstage with outstretched arms. Maybe there were supposed to be bouquets of flowers.

Undeterred, Setrákus Ra draws himself up a little taller and proceeds down the rest of the steps.

"We have much to offer your people!" he continues in his booming, charitable voice. "Advancements in medicine to heal your sick, farming techniques to feed your hungry and technology that will make your lives easier and more productive. All we ask in return, after our long journey, is shelter from the cold of space."

I glance over the crowd to see if any of them are buying it. I end up locking eyes with a young guy in the front row, pushed up right next to some TV cameras, his dark eyes seeking mine. He wears a hooded sweatshirt, long black hair spilling out from inside, and he's tall and athletic, and—

In my condition, it actually takes me a moment to recognize him. Not so long ago, I balanced on his shoulders and he taught me how to fight.

Nine.

Seeing him, knowing that I'm not alone, that all isn't lost just yet—it makes me snap back to my senses. The pain in my shoulder increases exponentially, like something is trying to crawl its way out of me. Whatever's inside me doesn't want me to use my Legacies. I ignore it and reach out with my telepathy.

Nine! His cane! It's how he changes forms! Get his cane and smash it!

A feral grin spreads on Nine's face and he nods to me. My heartbeat quickens.

Next to me, Setrákus Ra's posture has stiffened. My hand is trapped in the crook of his elbow. He knows that something is up, yet he proceeds with the show all the same.

"I expected more of them to be here on this momentous occasion, yet I see one of your leaders has come out to greet me!" Setrákus Ra extends his hand to the old man. "I come to you in peace, sir! Let this cement the friendship between our two great races."

Instead of clasping Setrákus Ra's hand, the old man takes a step away. There's deep fear in his eyes, but it's not run-and-scream fear. It's cornered animal fear. The old man has a microphone of his own and, as the TV cameras swing in his direction, he begins to yell.

"This man—this *thing*—is a liar!"

"What—" Setrákus Ra takes an aggressive step towards the old man, and I'm loosed from his elbow. For the first time since I've been in his company, the Mogadorian leader actually looks surprised.

Surprised and furious.

A murmur of uncertainty passes through the crowd. The old man shouts something else—I hear the words "enslavement" and "death," but otherwise I can't really hear him. No one can. Setrákus Ra has used his telekinesis to crush the old man's microphone.

"You must be confused, my friend," Setrákus Ra says through gritted teeth, still trying to salvage this farce. "My intentions are pu—"

Setrákus Ra is suddenly knocked off balance. I know why. A telekinetic attack. I watch as his golden cane is ripped out of hand. Nine plucks it out of the air as he hops onto the stage, grinning at Setrákus Ra.

I sense movement to my left. I turn my head to see John also hop onto the stage. They're flanking him, just like we practiced in the Lecture Hall. Peppered throughout the crowd, I see men and women in dark suits, all of them slyly pulling firearms into view. The crowd is beginning to buzz as some civilians—the smarter ones—begin to back away from the stage.

It's a trap, I realize gleefully. The Garde are here!

Now, Setrákus Ra really looks surprised. And, dare I say, a little frightened.

"You have been led astray!" Setrákus Ra screams, pointing his now empty hands at Nine and John. "These boys are fugitives! Terrorists from my home world! I don't know what they've told you—"

"We haven't told them anything," John says, interrupting. His voice doesn't carry like Setrákus Ra's, but people in the crowd crane their necks to listen. "We'll let them make up their own minds. A genocidal maniac is easy to spot."

"Lies!"

Do it now! I urge Nine telepathically.

"I wonder what will happen if I do this?" Nine asks, fiddling with Setrákus Ra's cane. Before Setrákus Ra can lunge in his direction, Nine raises the cane over his head and smashes it down on the stage. The obsidian eye in its center explodes in a cloud of ash.

Things happen quickly after that.

Setrákus Ra's body begins to thrash and spasm. The handsome human form he's been so attached to begins to slough off him, like a snake shedding its skin. The real Setrákus Ra—pale verging on bloodless, ancient and hideous, tattooed across his bald skull, a thick scar around his neck, clad in spiky Mogadorian armor—stands revealed on the stage.

Many in the crowd scream. Even more recoil in horror and turn to run. A gunshot goes off—I hear the bullet whistle past my ear before it ricochets harmlessly off the Mogadorian ship behind me. The gunshots only frighten people more and now it's a full-blown stampede in front of the stage. More shots are fired, this time into the air. One of the agents taking aim on Setrákus Ra goes down, bull-rushed by the terrified spectators.

It's chaos.

With a monstrous howl, Setrákus Ra grows to fifteen feet in size. The stage beneath us groans. The old man who was onstage with the Garde tries to run into the crowd, but Setrákus Ra grabs him with his telekinesis and hurls him like a missile into Nine. The two of them fall off the stage in a heap.

Fireballs come to life in John's hands. They go out immediately as Setrákus Ra triggers his Dreynen field. That doesn't stop John from charging in, pulling his Loric dagger out of his sheath as he comes.

"Yes!" Setrákus Ra screams, beckoning John in. "Come racing towards your death, boy!"

Unaffected by Setrákus Ra's version of Dreynen, I pick up a broken piece of his cane. My fingers are clumsy and I nearly drop it twice before I'm able to grasp it tightly enough. I concentrate, ignore the shredding pain under my skin and charge the shrapnel with my Dreynen.

When the broken shard glows bright red, I jab it into

the back of Setrákus Ra's leg.

The Mogadorian overlord cries out and shrinks down to his normal size. I sense the Dreynen field canceling Legacies lift. Too late, Setrákus Ra stumbles forward in a futile attempt to get away from me. The Dreynen-charged cane is buried an inch deep in the back of his calf. When Setrákus Ra yanks it out, a trickle of night-black blood darkens his pant leg. Now that it's off him, I'm not sure how long the effects of my Dreynen will last.

Wait a second. He's bleeding. The damage wasn't transferred to me. Every charm has a weakness, that's what Setrákus Ra said right before he burned the terrible thing into my ankle.

I can hurt him. I'm the only one who can hurt Setrákus Ra.

I barely have time to process this information before Setrákus Ra rounds on me, his eyes wide with outrage. He backhands me, hard, and I'm tossed into the air. The wind goes out of me when I hit the stage, my head swimming again. He must've known that even if I figured out the loophole with the Mogadorian charm, I wouldn't be strong enough to fight him.

Setrákus Ra stands over me, his hideous features creased with fury. He reaches down, fingers grasping for my throat.

"You treasonous little bi—!"

John barrels into him shoulder-first and knocks Setrákus Ra off his feet. Setrákus Ra lands hard on his side and I feel bruises puff up immediately on my own elbow. I accept the pain. There's more to come.

I'm not strong enough to fight him, but I've done my part. I drained his Legacies.

Now, the others can do what has to be done.

John doesn't let up. He pounces on Setrákus Ra, who tries to scramble away. The Mogadorian ruler doesn't look so frightening now, trying to crab walk away from John. I'm happy to see him so pathetic and desperate. He should know how that feels before he dies.

Before *we* die.

John manages to straddle him. He raises his dagger above his head. I take a deep breath and brace myself.

"This is for Lorien! And for Earth!"

I know what happens next. John will stab Setrákus Ra, and I'll die. It will break the Mogadorian charm, and then the Garde will be able to kill Setrákus Ra for real. It's worth it. I'll gladly die if it means ending Setrákus Ra's miserable life.

Do it! I scream at John telepathically. *No matter what happens! Do it!*

As John brings his dagger down, I hear a whooshing sound. Something is flying in this direction. Fast.

A bead of blood tickles my throat, a small cut opening up. That's how close John's blade comes before a chrome-plated cannonball flies through the air, knocks him off Setrákus Ra and sends him crashing through the stage.

Five. He's alive and he just saved my life.

Saved my life and doomed us all.

Before I can react, the stage creaks and collapses. I slide down the tilted piece of wood and land hard on the pavement below. All around me, people are running and screaming.

Setrákus Ra lands next to me.

He reaches down and grabs me by the hair, yanking me viciously to my feet.

"You'll die for this embarrassment, child," he snarls, and begins dragging me over the wrecked stage towards his ship.

Nine stands in his way.

CHAPTER TWENTY-EIGHT

MY SHOULDER IS DISLOCATED, THAT MUCH I know for sure. I'm on my back with jagged pieces of the destroyed stage digging into me. I'm seeing double and it's hard to breathe. I feel like I just got hit by a car.

Not a car. Five.

The traitor stands over me, gulping down deep breaths. His skin is metallic, but he still looks badly injured. He's wearing an eye patch, for starters. One side of his face looks swollen, and I think I actually see dents in the metal carapace that covers his skull. He's missing a couple of teeth. I'm not sure where he picked up those injuries, and I don't care.

The bastard blindsided me. I was so close. Setrákus Ra was as good as dead.

My dagger is still attached to my wrist, but it's the arm that's dislocated. I grope for it, trying to switch hands. Before I can manage it, Five lifts me by the front of my tattered sweatshirt.

"Listen to me!" he shouts in my face.

"Go to hell," I reply.

With my working arm, I grab Five's metal forearm and heat up my Lumen as hot as it can go. Whatever metal he's turned into, it definitely has a boiling point. I wonder if I can get his metal shell to melt off before he can do whatever he's got planned.

"Stop it, John!" Five yelps, shaking me.

"You murdered Eight, you son of a bitch!"

Noxious-smelling steam curls up from between my fingers. Five's eye widens a fraction, but he doesn't let me loose and he doesn't pull away. I'm hurting him and he's just taking it.

"You arrogant asshole," Five snaps, and he cocks back his fist like he's going to strike me. I'm not sure I have the strength to stop him. His clenched fist trembles, and he seems to reconsider. "Listen to me, John! If you hurt Setrákus Ra, the damage will be done to Ella!"

I let the heat of my Lumen die down a fraction. My hand feels sticky with molten metal.

"What? What are you talking about?"

"It's a charm, like the one the Elders used on us," Five says. "He's twisted it somehow."

I turn off my Lumen entirely. Is Five trying to *help*

us now? Did he knock me off Setrákus Ra not to protect his Beloved Leader but to save Ella? I don't know what to think.

"How do we break it?" I shout at him. "How do we *kill* him?"

"I don't know," Five replies, glancing over his shoulder. His expression suddenly goes dark again, that fury I'd seen when he was about to punch me reignited. "Damn him!"

Five rips away from me and takes flight. I climb back to my feet just in time to see Nine charging at Setrákus Ra. He holds a broken piece of the stage out in front of him like a spear.

"Nine! Don't!"

Nine doesn't hear me, probably because he's too busy getting sideswiped by Five. The two of them go crashing into the wreckage of the stage, broken pieces of wood flying everywhere. Once they hit, it looks like Five tries to take flight again, but Nine gets hold of his ankle.

"Where you going, fat boy?" I hear Nine yell.

Nine gets back to his feet, still holding Five's ankle, and then swings him with all his might. Five flaps his arms in a futile attempt to get some momentum, but he's overpowered. Nine slams Five face-first onto the pavement. Chunks of concrete fly up from the impact, and Five's head makes the sound of a bell ringing when it hits. I notice his metallic shell momentarily switch back to normal skin—that must've hurt Five enough to make it hard to focus on his Externa.

"Nine! Enough!" I shout, pushing loose of my own pile of broken wood.

Nine glances in my direction, and that's when Five uppercuts him. With a roar, Nine dives back at him, and they slam together. They hurl punches at each other, a tangled mess of limbs that I lose sight of when they go crashing through the front window of the United Nations building.

I can't worry about them now. I have to get to Setrákus Ra.

I have to save Ella. I won't let her be taken for a second time.

My left arm hangs limp at my side. I'd need to pop my shoulder back in before I could heal myself, but I don't have time for that. I shake crusty flakes of metal off my hand and strap my dagger to the wrist of my working arm. I'll have to do this one handed.

Surprisingly, Setrákus Ra doesn't seem the least bit interested in staying to fight. He drags Ella through the rubble, heading for the pearl-shaped ship he arrived in. Ella looks a lot like she did in that vision we shared of Washington, D.C.—like she's been drained of something essential. I wonder what they did to her on that warship.

No matter what happens! Do it! Ella had shouted in my mind. *No matter what happens.* Five must not be lying. Ella knew what the consequences of me stabbing Setrákus Ra would be, and she accepted them.

Whatever they did to her, the Mogs didn't break her. She had enough fight left in her to help us. It was like Dulce Base all over again. She stuck Setrákus Ra with a glowing piece of debris, and my Legacies instantly came back.

She drained Setrákus Ra's powers, I realize. And, judging by his cowardly retreat, they still haven't returned to him.

I might not be able to kill Setrákus Ra, but that doesn't mean I can't subdue him. Let's see the Mogadorians invade while I'm holding their Beloved Leader hostage.

I race across the lopsided and broken stage, trying to cut off Setrákus Ra before he can reach his ship. Ella sees me coming and digs her heels in. She struggles against Ra's grip and this slows him up just enough. I'm going to catch him.

"Setrákus Ra!"

Damn it. Not now.

The Mogadorian leader doesn't even acknowledge Agent Walker as she comes at him from his other side. Does she expect him to freeze? It's her and two other agents who have managed to extricate themselves from the riotous, panicking crowd. Sam is with them. They stop a few yards off, their guns leveled. Even Sam looks ready to fire—his eyes narrowed, his mouth pressed into a firm line. I remember those acid burns on Sam's wrists. They came courtesy of Setrákus Ra. I'm sure he's ready to settle that score.

"Wait!" I yell at Sam and Walker, but I'm too late.

Setrákus Ra jerks his head in the direction of the agents and Sam, like they're an annoying bug that needs to be swatted. With the hand not holding Ella, Setrákus Ra produces that three-headed whip of his from where it's hidden under his torn uniform. Before he can lash out at them, the agents and Sam open fire.

I can't believe what I'm about to do.

I stop the bullets in midair with my telekinesis. I'm not sure if they would have even penetrated Setrákus Ra's armor, but I can't risk it. I don't let Sam and the others have a chance to realize all their shots have missed. Instead, I shove the entire group backwards with my telekinesis. Not hard enough to hurt them, but hard enough to knock them over some of the broken stage debris. It's also enough to put them out of range of Setrákus Ra's whip. I'll apologize later.

Setrákus Ra doesn't give the agents a second look. The brief distraction was all he needed to reach the steps of his ship ahead of me. He bounds up them, dragging Ella along behind him, and disappears into the vessel.

I sprint forward, determined not to let him escape. The ship begins to rise up before the staircase has fully folded back into its smooth body.

I can still catch them. I can still stop him. I'm so close.

I dive forward and manage to grab the bottom step with my good hand.

The ship continues to rise while the steps recede back towards the open doorway. They pull me closer towards Setrákus Ra and Ella, even as the ship rises farther away from the Earth. I swing one of my legs up so that I'm hooked around the bottom step. Soon, we're almost a hundred feet in the air, getting closer and closer to the warship above.

The steps fold up like an accordion into a panel at the base of the ship's entrance. I push off the step I'd been grasping before I'm crushed in the mechanism and lunge for the open doorway. It isn't easy to do with only one good arm. I end up hanging from the doorway's edge, my good arm starting to feel hyperextended. My legs dangle above what is now a two-hundred-foot drop.

Setrákus Ra stands over me. His three-headed whip dangles in my face, the tips alive with crackling fire. I don't think he plans to pull me the rest of the way in.

I catch a glimpse of Ella through his legs. She's slouched in one of the cockpit's chairs, looking totally sedated. I won't be getting any help from her.

"John Smith, isn't it?" Setrákus Ra asks conversationally. "Thank you for the help down there."

"I wasn't trying to help you."

"But you did, regardless. That is one reason why I will let you live."

I grimace. My grip slips a little. I need to come up with a play soon. It's hard to chuck a fireball with one arm dislocated and the other holding on for dear life. It'll have to be my telekinesis. Maybe if I can push him back . . .

It's gone. My telekinesis is gone. Drained, just like before.

Setrákus Ra smiles at me. His Legacies are returning. I've failed.

He crouches down so he can get right in my face.

"The other reason," he hisses, "is so you can see how I make this planet *burn*."

Setrákus Ra straightens up again and nonchalantly flicks his whip at me. The three heads strike me right across the face. I'm immune to the fire, but the lashes still dig three grooves across my cheek.

It's enough to make me lose my grip. I'm falling.

As I plummet towards the river below, I feel my

Legacies snap back on. I must be far enough away from Setrákus Ra. Quickly, I push down with my telekinesis, doing everything I can to slow my fall.

I still hit the East River hard. It's like getting slapped across my whole body. Dirty water floods my lungs and for a terrifying second I'm not sure which way is up, which way to swim. I manage to resurface, choking and spitting, and trying to swim against the current with only one arm. I end up doing an awkward backstroke, gasping for breath the entire way. I'm exhausted by the time I reach the bank, slightly downriver from the chaos at the UN, surrounded on all sides by trash and dead fish.

"John! John! Are you all right?"

It's Sam. He runs across the mud towards me. He must have seen me fall and followed me here. He skids into the muck next to me. I can only manage a groan by way of greeting. I think some of my ribs are broken.

"Can you move?" Sam asks, gingerly touching my screwed-up shoulder.

I nod. With Sam's help, I make it back to my feet. I'm soaked, bruised, broken in places, with three long cuts across my face. I'm not sure what to heal first.

"Where's Nine?" I manage to ask.

"I lost him in the chaos," Sam replies, his voice breaking. "He and Five were *killing* each other. Walker and her people are trying to evacuate civilians. It's crazy up there. John, what do we do?"

I start to open my mouth, hoping a plan will come to me if I just start talking, but a nearby explosion cuts me off. The impact is powerful enough that my teeth click together.

I look up at the sky just in time to see the Mogadorian warship open fire on New York.

CHAPTER TWENTY-NINE

EIGHT'S EYES, BRIGHTLY GLOWING EMBERS OF pure Loralite, assess each one of us in turn. They linger for a particularly long time on Adam—long enough to make our Mogadorian ally take a nervous step backwards. Like Marina, I'm rooted in place, staring at our friend brought back to some kind of life. Eight floats over the Sanctuary's well in a column of unleashed energy. No, he doesn't just float in the energy. The energy is a part of him.

Or *it.* I'm pretty sure that's not our sarcastic, goofy friend floating up there. Whatever it is, I feel a strange kinship with the entity, almost like the same energy now reanimating Eight is flowing through me, too. It's the same electric rush I get when I use my Legacies. Maybe I'm looking at the essence of what makes me Loric, what makes me Garde.

Maybe I'm looking at Lorien itself.

"Two Loric and a Mogadorian," the entity says at

last, its appraisal of us complete. Its voice is nothing like Eight's used to be—it's like a hundred voices speaking at once, all of them perfectly in tune. The flashing pools of energy where Eight's eyes used to be linger on Adam again and the entity's lips purse in curiosity. "Except not quite. You are something different. Something new."

"Uh, thank you?" Adam replies, and takes another step backwards.

Marina clears her throat and steps closer to the well. There are tears in her eyes. Her hands extend out in front of her, like she wants to grab at the entity's hand and make sure he's real.

"Eight? Is that you?" Her voice is hard to hear over the rhythmic pulsing beneath the well.

The entity turns his gaze on Marina and frowns. "No. I am sorry, daughter. Your friend is gone."

Marina's shoulders heave with disappointment. The thing in Eight's body reaches out to comfort her, but energy crackles between them and it ends up pulling back.

"He is with me now," the entity says, soothingly. "He does me a great service, letting me speak through him. It has been a long time since I had a voice."

"Are you Lorien?" I ask, at last finding my own voice. "Are you, like, the planet?"

The entity seems to consider my question. Through the thin fabric of Eight's shirt, I can see his wound light up. It glows cobalt blue like the rest of him, his entire body filled up with the energy. It's seeping out of him.

"I was called that once, yes," the entity says, and waves its hand at the glowing carvings on the walls. "In other places, I was called other things. And now, on this planet, I will be called something new."

"You're a god," Marina breathes.

"No. I simply *am*."

I shake my head. God or not, we need this thing's help. We don't have time for riddles. I'm suddenly really, really tired of cave drawings and prophecies and glowing people.

"Do you know what's happening?" I ask Eight—Lorien—whatever it is. "The Mogadorians are invading."

The entity's eyes turn once again to Adam. "Not all of them, I see."

Adam looks uncomfortable. The entity quickly turns away. It stares up at the ceiling and it's as if those crackling eyes can see outside of the temple. Like it can see everything.

"Yes. They are coming," the entity says, his echoing voice apparently bemused by the impending Mogadorian invasion. "Their leader has chased me for a very long time. Your Elders foresaw the fall of Lorien and chose to protect me. They hid me here in hopes that it would delay him."

"It didn't go so hot," I reply. Marina elbows me.

The entity's eyes slowly turn to the ceiling again. For a moment, a deep sadness passes across its face.

"So many of my children gone forever," the entity muses. "I suppose you would be the Loric Elders now, if such a thing still exists."

"We're Garde," I say, correcting this billion-year-old godlike energy force, because what the hell, we've come this far. "We're here for your help."

The entity actually chuckles. "It does not matter to me, daughter. Elders, Garde, Cêpan—these words are how the Loric chose to understand my gifts. It does not have to be that way here. It does not have to be *any* way." The entity pauses thoughtfully. "As for help, I do not know what I can offer, child."

More confusion, more riddles. I didn't think coming to the Sanctuary would go like Nine had joked—that we'd unleash some massive power that would wipe out all the Mogadorians. But I expected to find something that could *help*. Our friends could be dying right now in the first wave of a Mogadorian invasion, and I'm down here making small talk with an annoyingly mysterious immortal.

"That's not good enough," I say.

Frustrated, I take a step towards the entity. Energy crackles around me and I feel my hair stand up from static.

"Six," Adam whispers, "be careful."

I ignore him, raising my voice to yell at the all-powerful Lorien. "We've come far to awaken you! We've lost friends! You have to be able to do *something*. Or are you cool if Setrákus Ra just marches down here and destroys this planet? Kills everyone on it? You're going to let that happen *twice* on your watch?"

The entity's brow furrows. A crack opens in the skin on Eight's forehead, and energy begins to spill forth. Marina covers her mouth but manages not to cry out. It's like Eight's body is hollow inside and the energy is gradually breaking it down.

"I am sorry, daughter," Eight says to Marina. "This form cannot hold me for long."

Then, the entity turns back to me. There's no sign that my words have offended it, or had any effect at all. Its voice is as melodic and patient as ever.

"I do not condone the senseless destruction of life," the entity explains. "But I do not choose fates. I do not judge. If it is the will of the universe that I cease to be, then I will cease. I exist merely to bestow my gifts upon those who are open to them."

I spread my arms. "I'm open to them. Load me up. Give me enough Legacies to destroy Setrákus Ra and his fleet and I'll leave your glowing ass alone."

The entity smiles at me. More cracks form along the backs of Eight's hands. The energy is escaping.

"It does not work that way," it intones.

"Then how the hell does it work?" I shout. "Tell us what to do!"

"There is nothing left to do, daughter. You have woken

me and restored my strength. I am of the Earth now, and so are my gifts."

"But how will that help us win?" I yell. "What was all this shit for?"

The entity ignores me. I guess that's all the wisdom it's willing to impart. Instead, it gazes upon Marina.

"He won't have long, daughter."

"Who won't?" she replies, puzzled.

Without another word, the entity's eyes close and Eight's body begins to tremble. To my surprise, the energy actually recedes from his body. The cracks along the backs of his hands stop glowing and close up, as does the one that opened across his forehead. After a few seconds, the only thing left glowing on Eight is the wound over his heart. He floats out of the column of energy and ends up right in front of Marina.

When Eight opens his eyes, they don't glow. They're green, just like I remember them, serene, but with a spark of that old mischief. Eight's lips curl into a slow smile as he sees Marina.

"Wow, hi," Eight says, and when he speaks it's with his own voice.

It's him. It's really him.

Marina nearly doubles over with a delighted sob. She collects herself quickly, though, and grabs Eight first by the shoulders, then on the sides of his face. She pulls him in close.

"You're warm," she says in wonder. "You're so warm."

Eight laughs easily. He puts his hand over Marina's and gently kisses the side of it.

"You're warm, too," he says.

"I'm so sorry, Eight. I'm sorry I couldn't heal you."

Eight shakes his head. "Stop, Marina. It's okay. You brought me here. It's—I can't even describe it. It's *amazing* in there."

Already, I see the energy spreading outward from Eight's heart. It races through his body, fissures opening on his arms and legs. He doesn't seem to be in any pain. He just smiles at Marina and looks at her like he's trying to memorize her face.

"Can I kiss you?" Marina asks him.

"I really wish you would."

Marina kisses him, pressing in close, squeezing him. As she does, the energy swells up from within Eight and, slowly, his body begins to break apart. It's different from when a Mogadorian disintegrates. It's as if, for a moment, I can see every cell in Eight's body and see how the energy from the well glows in between each of them. One by one, those pieces of Eight dissolve, and he becomes one with the light. Marina tries to cling to him, but her fingers pass right through the energy.

And then, he's gone. The light flows back to the well and recedes deep under the ground. The heartbeat we triggered grows fainter. I can still hear it, but only if I really listen. The chamber is peaceful again, lit only by the glowing Loralite carvings on the wall. I feel fresh air on my back and turn around to see that a door has opened up in the wall. It leads to a staircase, sunlight coming in from the outside.

Marina collapses against me, a sobbing wreck. I hug her close and try not to break down myself. Adam watches us without staring too hard and wipes at something in the corner of his eye.

"We should go," Adam says quietly. "The others will need our help."

I nod at him. I wonder if we even accomplished anything down here. It was beautiful seeing Eight again, even for a few fleeting moments. Yet my conversation with the intergalactic entity that grants us our Legacies sure didn't yield a lot of answers. Meanwhile, the time until a Mogadorian invasion is probably running out, if it hasn't already.

Marina squeezes my arm. I look down at her.

"I saw it, Six," Marina whispers to me. "When I kissed him, I saw inside the thing—Lorien, the energy, whatever you want to call it."

"Okay," I say, wanting to be gentle with her, but not sure we have time for this. "And?"

Marina grins at me. "It's spreading, Six. Through the

Earth. It's spreading *everywhere*."

"What does that mean?" Adam asks.

"It means," Marina says, wiping her face and standing up straight, "that we aren't alone anymore."

CHAPTER THIRTY

SKYSCRAPERS BURN.

We run.

The Mogadorian warship crawls across New York's skyline, its massive energy cannons bombarding the blocks indiscriminately. The warship already disgorged dozens of armed scout ships, the smaller vessels zipping up and down the avenues, ferrying warriors to the ground, where they blast whatever civilians they come across.

Other things leaped down from the ship, too. Hungry, angry things. I haven't seen any yet; I've only heard their terrible howls rising above the explosions.

Piken.

New York City is lost, that much I know for sure. There's no turning back the Mogadorians at this point. I have no idea how the other cities where Mogadorian warships were spotted are doing. The network is down in New York, and my satellite phone sunk to the bottom of the East River.

All we can do is run. Just like I've been doing my entire life. Except now, unfortunately, there are a million people running with me.

"Run!" I shout at anyone we come across. "Run until you can't see their ships! Survive, regroup and we *will* fight them!"

Sam is with me. His face is ashen and he looks like he's going to be sick. He never saw what the Mogadorians did to Lorien. He's been through some hard times with us, but never anything like this. I think he always believed that we would win. He never thought this day would come.

I've let him down.

I don't know where Nine and Five are. There aren't any new scars burning their way across my ankle, so they haven't killed each other yet.

I lost Agent Walker, too. She and her agents are on their own. I hope they make it out alive. If they do, maybe they'll be smart enough to meet us back at Ashwood Estates.

If Sam and I can even make it that far.

We run down streets filled with smoke, darting around overturned cars, climbing over fallen chunks of buildings. When one of the scout ships cruises by, we duck into alleys or hide in doorways.

I could fight them. With all the anger I'm holding on to, I'm sure I could rip through them in no time. I could easily take down one of the scout ships on my own.

But I'm not on my own.

There are about twenty survivors following me and Sam. A family I pulled off a burning balcony with my telekinesis, a pair of blood-splattered NYPD officers who saw me take down a pair of Mog warriors, a group that came out from hiding in a restaurant when I flashed my Lumen inside, and others still.

I can't save everyone in this city, but I'll do what I can. That means not picking fights with the Mogadorians. At least not until I can get these people to safety.

I avoid trouble wherever I can. It isn't always possible.

We cross an intersection where slashed power lines are draped across the burned husk of a city bus, and we run right into a dozen Mogadorian warriors. They bring their blasters around on us, but I blow them back with a fireball before they can squeeze off any shots. The ones who aren't immediately incinerated get popped by the cops standing behind me.

I look over my shoulder, nodding to the officers. "Nice shooting."

"We've got your back, John Smith," one of them says.

I don't even think to ask how he knows my name.

Our group runs a few more blocks before I'm drawn

to the sound of nearby screaming. Around the corner, we find a young couple trying to escape from their burning apartment building via the fire escape. The bolts look like they've come unmoored from the wall near the roof, and now the whole fire escape hangs like a crooked finger over the street. Still five stories up, the guy has fallen over the railing. His girlfriend desperately tries to pull him back over the side.

Sarah's face flashes into my mind. *Just stay alive,* I think. *Survive this, and we'll be together.* I'm going to make it back to her.

I run towards the fire escape, bracing it from a distance with my telekinesis.

"Let go!" I shout up at the couple. "I'll catch you!"

"Are you freaking nuts?" the guy yells back.

None of us have time to argue, so I reach out with my telekinesis and just yank the couple off the fire escape. As I'm lowering them to the ground, I hear the beats of heavy footfalls bearing down on me.

"John!" Sam screams. "Look out!"

I turn my head. It's a Piken. The beast gallops towards me at full speed, its jaws covered with slobber, its razor-sharp teeth bared. I hear screams from my group. The cops take some shots at the monster, but they don't even slow it down. The others have the good sense to run from the rabid Mogadorian beast.

Except the direction they run in puts them right

beneath the fire escape. Which, of course, chooses that exact moment to tear fully away from its building and come clattering down into the street.

I've still got the couple suspended in the air, and now I'm holding up the fire escape with my telekinesis, too. I try to divide my focus enough to turn on my Lumen, but it's just too much. I'm too exhausted, the strain is more than I can manage.

The Piken is almost on top of me.

Sarah's face flashes again to the forefront of my mind. I have to try. I grit my teeth and dig down deeper.

With a massive *woomf*, a wave of telekinetic force hits the Piken and knocks it into the air. The beast's muscular legs flail wildly. It lands back-first on top of a stop sign, the pole impaling the beast right through the heart.

That didn't come from me.

I lower the couple safely to the ground, toss the fire escape aside and turn in the direction the telekinetic blast came from.

Sam stares at me. He's frozen. His hands are extended out in front of him like he just shoved the Piken and still hasn't finished with the follow-through. Slowly, he blinks his eyes. Sam looks down at his hands, then over at me.

"Holy shit," he says. "Did I just do that?"

WITNESS THE RETURN OF AN OLD ALLY WHO UNCOVERS A VITAL MOGADORIAN SECRET!

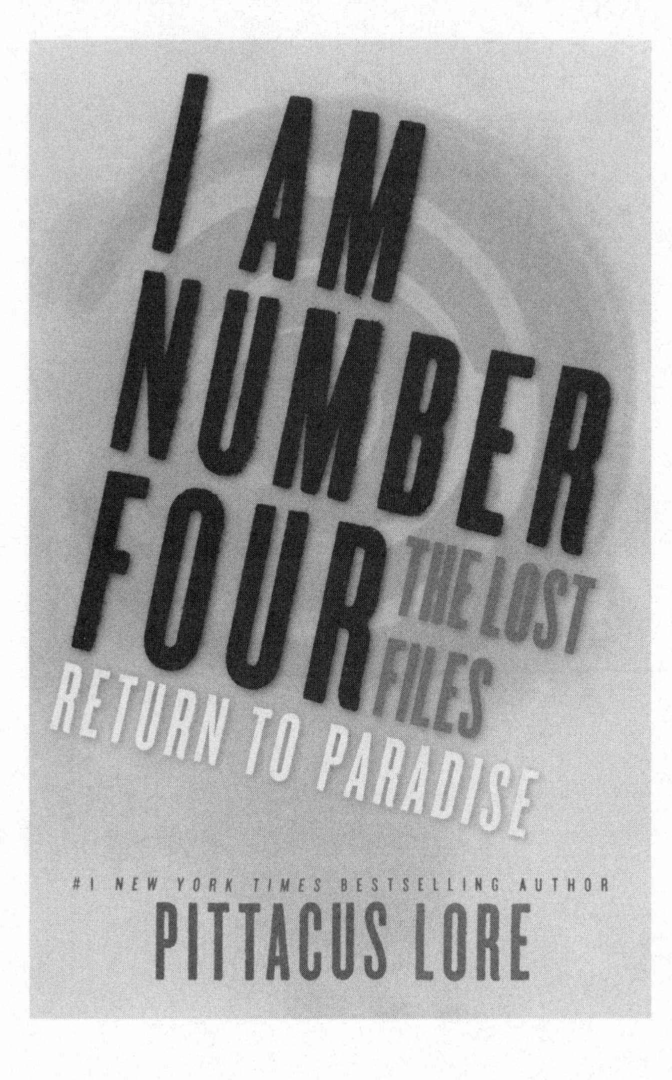

CHAPTER ONE

I HAVE TO KEEP REMINDING MYSELF WHO I AM the first week at the new school. Not, like, I lost my memory or something. I *know* who I am in a literal sense. But I have to keep forcing myself to remember what being me means. So all week I keep a single thought repeating through my head:

You are Mark James.

It's what I think on Monday when some douche bag trips me while I try to find an empty seat among a precalc classroom full of strangers.

You are Mark James, the guy everyone at your old school looked up to. These idiots will learn.

And Wednesday when someone loots my locker during weight training and forces me to walk around in sweaty gym clothes for the last two periods.

You are Mark James, all-conference quarterback. They're just jealous.

And at lunch on Thursday when I sit on the tailgate of my truck and someone in a loud old Camaro zips past, hurling an oversize Styrofoam cup of orange soda at me while yelling what I think is "ass pirate."

You are Mark James, and you are the best fucking athlete the Paradise High Pirates ever saw.

If someone had asked me a year ago what my future held, I'd probably have said something like "Mark James, Ohio State star quarterback." Maybe if I'd had a beer or two I'd go so far as to say, "Mark James, first-round NFL draft pick."

What I wouldn't have said—what I couldn't have even imagined thinking—was anything remotely close to "Mark James, survivor of an alien attack."

For my entire life, the future seemed set for me. As soon as I threw my first pass, I knew what I wanted to do. Paradise High QB, college football star, NFL hopeful. But now the future is this stupid, dark thing I can't predict, and I feel like my whole life has been heading towards something that doesn't even matter. Might not even exist if we end up conquered by a bunch of superpowered aliens. I mean, my all-conference trophy was used to *murder* an alien. A Mogadorian. A bunch of pale, janky-looking assholes from another planet came to Earth hunting for a very human-looking alien named John Smith—*ha*—and his invisible friend. Then they destroyed my school. My kingdom. Almost killing me in the process.

Some people did die. I guess I should count myself lucky, but I don't *feel* lucky. I feel like someone who's just found out that vampires exist or that reality is actually an elaborate video game. Everyone else keeps going on as usual, but the world has changed for me.

There are only a few people who know what really happened at Paradise High. Everyone thinks the school's in shambles because weirdo-drifter/new student John Smith went crazy and jumped through the principal's window one day, then came back that night and caused massive amounts of damage that took out half the building. Then he fled town. Word is that he's some kind of teenage terrorist or member of a sleeper cell or a psychopath—it depends on who is telling the story.

But one exploding school can't stand in the way of education, so now everyone from Paradise is being shipped to the next town over where there's an actual building for us to go to. It just so happens that the next school over is Helena High, our biggest rival, who I beat in the best football game of my life, capping off an undefeated season by completely annihilating their defense. So, yeah, I guess I can see why I'm not the most loved guy in school. I just never thought I'd spend my last semester of high school washing orange soda out of my hair. Maybe if I was still the same old Mark James I'd think it was kind of fun even. I'd be dreaming up ways to get back at the other students, ways for me and my football buddies to prank them and get the last laugh. But filling someone's locker full of manure isn't as high on my list of priorities now that I know beings from another world are walking among us and that a complete alien invasion is possible at any time. I *wish* manure were still higher on my to-do list.

A bunch of my teammates have told me I've gotten quiet and seem different since it happened, but I can't help it. It's kind of pointless to talk about cars and partying when I was literally almost squashed by some kind of extraterrestrial monster. How am I supposed to go back to being fun-loving, beer-chugging Mark James after all that? Now I'm "Paranoid That Aliens Are Going to Hunt Me Down" Mark James.

I can deal with the new school. Hell, I probably deserve it for the shit I put people like John through back in Paradise. It's only a semester, and then I'll have graduated. Maybe they'll even be able to fix up the school auditorium in time for me to walk the stage in Paradise. What sucks is that I can't tell everyone what's going on. They'd throw me in a mental institution. Or worse, those bad aliens—the Mogs—would be after me to try and shut me up.

At least I have Sarah to talk to. She was there. She fought with me, almost died beside me. As long I have Sarah, I don't feel like I'm going to go crazy.

CHAPTER TWO

THERE ARE BIG SCHOOL BUSES SHUTTLING KIDS back and forth between Helena and Paradise, but I was able to talk the principal into letting me drive myself. I told him I wanted to stay late and work out—that I didn't want what happened in Paradise to keep me from being an unstoppable college football machine. He said that was fine: I'm guessing partly because he hopes anything I do in the future will make Paradise High look good, and partly because everyone in town still feels kind of bad for me because I threw a party and some kids accidentally burned down my house.

I don't *think* that had anything to do with aliens. At least, I've made sure to tell everyone who insinuates that John blew up my house that it was really a couple of stoners down in the basement who were lighting stuff on fire for fun. That usually shuts people up—especially adults who like to pretend that stuff like that never happens in good old Paradise. Besides, John saved Sarah and both of my dogs. There's a YouTube video to prove it. No one should be giving him shit for that night. He gets a free pass on that one.

I meet Sarah in the parking lot after the last bell on the Friday of our first week in Helena. She waits for me at my truck. It's kind of gray outside, and she's got on a plaid sweater that makes her eyes look like they're practically glowing blue. She looks gorgeous.

She always does.

Sarah Hart was—*is*—the love of my life. Even after she dropped cheerleading and came back to school as some kind of emo hipster who suddenly didn't want to be dating the star QB. Even after she dumped me and started sorta dating an alien.

I smile at her as I approach, all teeth. It's a reflex. I can't help it. She smiles too but not as wide as I'd like.

Even with the "You are Mark James" mantra in my head all day, sometimes I don't feel like me at all. Instead of being the cool, put-together guy I've always been, I start worrying about intergalactic war and if Mogs are watching me have breakfast. But even when I start to wonder if I should be building a bomb shelter out in the middle of the woods or something, part of me wants to stay planted in the world I knew before there was definite proof of aliens on Earth, where I'm just a dude who's trying to win back his ex-girlfriend.

If this whole ordeal has had any bright side, it's that I see a lot more of Sarah than I did before. I like to think that me saving John's life impressed her, maybe even showed her that there's more to me than she thought. Someday when this is all said and done, Sarah is going to come to her senses and realize that even if John is a good alien, he's still freaking E.T. And I'll be waiting, even if it means fighting off space invaders to keep her safe and show her I'm better than he is.

The waiting totally blows.

"You're begging to get jumped, aren't you?" she says as I get closer.

At first I'm confused, but then I realize she's nodding at my chest, where my name is embroidered in gold over the heart on my Paradise High varsity letter jacket.

"What, this?" I ask, flexing a little and puffing out my chest. "I'm just repping our school. Trying to bring a little bit of Paradise to hell. That way we all feel like we're at home."

She rolls her eyes.

"You're provoking them."

"They're the least of my problems these days."

"Whatever," she says. "Your truck still smells like orange soda."

Once we're in my truck, Sarah leans her head against the passenger window and exhales a long breath, as if she's been holding it in all day. She looks tired. Beautiful but tired.

"I got a new name in bio today," she says, her eyes closed.

"Oh yeah?"

"'Sarah Bleeding Heart.' I was trying to explain that John wasn't a terrorist who was going to try to blow up the White House. Like, literally, someone said that they heard he was going to blow up the White House."

"Now who's the one asking for it?"

She opens her eyes just enough to glare at me.

"I feel like all I do now is defend him, but everyone else refuses to listen. And every time I try to say something about how they don't know the whole story, I lose a friend. Did you know that Emily thinks he kidnapped Sam? And I can't even tell her that it's not true. All I can say is that John wouldn't do that, and then she looks at me like I'm part of some big plot to destroy America or something. Or worse, some lovesick loser who's in denial."

"Well, you've still got me," I say reassuringly. "And I try to defend John whenever I can. Though I don't think I've been very good at it. All the guys on the team think he was able to kick our asses after the hayride because he was trained as a special agent from Russia or something."

"Thanks, Mark," Sarah says. "I know I can count on you. It's just . . ."

She opens her eyes and looks out the window as we speed past a few empty fields, never finishing her sentence.

"Just what?" I ask, even though I know what's coming. I can feel the blood in my veins start to pump a little faster.

"Nothing."

"*What*, Sarah?" I ask.

"I just wish John was here." She gives me a sad smile. "To defend himself."

Of course, what she really means is that she wishes John was here because she misses him. That it's killing her not to know where he is or what he's doing. For a moment, I feel like my old self again as my hands tighten around the steering wheel. I want to find John Smith and punch him square in the jaw, then keep hitting him until my knuckles bleed. I want to go straight into a rant about how if he really loved her, he wouldn't have left her here to get picked on and laughed at. He would have manned up. Even if he did leave to find other aliens like him to save our planet. If I were in his shoes, I'd have figured out a way to keep Sarah *and* the world safe. And happy.

I can't believe these are the types of conversations I have with myself on a daily basis now.

LEARN THE TRUE STORY
OF FIVE'S SECRET PAST!

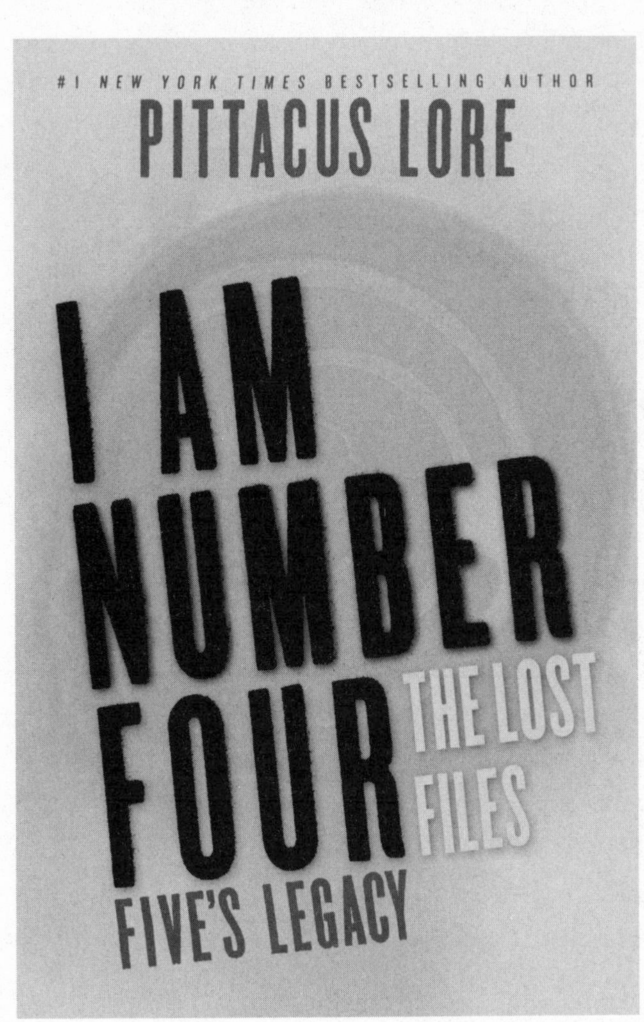

CHAPTER ONE

"THE MOGS ARE HERE!"

My eyes shoot open as I jerk upright, hoping that sentence was just something from a bad dream.

But it's not.

"They're here," Rey whispers again as he crosses over the floor of our little shack to where I'm sleeping on top of a pallet of blankets.

I'm off the floor in seconds. Rey's solar-powered lantern swings in front of my face, and it blinds me. I flinch away and then he turns it off, leaving me in complete darkness. As he pushes me towards the back of our home, all I can make out is a sliver of silver light peeking through the window.

"Out the back." His voice is full of urgency and fear. "I'll hold them off. Go, go, go."

I start grabbing at the air where he'd stood moments before but find nothing. I can't see anything: My eyes still burn from the lantern.

"Rey—"

"No." He cuts me off from somewhere in the dark. "If you don't go now, we're *both* dead."

There's a clattering near the front of the shack, followed by the sound of something—or someone—slamming against the front door. Rey lets out a pained cry but the inside of the shack is still nothing but an abyss of black in my eyes. I know there's a metal bar over the door that's not going to hold up against much more than a little force. It's for show more than anything else. If someone *really* wanted into our shack, they could just blow through the flimsy wooden walls. And if it's the Mogs . . .

There's no time to think, only to react. It's *me* they're after. I've got to get to safety.

I rip away the piece of cloth that serves as a makeshift curtain and throw myself through the little window. I land with a plop in a three-inch puddle of mud, slop, and things I don't even want to imagine—I'm in the hog pen.

A single thought runs through my mind. *I'm going to die a thirteen-year-old boy covered in pig shit on an island in the middle of nowhere.*

Life is so unfair.

The hogs squeal—I've disturbed their sleep—and it snaps me back into the moment. Old training regimens and lectures from years before take over my brain and I'm moving again, checking my flanks to make sure there are no Mogs that have already made their way to the back of the hut. I start to think about what their plan of action might be. If the Mogs actually *knew* I was on the island, I'd be surrounded already. No, it must be a single scout that stumbled upon us by accident. Maybe he had time to report us to the others, maybe not. Whatever the case, I have to get out of the line of fire. Rey will take out the scout. He'll be fine. At least that's what I tell myself, choosing to ignore how frail Rey's looked lately.

He *has* to be okay. He always is.

I head for the jungle behind our shack. My bare feet sink into the sand, as if the island itself is trying to slow me down. I'm dressed only in dark athletic shorts, and branches and shrubs around me scratch at my bare chest and stomach as I enter the cover of the trees. I've done this sort of thing before, once, in Canada. Then, coats and a few bags weighed me down. But we'd had a little more warning. Now, in the sticky-hot night of the Caribbean, I'm weighed down only by my lack of stamina.

As I hurl myself through the dense vegetation, I think of all the mornings I was supposed to spend jogging along the beach or hiking through the forest that I *actually* spent playing solitaire or simply lazing around. Doing what I really wanted to do, like drawing little cartoons in the sand. Coming up with short stories told by stick figures. Rey always said I shouldn't actually write anything down—that any journal or notes I wrote could be found and used as proof of who I am. But writing and drawing in the sand was temporary. When the tide came in, my stories were gone. Even just doing that caused me to work up a sweat in this damned climate, and I'd return to Rey, pretending to be exhausted. He'd comment on the timing of my imaginary run and then treat me to a rich lunch as a reward. Rey is a taskmaster when it comes to doling out things to do, but his lungs are bad and he always trusted that I was doing the training he told me to do. He had no reason not to—no reason to think I wouldn't take our situation seriously.

It wasn't just the avoidance of having to work my ass off in the heat that kept me from training. It was the monotony of it all that I hated. Run, lift, stretch, aim, repeat—day in and day out. Plus, we're living out in the middle of nowhere. Our island isn't even on any maps. I never thought the Mogs would ever find us.

Now, I'm afraid that's coming back to haunt me. I wheeze as I run. I'm totally unprepared for this attack. Those mornings lazing around the beach are going to get me killed.

It doesn't take long before there's a stitch in my side

so sore that I think it's possible I've burst some kind of internal organ. I'm out of breath, and the humid air feels like it's trying to smother me. My hands grasp onto low-hanging branches as I half-pull my way through thick green foliage, the bottoms of my feet scraping against fallen limbs and razor-sharp shells. Within a few minutes the canopy above me is so dense that only pinpricks of the moonlight shine through. The jungle has given way to a full-blown rain forest.

I'm alone in the dark in a rain forest with alien monsters chasing after me.

I pause, panting and holding my side. Our island is small, but I'm only maybe a fifth of the way across it. On the other side of the island a small, hidden kayak is waiting for me, along with a pack of rations and first aid gear. The last-chance escape vessel, something that'll let me slip into the dark of the night and disappear on the ocean. But that seems so far away now, with my lungs screaming at me and my bare feet bleeding. I lean against a tree, trying to catch my breath. Something skitters across the forest floor a few feet away from me and I jump, but it's only one of the little green lizards that overrun the island. Still, my heart pounds. My head is dizzy.

The Mogadorians are here. I'm going to die.

I can't imagine what Rey is doing back at the shack. How many Mogs are here? How many can he take on?

I hope I'm right, and it's just a single scout. I realize I haven't heard any gunshots. Is that a good sign, or does it mean the bastards got to him before he was able to fire off a single round?

Keep going, I tell myself, and then start out again. My calves are burning and my lungs feel like they're about to split open every time I inhale. I stumble, hitting the ground hard and knocking what little breath I had out of me.

Somewhere behind me, I can hear movement in the trees.

I glance around. Without a clear view of the sky, I can't even tell which direction I'm going anymore. I'm totally screwed. I have to do something.

I abandon the plan to cross the island. I'm in no shape to do so. For a moment I think of burrowing down into the brush—maybe finding something to hide in until I can slip through the forest—but then I think of all the fist-sized spiders and ants and snakes that could be waiting there for me, and imagine a Mogadorian scout stepping on me by accident.

So I head up instead. Gathering every ounce of strength I have, I use a few sturdy vines to pull myself hand over hand up to a low branch on a nearby tree. All I can think of are the many different types of beasts Rey's told me the Mogs can command, any one of which would like nothing more than to tear me apart.

Why don't *we* have giant hell-beasts to fight for us?

My arms are shaking by the time I squat on the limb, the wood creaking under my weight as I stare into the blackness, hoping over and over again that nothing will emerge from it. That I can just wait this out.

That it will all just go *away*.

There's no telling how much time passes. If I'd been more put together or hadn't been so taken by surprise, I might have remembered to grab my watch on the way out the window. It's weird—time always seemed like it didn't mean anything on the island, and now it means everything. How many minutes before more of them arrive? How many seconds before they find me? I try to keep from trembling, and my stomach from turning over—between the running, my fear, and the damp smell of pig that clings to me in a thick coat of sludge, I'm teetering on the edge of vomiting. Maybe the stinking layer of crap will help keep me camouflaged, at least.

It's not a very reassuring silver lining.

Finally, a silhouette starts to take shape in the darkness. I draw in closer to the tree. The figure is human sized. Maybe even a little hunched over, leaning on a cane as he steps into the dim moonlight. He's wearing a blue linen shirt, khaki cargo pants, and sneakers that might have been white at some point. His beard is white, streaked with black, his wild hair almost silver.

I recognize him immediately, of course. Rey.

He's got something held against him, wrapped in a piece of cloth. I start to call down to him, but he's already staring holes into me, his lips quivering, as if he's fighting every urge to yell. He simply stands there, the silence hanging in the thick air between us. Finally, I break it.

"Well? Did you get him?"

Rey doesn't respond immediately, just looks away, staring down at the ground.

"What'd you forget?" His voice has a slight rattle to it.

"What?" I ask, my breath short.

He throws his parcel down on the ground. Part of the cloth falls back, and I can make out a familiar corner.

"The Chest?" I ask. My *Loric* Chest. The most sacred thing I own. The treasure I'm not actually allowed to look into. The container that supposedly holds my inheritance and the tools to rebuild my home planet, and I can't even peek inside until Rey thinks I'm ready to—whatever *that* means.

"The Chest." Rey nods.

I scramble down the tree, half falling to the earth.

"We should get going, right?" I ask. My words are spilling out now, my tongue stumbling over the letters as I try to say a million things at once. "You don't have any weapons? Or our food? Where are we going now? Shouldn't we be—"

"Your Chest is the second most important thing you have to protect after your own life. It was stupid to leave it. Next time, it's your priority to keep it safe."

"What are you—"

"You made it half a mile into the forest," he says, ignoring me. His voice is getting louder now, filled with barely restrained anger. "I didn't want to believe it, but I guess this is proof. You haven't been doing your training. You've been lying to me about it. Every day."

"Rey . . ."

"I already knew that, though." He sounds sad now. "I could tell just by looking at you."

My mind is racing, trying to figure out why we're still standing here. Why he's worried about my training when there could be a whole fleet of Mogs on their way after us. Unless . . .

"There aren't any Mogs here," I say quietly.

Rey just shakes his head and stares at the ground.

This was a test. No, worse than that: This was Rey's way of trapping me and catching me in a lie. And even though, yes, I technically have been less than honest about my training regimen, I can't believe Rey would scare me like this.

"Are you kidding me?" Unlike Rey, I don't have the power to keep my anger from clouding my voice. "I was running for my life. I thought I was going to *die*."

"Death is the least of your worries for now," he says, pointing at my ankle. Underneath the layer of mud and crap is an ugly red mark that appeared a few days ago. A mark that's starting to scab over, and will soon turn into a scar. The mark that—thanks to some otherworldly charm—shows me that another one of my fellow Garde has been murdered. Two is dead. Three and Four are all that stand between death and me.

I am Number Five.

I suddenly feel stupid for thinking I was about to be killed. Of course I wasn't. Numbers Three and Four have to die before I can. I *should* have been worried about being captured and tortured for information. Not that Rey ever tells me anything.

And I realize what this is about. Ever since the scar appeared, it's like something within Rey snapped. He's been getting sicker the last few years, and I'm not anywhere as strong as he thinks I should be. I haven't developed any of the magic powers I'm supposed to have. Neither of us can put up a good fight. That's why we're here on this stupid island, hiding.

CONTINUE FIVE'S STORY AND DISCOVER WHY HE JOINS THE MOGADORIAN ARMY!

CHAPTER ONE

THERE WAS ONCE A PLACE THAT WAS BEAUTIFUL and lush and full of life and natural resources. Some people lived there for a long time, but then others came along who wanted or needed the land and everything on it. So they took it.

There is nothing special about this story. Open any history book on Earth—and probably every other planet—and you'll see a version of it play out continuously, on loop, over and over again. Sometimes the land is taken in the name of spreading a better way of life. Or for the sake of the native people. Occasionally the takers seize it based on some intangible reason—some divine right or destiny. But all of these reasons are lies. At the center of every conflict is power, and who will wield it. That's what wars are fought over, and why cities, countries and planets are conquered. And though most people—especially humans—like to pretend that gaining power is just an added bonus on top of whatever a conflict is *supposedly* about, power is the only thing that anyone is really after.

That's one great thing about the Mogadorians: they don't really bother with pretense. They believe in power. Even worship it. They see its potential to grow and serve their cause. So when you're someone like me who has extraordinary abilities, you become one of two things to the Mogs: a valuable asset, or an enemy who will eventually be destroyed.

Personally, I like being alive.

The Mogs don't pretend that they took my home planet of Lorien—which I barely remember—for any reason other than because they needed its resources. It's the same reason they're on Earth now. A planet as big as Earth will serve the Mogs well for decades before they have to go looking for another home—maybe even centuries. And the humans . . . well, it's not like there's anything really special about *them*. They're pretty weak for the most part and are only barely managing to keep the planet alive as it is. One day soon there will be a full-scale invasion, and all their petty problems won't mean anything, because suddenly there will be some incredibly powerful extraterrestrials lording over them. Showing them how to live. Giving their lives purpose.

And I'll be one of their new rulers. Because the Mogs

have seen the potential in me. They've promised me a spot as a commanding officer in the Mog ranks, with North America as my kingdom. My personal playground. And all I have to do is fight alongside them and help them capture the other Garde remaining on Earth. Then I can help the Garde see that there's no way the Loric are ever going to defeat the Mogs. I'm assuming they were spoon-fed the same stories Rey, my Cêpan, told me when I was growing up: that the Mogs were our enemies.

But that's not true. Or at least it doesn't *have* to be true. Not if we join them.

After sitting around training and waiting for almost my entire life, it feels good to finally have an actual mission. To have a purpose. To not just be hiding and waiting for something to happen to me. It makes me actually *want* to train and study and get better, because what I'm working towards now isn't some fairy tale Rey fed me over dinner on the island, but a future I can see.

I've learned a lot about the reasons why wars are fought and won in the last few weeks since I've been living in a Mog compound somewhere in the middle of West Virginia. In fact, most of my "research" hours are spent in an interrogation room that's been converted into a study for me, where I learn about famous battles and conflicts or read the Great Book, which is the story of the Mogadorians and how their intellect and abilities outgrew their planet and forced them to seek other worlds to rule and guide. About how the Loric refused to share their resources or listen to reason when it came to adopting the Mogs as rulers. It's a book written by Setrákus Ra, the unstoppable leader of the Mogs, and, well, let's just say if I'd read it earlier, I would have had a much clearer viewpoint of the fight between the Mogs and the Loric than I did when I was hiding in a lean-to shack on a deserted island. I've begun to wonder if all my memories of being so young and happy on Lorien are just because I was too dumb and little to know what was really going on. I mean, any civilization that puts their last hope in a bunch of toddlers on spaceships has got to be a little bit out of whack, right?

Ethan's helped me see these things. He's helped me realize that I have a choice in this war, even though the Elders didn't want me to have one. It was strange at first to find out that my best friend was working for the Mogs—and that I'd technically been under Mog care for the better part of a year without knowing it—but I can't blame Ethan for keeping things a secret from me at first. I'd been so brainwashed by my Cêpan's stories of the Garde triumphing over the armies of the Mogs and returning Lorien to its former glory that I probably wouldn't have seen reason if he'd been up front with me at the beginning. Ethan is what some of the

Mog commanders here have called a rare example of a human who has the intelligence to side with the winning team.

Still, it's so strange to be here underground. I'm technically an honored guest of Setrákus Ra, but I haven't proved myself yet. All they have is my word that I'm now loyal to them, but words don't carry a lot of weight with the Mogs. They believe in action, and results. And so I study and train and wait for the day when I get the chance to show them I am capable and ready to lead in their name. I follow orders. Because even though someday in the future I'll become invaluable to the Mogs, right now I'm just a former enemy living under their roof.

I'm buried in a book about the founding of America—particularly the expansion of European empires across the country—when Ethan comes into my study, flashing the toothy grin he always has plastered on his face.

"Good afternoon, Five," he says.

"Hey," I say, closing the book in front of me. Ethan's arrival means study time must be over. As much as I'm looking forward to being in charge of Canada and the United States, reading about the endless cycles of wars they've been caught up in can be monotonous. At least once the Mogs take over, war will be a thing of the past. There'll be no armies capable of standing up to them.

"How did you find today's reading?"

"There was some pretty dirty chemical warfare going on back when Columbus and other explorers were first coming over. Smallpox blankets? It's kind of insane."

Ethan's grin doesn't flinch.

"The beginning of every great empire is stained with a little blood," he says. "Wouldn't you say it was worth it?"

I don't answer immediately. Ethan's eyes shift almost imperceptibly, but I catch them. He's glanced at the one-way mirror at the other end of my desk. It's easy to see what he's getting at. Others are watching. Here in the Mog compound, someone is *always* watching.

I tense up a little. I'm still not used to being under constant surveillance. But it's necessary, as Ethan's explained, so that the Mogs know they can trust me. It makes me only want to say things that will impress whoever's watching, or show off how smart I am. I'm getting better at keeping my brain focused on that.

"Definitely," I say.

Ethan nods, looking pleased. "Of course it's worth it. Keep reading that book tomorrow and write down a few positive things about the conquerors' tactics."

"Whatever our Beloved Leader requires of me." I say this almost as a reflex. The first few days I was here, I heard it so many times that I just kind of adopted it. I probably say it ten times a day now without even realizing it half the time.

"Did you read the assigned passages from the Great Book?" Ethan asks.

"Of course. Those are the best parts of the study sessions." This is completely true. The other books are boring and make me suddenly understand why teenagers like me were always complaining about homework on TV shows I saw before coming to the Mog compound. But the Great Book is, well, great. Not only is it written much simpler than the other books, it also answers a lot of questions I've had throughout my life. Like why the Mogs went after Earth even though they had Lorien, and why they started hunting down the Loric once they got here, even though there were so few of us. The book explains that the Loric were weak but sneaky, and the Mogadorian belief that leaving even one enemy alive gives them the power to recruit others and multiply, gain power and one day rise against you.

Also, it's really bloody and violent, which makes it much more fun to read. I can see it play out in my head like one of the action movies I used to love to go see when I was still in Miami.

"And what did you learn about today?" Ethan asks.

"About how Setrákus Ra bravely fought our Elders.

How they tried to trick him and poison him, but our Beloved Leader was courageous and bested them, anyway."

"*Our* Elders?" Ethan asks, slight concern on his face.

I correct myself. "I mean the *Loric* Elders. It makes me even more excited to meet our Beloved Leader."

I have not had the pleasure of meeting Setrákus Ra in person yet. Apparently someone higher up thought it wasn't a good idea to give a superpowered guy like me an audience with the future ruler of the solar system until I've proved myself.

I AM NUMBER FOUR

THE LEGACIES DEVELOP...

DON'T MISS A SINGLE PAGE OF THE ACTION-PACKED,
#1 *NEW YORK TIMES* BESTSELLING
I AM NUMBER FOUR SERIES

VISIT THE OFFICIAL SITE AT **WWW.IAMNUMBERFOURFANS.COM** FOR THE LATEST SERIES NEWS AND TO SHARE YOUR THOUGHTS!

HARPER
An Imprint of HarperCollins*Publishers*

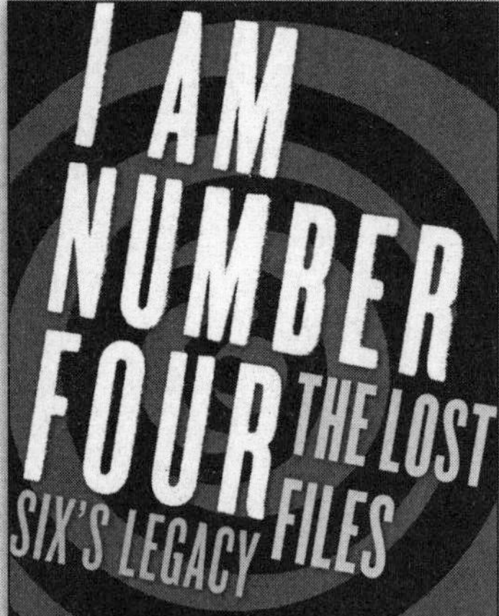

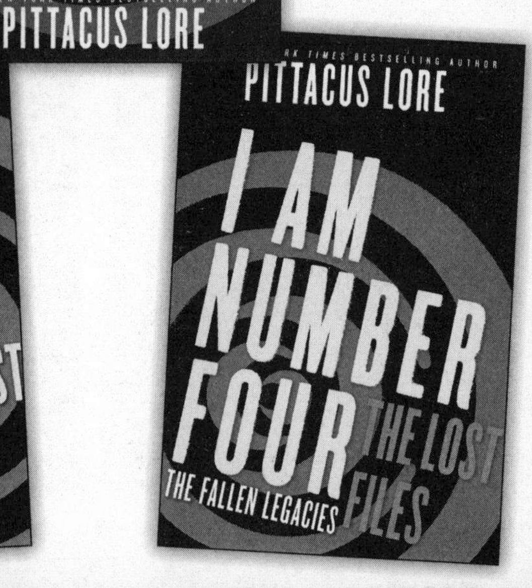

READ THE FIRST THREE NOVELLAS IN ONE THRILLING PAPERBACK,
I AM NUMBER FOUR: THE LOST FILES: THE LEGACIES

HARPER
An Imprint of HarperCollins*Publishers*

www.iamnumberfourfans.com